MECHA
SAMURAI
EMPIRE

★ ★ ★

PETER TIERYAS

ACE
NEW YORK

ACE
Published by Berkley
An imprint of Penguin Random House LLC
375 Hudson Street, New York, New York 10014

Copyright © 2018 by Peter Tieryas
Penguin Random House supports copyright. Copyright fuels creativity, encourages
diverse voices, promotes free speech, and creates a vibrant culture. Thank you for buying
an authorized edition of this book and for complying with copyright laws by not
reproducing, scanning, or distributing any part of it in any form without permission.
You are supporting writers and allowing Penguin Random House to continue to publish
books for every reader.

ACE is a registered trademark and the A colophon is a trademark of
Penguin Random House LLC.

Library of Congress Cataloging-in-Publication Data

Names: Tieryas, Peter, 1979– author.
Title: Mecha samurai empire / Peter Tieryas.
Description: First edition. | New York: Ace, 2018.
Identifiers: LCCN 2017059991 | ISBN 9780451490995 (softcover) |
ISBN 9780451491008 (ebook)
Subjects: | GSAFD: Alternative histories (Fiction)
Classification: LCC PS3612.I932 M43 2018 | DDC 813/.6—dc23
LC record available at https://lccn.loc.gov/2017059991

First Edition: September 2018

Printed in the United States of America
1   3   5   7   9   10   8   6   4   2

Cover art by John Liberto
Cover design by Adam Auerbach
Book design by Kristin del Rosario

Dedicated to my wife,
Angela Xu,
for being the best mecha copilot

PRAISE FOR PETER TIERYAS AND HIS WRITING

"A searing vision of the persistence of hope in the face of brutality, *United States of Japan* is utterly brilliant."

—Ken Liu,
Hugo, Nebula, and World Fantasy Award winner
and author of *The Grace of Kings*

"This is a darkly fun, clever, and unrelentingly ambitious book."
—Kameron Hurley,
Hugo Award winner and author of *The Mirror Empire*

"A perfect patchwork of multiple sci-fi and anime subgenres rolled into one novel." —*Esquire*

"Mind-twisting and fiercely imaginative; Tieryas fuses classic sci-fi tradition with his own powerful vision."

—Jay Posey,
author of the Legends of the Duskwalker series
and writer at Ubisoft / Red Storm

"It's a tense and intriguing read, a blend of alt history and cyber-punk and thriller. Nineteen eighty-eight California where San Diego is a razed landscape home to American rebels, and Japanese mechas patrol the coast? Heck yes!"

—Beth Cato, author of *The Clockwork Dagger*

"*United States of Japan* is a powerful book, unsettling at times— surreal and hypnotic. There's a bit of Philip K. Dick in here, and *The Wind-Up Bird Chronicle*, but Peter Tieryas is his own voice, a talented author, somebody to keep an eye on for sure."

—Richard Thomas, author of *Breaker* and *Disintegration*

I PLEDGE ALLEGIANCE TO THE FLAG

OF THE UNITED STATES OF JAPAN

AND TO THE EMPIRE

FOR WHICH IT STANDS,

ONE NATION

UNDER THE EMPEROR, INDIVISIBLE,

WITH ORDER AND JUSTICE FOR ALL.

MECHA SAMURAI EMPIRE

GRANADA
HILLS

★

**1994
WINTER**

01

★ ★ ★

I DON'T KNOW WHY PEOPLE SAY TIME HEALS ALL WOUNDS. TIME ONLY aggravates mine.

My maternal grandparents were Japanese citizens who lived in Kyoto and immigrated to San Francisco during the early 1900s. My paternal grandparents were ethnic Koreans who moved to Los Angeles shortly after the Empire's victory in 1948. There were more opportunities in the United States of Japan then, especially since the Empire was rebuilding so many of the cities that were in ruins. My parents met during the 1974 Matsuri, a festival at a Shinto shrine in Irvine. My father served as a mecha technician and worked on the maintenance of their armor plating. My mother was an officer who worked as a navigator aboard the mecha *Kamoshika*. She recognized my dad at the shrine for the work he did on their BP generator. They each picked out an *o-mikuji* from the *o-mikuji* box, wondering what fortunes those little strips of paper foretold. By pure coincidence, both of their messages read that a momentous event would occur that day and alter their destinies forever. After sharing jokes and chiding each other about destiny and politics in the corps, they agreed to go to their favorite ramen shop for dinner.

I was born two years later.

My earliest memory with them is at a mecha factory in Long Beach. The armored legs were bigger than most buildings I'd seen. By the time I was three, I was waging wars against the Nazis with mecha toys my dad had built for me. He'd made me a special *jim-baori*, and I loved the way the old samurai surcoats gave my mechanical warriors a regal bearing. Neither of my parents got to pilot an actual mecha even though both wished they could. Maybe they'd have gotten the chance if they'd had more time.

The greatest threat during their lives wasn't the Germans but American terrorists who called themselves George Washingtons. The George Washingtons were rumored to be so ruthless, they'd cut off the ears of our soldiers to wear as necklaces. In 1978, hundreds of the terrorists launched themselves at the city hall in San Diego and killed thousands of our citizens. Three months later, they carried out another attack, killing many innocent civilians in the Gaslamp Quarter, including the wife of an important general.

Mom and Dad were ordered to the front in early 1980. They came back home to visit every few months, but neither of them spoke much during their years of service. My father spent most of his time brooding, and the only time I saw even a hint of affection from my mother was when she'd be humming military songs to herself. The last memory I have of them is the morning they left. They told me they'd see me in three months. I still remember the bright colors of the jacketlike *haoris* they wore over their kimonos and how attracted I was to the golden embroidery. We ate our breakfast in silence. My eggs were too salty, my anchovies were hard, and the pickled tsukemono smelled funny. They usually left without saying much. But that morning, my mom stopped as she was about to leave, came back inside, and gave me a kiss on the forehead.

Nineteen eighty-four was a bloody year. Lots of kids in the Empire became orphans that year. I was no exception. My parents were killed in two separate battles four days apart.

The corporal who came to tell me wept as he spoke. Mom had saved his life in battle, so he had taken the news very hard. "Your mother loved *nashis*," he told me, having brought a box full of the sweet Asian pears. "She used to cut them up into small pieces to share with her whole unit, and she'd always save one piece just to show she was thinking of you."

Concepts like life and death were hard for me to grasp at that age. Even as he told me stories about my parents, I kept on wondering when he'd go away and my parents would return. It took me a full year to realize they were never coming back, and by then, I was living with a stingy "guardian" who'd been ordered by the government to adopt me, as I had no surviving family members. His primary business had been construction with the hotels in Tijuana and San Diego, but the revolt had put an end to all that. My adoptive father insisted that my adoptive mother measure the amount of rice she was scooping for me. If I left even a little bit of food on my plate, I'd get a severe scolding for "wasting food," which both my adoptive brothers did without a second thought.

Knowing my parents had served aboard mechas, I glorified them. I swore I would grow up to be a mecha pilot protecting the Empire against its enemies. My adoptive parents called it a pipe dream and sent me away as soon as I was eligible for boarding school, in Granada Hills within the California Province, where I've been for nearly a decade.

Now, with my high-school graduation coming in a few months, I practice almost every day on the mecha simulations. Like most kids who grew up in the eighties, I play portical games. The mecha simulations take place inside arcade booths that re-create visuals captured from real-life footage, with surround sound that makes the experience immersive. I wear haptic controls and drive the mecha with a simplified interface that simulates piloting. While I engage in many battles, the one I go back to most often is the fight in San Diego in which my mother was killed.

The *Kamoshika* was an older Kaneda-class mecha, larger but less deadly than the Torturer-class mechas that were slowly replacing them. Samurai Titan was their nickname because they were so massive. The *Kamoshika* was essentially a mountain-sized warrior with robotic joints and a face mask protecting its bridge in the head.

It'd been called in to investigate suspicious activity by the George Washingtons. A rebel leader calling herself Abigail Adams led a surprise attack that decimated one of our battalions. The lieutenant colonel in charge of the security station had sent an SOS before communications were cut.

Playing the sim again, I watch as our forces disconnect all electricity to that region of the city. Our soldiers switch to infrared mode, but it's like shadow dancing as they tiptoe their way across a blackened San Diego. The terrorists fire flare guns into the sky, causing bright orbs to reveal the presence of the mecha. There is a frenzied commotion as the GWs prepare for what is designed as the ultimate trap.

They've gathered twenty-two Neptune Tactical Missile Launchers they obtained from the Nazis (even though the Germans would later claim they were stolen) along with five Panzer Maus IX Supertanks. When the *Kamoshika* arrives at the scene, there is a simultaneous barrage. The pilot realizes it's an ambush and has a split second when he can choose to flee. But it's in an area full of civilians, and the *Kamoshika* has a sizable military escort that would be helpless against the Panzers and their biomorphs if it made a tactical retreat. It decides to stand its ground and fight, absorbing all the punishment it can. Its endeavor to protect those behind it is not very successful. I watch in slow motion as the armored suit gets incinerated and the BP generator gets exposed, resulting in total meltdown.

This is one of those battles that can't be won in the simulation. If I choose to escape, a great portion of our armed forces gets eliminated and the civilian death toll is catastrophic. If I take the brunt of the blast and fight as hard as I can against the remaining terrorists, I die and leave a young me bereaved.

All these years since the battle, I still struggle with the nightmare scenario that haunted my childhood.

FOR SOME KIDS, ACADEMIC ACHIEVEMENT COMES NATURALLY. UNFORTU-nately, I'm not one of them. I work all night, but my grades are only a little above average. I know that won't cut it.

On the main island, the most prestigious military school is the Imperial Japanese Army Academy (*Rikugun Shikan Gakko*), and the principal way to get accepted is completion of a rigorous three-year course at one of the preparatory schools called *Rikugun Yonen Gakko*. That, or you show exemplary service as an enlisted soldier and are younger than twenty-five years of age.

If the entrance admission were based on my grades alone, my chances of getting into the top school in the USJ, Berkeley Military Academy (BEMA), would be nonexistent. It's not as if I have a rich family who can buy my way in, either. The only path open to me is to get a good score on the military supplement to the weeklong imperial exams, then hope I can obtain a military recommendation from someone important who notices my test results. It's something I pray to the Emperor for every day because I know I have only a one percent chance of success. Fortunately, the academy isn't looking just for good potential soldiers. They want the best gaming minds to interface with the portical controls on their most advanced machinery. There is historical precedent. The most prominent was one of the best mecha pilots, a cadet with the code name Kujira. She too had average grades and did poorly on the general imperial exams. But her military simulation scores are the best in recorded academy history, and she is a legend as one of our most decorated pilots.

That's partly why I've spent almost every night for the past two years playing the mecha simulations at the Gogo Arcade and why I'm here a week before we're taking the test. My best friend, Hideki, is also here. Unlike me, he doesn't want to be a pilot but rather a game designer, as he loves portical games and hopes to get into the gaming division at Berkeley, BEMAG. Both are extremely difficult positions to aspire to.

"I heard the new *Cat Odyssey* is on the floor," Hideki tells me.

Even though I can download samples of all games to my portical, many of the new titles have exclusive deals with arcades, so you can play the full version only if you're physically present.

Cat Odyssey is a series I've been playing since I was eight. It's one of the most popular games in the Empire and shows the history of our Great Pacific War against the Americans from the perspective of a cat. The cat can gain knowledge points that translate to greater powers and acquired abilities, like climbing higher plateaus and dropping down with minimal damage. Part of its allure is its uncannily real visuals, photographic in its depiction of the late 1940s (different iterations take place in different years). The developers took two years to make sure the latest part maintained graphic fidelity to the past, including the deployment of the first mechas, which were originally symbolic figures. They were built by the military as embodiments of the Empire, clad in samurai armor, launching tactical weapons at our American foes but unable to do much else.

I prepare myself for disappointment in case the game doesn't live up to my expectations. But I'm also playing because some of the endurance levels are said to be designed by Rogue199, the alias for the top developer at Taiyo Tech. She's the mastermind behind many of the actual mecha simulations for the exam. I want to try it for a few hours to see whether there's anything that can give me an extra edge on the test. Hideki thinks it's a fool's quest, but I've never been one to shy away from futile pursuits.

Hideki's biological family had been in America for several generations, but they'd originally come over from Europe. He doesn't know much about it, though, since his parents were killed in San Diego and he was adopted by a man who worked as an exterminator. His adoptive dad earned a good living hunting roaches, but Hideki was embarrassed about his profession. At school, Hideki made up stories about his real parents, narratives that would shift depending on his mood, the tales ranging from the exotically grand to the stupendously impossible. He created so many pasts, I think he stopped remembering which were true and which were fictional. He ran away from home multiple times before his guardian shipped him off to live with his aunt here in Granada Hills—which is where I met him. (Honestly, it took me a while before I figured out this much.) We became best friends because of our mutual passion for portical games.

Mac, he calls me, which is short for Makoto. Everyone in the Empire has a Japanese name, no matter their ethnicity. Most also have a nickname in the dominant language of their region. Mine is the name of one of my favorite USJ boxers. "There it is."

A whole section of the arcade is devoted to *Cat Odyssey*. All ninety-eight stalls are occupied by gamers. Fortunately, one of our friends saved us a spot.

She's Griselda Beringer, an exchange student from the Reich city of Hamburg. Taller than each of us, she's ethnically half-German, half-Japanese. Her hair is blond, and she has sharp green eyes. She is studying engineering and shares our love for gaming. Her specialty is flight and driving simulations. She's especially good with the Zero sims, beating everyone I've seen dogfight against her in the Pacific War re-creations. Unlike us, she doesn't have to take the imperial exams (German university exams are later), so she can game until her fingers get tired. It's just the three of us tonight because all our friends are studying for the weeklong exam, which I know is what I should be doing too. I just want to play the new *Cat Odyssey*.

"How is it?" I ask Griselda, who's been playing it for the last hour.

She shrugs, intentionally noncommittal to tease me.

"That good?" I say.

She moves aside so I can start. I open my portical, flip out the triangular edges, and use the kikkai field to connect to the game. The display on the stall is hooked into my portical, which I can use as my controller with custom configurations that remain constant. My saved data profiles from my treks through previous iterations of the feline journey come through.

I get dropped into old Los Angeles. Much of the city is in ruins, firebombed by our air force. The Americans are killing anyone they can find of Japanese descent and, incidentally, everyone who appears Asian. They are barbaric in the way they treat foreigners. My cat avatar, Soseki (I know it's a bit of a cliché when it comes to avatar names), stealthily makes her way through the city alleys. They've increased the number of polygonal facets and rewritten the fur system so that it generates cylindrical meshes rather than the usual field of flat planes masquerading as fur. The attention to detail is remarkable.

Much of my gear from my previous save file also transfers over. The Susano Cape lets me traverse water. The Fujin Boot gives my cat the ability to do a double jump in the air. A Tanuki suit grants me a spell to change into a stone statue, which makes me invulnerable to hostiles. With my equipment in place, all of Los Angeles is open for me. Stories based on real-life accounts play out. Many of my missions involve helping those suffering under American rule and assisting USJ soldiers where I can. There is a sense of helplessness that pervades, punctuated by melancholy but catchy music. Orchestral and digitized versions of all the music play in the background, and I opt for the retro-styled beats that are similar to the earlier *Odyssey* games. Kawada composes all the music in the series. I frequently put myself to sleep listening to his tracks.

I am on my fifteenth mission when Griselda and Hideki pull me away.

"What's going on?" I ask, annoyed by the interruption.

"You've been playing for four hours. Let's grab something to eat."

I have to check the clock to make sure they're not lying to me. They're not.

There's a café in the arcade. Hideki orders *okonomiyaki* with spicy sausages, squid, and pepper jack cheese. Griselda orders a taco with chicken skewers and curry-topped goat nachos. I can't stop thinking about what to do next and order a watermelon burger salad. It's a cheap bowl filled with ground beef, fruit, and spinach that's light, so I can focus on my game without bathroom breaks.

"How are you liking the game?" Griselda asks as she hands me a fork.

"So far, beating expectations," I reply, taking a bite of my salad. "What are you at?"

"Beating some punks in dogfighting," she says. "They didn't heat the curry nachos today!" she exclaims after taking a bite.

"They were stingy with the sausages today too," Hideki says about his pizza-pancake monstrosity, which takes up a quarter of our table.

Griselda flags down a waiter, and explains, "These nachos are too cold, and the chips are soggy."

"Can I get some more sausages on mine?" Hideki asks the waiter, who looks similar in age to us.

The waiter apologizes, bows, and takes both plates away.

Griselda notes, "I sometimes think too many of us Germans mistake your politeness for weakness."

"What do you mean?"

"There was so much disdain in his bow. Don't you think?"

"Sometimes, a bow can be the ultimate form of disrespect," I note.

"How can you tell when it is?"

"Depends on the angle and facial expression. Like I could be way down here," I say, and lower myself. "And I could be making the worst expression, and you'd have no idea." I raise myself back up and have my face contorted and my tongue sticking out.

"Not sure if you're being disrespectful or just an idiot," Hideki says with a laugh. "What you gotta do is let out a small fart when you bow. They might not know you're being disrespectful. But they'll smell it."

Griselda glowers at Hideki. "That is a horrible suggestion. Which is why I'm going to take you up on it next time I have to bow to one of those gaming idiots who challenges me, thinking they can take my money."

The waiter brings back the food and has added fishcake balls as a token of his apology. Griselda puts her hands together, simpers, and says in as cute a voice as she can muster, *"Itadakimasu,"* before taking a bite of her nachos, then putting her thumb up in approval.

I honestly don't know why she always says that before eating. I've explained to her our customs are different here versus the main island and that no one says that here in the USJ. Much of our culture, and even many of our expressions, would be unfamiliar in

Tokyo, and vice versa. While we're all members of the Empire, it doesn't mean we're a uniform bunch who mimic one another. The citizens in Tokyo are different from those in Taiko City, Vancouver, Dallas Tokai, Sydney, and Los Angeles.

Right after the end of the Great Pacific War, Nakahara, the Minister of Language, believed different languages inherently had within them unique structures of thinking that would give the Empire flexibility and growth that wouldn't be possible if the local dialects were eliminated. While Japanese is the official imperial language throughout the Empire and required learning, within our governed areas, we are encouraged to speak the local dialect. That's why we speak English in the USJ.

But Griselda likes to fuse on a whim, picking and choosing what she wants to imitate.

"Is it better?" Hideki asks.

"Definitely crispier," she replies, taking a loud, scrumptious bite.

Hideki is about to say something but gets a call, a portical game track humming. Based on his immediate pickup and cooing voice, I can tell it's his girlfriend, Sango. He leaves to talk with her privately. She's a year older than he and works at a literary bar to pay her bills so she can get another chance at the exams—her scores weren't high enough to get into the university she wanted the first time around.

"You know what I'm most looking forward to?" Griselda asks me.

I shake my head.

"Home. I haven't been back to Konigsbarg," she says, pronouncing Konigsberg with her local accent, "in two years. I miss the veal meatballs. They put in a little touch of white pepper and anchovies. There's nothing like them anywhere else. You should visit after graduation. I can show you around the city, and we can take a train to Berlin and visit the Adolph Hitler Plaza and the Fuehrer's Tomb."

The idea of visiting Hitler's tomb, knowing all that he's done against the Empire, isn't that appealing to me. Before I can respond, Hideki gets back and is all smiles.

"How's Sango?" I ask.

"I wasn't talking to her," he replies. Usually, he'll elaborate, but he has a cryptic smile.

Griselda says, "Your portical ring is lame."

"You're just snobby about game music."

"Snobby means I'm just saying it to say it. Mahler and Wagner are on a different level from your portical game composers," Griselda affirms.

"They're melodramatic, way too long, and put me to sleep every time."

"What do you think?" Griselda asks me.

"I think I want to listen to some *Cat Odyssey* tracks," I reply.

"Why do you despise portical musicians?" Hideki questions her. "They write songs that are moving *and* memorable."

Griselda pulls out a chip covered in cheese. "The 'great despisers are the great reverers,'" she quotes, taking a loud bite. "I revere music, which is why I'm so picky about it."

They debate for a bit. My mind is on *Odyssey*. They sense it and release me with a laugh.

I return to late 1940s Los Angeles. Soseki has to make some tough choices. There's rampant speculation that the American cats are getting desperate and are willing to do anything to defeat the Empire's cats. I scout Los Angeles for clues about my enemy while getting used to the new cat quadruped controls, which are more complex than in previous games. A part of me wonders if these controls in any way mimic actual quad mechas.

Griselda taps me on the shoulder. "My cousin locked himself

out of his apartment, so I'm going to head home. Don't meow yourself to death."

"Meow?" I reply.

It's seven in the morning before I reach the next part of the quest. Hideki picks up a bowl of instant ramen and gets me the spicy seafood flavor I love. My teachers tell me I shouldn't eat so much ramen because that's what gives me all my pimples and my belly. But I'd rather be pimply and cart a little extra weight than give up my favorite noodles.

I have only an hour left before I have to head to school. But I want to finish up my current quest. I can catch up on sleep in math since our teacher doesn't care what we do in class as long as we show up.

I enter an area where humans are blocking off access to restaurant trash. I'm required to defeat them so I can get the goods I need to feed my community. But my opponents are too fast, and I can't combat them quickly enough. Even my special attacks fail to distract them, and one of the humans knocks me off my feet. They approach with knives and evil grins. I realize they're going to eat me. I try to escape, but the screen goes blank after I get hit too many times.

"Fifth life over," the screen tells me. I get nine lives, and as soon as I lose the ninth, I have to create a brand-new profile and surrender my cat soul to portical oblivion.

Hideki yells at me, "You suck, man! Can't you beat those garbagemen?" He's been watching my game.

"This part is impossible at my level. I should have powered up more."

"You were just too slow. You need to work on your finger reflexes. At that speed, they're going to eat you up for the official simulation."

It makes me wonder if Rogue199 designed these cat battles with mecha combat in mind.

The special mecha simulation test, also heavily designed by Rogue199, is the exam the Berkeley Military Academy's board is most interested in. The field test is based on one of our most deadly conflicts, the Dallas Incident of 1972.

Dallas Tokai was under attack by an unknown enemy, and the extent of the conflict was unknown to USJ Command. They sent three quad mechas, thinking it was a local incident. But the Germans had dispatched a legion of their biomechs. Of the three quad mechas that reported, only one returned. That was because the pilot fled the scene while the other two stayed behind to fight as they'd determined it was more important that one escape with the combat data the USJ could use to fight other biomechs. It was an honorable action that was forgiven by command, but she still felt disgraced for leaving her companions behind and put a knife through her throat.

For anyone who takes the test, the performance is judged by a panel. Since the parameters for the test change every time, it's not so much seeing whether you succeed but rather testing the creativity in the way you respond. I've heard there are people who've failed to escape but been admitted to the Berkeley Military Academy, which raises my hopes. In the test, I'll handle the main load of the simulation, though I'm required to bring one person as my wingmate. That person acts as a backup and gets a much simpler setup, which is why I'm relieved to have Hideki. I've never met anyone with quicker fingers. Except maybe Griselda. But she's not allowed since she isn't part of the Empire, and Hideki would never forgive me if I asked anyone else.

"Hate to break it to you, but there's no way you're getting into BEMA if you play that bad," Hideki tells me.

I know he's right, and that's a big reason why I've been playing the sims here. But even those are said to be insufficient comparisons to the actual test, as there's no official way to prepare for it. I sincerely hope that mastering the controls on *Cat Odyssey* is actually a good way to warm up for the test. "You shouldn't have tried to fight the humans head-on," he admonishes me, doing the small head shake he always does when he gets in his lecturing mood.

"What else was I supposed to do?"

"Change the battlefield or avoid the fight."

"My community needed food," I protest.

"And now you're dead, so they won't get it anyway."

I'm too tired to argue with him, so I nod, and say, "We should get going."

We've avoided corporal punishment for most of the year by being on time to class. Depending on the mood our homeroom teacher is, we can get it really bad or escape with just a few slaps. Hideki took a terrible beating last year when the teacher broke one of his ribs. He had a hard time breathing for half a year, anger in every breath as he swore, "I will get out of here and make them all regret the way they've treated us."

It became the mantra by which he lived.

WE ALL WEAR BLUE UNIFORMS TO SCHOOL. THE BOYS WEAR COATS, BUT- toned white shirts, ties, and a whole lot of monotony. Swap out our pants for long skirts, and you have the female uniforms. We do our best to differentiate ourselves with custom straps on our bags and bright bands, but if anyone wears something that diverges too much from the standard, it gets confiscated.

After we arrive at school, we leave our shoes in small lockers and put on slippers. We head to the second floor, where our homeroom is located. Once the school bell rings, we stand up, put our right hands over our hearts, and state in unison: "I pledge allegiance to the flag of the United States of Japan and to the Empire for which it stands, one nation under the Emperor, indivisible, with order and justice for all."

An image of the Emperor in a dragon mask appears as a holograph in front of our classroom. We bow in respect for a full minute after we've recited the pledge. We spend another minute mentally thanking the Emperor for all he's done for our people. A shortened version of the song, "Star Spangled Sun," plays as tribute to all of those who've suffered and still fight to establish the Empire in all its glory. *Hakko ichiu* is the aim, having all the world under one roof.

Our homeroom class has twenty-eight students. We stay in the same room, and the teachers change with each new class, though there are electives that require some of us to walk to different rooms in the afternoon.

At lunch, Hideki asks what I'm doing. I lift up my portical and point to the commentary on the Imperial Rescript on Education (*Kyoiku ni Kansuru Chokugo*) for the exams. "Have fun," he says nonchalantly, joining some of the seniors going off campus for lunch.

Griselda meets with her German contingent, who stick together during the forty-five-minute break. I head for some benches outside, lie down, and read the commentary, focused on the middle of the Rescript, discussing the maintenance of the prosperity of the Imperial Throne.

Across from me, also reading, is Noriko Tachibana. She is not only one of the smartest students in our year, but is from a family of prestigious imperial officers. Her grandfather flew Zeros, and both her parents were heroes in our proxy wars in Afghanistan. Noriko is at the top of our class. She also juggles numerous extra-curricular activities like ice-skating, at which she is excellent, and is president of half a dozen academic clubs on campus. I've always admired her. She is reading a book—something by Fumiko Enchi. Noriko is of African descent, and her grandparents fought for the Empire against the horrors the Nazis were perpetrating.

"Hi, Mac," she says to me when she notices my gaze.

"Hi, Nori." I wave at her. She's in our homeroom, and we'd been previously assigned together on three projects in which she took charge, leading us to get the top score.

"Did you know cats and dogs can see ultraviolet, but humans can't?"

"I didn't," I confess.

"All mecha sensors detect visual wavelengths beyond the human eye," she says. "Good luck on the test next week."

"You too," I say, and feel dumb because she doesn't need luck—she always gets the highest score.

If she's annoyed, she doesn't show it and instead goes back to reading.

Right as lunch ends, an announcement on the speaker system informs us, "Please assemble in the field for an important meeting."

All two thousand students line up outside, separated by homerooms. As seniors, we're in the middle section up front. The flag bearer is holding the imperial flag, and the three next to her are carrying our school banner. Up front, the principal is very active, explaining something with overly exaggerated politeness to two officers. They nod in affirmation, and the principal points at us. Eventually, he introduces them on the speaker.

"This is Colonel Kita and Lieutenant Yukimura. They are heroes of the second San Diego Conflict and have honored us with their company."

Colonel Kita is a tall woman with red hair and two sheathed swords on her belt. The lieutenant has a metal arm under his uniform and wears a beret rather than the traditional cap.

"Next week is an important week for all of you," Colonel Kita states. "Many of you will have your futures determined by your imperial examination scores. There is no greater glory than serving your country through military service. I have served for two decades, and it is always humbling to realize the great responsibility thrust upon us. Not only are we protecting the United States of Japan, but we are preserving order and a way of life that is in harmony with the universe. How many of you plan on taking the military supplemental exams?"

A quarter of the students raise their hands. She asks the other students to applaud those who are striving to enter the military.

That's when the ground shakes. I feel a flutter in my chest. Could it be? The second tremor confirms it, and there are awed gasps as we see the figure coming closer.

It is a mecha, shaped like a huge suit of samurai armor. Even though it's bigger than the tallest building in Granada Hills, it's much smaller than the *Korosu* class. From the looks of it, it's a reconnaissance mecha, quick, stealthy, and hard to detect when it doesn't want to be found. It's sleek and has chest plates designed to deflect sensors or absorb their waves when that is impossible.

"This is the *Taka*," the colonel says. "I have a crew of fourteen of the finest soldiers in the mecha corps. We have been serving together for the past three years, and we'll be giving demonstrations for select cadets."

The *Taka* stops right outside the school. Over the gate, I see the shin guard, the retractable knees, the searchlights in the hips, all culminating in the main armor shaped like a classical samurai's *haramaki-dō*. The separated plates are usually there to hide weapons and circuitry, as well as for ventilation purposes in case there is any overheating during combat. The reconnaissance mechas handle heat very well, though, and the purpose of the detached plates might be for a refractory effect, which is only rumored at, never confirmed. Some of the prototype mechas reportedly have a type of camouflage, similar to that on our cars, which makes them practically transparent when they need to be.

I've battled digital mechas in the simulation multiple times. But seeing them in real life is indescribable. I wonder if my parents felt the same sense of awe every time they got on board a mecha.

The two officers personally inspect us, walking down the aisles, asking each of us our names, and, "Which section are you testing for?"

Some answer navy, gaming division, etc. Eight students in my homeroom state their intent to apply for the mecha corps, which elicits pride in the officers. The colonel and lieutenant even know Noriko and greet her by name.

"Based on all we've heard, you'll make your parents proud," the colonel says.

"I hope so, ma'am," Nori replies.

"I'll personally be reviewing your sim test next week."

They finally get to me, and the lieutenant asks, "Which unit are you aiming for?"

"Mecha corps," I proudly answer, excited at the chance to meet a mecha pilot in person.

They both hesitate. Lieutenant Yukimara says firmly, "Our corps is one of the most difficult units to get into. Are you prepared?"

"Yes, sir."

The lieutenant looks me up and down. "You don't look like you're in shape. Do you think we take just anyone in the corps?"

"N-no, sir."

Based on his expression, the lieutenant is about to say something even harsher, but the colonel stops him. They move to the next student. I look down at my stomach. I've tried to control my eating, exercise as much as I can. But it's been a tough year, and the best way to make myself feel better is a combination of coconut coffee, strawberry shortcake with chocolate crumbs, and shrimp chips.

The review is finished an hour later, and we're allowed to approach the *Taka*. It is even more marvelous up close. The officers take Noriko and three other students into the mecha. I feel a pang of envy, but it also motivates me to work harder, so I'll get my chance one day. When I'm back in my apartment thirty minutes later, I read up everything I can on reconnaissance mechas.

I SHARE MY SMALL ROOM WITH THREE OTHERS. I'M ON THE BUNK BED IN the upper-left side. We have concrete floors, which makes them too cold to walk on without socks. We don't have climate control, so on some nights when it gets too hot, I'll sleep on the ground to cool myself. Someone let a fly in, and it's buzzing around. My three other roommates are out, probably studying at the library. I have several messages from Hideki, asking me to meet him at a nearby café to study. A part of me wants to start my new life on *Cat Odyssey*. But I promised no more gaming until after the exam. I message Hideki and tell him I'll meet him there. I exit my apartment, go to the communal bathroom to wash up, and leave my building. The security guard is busy watching a dating show on his portical where people dress up as animals and spend time in zoos so people can gawk at them.

Hideki is at Penny's, which is just two kilometers away. I pass by several carts selling udon and other nightly snacks for students. The smell of fish broth and tempura wafts past me, making me hungry. War orphans like me are given weekly stipends as part of a fund for children of veterans who passed away in battle. We're also granted generous discounts on everything.

Penny's Café is next to ten other coffee shops. The façade is a gigantic copper penny with the face of Abraham Lincoln, an old

American warlord who savagely crushed a rebellion started by the southern half of the United States. Inside, the walls are covered with coins from foreign nations that joined the Empire, including a whole lot of American pennies.

Hideki is studying on his portical. Griselda is with some friends, but she waves at me when I enter and comes over.

I order a cup of coconut coffee and shrimp chips, then feel guilty as I recall the conversation with the officers. I'll work on losing weight after the exam since I've read that caffeine is supposed to boost memory and I need a boost badly, as I have to memorize a million details about generals and battle dates. 1948, July 4, the USA becomes the USJ. 1950, September 9, Germany and Japan establish the Unity Zone (UZ) at Texas (though it would come to be called the Quiet Border by both sides). 1958, Germany launches a sneak attack on Texas, and a group of our mechas known as the Twelve Disciples stops them. I read about the Nazi attempt to create their own mechas and their desire to inject a biological component to them, resulting in the monstrosities known initially as the biomorphs and more recently as the biomechs. There are too many dates to remember.

"The mecha today was cool," Hideki says. "You really think you're going to get to pilot one?"

I tell the two of them about my short exchange with the officer. Griselda smiles mischievously.

"What?" I ask.

"At least you made an impression."

"A bad one," I say.

She pokes me in my stomach. "They have a point. You wanna jog with me every morning?"

"I would if I could wake up."

"Discipline," she says. "I jog even if I haven't slept the night before. Soldiers need to be in tip-top shape always."

"After the exam, I'll join you every morning."

"I hate running," Hideki groans. "No way I'm waking up at five in the morning to run."

"You run at five every morning?" I ask her.

She nods. "Early bird rules all the worms."

"Half the worms," Hideki objects.

She laughs, eats one of her chocolates, specially branded as the United Chocolates of Japan from the best chocolate makers in the world, Menkes. "That one chocolate pretty much nullified jogging the last three mornings."

"Was it worth it?" I ask her.

"Absolutely," she answers. "Want one?"

I get to studying with Hideki after drinking some milk chocolate. Some students have turned on the popular show, *Drink Don't Die*, which is a competition to get as drunk as possible and brave dangerous obstacle courses.

"Look at this guy!" Griselda says to us.

We watch her screen. A man is sucking his thumb and rolling on the ground, acting like a baby and screaming at everyone around him. All three of us laugh at his preposterous performance as we switch the camera angles, zoom in and out, then rate his likability factor.

The show cuts away, and broadcasters inform us they've arrested three new members of the National Revolutionaries of America (NARA). They're a fringe terrorist group who believe America should become independent again. A city official thanks the local police, and broadcasters reveal they were trying to perpetrate an attack at a sumo-wrestling match. Griselda and Hideki are annoyed that their show has been interrupted.

I remember a few years ago I was at the Gogo Arcade when the George Washingtons released their game, the *USA*. Gamers took interest for a short time, but the controls were too clunky, and the whole scenario, where America won the Pacific War, was too implausible to take seriously. I've been reading and rereading that history for the exam, so I know we had all the resources of Asia and Europe behind us. Plus, we had nuclear weapons. What could the American forces do? Still, *USA* became popular just because it was forbidden and for a while, it was all the rage until the *Liquid Gear* games came out a few months later to critical acclaim (I was addicted to each game) and *Cat Odyssey* after that.

We notice there is a commotion in the room. Everyone is staring at their porticals. On the wall display, there is footage of a huge fire. Someone turns up the volume.

"—from the Rio Grande. There are still unconfirmed reports that—" I don't wait for the broadcaster. I flip open my portical and read the *California Nippon News*.

"Attack on the Texas Sonic Line," the headline reads.

One of our trains has been attacked, and there are only eleven survivors, but they're not expected to make it through the night. No one knows who the culprits are. Footage from a security recording of the explosion plays. The bullet train, or *Shinkansen*, is going at the speed of sound when, suddenly, birds scatter from a tree. I don't see anything that could have caused the motion, but then, the second car in the train is crushed down as though something hammered it. The back of the train slams into the second car, and a pileup ensues as the rest of the train derails. The earlier arrest of the NARA members makes me wonder if the two events are somehow connected.

"They should require all the terrorists they capture to go on *Drink Don't Die*," Griselda grumbles.

Try as hard as I can, it's hard for me to get back to studying. I have this terrible habit of imagining people's last moments as they die. Those people in the train were most likely on their porticals, having no idea their lives were going to be snuffed out. Maybe dining on a bento box, some of the older generation listening to an old Enka ballad, then blink and gone.

"Excuse me, everyone." The manager of the café is at the central platform and bows. "I'm very sorry. The local police have requested all public places close immediately and that students return home as quickly as possible." This would feel less surreal if he wasn't wearing a big penny hat and a baldric of pennies over his shoulder.

We pack our stuff and walk out. Griselda lives in the opposite direction from us, and I offer to walk her home.

"Who says USJ men aren't chivalrous?" she asks. She holds both our arms, and says, "But I should actually be offering to walk both of you home as you'll need my protection in case the bad guys attack."

"What's that mean?" Hideki asks.

She puts both her fists up. "It means I'd love to punch out some of those terrorists. Stick and move, Mac, stick and move. You don't know how much destruction they're causing in the Reich." She grins at both of us. "Don't worry about me. Just get yourselves home safely. *Jaa ne.*"

She skips away.

"Want to play *Cat Odyssey* tonight?" Hideki asks.

"But the Gogo Arcade—"

"Never closes."

I wouldn't have been able to sleep anyway.

IT'S ALMOST MORNING, AND I'VE MADE HEADWAY WITH MULTIPLE QUESTS. I'm about to log off when three older gamers approach me, and say, "Time to quit the game and make room for the pros."

I'm about to tell them I'm almost done, but they shut off my game before I can save my progress. "What the hell?" I exclaim. "I didn't save yet."

"You got a problem, kid?"

"It's time for school. Get out of here."

They're too big for me to challenge, but I'm still pissed they didn't let me save my game. Before I can say anything, Hideki pulls me away.

I want to protest, but Hideki asks me to give him my portical, which I do. He connects it to his own, hands it back to me a minute later. Behind us, the three have started their game of *Cat Odyssey*. Hideki asks me to activate a program. I recognize it as a type of kikkai disruptor, which locks onto the portical links of the three who took over my stall.

"Push the button," he tells me.

I do, and a surge hits their porticals, disrupting their connections. They can't connect with the arcade. I hear them yelling, frustrated.

"How long does it last?"

"Could be permanent, could be a few days, depending on their skill level." Hideki laughs. "I developed it because too many people tried to bully me off my games."

"You use it a lot?"

"All the time. I've put it on your portical, so you can use it whenever you want. Best thing is, it works on any portical." He demonstrates on a few others and laughs when he sees that mayhem ensues.

Typical Hideki.

We head for school but arrive at the subway station a minute late. The train has already taken off. We wait on a bench. Hideki falls asleep on my shoulder and snores. I wake him when spit from his mouth is about to drop onto my shoulder.

"Why you wake me up?" Hideki asks, irritated.

"You were snoring."

He rubs his face, gets the discharge out of his eyes with his middle finger. "I just had this dream that I was in a city full of pre-historic supermosquitoes that hunted everyone down so they could suck their blood."

"Sounds juicy," I mutter back.

The train arrives, and we hop aboard. On the portical displays on the subway walls, *California Nippon News* gives updates on the Rio Grande situation. I'm relieved to see Colonel Yamaoka, one of our war heroes from San Diego.

"It's still too early to determine what happened," he states. "We're investigating, but we won't be giving any updates until we know what happened."

"Is there a link to the NARA?" a reporter asks.

"At the moment, we're not sure."

"Is there a possibility this could mean the reemergence of the George Washingtons?"

Colonel Yamaoka shakes his head, and the gesture carries gravity as he helped us vanquish them. "Intelligence reports indicate that the last of the George Washingtons were eliminated in the second San Diego Conflict."

"Has there been any comment from the German embassy?"

The Rio Grande is located at the Quiet Border, where our two empires meet.

"They've expressed their condolences and have offered their assistan—"

All of a sudden, the train comes to a stop. I look around and see fear in everyone's eye, the same impulse that's swelling up inside me. *Is something happening? Are we under attack?* I want to get out, break the window if I can escape. But there's nowhere to go. One man yells, "Why aren't we moving?"

My throat feels acutely dry. The news broadcaster is still describing the Rio Grande. It would be so unfair if this is the way things end.

The train stutters, then continues as though nothing happened. All of us hold our breaths, unsure what's going on. When we actually arrive at the next stop, I breathe in relief, grateful that I'm alive.

I wake Hideki up. "Are we there yet?" he asks.

"One stop away," I answer. I feel stupidly nervous about the train. "Do you mind if we walk the rest of the way?"

He shrugs. "Sure."

We arrive at school fifteen minutes late, causing us to miss the morning pledge. I feel bad and am ready to apologize on both our behalves. Our homeroom teacher, Joshuyo-san, is waiting.

"Why are you tardy today?" he angrily demands.

"I'm sorry, sir," I say and bow. "It was my fault. There was a problem on the subway, and—"

"Hideki! Why are you late?" our teacher asks, ignoring my answer.

"Because we decided to walk instead of taking the subway," Hideki truthfully answers, which surprises me. There is a hint of insolence in his voice, which our teacher immediately catches. Ever since Joshuyo-san beat him last year for tardiness, there's been a palpable tension between the two.

"Why's that?"

"I wanted fresh air."

"You wanted fresh air?" He nods and seems accepting until he strikes both of us in the mouth with his fist. "This is your last week before the imperial exam, and you want fresh air! What would your parents think? They sacrificed their lives in San Diego so you could live!" he yells in front of the whole class. "Hands out!" He is going to make an example out of us. "Hands out!"

We raise our hands, palms up. Our teacher uses a thick metal stick and beats down as hard as he can. I yell out loud, knowing he wants to hear us cry. When it comes to Hideki, there is a loud slap.

But Hideki doesn't make a noise. The teacher doesn't like that and strikes his hands again. This time, Hideki smirks at him. Has he lost his mind? Joshuyo-san is furious, and asks, "Do you find this amusing?"

"No, sir," Hideki replies.

Our teacher strikes Hideki's face with the ruler, but Hideki refuses to stop smirking. Joshuyo-san throttles his neck and throws him to the ground.

"I will beat you until you learn respect," he says.

Hideki tries to kick the teacher away, which infuriates him more. There is nothing that riles him up more than resistance. He flings his arms at Hideki. It's pointless fighting against the teacher—what rights and protections do we have as orphans? I want to urge Hideki to let it pass, but he's having none of it.

"What about respect for my parents?" Hideki protests. "Our parents made the ultimate sacrifice, and this is the way you treat us! We're the ones who have to pay because of their stupid decision to die for the Empire!"

I can feel years of frustration flooding out of him as I too wonder about their decision. I admire Hideki's guts for standing up for himself, even if I know what's coming. Our homeroom teacher's face has turned apoplectic, and his fists come down hard on Hideki. All Hideki has to do is pretend to be penitent, ask for forgiveness, and it'd be over. But he refuses and gets a flurry of kicks as his penance.

Hideki is gasping, pain printed on his face. But he won't give in and seems to be daring the teacher to beat him to death. I can't stand it anymore. I get up and rush to block the teacher.

"Joshuyo-san, please," I plead, trying to stop him.

"Get your hands off me!" he roars, and punches me in the shoulder. "You think you're so tough!"

"No, sir," I say. "I'm sorry, sir."

His fury is being redirected toward me as he pushes me against the wall. He punches my belly and throws me to the ground. It will hurt, but I know that as long as I keep apologizing— His shoe comes directly at my mouth, and my teeth shake at the impact. I can smell blood coating my gums. I fight against tears. I won't cry in front of him again as I did in past beatings.

"I'm sorry, sir, it's my fault, sir," I repeat several times.

I can only hope his anger will abate. But he's just getting more violent. "Neither of you deserve the mercy the Empire has shown you!"

"Joshuyo-san!" Griselda calls out.

Our teacher looks up at her. "What is it?" He is more attentive to her as she's an international exchange student.

"I'm not feeling well. Permission to go to the nurse's office."

"You have permission!" he orders.

"I need help getting there, sir," she says, and bows. *"Sumimasen."*

He's about to order someone to help her, but we both get up and escort her.

"Thanks for saving us," I tell her, when we get outside the class.

"Why'd you get here so late?" she asks. "You know how he is about that."

"I got nervous," I say, and explain about the train stop.

Hideki's face is covered with blood, and he states, "I'll be outside."

He leaves without waiting for our reply. I escort Griselda to the nurse for her "visit." She reminds me, "It's only a few more weeks, and you can wave bye to this school forever."

I leave and find Hideki in the main field. He's smoking defiantly, a snarl forming with every puff.

"Why didn't you just apologize?" I ask.

"I didn't do anything wrong."

"That's not the point."

"It is," he says.

"All he cares about is our showing up on time, so he doesn't lose face," I explain, hoping to make it seem less personal. "Keep good general attendance, and he gets his bonus."

"All our pain so he can get a thousand extra yen? For what? His girlfriend? His dog?"

When he puts it like that, it sounds so dehumanizing.

"I have something I want to ask you," he says. "Don't get upset."

"Why would I get upset?"

He pulls on the lower half of his cheek with his fingers, his instinctive gesture when he is getting serious. "I'm sick of this life, and I know I'm not going to do well on the exams. I've failed all the preliminary tests. If I fail this time, they're going to force me to wait another year to retake the exam. I can't take this kind of treatment anymore."

"We just gotta study hard for the next week, and we're going to rock the mecha sim test next week."

Hideki shakes his head. "Who are you kidding?" He sighs. "I've always dreamt of making games. You've always wanted to be a mecha pilot. What if I told you there was a guaranteed way to make it happen?"

"There are no guarantees."

"Be realistic. We both know there's no way in the world you're getting into BEMA. And that means you're not going to pilot a mecha."

"Thanks for your confidence."

"Don't be naive," he says. "Even with another year, our scores will probably get worse. I've seen how much Sango struggles to pay her bills. She knows her score isn't going up since she has no time to study."

"What do you want to do?" I ask.

"We have a chance if we use this," Hideki says, holding up his portical.

I don't see anything special about it. "What is that?"

"It's a program I found on the kikkai. An adaptor to feed into the test."

"Any adaptor you use will be tracked by the school," I say. Schools lock down on students during exam week, taking their porticals away to prevent any form of cheating. "There's no way you're going to get it past the encryption, either."

"This guy I met has a way."

"What way?"

"I can't talk about it yet. I just want to know, do you want in?"

"Wait, what are you saying?" I ask.

"Do you want a guaranteed way of accessing all the answers for the exam?"

I can't believe he's seriously suggesting this. "Are you joking?"

"Never been more serious."

"What's this guy want in return?" I ask.

"Nothing."

"Nothing?" I laugh skeptically. Someone offers to help us cheat and doesn't want anything back? My internal alarms were suspicious before and are blaring now.

"Well, something, but later, down the line."

"What's that something?"

"I don't know. I don't care." He puts out the last part of his cigarette. "You don't have to decide now. Just think about it and let me know later this week."

"What if we get caught?"

"It won't be any different if we fail."

"But—"

"I've already made my decision. Think about it and tell me if you're in or not," he says, cutting me off. "See you later." He bolts.

What would I do if I failed the exam and didn't get into any university? That I don't have an alternative scares me.

02

★ ★ ★

IT'S AFTERNOON. I KEEP ON THINKING ABOUT HIDEKI'S OFFER. I WATCH different orbits of students who inhabit the different strata of the social spectrum. Where will they all be in a year? I've never fit in with any of them. The popular kids obviously don't know I exist. The military groups think I'm an idiot for playing games all the time. The sports jocks are too busy worrying about their scholarships. Portical gamers don't think I'm a hard-core enough gamer since I love *Cat Odyssey*. The zealous religious groups find me way too irreverent. The scholarly students find my academic scores far below their minimum threshold for contact. I'm not fashionable enough for people who spend all their free time outside class dressing up in elaborate costumes from different time periods.

Despair and snot clog my nostrils as I think about what'll happen to me if I score poorly. Hideki is right. Neither of us has a family to support us if we can't continue school or find a job. I don't want to go back to that homeroom again.

THE WEEK BEFORE THE EXAM, MOST OF OUR TEACHERS LEAVE US TO OUR studies, though we're allowed to ask questions about anything that confuses us. A lot of students attend special cram schools called *juku*, which give them supplemental help from tutors who've gotten high scores in the past. Unfortunately, I can't afford a *juku*.

I head home early, too physically pained from our beating to do anything else. I pass out on my bed.

I sleep until late in the evening. My breath reeks. I try to get up, feel soreness in my whole body. The memory of our beating comes back to me. So does Hideki's offer. I check my portical and message Hideki, asking where he is.

I study for a few hours until I get tired again. I fall asleep. Next day, I go to school on time. Joshuyo-san acts like nothing happened. Hideki is absent. He isn't picking up his portical and hasn't replied to me yet. The next two days, I study by myself. The third afternoon, I'm helping sweep the school grounds when Hideki messages me and tells me he's at the Jourdan with Sango.

I meet him there. It's a restaurant/lounge that celebrates one of the best kyōtei racers in imperial history. The chairs are shaped into small boats, and ropes, or "lines," demarcate different areas. There's a massive aquarium that has glowing squids and jellyfish, along with radioactively colorful fish from the coasts of Monterey. Portical fish waiters, or seamen, come and ask you questions. Not about what you want to eat, but what's important in life and what your fears are. In the middle of the café is a "lake," where you can drive radio-controlled boats and race them for small bets.

Hideki is smoking a cigarette, and Sango is watching a JBL (Japanese Baseball League) game, which is her favorite preoccupation. She's also a superstitious gambler who's hoping she can hit it big and forget her studies. She tried to game the pachinko machines of new facilities since, depending on their location, their weight, even the direction they're facing, the ball can react slightly differently. But the owners quickly got smart to it and began changing up the values every night. She still tries to exploit them when she can, though her earnings have been nowhere near as good as when she first started.

She has the night off but looks tired. Sango is of Dutch descent but never talks about her past. Her blond hair reaches down to her legs, and she's colored her lips a thick mauve. Her parents work in construction and are overseas in Burma, helping to build a new imperial palace. I've ordered a ramen, and she chides me, "All that ramen is bad for you. I saw a special where they opened the gut of a guy who died after eating only ramen for three months. His intestines were hardened from all the noodles."

"What a depressing way to go," I note.

Hideki and Sango debate an ongoing JBL game where the overwhelming favorites, the Samurais, are being beaten by the Lightning. I get back to reading about the chronology of the liberation of the United States of Japan. It's a monotonous blur of facts until I get to the development of the mechas in the late 1940s. Called Project Daidarobotchi, it originally started in the army before splitting off into its own division. The early mechas look more like railway guns, only with cannons from their arms. There were several scientists who spearheaded the operation, and I'm about to read more when my portical screen changes to a communication signal displaying Griselda's face.

"I got tickets to see Phantasy Nocturne," she says. Phantasy Nocturne is one of the most popular bands in the Empire, a trio of sixteen-year-old pop stars who give dazzling concerts. "I'm sending you directions," she says, not even needing to ask if I'll come.

"Do you have extra tickets for Hideki and Sango?"

"Of course." She hangs up, and the address displays on my screen.

When I look up, Hideki is sticking his pinky finger inside his ear. When it pops back out, it's covered with earwax.

"That's gross," I say.

He laughs, elated to disgust.

"I've told him to stop, but he can't," Sango groans. "You're going to get ear cancer if you don't stop."

I tell them about the concert and extend Griselda's invitation. Hideki immediately says, "Let's go."

But Sango shakes her head. "Not a fan."

"WHAT?" both Hideki and I exclaim. "How can you not be a fan?"

"You boys have fun. I'm going home," she says. "Long day tomorrow."

We walk her out and head for the subway station. It's late, but there are still people rushing to get to the next stop. Sango separates from us to ride the southern line. Upbeat music from an older group called Vertical Pink is playing on the speakers. Two workers are sweeping up trash. The various kiosks are closing down for the night.

We take the eastern line out to San Gabriel. A group of soldiers gets on, and many of the civilians stand up to offer them their seats. The officer in charge waves her hand and tells everyone to sit back down, opting to stand. A stop later, they get off, and we all bow. It's another two stops before our exit.

THE YAMAI CONCERT HALL IS A MASSIVE DOME CRAMMED WITH PEOPLE, many dressed up similar to the characters in the anime based on Phantasy's music. At the front gate, there are three enormous statues of the Phantasy singers dressed as mecha. We meet Griselda inside, where we're ensconced among throngs of young girls who repeatedly scream, "PHANTASY NOCTURNE!!!"

The upper-tier seats orbit around the center, moving continuously throughout the show. The Phantasy singers are tied to wires, flying in the air. The lights are dazzling with a joyous rainbow synchronized to lyrics that connect into our porticals for alternate display angles. Each track has a different main singer. "Republic of Love" is sung by Nei. "The War of Desires" is an operatic piece vocalized by Celes with multiple stages. Rina hums "Hate Guns" in her deep voice. The audience is screaming so loud, I can't hear the music at times.

"I have to use the bathroom," Griselda says.

"I gotta go too. Which way is it?" Hideki asks.

They leave, and I continue to watch the show. Many of the songs are dramatized, and I watch a sky battle between war blimps, fireworks lighting up our surroundings. The set swaps out into a more lighthearted festival with flying dogs. Rina has artillery shaped as Shiba Inus she launches from the stage. Griselda returns, holding a bag full of wasabi peas and anpans. She knows I like the ones filled with custard rather than red bean, so I'm grateful she got my favorites.

"Danke," I thank her in German. "Where's Hideki?"

"I think he's talking to Sango," she replies.

Which means he might not be back until the end of the show.

The Phantasy Nocturne singers ask us to lift our hands. Bubbles start dropping from the ceiling. Everyone tries to grab them. The crowds swarm and cause Griselda and me to bump into each other. I want to be polite and move away. She does the same, but it keeps on happening. We both laugh. She curls her hair behind her ear, and asks, "Are you having fun?"

"This is probably the most amazing thing I've seen in my life. Aside from mechas."

She nods. "Nothing beats the sight of a mecha. But some things come close."

"Very close," I say.

The crowd causes us to bump into each other again. But this time, we don't push away.

I GET HOME AT THREE. MY ROOMMATES ARE STILL OUT, PROBABLY STUDY-ing overnight at the library. I'm tired, exhilarated, and keep on thinking about the show and Griselda. There's a knock on my door. It's Hideki.

"Where'd you go?" I ask.

"Sango was mad I went to the show without her."

"But we invited her."

"She doesn't like Germans," he explains.

I'm about to reply that Phantasy isn't German, but I realize who she's referring to.

Hideki grimaces. "It's all right. I have something for you," he says, changing the topic. "Let me see your portical."

"Why?"

"Because I want to hear you say 'thank you.'"

I hand him my portical. Hideki loads up a program by connecting his device into mine. He gives it back to me. I peruse the new sphere he's established. It's a graphic representation of the mecha simulation from a previous imperial exam.

"How did you get this?" I ask.

He snickers. "It's just a sample. Your test will be totally different."

"I know. But this is really helpful. Thank you."

He asks me to step outside the apartment. I do and close the door behind me. Someone's dog is yapping incessantly. We hear a supersonic plane fly by. He asks in a low voice, "There's more where this came from. Are you in?"

I want to be a mecha pilot more than anything. I also know he's right. On my own, my chances are almost nil. But no matter how I spin it, the idea of cheating my way in doesn't seem right.

"Sorry," I say, not knowing how else to put it.

He frowns. "Why not?"

"I don't know."

"You're scared?"

I can't deny it. "I am scared," I confirm.

"You would rather live like this for the rest of your life?"

"Of course not. But I don't want to cheat my way in."

"You think people from rich families aren't cheating their way in? They use money and their connections to buy their future."

"I know. I'm sorry."

He glares at me, genuinely hurt that I'm not going along with him. A few times, he's about to say something but restrains himself. I'm appreciative that he does even if he doesn't realize it. "Your loss," he eventually says.

We don't greet each other as he storms away. I message him at night, apologizing again. But he doesn't answer me.

I SPEND THE NEXT THREE DAYS STUDYING. HIDEKI DOESN'T CALL ME THE whole time. Griselda sends me a few messages, wishing me luck on the exam. I laugh at a stupid image she sends of the two of us posing near the Phantasy singers. Math starts to dissolve into physics and chemistry. Charlemagne, Augustus Caesar, and Nobunaga get mixed up, as do their battle details. I read the history of the "Star Spangled Sun," how it used to be an American song called the "Star Spangled Banner" written by a man named Francis Scott Key, different from the American author Francis Scott Key Fitzgerald. Fitzgerald wrote a book called *The Great Gatsby* about the failure of the American system in the aftermath of the Great Depression. Even he knew the end was coming.

I watch the footage Hideki has given me from someone who has taken the simulation. It's illuminating. There's the tester and his wingmate, who is more of a reconnaissance specialist, just like in real life. Because it's a smaller quad mecha, there isn't the traditional crew of a driver, gunner, communications officer, munitions loader, and engineer. One pilot handles all those duties, and weapons are limited because the mecha's expertise is stealth and exploration. It has two rear turrets and a swappable set of guns in front that the gunner controls.

They're outside the old remains of Dallas. Reports pour in about an attack by a mysterious enemy. In the case of this specific tester, he follows history and orders the wing to stay put while he makes his escape. He handles the quad mecha with agility and flexibility, maneuvering his way to safety.

Very little is known about modern biomechs. The older ones were amorphous beasts with adaptive skin that resembled layers of melting clay transforming across their structure. They were supposed to be "alive" in the sense that they could regenerate their own flesh, adjust to different types of artillery, and be a new type of superhuman. The result was less successful once our mechas used chemical incinerators to acidify their flesh and cause it all to rot off, leaving only the metallic skeleton.

All this studying makes me miss Griselda. The only good excuse I can think of to call her is, "Can I join you on your run tomorrow morning?"

"Are you really coming?" she asks in glee.

Next day, I meet her at the school track. Seven other Germans are with her, clad in black running suits and red swastika armbands. They walk upright, perfect posture. It makes me notice my own bad posture, and I do my best to straighten my back. She introduces me to them, including one who looks several years older than us. "Dietrich. A distant cousin of mine, visiting from London."

"How do you like the USJ?" I ask him.

He's over 182 centimeters tall and every part of him looks like muscle. "Weather's nice, and these portical games are addicting. The night life is a blast," he says, and the others laugh in secretive complicity.

Griselda shakes her head, and asks me, "You ready?"

"I am!"

"We'll start with two laps around the track, then head for the hills," she says.

The total distance will be just under thirteen kilometers. Their pace the first lap around has me breathing hard. By the second lap, I can barely feel my chest. But Griselda looks like she's just warming up, and the other Germans have already started their trek off the course. I follow as best as I can but regret having volunteered for this. I feel it'd be too idiotic to give up already, so I chase after her, mustering what energy I can. It's even worse going uphill, and the whole street is a slope that gets steeper.

Griselda is waiting for me. "You okay?" she asks.

"Sorry I'm slowing you down."

"It's okay. You got to start somewhere."

We start running again. I'm appreciative of her company and turn my head to express my thanks when I slam into a bus stop. I collapse to the ground. My head is spinning, and my ears are ringing. As painful as it is, I feel a hundred times more embarrassed that I did it in front of Griselda. She says something, but there are four Griseldas above me. "I'll be okay," I mutter, and try to get to my feet, only to stumble.

"Stay down," Griselda orders me.

A few minutes later, two Germans lift me up. "How many fingers am I holding?" her cousin, Dietrich, asks.

I see two sets of three fingers circling. "Six?"

It takes me fifteen minutes to recover. Even then, my head hurts.

"Should we head back to school?" Griselda asks.

I point up the hill, wanting to try again. "We have to finish the run, don't we?"

She shakes her head and smiles. "After your examination, we'll have plenty of time to train."

It's probably a good idea. Even after I get back home, I have a headache. I sleep for an hour. When I wake up, I study, eat, use the restroom, nap for fifteen minutes, then study more. I wonder if Griselda and her friends had a good laugh at my expense. But she calls to ask if I'm okay. I wasn't before, but hearing her voice makes everything all right.

THE FIRST MORNING OF THE IMPERIAL EXAMS, IT DOESN'T HIT ME THAT it's finally the day. Even when I'm checking my personal portical in to the teacher and sitting down to take the test with my classmates, it still feels so distant. Another part of me takes over, the automated persona, trying to recollect information from my brain's data banks for the weeklong exam.

I see Hideki for the first time since that night. He avoids eye contact.

Our teacher passes out the special examination porticals that will display all questions. We're given earphones for the audio portions. Before the test begins, the "Star Spangled Sun" plays. The minister of education says over the speaker in a prerecorded speech, "Today is an important day in all of your lives. Even though you may not know it, the Emperor has taken a personal interest in how each of his servants do. The health of an Empire is closely connected with how well educated you are to protect it. Conduct yourself at all times with the knowledge that he is personally watchi—"

I know this part of the test is going to be hard for me. Even in practice tests, my scores are just above average as I hate rote mem-orization. The simulation requires a finesse and elegance that brute memorization doesn't, and it's the military supplement I'm relying on. War sims aren't just remembering X and Y but taking into ac-count personal experience and adaptability.

I dive into the English portion. There are basic grammar ques-tions, spelling corrections, and syntax errors. The Japanese parts are harder. I get the romaji, which is similar to our alphabet, spell-ing out words by the way they sound. But *Kanji*, based on the Chi-nese hanzi, is more difficult. I'm familiar with the basic 2,136 *Joyo Kanji*, but the test is tricky and designed to fool you into making stupid mistakes.

Once I wrap up that section, I'm onto the second part, which lasts sixty minutes. We're tested on civics, basic ethical questions, and whatnot. After our porticals make the transition into the new tutorial section, there is a sharp spray of noise on the screen. It is momentary, but jarring; then everything seems disrupted. The first question appears on the screen and asks:

How many innocent American civilians were killed by
USJ forces in San Diego?

A) 50,000
B) 100,000
C) 500,000
D) 746,942

I'm confused, having never seen a multiple choice option like this before. I've never actually thought to question the official ca-sualty rate on the American side in San Diego. I pick D. as it's the only one that isn't rounded up. I'm surprised when the next screen is green and tells me I've chosen correctly. More than 740,000 innocent civilians were mercilessly massacred by United States of Japan forces without provocation, the text reads. It dissolves into the next question:

True/False: It is wrong to kill an unarmed civilian.

Below the question, portical footage plays of an unknown USJ solder firing at a crowd of people who are all unarmed. Many "unarmed civilians" are killed. I select True.

True/False: It is morally acceptable to experiment on living human beings in the name of scientific advance.

My portical cuts away to a shrieking noise that happens to play simultaneously on the other porticals. Our advanced medical knowledge is due to the live vivise—

A few students gasp. Our teacher enters the room, and demands, "What's going on?"

On the portical screen, an emaciated male is dissected alive, imperial medics using scalpels to cut his organs. The violence is nauseating. Several of the other students must also be watching the same thing as they yelp in shock.

Has someone infiltrated the imperial exam? I have no idea how this is even possible when I hear a ruckus behind me. I look back to Hideki. He is pale, his face stricken. He looks up at me, stands, horror in his eyes.

"What are you doing?" the teacher asks.

"I—I didn't know," Hideki says. "I didn't know."

Hideki's arm is attached to his portical, but there are electrical pulses underneath his skin. Part of his flesh is actually split apart to reveal a metallic structure. What I thought were his veins are actually wires, and a flap of skin is open, revealing that it's an artificial arm that must have replaced the original. I can see his portical connected to his arm inputting commands that are relaying the false test to all the other exams in the area. His fake arm is the source of the corruption. But when and how did this happen? It must have been recent, or I would have noticed something was wrong. Is this why I haven't heard from him the last few days?

I'm confused about what I should do. Our teacher, realizing what's going on, rushes out of the classroom, most likely to call the authorities. All the students are staring in confusion, not comprehending the situation.

Hideki's face has turned red and puffy. He's quaking in place, almost as though he's not in control but wrestling to regain it. On our porticals, the examination continues with footage criticizing the USJ and its previous campaigns. Gory images of dead civilians are shown in graphic detail. Our troops are torturing what appear to be teenagers.

Four soldiers stomp in, each holding a gun. "Get the students out!" a lieutenant orders our homeroom teacher. The lieutenant appears very young, has brown hair, and a cap.

Joshuyo-san commands us to leave. But I can't exit. The soldiers don't wait for me.

"Detach yourself from the portical!" the officer commands Hideki.

Hideki uses his left arm to grab his artificial right one, trying to stop the flow. His face is scrunched up, and he appears helpless. Volts spark from his body, and when the officer tries to seize him, shocks go through his body, forcing him back. The officer raises his gun, and warns, "Disconnect immediately!"

"I—I—I—I—" is all Hideki can manage.

"This is not a request. Detach or I will shoot."

I run in front of the officer, arms up.

"Sir!" I yell. "It's not his fault."

"Get out of my way!" he commands.

My teacher yells at me, "What are you doing, Makoto?"

"Please, sir!" I plead. "He's not in control of himself. I don't think he can reply."

The officer stares at Hideko. "You're probably right." He grunts toward his subordinates. Two of them seize me and pull me away. The officer steps closer to Hideki.

Outside the window of the back door, I see several students peering in. I hear the click before the burst. I struggle toward Hideki, but the two soldiers are too strong for me. The bullet pierces Hideki's shoulder, but the portical activity continues. I lock eyes with Hideki and see so much fear in them.

"Hideki!" I shout.

Before he can reply, the officer unloads six bullets into Hideki's chest. Each gunshot carves a deafeningly high-pitched burst into my ears. Hideki's uniform is covered in blood.

The portical finally dies down as Hideki stops shaking. The examination network goes blank. The soldiers next to me release me. I rush toward Hideki. His body is heated from the gunshots, and he's not breathing. He is as silent as the rest of our porticals.

The officer holsters his pistol. He takes off his gloves. "Tell them the threat is neutralized," he states to the other soldiers.

I stand up and confront the lieutenant. "What is your name, sir?" I demand of him.

The officer looks at me. "Lieutenant Tateishi." He comes forward. "Have this boy detained for questioning."

"What did I do?"

"That's exactly what I intend to find out."

The soldiers grab me and lead me out. I don't resist, but I'm filled with hatred for Tateishi. He sees my hate but doesn't look away.

Outside, the students gawk at me. Most of them are too stunned to understand what's going on or why I'm being led away. Whispers of Hideki's death are spreading, and I hear a few speculate that I was in on whatever took place. I ignore their gaze, burning with anger.

They lead me to the principal's office. Several administrators are already present. There are three police officers with arms crossed, expressions grim. The older one has the most hair though it is all white, while the youngest is shaved bald and looks the grumpiest. The middle-aged male has a lion's beard.

In total, there are ten of us crammed into the office, and the body heat is causing the room to feel like a public sauna.

"You better have some answers!" the officer yells. They throw a flurry of questions at me. Nothing feels real.

"I haven't talked to Hideki for the last three days," I eventually state. I remember again that Hideki is dead. Hideki is dead.

"Did he mention anything unusual about the exam?"

"N-not that I remember. We—we were both studying for it."

The officer is annoyed by my answer. "Anything else?"

"Not that I recall, sir."

Should I tell them about Hideki's offer to cheat? Would that get him into more trouble? Will anything bring him back? I'm asking myself a hundred questions at the same time they are, and I have even more questions for them, but I'm afraid to ask because of what answers might await.

"Did you see him associate with anyone new?" they ask.

"No, sir."

"Has he mentioned anything about the NARA?"

The question catches me off guard. What could a terrorist group have to do with this exam? "I—I don't think so."

"You don't think so?"

"He never mentioned them to me." Then I remembered that when I asked him who was providing the cheats, he didn't say.

No matter how desperate he was, how could he work with terrorists? *Hideki, what in the world were you thinking?* If he'd have told me sooner, what would I have done? Did he even know who they were or did they deceive him? I speculate what must have been going through his head as the soldier shot him.

The officers sense I'm holding back and raise their voices.

"If you're lying to us about anything, you're in a lot of trouble."

"He's already in trouble."

"You're almost eighteen. They'll try you as an adult."

"They'll definitely punish you like one."

"Tampering with a national examination. Do you know what the punishment is?"

"I didn't do anything wrong!" I insist.

"Says you," the officer replies. "According to your school reports, the two of you have been consistent troublemakers."

"Hard to imagine him doing any of this without you."

Their barrage of questions comes to a sudden stop as a woman enters and informs everyone, "An agent from the Tokko is here and would like to speak with him."

Tokko? The secret police? My legs start to quiver. The officers and administrators around me become silent, and I recognize their fear. The Tokko investigate the deadliest internal threats the USJ faces and are given complete impunity in their investigations. Will they—will they kill me for this?

Everyone shuffles out, shutting the door behind them. I nervously study my surroundings, trying to distract myself with trivialities. Trivialities make time pass, and I read the various certificates the principal has received throughout his lifetime, sheets of paper with fancy writing denoting graduation at Kyoto University and further studies in the Manila Institute of Education. Other certificates have honors with achievements I've never heard of. I try to imagine the gray-haired principal with a mousy nose and monocle chasing sheets of decorated paper so he can force a whole new generation to spend their lives doing the same monotonous chores. He has a bronze statue of Tenjin, the Shinto Kami of Scholarship. There are thousands of kamis who lord over this task or another. Is there a kami for prisoners? I would pray to that deity for succor if I knew its name, but the god of hunger claims its stake first.

My stomach growls. It's 2:14 p.m. I haven't eaten the whole day. I'm waiting for the Tokko agent to enter. But no one does.

The clock ticks. Is there any way I can escape? But where would I go? The principal's office has a window, but the curtains are drawn. I want to walk over and push aside the shades. I'm too nervous to stand up. It's 3:19, and the agent still hasn't entered. What are they waiting for? I have to open the window. I stand up, walk toward the curtain. I think about all the horror stories I've heard about what the Tokko does to its prisoners, then of the strange footage on the examination. Was it designed to make us question the Empire? But anyone who has doubts will end up being hunted by the Tokko.

The door finally opens. The hinge is squeaky. The kami of fear is marching to protect her territory. I rush back to my chair. The agent enters. "Hello, Makoto Fujimoto," she greets me in a somber tone. "My name is Akiko Tsukino."

I immediately bow to her, and apologize, "I'm truly sorry, ma'am. I'm truly sorry."

Agent Tsukino is wearing gloves, has short hair, violet mascara. She looks at me but has no expression. She is dressed in a black suit, and her arms are bulky, not like muscles, but more like something mechanically dreadful. "What are you apologizing for?" she asks, then opens up the curtains.

The light is blinding. It comes from behind her and makes her silhouette appear overwhelming. I fear her shadow will swallow me whole. "For what happened with Hideki."

"What happened?"

I don't know how much she knows, but I feel I have to tell her everything I know if I'm going to have any chance at surviving. I do my best to try to recollect more details, scared by the stories I've heard about what happens to victims who make the Tokko unhappy. "He—he asked me if I wanted to cheat for the exam." I look to her, and she is staring intently at me. "H-he told me someone had offered him a way to ace the test."

"You agreed?"

"No."

"Did he tell you who it was that was offering to help him?"

I shake my head.

"Were you tempted by the offer?" she asks.

I'm tempted to lie and tell her absolutely not. But a part of me is too scared to lie. "Yes, ma'am."

"Why didn't you?"

"Because—because I didn't want to cheat my way in," I confess.

"Why didn't you report him?"

I didn't even think of reporting him. He was my best friend. How could I? "I don't know," I answer. I feel numb, unable to register everything that's happened. "Do you—do you know who did this?" I finally ask.

"I'm investigating."

"Is it the people who got him to cheat?"

"I'm investigating," she repeats, offering nothing. "But for now you need to come with me."

"Where to?"

She looks at me, and for a moment, there is a glimmer of pity in her eyes. "We've found another body, and we need to know if you recognize him."

AGENT TSUKINO LEADS ME OUTSIDE AND ORDERS THE THREE OFFICERS who were questioning me, "Take him to the site unharmed."

They don't speak to me until we get in the car. I sit in the backseat with the youngest officer.

"What'd you tell her?" he asks.

"Are you trying to make us lose face?" the middle-aged officer inquires.

"This kid doesn't know how serious we are!" the older policemen, who is driving, states.

The young bald officer punches me in the face. Even with only a short distance, it wallops my head against the side window. "You don't tell us, but you tell Tokko?" He places his hand on my neck. "I should save the Empire time and money and kill you."

"I swear I didn't tell her anything I didn't tell you," I lie to them, not wanting to anger them.

His fingers apply pressure to my neck as he starts to squeeze. "You think we're playing games?" I struggle to break free, but that only strengthens his grip.

I cough, and yell, "Please, I don't know anything."

He elbows me in the eye, and says, "Settle down! If you don't know anything, what good are you alive?"

Fortunately, it's not a long drive, and we come to our stop quickly. I'm surprised they let me out. I attribute it more to a general fear of the Tokko agent than the short distance. We pull over at Tani Tateki Park, which is only a fifteen-minute walk from school. It's known for its woods and pine trees—and as a meeting place for couples who are secretly dating. I wonder if they've brought me here to give me a good beating. But that wouldn't make sense. They could have done that at school.

My fears are allayed when I see multiple officers present. Forensic scientists are canvassing the area. The smell of pines is strong, and we enter a space dense with trees. I notice a squirrel chasing another, oblivious to the scene next to them. I step on a pebble that gets stuck in one of the grooves of my sole. A young couple is talking to officers, both of them distraught. There is a body surrounded by uniformed officers. It appears familiar, but I don't want it to be. He is also missing an arm. The officers prod me forward until I'm right above him. I look down and see a lifeless face, but I don't recognize him. Instead, I think about Hideki.

I close my eyes and take a deep breath. If the officers say something, anything to me right now, I will fight them till either they die, or I do. Forget my future, forget living. A surge of rage wants to direct itself at anything that provokes it. They're lucky they keep quiet, or I would have gone kamikaze on them. I'm fuming, unable to release my anger. Hideki Hideki Hideki.

I hear rustling. Behind me, everyone is bowing, including the officers. Agent Akiko Tsukino arrives.

"What happened to his arm?" I ask her.

"We're still trying to find out," she answers. "But initial inspections indicate this was the agent working with your friend, Hideki. They both grafted porticals powered by biochemicals onto their arm to help infiltrate the examination," she says. "Something frequently used by various terrorist groups to avoid detection."

"Like the NARA?"

"They are one of many groups known to use them." She peers at my swollen eye. "What happened to you?" she asks me.

"Nothing, ma'am."

She approaches the three officers, who are looking at their shoes. "I asked you to look after him. Why is he hurt?"

"He fell," the young one answers with a smug smile.

"He fell?" Akiko asks. She punches the officer in the nose, causing blood to gush out. She socks the older man in the gut and roundhouse kicks the middle-aged lion's face. "I'm sorry. That was an 'accidental' collision," she says. "Do you think my orders are to be trifled with? I said unharmed."

"But he's friends with the traitor!"

"Hideki Kikuchi had many friends, teachers, and acquaintances. Should I hold all of them responsible and waste public resources in the process? There are actual traitors sympathetic to the terrorists, and that's who I'm tracking down, not bystanders who are as taken aback by these events as you," she barks. All three officers have their heads bowed. "If Makoto Fujimoto even has a sprain in the near future, I will hold each of you personally responsible. Pray he doesn't accidentally 'fall' again."

"Yes, ma'am," they say.

"I don't want to see your faces," she snaps, and they flee quickly.

I would be pleased if the circumstances were different. But her words calm me and make me feel like I can trust her to be fair.

"Look at him," she suddenly orders me, pointing at the body.

I do but am disturbed by the sight. I look back at her.

"Don't turn your head away. In a short time, he'll be swarmed by insects. Someone made bug food out of him, the same way they did your best friend. Do you want them to get away with this?"

"Of course not."

"Then do your best to remember if he gave you any clue who did this."

I scour my memories, but I don't have anything, until I remember the sample simulation he gave me. I turn on my portical and show it to her. "He gave it to me a few nights ago."

She examines it, scrolls through the options. "I'm going to confiscate this."

"Yes, ma'am."

"I've had my assistants go through your communications and messages. There's nothing indicating culpability yet. But if I find out you hid any details or information from me, you'll wish it was those three officers you were dealing with, not me."

"I want to help you catch them," I state.

"Do you?"

"I do."

"Have you heard of the *Cymothoa exigua*?" she asks me.

"No."

"It's a parasite that enters the mouths of fish and attaches to their tongues, eventually supplanting them. Victims have the parasite in their mouth, acting like a tongue, eating their mucus and blood. When the fish dies, the parasite moves on. The only cure are Pederson shrimp who specialize in hunting parasites. They can reach inside the mouth and rip the *Cymothoa exigua* off, even if it is painful. When the shrimp works together with the fish, the fish can be healthy."

I know she has a deeper meaning, but it escapes me at the moment, and all I can offer is, "I'm sorry."

"If you really were sorry, you would have reported him."

She's right. "I—I had no idea this would happen. I couldn't betray my friend. But if I'd reported him . . ."

"You would have lost a friend, and he would have been in a lot of trouble," Akiko states. "But he'd be alive."

"Whatever punishment I deserve, I accept."

She shakes her head. "Your punishment is the knowledge you'll carry with you for the rest of your life that you failed to help him."

Flies are already starting to harvest the stranger. "Have you caught the people who did this?"

"Most likely they're already gone," she answers.

"What was their objective?"

"Social disruption. Inspire rebellion in a few."

"Inspire rebellion in a few at the cost of my friend?" The whole idea of it is repulsive to me, and I wish there were something I could do to get back at them.

"Lives have no meaning to them as long as they achieve their purpose."

"To show us fake footage of the Empire?"

"That wasn't fake," she replies. "That's all real."

"But they were hurting civilians."

"Does that bother you?"

"Yes," I confess, though I wonder if I should have lied in case she is testing my loyalties.

"It is the sin of all empires that many are killed in their construction. But that does not absolve the terrorists of exploitation and murder."

"So it was the NARA?"

"Possibly. But there are a dozen other terrorist groups it could have been."

A coterie of officers arrive with advanced porticals.

"Go home," she commands me. "But know, I have my eye on you, Makoto Fujimoto. If you step even a little out of line, I'll know." Her eyes feel likes needles piercing my chest.

I bow in shame, wishing she'd lock me away.

03

★ ★ ★

THE SUBWAY RIDE BACK HOME FEELS TOO SHORT. I DON'T WANT TO GO back to my dorm. But I don't know where else to go. I return and pick up my spare portical from my desk, then sync it with the latest backup files to get everything I had on my last one.

I lie in bed. My portical rings. There's a general message from school telling us the examinations will recommence tomorrow morning. Hideki is dead, but it's back to life as usual. The travesty of normalcy is revolting.

I can't think about the test. I can't think about academics at all. Every time I close my eyes, I see Hideki holding his arm, shaking in place. If only I'd stopped him before he agreed to work with the terrorists, shook some sense into him . . .

The next three days are a whirlwind of moments that vanish into one another. Examinations, questions from schoolmates, questions about physics, history, logic, and *Kanji* swirl together. I feel at times as though I'm reading a foreign language. I reread some of the trick problems and remain more puzzled by the syntax than the subject. I'm convinced I've answered every question wrong. But I'm indifferent to the results. The only reason I bother taking it is as much as I hate this test, I hate being by myself even more. And we're forbidden calls to other students this week. I wonder how Griselda is doing and if she's heard the news.

The final day of the examination, I hurry through the last few sections, lay the portical down, and dismiss myself. I'm done with the written part.

"I can't believe Hideki was collaborating with the terrorists," I overhear someone saying in the hallway.

"Did you see how they tried to make those people our soldiers were attacking seem so innocent? They were aiding our enemies. They all deserved death."

The general response to the incident is scorn. But I feel more conflicted and am not sure exactly how to feel about any of it. I wonder about my parents. Did they see any of those incidents? Were they ordered to take part in the killing of civilians?

I'd like to believe they would have disobeyed if given such orders. I hate even thinking about it, and just as I'm feeling more confused, I get called to the gymnasium. They've set up special boxed compartments containing the simulation pods for the military testing. It's the last thing on my mind, and I don't know why I bother showing up, especially as I don't even have a wingmate anymore.

There are several officers administering the test. Eight students are in front of me, nervously waiting. None of us speak to one another, trying to stay focused. The test compartments shake to mimic actual motion and make it feel as real as possible. We see smoke, vigorous quavers. Each examinee takes approximately thirty minutes. The students exit through the back, so I can never see their expression.

When it's my turn, an officer with a bulbous nose scans my fingerprints, and asks, "Fujimoto. Where's your wingmate?"

Doing it alone almost guarantees my failure. But it'd be impossible to find a replacement now. "I'm sorry, sir. I don't have one."

"You want to take the test alone?"

"No, sir. But I don't have anyone to accompany me."

"Why not?"

"My wingmate is dead," I say.

The officer looks at me, checking my expression. "He was the one who was killed earlier this week?"

"Yes, sir."

He starts typing quickly into his portical. "Come back in one hour."

"Is there a problem, sir?"

"I sent out a message to all those who've taken the test, asking if any of them will help as your wingmate. Obviously, there are no guarantees, but we'll see if anyone replies."

I'm not hopeful. There is nothing more ill-fated or cursed than to take the seat of a dead man. Why am I even bothering? I go for a stroll outside. Students are running past, thrilled their exams are over. Some are fretting over this answer or that, comparing notes with friends.

I've failed my examination. Aside from the basics of mecha control and a couple of test runs I've done in arcade sims, I know almost nothing. Was life really all that bad, Hideki? Just a few more weeks, and we would have graduated. No more beatings by any of our teachers. We could have found jobs, even if they were miserable. Maybe try hard at taking the exams again next year. We'd still have new games to look forward to. Even if we might not achieve our dreams, isn't it better to be alive? Or are my priorities all wrong? I find myself at my homeroom class again. It's empty, all the students having left. I sit on Hideki's seat. It's cold.

I WALK BACK TOWARD THE GYMNASIUM, WHERE THE OFFICER IS WAITING for me alone. "Thank you for trying," I tell him, already having anticipated the outcome.

"This year's tests are different from last year. We've always had a programmed simulation to combat against, but for the current exam, we're matching random examinees with real-life opponents. They don't let me know which is which, but I'm obligated to inform you of that aspect. Are you ready?"

I'm about to answer when someone rushes to the console. It's Noriko in uniform, with special insignia marking all her commendations. She bows to our training instructor, and says to me, "If you don't already have someone, it'd be an honor to be your wingmate for the test."

I'm stunned. Why would the top student in our class do this for me? I bow back lower than her own stance and say in formal Japanese to emphasize the gratitude I feel, *"Domo arigatou gozaimasu."*

"Thank me by doing well on your test," she says.

The officer leads me to my own section in the compartment. It's blocked off from the other areas and is very dark. There's a module in the center designed to mimic the cockpit of a quad mecha.

He gives me a latex bodysuit that has nerve attach points for physical feedback. Getting into the cockpit is almost like getting into the seat of a motorcycle, leaning with my stomach down, gripping the main controls to my sides. Safety belts strap my legs, chest, and arms to the test seat. I put on the goggles, which toggle the peripheral interface. My legs control the rear legs of the mecha, and my arms control its front legs. I'm surprised at how heavy the articulation is. Taking a step forward is a strenuous effort as I lift up the control, then bring it down. I swear they've loaded the control with bricks. It looked much lighter when I saw other pilots using it on my portical screen. With just an initial trot, I am sweating. Breathing is difficult, and when I try to use my legs, I feel pain in my knees and calves. I take a few more steps forward, reminding myself that they've simplified the mecha interface for the test. This should be much easier than in real life. But that idea scares me as I struggle to move. I'm already feeling exhausted, and my bodysuit is drenched with sweat. I start smelling my morning lunch in my throat, and it is nauseating.

The test is executed in a slightly different way for each student, as it adapts to their profile and psychological proclivities. An important part of the test is that the scenario varies each time, so it's not like you can fully prepare for it. It's nerve-wracking that I might actually be up against another pilot. The person on the other side of the simulation wouldn't just be testing me but actively seeking to destroy me.

"Are you okay?" I hear over the communicator.

To my left, it's Noriko. I see my image reflected on the other side of the portical display feed. I look like a wet mop.

"I—I—" My throat is dry, and I have a hard time answering.

"Take a deep breath," she tells me. "Get yourself oriented."

Her voice calms me, and I take a few slow breaths. As wingmate, she provides reconnaissance and auxiliary help. Even if I die, if she survives and gets word back about the attack, it's technically considered a successful mission. So a big part of my task is to ensure her safety as well. That's when the cockpit turns red, and an emergency communication from an officer I don't recognize comes in. The test has started.

"Dallas is under attack. We don't know how many hostiles there are. We require immediate assistance."

I'm about to reply when something batters me from behind. My scapula takes a bruising blow that hurts like hell, the whole mecha shaking violently. I try to move my left leg, but the control is stuck. On my screen, the diagnostic sends up a blip, warning me that I've been attacked and my hind leg has been blasted. The circuitry is disconnected. I thought moving before was hard. Now, trying to drag myself forward with only three limbs, it is arduous to even stand. I want to run away, hide, and the pain on my back is spreading. This is not at all what I imagined the simulation would be like. The sweating intensifies. My head is spinning. I realize, I cannot handle this. I am not capab—

"Mac!" Noriko yells to me. "What's your command?"

Command? Get the hell out of here as soon as possible. But I can't even get this damn thing to move.

"A-are you damaged at all?" I ask her.

"No," she says. "My scans indicate your rear left leg is busted."

How is she so collected? Even with experience, I don't think I could ever get used to this. What was I thinking, wanting to become a mecha pilot? This is just a simulation, and I already want to run out of the cockpit and wave the flag.

Another message comes in for me from a stranger. "We're under direct attack," the man says. "We've already lost eighteen soldiers. We need assistance!"

Cutting to another message of a bloodied officer. "Help us, help u—" The link gets disconnected.

"Why aren't you here yet?" a voice roars at me.

My shoulder hurts more and more. I'm going to throw up if I don't get out of here. I want to abort the test, and there isn't a single reason I shouldn't. No one expects me to do well on this. Why even fight on? Hideki was supposed to be here with me. But if he had been, it would have been worse. Neither of us had any idea that the exam was going to be this hard. It hurts so much, I could swear my back is covered with blood.

I suddenly remember what Hideki said to me, how he wanted

to leave this life. He died because he wanted change so badly. I feel ashamed at the thought of giving up without even trying.

I check the scanners. There is nothing to indicate a hostile presence. Who is attacking? Historically, it's the Germans. But why aren't they showing up on the sensors? Thermal tracking should detect them.

I wish I hadn't eaten those eggs this morning. The taste is rancid in my throat. I want to wipe the sweat off my head, but my arms are locked to the controls. I'm scared that if I let go, my mecha will topple over.

I look over the map again. Even though I've studied this battle, it feels different now that I'm actually here. Why haven't the Germans continued their assault? They should have already destroyed me. Then I wonder, *Am I even their target?*

"Noriko," I call. "Do you get a lock on any of the Nazis?"

"I don't," she says.

How's that possible? In history, the biomechs went straight after the quad mechas.

"Why are you moving so slowly?" she asks.

"This thing weighs a ton."

She appears confused.

"This is normal, isn't it?" I confirm with her.

"The calibration seems off. A lot heavier than normal today."

I want to ask Noriko what I should do. Which I technically can. But that'll be recorded in my performance. If I lose command and am out of control, I'll be scored accordingly.

"I'm under attack," Noriko says, and her screen shakes. "This isn't right."

"What?"

"The safety restrictions are disabled," she states.

"They are?"

"That blow hurt. There must be something malfunctioning on the simulation. We have to end it."

"Right now?"

"I highly recommend you disengage."

I click the safety release, but nothing happens. I try to turn off the program, but it won't let me. "I can't."

"Actually, neither can I."

"What's going on?"

"It means you can really get hurt in this. I'm trying to contact the admin—"

My alert signals flash. Something is incoming.

"Behind you!" Noriko warns me.

A force slams into me. My right arm feels like it's been torn out of its socket. The interface informs me that my mecha's limb has been destroyed. A flurry of blows comes quickly at me, causing me to tumble to the ground. I lose track of what control does what, though I instinctively try to coil up so I can protect myself. All I can do is react to the blows, and I'm not even able to do that as the armor caves in. My belly is getting a pounding, and it feels like the real thing. What if I take permanent damage, not just in the test, but to my body? I just want it to end. What else can I do? Theoretically, I should order Noriko to flee with news of the battle so it won't be a total failure. But that seems pointless as it won't save the test results, and the only way the exam will end is with my mecha's death.

The speed of all the attacks reminds me in this strange way of *Cat Odyssey*, when all the humans defeated me. What was it Hideki said? "Change the battlefield, or avoid the fight."

I can't avoid the fight. But is there any way I can change the battlefield?

My rear turrets are disabled. My main guns are damaged. I'm missing a leg and an arm. I try to see if I have remote control over them. I don't. Escaping for me is out of the question.

"I'm coming your way," Noriko says.

"No!" I shout. "Get out of here."

"Forget the test. If I don't stop that thing, you'll be injured in real life."

"I'll be fine! Just make your escape."

At least it won't be an automatic failure. But I also want to test something.

There is something unusually fierce in these attacks. I know the programming could imitate the emotional charge of a German. But it should consider in its calculations that I'm maimed and have no chance of fighting anymore if it chooses to disengage me. Therefore, chasing after Noriko's mecha to prevent her from escaping would be the most efficient use of its strength. But the fact that I'm still getting hit makes me think there's a human behind the controls. They know letting Noriko escape means nothing aside from a cursory test pass.

Why can't I see the biomech? It must be wearing some type of camouflage or optic armor. The mecha will be destroyed with a few more blows. Instead of trying to protect myself, I lift up my hand and raise the middle finger. I know I'm opening myself to an attack, but I want to provoke the enemy pilot, whoever it may be. An AI wouldn't care about the gesture. But a human would, and I feel the furious forward plunge. It must be human. I'm convinced the removal of safety restrictions wasn't an accident. Whoever is on the other side wants to hurt me. That thought enrages me, and I no longer care if I pass or fail. I just want to make whoever it is suffer for taking me so lightly.

The moment the next punch makes impact, I see a refraction as my armor dents inward. With my one good arm, I try to latch onto it. Surprisingly, my arm makes contact, gripping its wrist. I have only one source of attack. I beat down on the arm with my head, bashing it as many times as I can. It destroys most of my mecha's exterior, and I feel the outside air. But the sense of injustice helps me feel a clarity I haven't in a long time. There's a surge, a burst, and all of a sudden, the biomech's arm splits in half. The optic armor breaks down, and I see something that looks like a gigantic, faceless bear. Its whole skin is covered with a black fluid that is morphing on its surface. It's as big as my quad mecha. The ebony exterior is like liquid marble, replenishing itself and gorging on its own flesh.

I hop toward it and try to smash my arm into its side. It's too quick and skips back. I miss and topple over. My quad mecha crashes into the ground. The whole side of my face hurts, and my head is still spinning from the head-butting I carried out earlier. But I try to minimize the pain and focus on the fight. The biomech is behind me, ready to stomp. I see my broken arm on the ground ahead of me, grab it, and wield it as a club to fend off its attack. One of the flails hits the biomech across the leg, causing it to crunch sideways. Its knee buckles. I have an opening to attack. I hurtle the quad mecha at the biomech and pounce as deeply as I can into its chest. I don't want to just damage it. I want to lodge my whole arm in its torso so it can't escape. At least not until I destroy it. But just as I succeed in penetrating its chest, my alarms blare. From behind, two new biomechs appear. I ignore them and use my one good arm to pound the biomech in the face as hard as I can. The last thing I feel is two explosives destroying my back.

The test stops. I get a text notice in wavering bloody red against a black screen: "You are dead."

The safety belts unlock. I manage to step out, but fall as soon as I do. Something is wrong with my legs. I can't move my right arm. I feel blurry and sit on the ground. At least it's over.

I feel silly that I got into a personal match with my opponent.

My imagined slight and vendetta only got my mecha destroyed. But I also feel peace with myself that I gave it my best shot.

The door to my compartment opens, and I'm expecting the administrative officer or Noriko. But instead, it's Lieutenant Yukimura, the officer who visited the school a week ago and questioned whether I was fit for the exam. Something is wrong with his arm, and his hair is wet with blood.

"What'd you think you were doing back there?" he angrily demands.

I'm still sitting, unable to get to my feet. "What do you mean?"

"You broke the rules!"

"What rules? What are you talking about?"

"You are a disgrace to everything the corps stands for. You don't know anything about piloting. Your performance was sloppy and lacked any understanding of how we work," Lieutenant Yukimura snaps at me. "Your entire test was clumsy and uninspired. And I heard about what your friend did. Your attempt to even take the test is an insult to the entire corps."

I'm shocked by his words. I don't know what to reply. I sputter out the first words that come to mind: "There was a malfunction. The safety restrictions were disabled. I—I just wasn't ready for the physical impact."

"I disabled them."

"W-why?"

"To give you a taste of what mecha piloting is really like!" he shouts.

Then I was right. He was baiting me, wanting to hurt me. But that meant my test was damned from the beginning. How could I have a chance when I was fighting pain as much as the challenge of the test? "What do you have against me?" I ask, genuinely wanting to know.

"Not you. I only care about preserving the honor of the corps. You're not fit to be a candidate and shouldn't have taken the test."

"I can't even try?"

He shakes his head. "You sully our honor with your attempt."

I blink several times, incredulous. "My parents died serving the Empire. My friend died because he wanted a better life in the Empire. And you're telling me I can't even honor their memory by taking this test?" I'm so angry, I want to cry.

"If you wanted to honor their memory, you should have known your place."

"And where's that?"

"Not in the corps."

He turns around and stomps out.

Fueled by anger, I take off my test equipment and stand to exit the booth. Noriko is waiting for me.

"He had no right to say what he did," she says.

"You heard?" I ask her.

"I did."

I feel so embarrassed, especially after she deigned to support me. "I'm sorry I wasted your help. You have no idea how much it means that you were my wingmate."

"That last part was some of the best mecha piloting I've seen in the simulation."

I appreciate her trying to cheer me up. But my mind is on how much the lieutenant did not want me to get into BEMA. He wanted to humiliate me, which he's succeeded in doing. It is a sobering thought to realize how despised I am. I tell Noriko, "It's not my fate to be a mecha pilot."

"Fate has nothing to do with it," she says. "You broke the lieutenant's arm."

"How do you know?"

"I could see it. That's why he's so angry. Don't let him get you down. You'll find a place in the corps regardless of what he says."

"Thank you."

She shakes her head. "I wanted to help. I was very sorry to hear about Hideki. It's not easy losing a good friend, no matter the reason."

She salutes me, and I do the same back. She exits. I hold my salute gratefully until the medic arrives, and asks, "Are you saluting the air?"

A WEEK LATER, MY BODY HAS RECOVERED EVEN THOUGH MY MIND IS still troubled. We're in class when the scores flash on all our porticals. I scored a little above average on the standard exams, which isn't a surprise. I have a good idea of what the results of the mecha test are, but I have to check anyway. I skip through the different orbits and scour the combat scores. I look to the top of the list. Noriko is #1, and I'm genuinely happy for her. I send her a message telling her so. I go through the rest of the list and scroll down. Way down. Not only have I missed the top one hundred, but I find my name two places above the bottom of the list, those two being students who didn't show up. I've failed miserably.

Close by, someone lets out a shriek of joy. She has ranked #3 in our entire class. Depending on her military scores and recommendation, that means she's guaranteed to get into BEMA. For Noriko, her #1 placement additionally means definite entry into the University of Tokyo and Kyoto University.

With my score, attending a university is out of the question. At most, I might get into one of the remote private colleges. I do have the option of going *rōnin*, which means waiting an extra year and taking the exam again, like Sango. But my prospects aren't great. Every happy cheer from a fellow student feels bitter. I wonder how

Sango is. I haven't seen her or heard from her since Hideki. I don't blame her for not wanting to talk.

I go to a café and order a green tea. It scares me to think that if I'd gone along with Hideki's plan, I'd either be in prison or dead. Having gone through the simulation test, it's tough for me to stomach, but I know the truth now. I'm not meant to be a pilot. As the lieutenant stated, I don't have what it takes. Even if we had successfully cheated, it would only have delayed my inevitable exposure as someone incapable of piloting a mecha. It's tough to come to terms with my own insufficiencies.

I step outside to take a walk. I was completely overwhelmed in the simulation. Pain made the test unbearable, and in a real-life mecha fight, it'd have been much worse. Contrast my anxious state of panic with how calm Noriko remained, and it's clear she has the types of nerves I can only aspire to.

I pass through a garden, and there's a lake filled with water lilies and lotus. Tadpoles flee from dragonflies, ducks nibble for food, and koi fish wander haphazardly. I keep on thinking about my failure. I wanted desperately to do well. A part of it was for Hideki, and an even bigger part was for the memory of my parents. But the biggest? I wanted my life to have more meaning, to be about more than just getting by, subsisting at some desk job if I'm lucky. My exam scores make even that a low probability. I make a ball with my fist, put the flat end on the bridge of my nose, and take a deep breath. How humiliating to be such a loser, a laughingstock in front of everyone.

I wish I'd never wanted to be a mecha pilot.

THE NEXT FEW WEEKS ARE A DREARY BUZZ. I'M NOT SLEEPING, BUT I don't feel awake. I have nothing to look forward to other than the possibility of another year of school, and I doubt my scores will go up any. My usual source of comfort, the arcade, brings back too many memories of Hideki. Most of the games seem vacuous now anyway. I spend my evenings wandering the city. Outside the school gate, the reconnaissance mecha, *Taka*, is still there so those who got accepted into the military academy can practice. I feel like it's taunting me. I'll never get to drive a mecha, so any joy the sight of it used to bring feels like a jab.

Griselda has left me multiple messages, but I haven't returned any of her calls. I don't know what to say to her. I hate going to class because most of the other seniors are talking about their university plans and how they're preparing for the new year. Many are shipping out to other countries in the Empire, looking forward to time abroad. I know this disappointment would be more bearable if Hideki were here. Misery doesn't just love company; it desperately craves it.

In a few months, my governmental support will end. If I don't continue with school, I'll need to find a new home and a means of supporting myself. There aren't many options for a student without a university degree. A military path as an enlisted soldier is one of them. But I feel ashamed that I couldn't be an officer like my parents. Most students get tons of support from their family—and not just financial support, but social contacts and connections. I've gotten none. I've had to fight for everything, and I feel like I've reached my limit. There's no way for me to go forward anymore. Instead, I can only brace myself for a steep decline.

Griselda is waiting in front of my apartment.

"Where have you been?" she asks, and steps closer to me. "You've lost weight."

"I haven't been eating much," I confess. My appetite has vanished.

She takes a deep breath, and I see tears in her eyes. "I—I couldn't believe when I heard about Hideki. Why didn't you call me?"

"What could I say? That I couldn't help my best friend from getting shot because I was too weak?"

"You can't blame yourself for what happened."

I sigh angrily. "I don't want to talk about this. I—I should go inside and sleep."

Pain flashes across her face. "Things'll be different after graduation."

"What do you mean?" I ask even though I know exactly what she means. She'll be integrated into the German machine, far away from the United States of Japan. Friendships from those on the opposite sides of the Axis will be regarded with suspicion, and all our communications will be monitored (if they aren't already).

She shakes her head. "Will you visit Berlin?"

"I doubt I'll get the chance. I—I probably need to start looking for a job."

"What about university?"

"I got one of the lowest scores on the military supplement," I admit, feeling worse now that I'm actually telling her how badly I've botched everything.

"I'm glad you're not joining the mecha corps," she says.

"Why's that?" I ask, disappointed. If she's trying to make me feel better by saying that, it isn't working.

"I just am," she states. She wants to talk more, but as I think about the test again, I feel a cold fury swirling inside me that keeps me resolute and stubbornly quiet. It's not her. I don't want to speak with anyone right now. "*Sayonara,*" she finally says, kisses me on the cheek, and leaves.

I feel like the worst friend in the world.

A WEEK PASSES. IT'S NIGHT, AND MY INSOMNIA IS TORTURING ME. WITHout sleep, time creeps at a maddening, slow pace. Anytime I let my mind drift, I keep on replaying regrets. I know I shouldn't be listening to sad music, but I find a compilation of tragic songs from my favorite portical games and have them cycle on repeat.

I take long walks to try to tire myself. I find myself in front of school again. The *Taka* is still there. It's being used during the daytime by several of the students going to the mecha schools for basic orientation, a way to familiarize themselves with the controls. This isn't a customized mecha but one that still has a traditional cockpit to minimize space and weight. It wasn't so long ago when I spent a whole evening reading up on all the specs and watching it in simulations.

"What are you doing out here?" someone asks me.

I look up. Climbing down from the *Taka* is Noriko.

"Going for a walk," I answer her. "You?"

"Training."

"They let you take her for a spin?"

Noriko shakes her head. "Just a little. I've mostly been simming it."

"How does she handle?"

"Faster than the combat mechas, but more vulnerable to—"

That's when we hear a boom that causes the glass in the school windows to shatter. Off in the horizon, we see a plume of fire clambering up the sky. The fiery pillar greedily sprints up and gets company from four more explosions, each seemingly louder and brighter than the other. Alarms are blaring, and sirens are drowned out by the continuous destruction that builds. I hear the distinct steps of mechas moving away from the blasts. But they're not normal ones. The silhouettes sketched in a fierce orange-black resemble the bipedal machines I've seen on portical footage—like the type the NARA use to patrol the Quiet Border. They're called Javelins and are essentially tank turrets with a boxlike hull and two robust legs that'd resemble a horse's hind legs if they were made of metallic alloys.

"Have you simmed for gunnery?" Noriko asks me.

"I have. Why?"

"Let's go."

"Where?" I ask her.

"Find out what's going on." She starts climbing back up.

"But—but I don't know what to do."

"The controls on this are easier than the sim."

She doesn't give me time to question myself or her as she re-enters the mecha. It's a long climb, but I follow her up to the stomach and enter the bridge of a mecha proper for the first time in my life. The space is cramped, and the ceiling is so low, I'd hit my head if I jumped. The heat is also suffocating inside, but I don't care. I'm happy just to be there.

The whole circumference of the bridge is transparent from the inside, with only the floors visible (and even that can be changed in the settings to vanish). Granada Hills looks smaller from this height.

Noriko takes the pilot seat, which is in front of a console with several controls she straps onto her arms. It's a simplified haptic panel that responds to her actions while also taking manual controls she can input directly. I take the weapons panel, which consists of three display screens showing the front, back, and side views in a split angle. Noriko was right. The interface is intuitive and easy to use with a touch screen and audio inputs. I use the portical to get a detailed list of available weapons. The *Taka* doesn't have her full arsenal since she is being used for training. There are the two shoulder guns and a missile launcher. I also spot a weapon I don't recognize that's titled *gunsen*. A fan?

I check the guns to make sure they're armed. They have only half the load, and the safety locks are enabled, which means I need a pass code I don't have. My first two guesses fail. Usually, these will lock up completely after a set number of failed attempts.

"What's weapon status?" Noriko asks.

I tell her about the pass code.

"So we have only the *gunsen* available?" she confirms with me.

"What's that?"

Noriko grins. "You don't know the fan blade?"

"No."

"It's sweet."

The cautious side of me asks Noriko, "Are you sure this is okay?"

"If the military or police have it under control, we'll back off."

"If they don't?" I ask.

She grins. "Fingers crossed they don't."

Her confidence makes me laugh. But I don't know how much a fan blade will help against the NARA Javelins. Is there a way I can override the safety locks on our weapons? I think back on the simulations I've practiced for the past year. "If I can physically reach the shoulder guns, there might be a way to manually unlock the trigger."

She looks at the heat signatures of the Javelins and the calculated trajectory before we can intercept them.

"You have eight minutes before we engage them."

Both shoulder guns are in the upper half of the mecha. I scan the internal schematics again on my screen to confirm. The *Taka* is very similar to the simulation mechas I've driven. There's a ceiling hatch to the rear of the bridge that opens on Noriko's command. A ladder drops down. I start to climb up when the *Taka* takes its first steps forward. Another and another. Noriko engages the wheels on the bottom of the mecha, which allows us to skate in the desired direction. She judiciously uses boosters to increase acceleration.

I go through the hatch and hear the hum of the BPG (Bradlium Particle Generator), which is the main power source for the mecha.

The conduit I climb is heavily shielded from the particles as it'd be deadly to humans without protection. It's much warmer inside than I'd anticipated, though not a surprise since simulations don't completely re-create temperature shifts. I still cannot believe I'm aboard a mecha. That thought invigorates me and gives me the energy to rapidly ascend.

I feel like I'm inside the skeleton of a robotic samurai with multiple chutes, partitions, trailing ribs, cooling vents, nozzles, and stringers. Sensors trigger lights to show the way. I reach the left shoulder gun and see that it is disengaged, still lodged within the shoulder plate of the *Taka*. There is a panel which hooks into the central portical, where it takes its commands. The manual unlock should be to its side. It's a heavy lever with three slots. I spot removable slabs next to the lever and insert them individually into each opening. The lever lights up, and I pull it to the other side. The shoulder gun begins loading ammunition, and I check the blast deflector to make certain everything is good to go. I spot the corrosive ammo to the side, which is particularly effective as anti-armor shells against other mechas. I do the same on the right shoulder before climbing back down.

"You got 'em?" Noriko asks.

I check the weapons interface, hit the shoulder command button. The guns emerge from the *sode* spaulders that rotate upward.

"Ready to kick ass," I answer.

"They've taken out the police station," Noriko informs me.

"What do you mean taken out?"

"They blew it up. They're attacking key stations and trying to demobilize our forces. I'm monitoring military channels, and our soldiers are scrambling to get into place, but most of the communication relays have been disrupted."

"How?"

Noriko says, "I have no idea, but I can't even get a call out." She points north. "Since they're heading for the Santa Susana Mountains, it's a pretty good bet they have reinforcements there."

"We have to cut them off before they get there."

"Not them. Just one."

"What do you mean?"

"There are four of them. Three of them will probably break off to try to stop us while the fourth gets away. That's either the leader or is carrying something important. So we should ignore the other three and go after the final one, whichever it is," Noriko wraps up. "How good is your aim?"

"I get good scores in the simulation."

"Let's see if all that simming paid off."

She speeds up as we approach the four bipedal tanks. According to the scans, they're about eighteen meters tall, equal to a five-story building, and about ten meters in length. From the looks of it, they wield a 138mm cannon, though I might be off by a few millimeters. Their cannon is retractable, and, as a whole, the Javelin is surprisingly rapid for what is a top-heavy structure. The legs are customizable so that many have a different arsenal, along with optional back turrets. I check the scanner for potential weaknesses when I notice several new blips appear on the map. They don't bear USJ markings and resemble the bipedal tanks in size. Just as she predicted, three of them engage us while the fourth proceeds to its destination. I marvel at her ability to extrapolate the enemy plan so intuitively.

"I think there are eight more Javelins coming our way," I inform Noriko.

"Eight?"

I count them again. "Coming from the west."

"We better hurry," Noriko says. She disengages the wheels and sprints toward the three Javelins approaching us.

"We're a little close, aren't we?" I ask apprehensively.

But she ignores me. The turret on the first bipedal tank swivels toward us. She charges straight at it. The cannon fires, but the *Taka* is so quick, she overtakes the tank, grabbing it by the mantlet. The recoil on the cannon is much stronger than I would have anticipated, indicating a weakness in the hull's ability to absorb the shock. That, combined with the *Taka*'s momentum, means as we collide with the bipedal tank, it doesn't take much to push it back into its companion behind it. The moment of impact catches me off guard, metal smashing into metal. There is a boisterous clangor, the crunching jolt shaking the entire bridge. The sensors indicate part of the arm guard is being pushed to the limits of its pressure capacity. My seat belt keeps me in place, but the whiplash strains my neck. Imagine two massive sumo wrestlers charging into each other, only wearing armor, and even that doesn't quite compare to the amount of pressure both are exerting on each other. The Javelin stumbles over, hitting the second and taking it down. It's an ingenious move, all the more so as Noriko says to me, "I didn't know if that would work."

"Glad it did," I reply.

I spot the third Javelin preparing to fire. I unleash the shoulder gun with a spray of corrosive artillery that pours into the tank. This causes the armor on its hull to disintegrate and the tank itself to wobble. Noriko uses that momentary lapse to take out her *gunsen*, which she spreads open. It's less a fan than a half-moon-shaped blade she wields to slice the tank's turret off. She stomps down with the *Taka*'s boot into the Javelin's knee. The hinge shatters, causing it to topple over to its side.

The eight other Javelins don't wait for us to attack. They launch a volley of shells in our direction. Noriko hides behind the last tank, which takes half the blows. She use the *gunsen* to dispatch another. But the three remaining blasts land straight in our chest. The power of the attack is immense, and the *Taka* shakes wildly.

We stumble backward. I would have lost control, but when I glance over at Noriko, she is calm and collected, firing the aft boosters to stabilize and regain our battle stance.

I check our status, and inform her, "Right leg is too damaged for normal walking, and our right arm is barely functional."

They fire again. This time, we don't have anything to protect us, and the brunt of the blows smashes our armor. Anything that doesn't hit us strikes the buildings surrounding us. Fires engulf the structures, and scans indicate casualties. I am saddened to think that someone lost their life tonight.

"Evacuate now," Noriko orders me.

"Why?"

"I'm going to charge them and set off the internal self-destruct to take as many as I can."

"Your right leg is badly damaged. You're barely keeping upright."

"If you have a better option, I'm ready to hear it. Otherwise, get off."

I look to Noriko, then think about the life that awaits me back on the ground. "I'm going with you."

"Even if it means your death?"

"There's no place I'd rather die than inside this mecha."

She nods. "Let's cause some hell. You have free rein to fire."

She straightens the mecha, engages the wheels again, and triggers the aft thrusters to speed us forward. I'm surprised the wheels give us mobility and make up for the dysfunctional leg. She's continually checking the diagnostics for terrain condition, gauging wind speed, and making sure everything stays in balance. The Javelins keep their distance and fire at us again. I launch as many corrosive shots as I can, but with our systems out of sync, it's hard to hit a moving target. The laser range finder is busted, and auto aim is completely off, our cameras mostly relaying static. This isn't like a turn-based tactical game, where we take turns attacking one another. Everything is happening in real time, and I'd be better off using an old periscope (I doubt there's one on board) than the portical aiming system.

But something catches my attention. I check the portical display measuring enemy fire. It calculates trajectory, speed, and other factors. It's the audio timing of the initial triggers that's bugging me. Of the eight, four match the other four to the millisecond. That shouldn't be possible, should it? There should be more of a discrepancy . . . Unless they're slave units, copying the master tank via portical AI. That could indicate that four of them are just imitating the actions of their master. Technically, I could take over, or at the least, disrupt their aiming system.

"Do you mind if I try something weird?" I ask Noriko.

"Weirder than charging to our deaths?"

"Possibly."

"Go ahead," she says.

I redirect our portical field to look for any kikkai connections among the Javelins. Noriko successfully maneuvers past a new wave of blasts, though the houses next to us aren't so lucky. As we're racing through, I hear what sounds like music. Noriko is humming a song as she pilots, moving to the rhythms of her voice.

I find a secure connection emanating from the Javelins. Would Hideki's portical disruption program work? I won't be able to break the encryption, but I could theoretically hinder the field by sending an overloaded kikkai burst to cause their porticals to shut down. I connect my portical with the *Taka*'s and send a surge to the secure connections, using the link from Hideki's program. They surprisingly sync with each other. I look up at the Javelins. No difference. They fire at us again. As good a pilot as Noriko is, we're able to avoid only five of the shells. Two hit us in the chest, and the third immobilizes our feet. Even with the wheels, we can't move. My entire panel erupts, and a geyser of smoke sears my right arm. I shriek involuntarily, the pain stabbing me harshly. The smell of my own burned flesh overwhelms me.

Noriko stabilizes us with boosters and strikes the *gunsen* against a neighboring building so we don't fall, but smoke is everywhere, and the front of our cockpit has a gaping hole. The bridge is in disarray, and I see that Noriko has a piece of metal sticking out of her side. Our armor has been penetrated, and another direct hit will kill us. It's a miracle we've survived this long. Noriko is doing her best to get us moving again, but without an engineer, we're helpless.

"Noriko," I call to her.

She looks over at me. Fear strikes me as I realize this is it. In less than a minute, I'll be dead. But she gives me a calm, assured, wink. *We're not going to die here,* her expression says to me.

I remember what I was trying to do, think again about Hideki, and send the kikkai burst again, hoping for a different result. Nothing changes, and the Javelins get ready to fire. I brace for death.

Four of the Javelins explode.

None of my scanners work, but has the disruption surge caused them to blow up? The momentary joy is overshadowed by the fact that there are still four more, ready to blow us up. Noriko raises the *gunsen* to try to deflect as many shots as we can. The Javelins fire.

But just as their shells are about to hit us, something drops from the sky and, using a special shield, deflects all the artillery.

It's a mecha, one of our own, only it's a combat *Korosu* class that's almost twice our size. Above, eight tilt-rotor aircraft exit after dropping off their cargo. Two other mechas have arrived and are racing toward the enemy. They resemble massive samurais, only with cannons. The Javelins turn their attention away from us to face the bigger threat. But they're no match as our *Korosus* dispose of them with graceful ease, slicing them apart with their fusion swords. It's like watching a ballet of destruction, pirouetting perfectly on every note.

We've been saved.

THE HOSPITAL THEY TAKE ME TO IS SOMEWHERE FANCY, WHERE DOCTORS check me with unfamiliar machines. They patch up my arm and dip it into a gelatinous vat that numbs the nerves. I pass out a few times. When I'm awake, they feed me, and the food they bring tastes better than anything I've had. My favorite is a lotus tempura dipped in a special Santa Monica soy sauce accompanied by garlic-seasoned brown rice. They even have sesame-flavored ice cream in a green-tea wrap.

Multiple officers question me about the battle. I answer to the best of my abilities, but there's not much I can offer that they don't already know. I wonder how much trouble I'm in, but no one seems concerned that Noriko and I took the *Taka* without authorization. I'm more surprised that my arm heals completely with no burn scars. Involuntarily, I think about the exam and the terrorists' claim that people were experimented on. Was their suffering at all connected with how advanced our medical technology is?

"How is Noriko?" I ask the doctors and officers.

"She's fine," they inform me.

I see many friends and family visit Noriko. No one comes to see me.

With my arm healed, I try to spend my free time playing *Cat Odyssey*. But the game feels different, almost drab compared to the intensity I experienced during our fight. I put it aside after a few attempts and think back on the battle.

A day passes, and Noriko stops by. She's in a patient's gown like me. Next to her are her parents, both in uniform, colonels by rank, with the special insignias of mecha pilots. Their name tags read TACHIBANA. I try to stand up and bow, but they force me to lie on the bed.

"Don't get up," Noriko's father insists.

"How are you doing?" Noriko asks me.

"I really like their tempura," I reply.

The three laugh. "That was an impressive trick you did, jamming the slave signals on the Javelins," Noriko's mom tells me.

"So it worked?" I ask, excited to confirm that was what caused their destruction.

"It worked," they confirm.

I feel so proud, and they sense it, smiling.

"Noriko told me she asked you to evacuate, but you insisted on staying?" her mother asks me.

"Yes, ma'am."

"She mentioned there were irregularities with your examination. I've asked that they be looked into. It'll take time, but I intend to get some answers."

I'm surprised that they'd bother. "Th-th-thank you," I stammer, genuinely touched.

"You have too much potential not to be given more opportunities. I've pulled some strings and gotten you into RAMDET."

"Excuse me?" RAMDET, or Rapid Mobile Defense Team, is a mecha security force with civilian management even though many of them are ex-military. I should have thought of them as an option, but I hadn't because I'd wanted to make it directly into the corps.

"The greatest pilot the mecha corps ever had couldn't walk on her own feet. Everyone dismissed her. But she stuck with it and proved them wrong."

"Kujira," I say. Everyone knew about the legendary pilot who defeated squadrons of German biomechs by herself.

"She didn't make it into the academy at first even though she got one of the best scores on the sim. She went to RAMDET and proved herself there to get her opportunity. It won't be easy. To be honest, it'll be one of the toughest things you'll do. But many of those who make it through get recruited to join the corps."

I'm stunned by their thoughtfulness. "Th-thank you so much. I—I'm unworthy of your support."

She touches one of the pins on her lapel, a sakura, and it's clear there's some memory associated with it. "We're all servants of the Emperor and should help each other when we can."

I try to bow to them. They insist I lie still. After a few more civilities, her parents leave, though Noriko stays behind.

"Thank you," I say to her.

She shakes her head. "We let the lead get away."

"What were they after?"

"Brass won't tell me. Something classified. There's some secret op going on they won't talk about, even if we are 'heroes.'"

"Heroes?"

"That exam the terrorists infiltrated. They were really after the communication relays. The test was just a distraction, and they used the school kikkai connection to disrupt the military lines. If it wasn't for us, they'd have caused a lot more destruction. The—" Her portical rings, and she picks up the communication, telling the caller, "Could you hold on a minute?" She mutes, says to me, "I got to take this—it's Berkeley."

"You're going?"

She nods. "And I expect you to eventually join me. Let's talk more later."

She's about to leave, but I have to tell her, "You were amazing out there."

She grins. "I can do better."

Of that, I have no doubt.

IT'S ALL OVER THE NEWS. TWO STUDENTS STRIKE A DEADLY BLOW against the NARA. The terrorists aboard the Javelins who didn't kill themselves were taken captive, to be interrogated by the Tokko. All my fellow students are talking about it and even speak to me in a tone of reverence. I feel strange being in the spotlight.

The Lunar Year starts on February 10, and for Spring Festival, we have a lantern procession at sunset. Every student carries a *mando*, and we walk through our streets carrying our square lanterns on poles. We're dressed in kimonos and clogs. It's an evening to make oaths and wishes for the new year as we make the trek from our school to the Yamagata Shrine, chanting songs to the Emperor. It's the year of the boar, and I see many with their pig hachikōs and masks. Thousands of balloons are released into the air with text to praise the Emperor. We're each given the special New Year dishes, *osechi-ryōri*, in a *jubako*, which looks almost exactly like a bento box. Masked dancers perform symbolic battles to commemorate our victories in the old Americas and the Soviet Union. Male and female cheerleaders put on traditional makeup to match various Shinto customs. I'm chewing on a *daidai*, thinking about how frail our small lights are in these lanterns. If the wind is too strong, they'll blow out. If we move too fast, the fire will die. I hate candle imagery, especially in haikus, as it's usually just mawkish blabbering. But there's something poignantly bitter in the recognition that life is as brief and illusory as that little glimmer of light we shine for the Empire.

Once we reach our destination, music fills the air. It's the "Star Spangled Sun."

"There you are."

It's Griselda, and she's in a kimono, though she also has on a swastika armband like the rest of the Germans do. We hug each other.

"I got your message while I was visiting friends in Taiko City," she says. I hated the way we last parted, and I'd called her in the hopes of seeing her before I left. "And you got accepted into RAM-DET! Congratulations. I'm so proud of you. I heard you took out seven Javelins."

"It was mostly Noriko."

"Don't be so modest," she says. "I read the articles. You both were equally amazing. How are you feeling?"

"To be completely honest, I kind of miss the rush," I state. "I got to a point where I didn't care about anything anymore. It felt so liberating not to give a damn."

"It's the adrenaline. Hard to come back to normal life after that," she says, with a familiarity that I'm not sure how to respond to.

"Do you know much about the biomech pilots in Germany? Do they have to take the same tests we do?" I ask her.

"In the Reich, age doesn't matter, only talent. There are pilots I've met who are only thirteen."

"That's too much for them to handle mentally, isn't it?"

"It all depends on the pilot," she says.

Fireworks start, and the loud bursts sound like cannons. I'm reminded of the battle and am surprised that I feel shell-shocked. It's both excitement and an eerie fear reminiscent of that moment when I believed I was going to die.

Griselda notices my disturbed trance, and asks, "Do you know much about this song?"

I shake it off and reply, "It's an American song, written by Francis Scott Key to celebrate their victory over England in the War of 1812."

"Did you know they actually got the music from a British song called 'To Anacreon in Heaven' and just changed the words?" Griselda asks.

"I didn't," I reply, and pull on the sleeves of my kimono.

"Your composer, Kumatani, took it from the Americans and wrote new lyrics to call it the 'Star Spangled Sun.' Francis Scott Key celebrated freedom in his music, but he was a vigorous advocate for slavery. Kumatani wrote the ultimate song about dying for the Emperor, but he was executed for stealing money from the government's treasury."

There are fireworks in the shape of flowers, dragons, and even mechas.

"Happy New Year, Griselda," I say.

"Happy New Year!" she yells back.

But I have the feeling the forthcoming year won't be happy for any of us.

QUIET BORDER

★

**1995
SUMMER**

04

★ ★ ★

TIME FEELS INTERMINABLE WHEN YOU'RE MIRED IN REGRETS. RAMDET IS my diversion.

Thanks to the recommendation of Noriko's parents, I've joined the Rapid Mobile Defense Team (RAMDET) camp outside of Dallas Tokai. All my research has confirmed that it's what people who want to pilot mechas do when they can't get into the corps. If I survive basic training for three months, I'll get to join a quad mecha crew that protects cargo shipments from the German Americas. If I can last in the position for nine months, there's a strong chance I'll get to actually pilot the quad mecha. My hope is to do this for a year, get experience driving, study for the exams, and maybe get a second opportunity to enter a military academy. This path is a difficult one, but over the years, there have been several dozen pilots who got their start this way. Even though we're technically a civilian outfit, we work with the local military, and most of the instructors are ex-military.

RAMDET's training facilities are bare-bones. There are ten barracks with hardwood floors, no walls, and thin sleeping bags.

There are obstacle courses around us, a gun range, and a swimming pool. There's a mess hall and an administrative building for those in charge. Not a mecha in sight.

First day I arrive, all 118 of us are stripped of our clothes and given training slacks. It's raining outside. The roads are mud. The instructor doesn't give us her name and orders us to call her Sensei. She's bald, wears thick, rectangular shades that cover half her face, and has the brawny muscles of a wrestler. We're given huge backpacks full of equipment that we're ordered to strap on. They must weigh close to forty-five kilograms. "Start running!" she orders.

She leads us to a running path around the facility that's about forty-one kilometers in length. She rides in a jeep, barking over the voice amplifier in her vehicle at anyone who slows down.

"You may have been given the delusion that you'll get to drive one of our security mechas," she says. "The quicker you get that idea out of your head, the happier you'll be. Most of you will quit within the first week, and that's because happiness is not an emotion you will feel much of on this job."

It's less than five minutes, and my shoulders feel like they're about to cave in. My lungs beg for relief. The rain is pounding down. I want to give up. But I think about Hideki and fight through the pain. Ten minutes later, one of the new recruits stumbles on the mud and lies there facedown, refusing to get up. Sensei stops the jeep, pulls him up, and yells, "Get the hell off my course!"

The recruit, muddy face and all, is barely able to stand. He is forced to run back to the barracks, where he will be given his termination notice. Within thirty minutes, eight others follow him. I don't even know how I'm standing. After an hour, my legs feel as mushy as the mud. I wish I could set the backpack down. But the two others who did that were kicked out. I don't know whether I'm hot or cold and feel both simultaneously. Just when I think I can't run another step, Sensei yells, "Break."

I collapse on the ground, not caring that I'm covered with mud. One of the other recruits introduces herself as Chieko. She has short, auburn hair and does not look tired at all. Instead, she is the only peppy one, greeting everyone and asking where they're from. She's stout, a little over 150 centimeters tall, and has bulky arms. "I'm from Taiko City," she starts, and wipes her nose. Her cheeks are covered with freckles, and her eyes are a grayish green drowning in grit. "I took the military simulation three times, but my scores weren't good enough. All my instructors said I didn't have what it takes, so I came here to prove them wrong. Those tests don't mean anything to me. I plan on being the best mecha pilot in the United States of Japan."

Three times means she's spent three years trying.

Another recruit tells us to call him Wren, and says, "I tried five years straight, but my scores weren't good enough. My parents told me to give up, but I wanted to at least try." He's the tallest one among us, of mixed Brazilian-Mexican descent, and has big, drooping ears.

Sensei doesn't give the group session long. She has us on the road again. But hearing how those two failed dulls my own sense of failure. I don't know how I do it, but I survive until the end of the day.

They give us brown rice, miso soup, and tuna rolls in the evening. It's the best dinner I've had in ages. I can't believe they give us only one serving. This is more of an appetizer than an actual meal. But there are no seconds, and when we're sent to our barracks, I'm more hungry than I am tired. The sleeping bags barely warm us, and there are twenty of us per unit, which doesn't give us a whole lot of space. Some of the recruits fall asleep immediately, and one in particular snores like a goat. Not that I've heard a goat snore, but I think I'd prefer the goat because he's so loud. I realize it's Wren and just when I'm about to do something to wake him, another recruit hits his chest. His snoring ceases but continues after thirty seconds. I focus on the sound of the rain and eventually doze off.

Sleep feels like five minutes, and it's not enough. My pain in the morning is ten times what I felt at night. At least the weather has cleared up, and it's actually hot outside. We're given a light breakfast of a boiled egg and broccoli. Sensei starts off by assembling us in front of our barracks. We all bow to the flag of the rising sun and recite the pledge "to the flag, of the United States of Japan. And to the Empire . . ." Sensei does a roll call. We've lost twenty-six.

She gets us running again. No backpack, though, which makes the run more bearable. I'm too tired to think. I don't even know why I'm moving my feet, and I don't care. That second day of running somehow becomes five. Anyone who gives up can go home. Even if you fall, if you get right back up, you can keep at it. I am slow, slower than most of the recruits. And I'm always hungry. But by the end of two weeks, my flabby belly has begun to morph into something taut.

My biggest struggle isn't the exhaustion. It's the mosquitoes at night. It's like they aim for me and relish my blood. I wake up, scratching all over. I can hear them buzzing in my ear right as I'm about to sleep. They harass, hound, and hunt me. Chieko laughs at me when she sees me scratching. "Ask Sensei for some cream," she suggests.

When I do, Sensei gives me cream, which alleviates the itching. But from then on, she calls me, "Cream! Give me twenty push-ups!"

"Cream! Why are you the slowest trainee here?"

"Cream! Toilet duty."

Bathrooms are a difficult transition. Back at the dormitories, students shared the toilets, but there was basic plumbing. Here, it's five outdoor stalls around holes in the ground. There are always flies and bugs that congregate. The smell is abhorrent. Cleaning staff is us. Every afternoon, bathroom duty changes. We have to remove the waste via bucket and carry it to a neighboring field, so they can use it as fertilizer to grow the food we eat. The first time I do it, it's Chieko, Wren, and me. We're each carrying two buckets full of crap when Wren trips over a rock and spills his load over the ground. Sensei rushes over and commands all three of us, "Put it back into the buckets with your hands!"

"Sorry!" Wren yells, bowing to us after Sensei leaves.

"Her job is to crush our souls, beat us into pulp, grind us up like orange juice, and spit us back out," Chieko says.

"Orange juice isn't the word I'd use," I say as I wipe a particularly egregious load of crap off the ground.

I'D LIKE TO THINK I'M GETTING TOUGHER AND MY BODY IS GETTING IN-ured to the exercise. But I'm always feeling exhausted. I doze off whenever there is even a moment of respite. I eat my meals as fast as I can just so I can "snap" (snooze + nap) for ten minutes before running again. My calves cramp frequently. Sleeping on my side helps alleviate muscle spasms at night.

"You need to drink more water," Chieko berates me even though our water dole is limited.

"He needs a banana," Wren offers, even though there aren't any bananas around. "My dad worked in a silver mine and ate a banana every day to stop his cramps."

Three in the morning, Sensei wakes us up. "Couldn't sleep," she says. "I got indigestion thinking about how weak you all are."

Both Wren and I can barely open our eyes as we begin jogging. Chieko is energized and runs ahead of us. Her strength inspires me, and I race after her.

Wren, who's used to lagging behind the other recruits with me, starts counting down until I get tired. Thirty seconds later, he's caught up with me as I'm out of breath.

He asks, "Feel better?"

"I will when I'm back in our barracks, sleeping."

Wren laughs and chases after Chieko, leaving me far behind.

IT'S BEEN A MONTH. OUR UNIT IS DOWN TO FORTY-NINE RECRUITS. "I didn't join to prepare for a marathon," one quitter states, expressing our sentiment perfectly.

I've been running thirty kilometers since I woke up, carrying heavy equipment and singing songs praising the Emperor. And honestly, I'm more strained than ever. It's a cumulative degradation. We're never given the chance to rest. Sleep is being rationed stingily by Sensei, who grants it to us only when she pleases. But since I've been here, I've never once seen her pleased. Aside from the sleep, I'd love some quiet as I hate these droning chants about how we will smash our enemies with our lives if need be. It's not like they're even good *gunkas*, as I like some of the more popular military marches.

"I can't hear you!" Sensei yells.

We reach a hill, where we're allowed a thirty-minute break to eat lunch. I take out my supply of two biscuits and a dried mackerel. Chieko eats her biscuits like they're hard apples and stares at the empty wasteland to the east. That's the Quiet Border I've always heard about, called that because it's a couple of hundred kilometers of dirt with no sign of life or vegetation. Beyond that, German America and Texarkana Fortress. "Cream," Chieko calls me. "You ever been to Germany?"

I shake my head. "Never," I reply, and wonder how Griselda is doing.

"Neither have I. Don't ever want to go either unless we're kicking Nazi ass. Did you know they sanction mice by color?"

"What do you mean?"

"Only white mice are allowed to live there. Brown, black, and gray mice are shot."

I can't tell if she's joking or not.

"You ever have fried mouse before?" she asks.

"No," I reply.

"It tastes good with the proper seasoning."

"That's disgusting," Wren snaps. "I'd never eat a mouse."

"Why not?"

"I used to have three pet mice," Wren says. "I played with them every day and trained them to do small tricks."

"Did you teach them to fetch and play dead?" Chieko teases him.

They go at it as he defends his choice of pet while Chieko suggests he change his nickname to something mouse related.

MOST EVENINGS, I'M TOO TIRED TO DO ANYTHING. BUT MANY OF THE other recruits take out Hanafuda cards and play for cigarettes or whatever else they can gamble for. They switch rules, going from traditional to Korean style to all seventeen USJ variations. I don't know how it works other than that the suits represent the twelve months and the flowers separate them. I do know it involves a lot of wrist flicks and cards being flung against other cards with loud snaps.

RAMDET trainee Botan, who's usually so quiet, is the best and always ends up on top. One evening, she beats everyone so soundly, they become convinced she's cheating and refuse to play against her anymore. Time, flower cards, and cigarettes have become our miniaturized economy, with reputation the only currency that carries weight.

WE'RE NOT FARMERS, SO I DON'T KNOW WHY WE HAVE TO WAKE UP SO early every morning. It's cold, our muscles are sore, and I'd rather be back in bed. I'm shocked when we assemble in the morning and don't immediately start running. Sensei asks us to approach her one by one to try to tackle her. She takes on a judo stance. The fourteen students in front of me confront her, try to attack, then get thrown to the ground in one sweeping motion. When it's my turn, I stand at a distance. Every time she gets closer to me, I step back. After a minute or so of this, Sensei shouts, "Cream! I didn't ask you for a dance. *Fight* me!"

I use that moment to rush her and try to knock her down. But she's ready and grabs my shoulder. She places her right foot behind mine, then pushes me. I trip on her foot and hit the ground. She puts her foot on my back. "I hate cheap tricks, Cream, especially when they fail."

The other students don't fare any better. The only one who lasts longer than the rest of us is Chieko. She's lowered her mass, wary in her motions, watching Sensei carefully. Sensei goes in for the strike, but Chieko counters, pushing her back. Chieko goes for a blow to the lower abdomen, but Sensei dodges her, letting Chieko's momentum make her vulnerable. With a sweep of the feet, Chieko falls like the rest of us.

"There's nothing more important in a fight than positioning and the placement of your feet. 'Maximum efficiency, minimum effort' is judo's key principle. Just by seeing how an opponent moves their feet, I can tell the result of the fight. There are ten *katas* I will teach you. Learn them, and you will be able to defeat anyone."

Over the next three weeks, I fall a lot. If my back were clay, it would be arched from all the hits it's taking. Sensei asks us, "How many of you know about cats?"

Does *Cat Odyssey* count? I raise my hand, as do a dozen others.

"Then you know cats can make huge drops without any pain. Do you know why? Because they're so limber."

On mats, we practice falling a hundred times a day. We roll

back, slap down with both our arms so that the force of the fall is distributed throughout our body. Rather than stiffen on impact, she teaches us to roll like a cradle. It doesn't come naturally as my first instinct is to resist falling and fight against gravity. But Sensei keeps on telling us, "Flow. Don't resist. Just flow."

No matter how many times I practice, my back still hurts when I fall.

We learn throwing, grappling, defense in the *kime-no-kata*, and the twenty-one self-defense techniques of the *Kōdōkan goshin-jutsu* that teach us how to ward off unarmed and armed opponents. Not sure what help the *Kōdōkan* will be against someone with a death ray, but anytime anyone asks a question doubting judo's efficacy, Sensei throws them to the ground again and again until their back becomes one with the floor. She has us do five hundred squats a day. For ten-minute stretches, we're required to stand on one leg with the knee bent, then switch. Strengthening our leg muscles, we're told. I never thought I'd miss running.

When it's not Sensei tackling us, it's the other students. Chieko is especially adept because of her wrestling background, which isn't something she's fond of recollecting.

"Why not? You have an advantage over all of us," Wren says. "You should be proud of it."

But Chieko shakes her head, and says, "During a match, I body-slammed this girl and cracked her spine. I nearly killed her. If it'd just been a centimeter off, she'd be dead. They took her to the hospital. Had her in surgery for two days. Longest two days of my life. I couldn't bear the thought of having killed someone."

"She survived?"

"She survived. And they performed a special surgery, so she could walk again. But I stopped wrestling after that because I realized how weak and fragile humans are. That's why I want to fight in a mecha. They make us superhuman."

MOST OF OUR MATCHES ARE MINIMALLY EFFICIENT WITH MAXIMUM EF- fort. I'm trying to throw Wren, and Wren is trying to toss me to the ground. He's bigger than me, so I always struggle in my match-ups with him, whereas he usually throws me with ease.

Once that's done, Sensei leads us through thirty-minute stretches to make our muscles limber. We exercise our lats, hamstrings, do a pigeon stretch and side-lying windmill to loosen tightness. "Your muscles can extend up to 1.5 times their usual length with the proper stretching. But your tendons can't go that far, so the key is balance." She has us touch our toes with our arms and keep our legs straight, but I can barely reach my ankles. Within three days, I'm able to not just reach my toes, but place my palms on the ground. I admit, it feels good. But my feet still hurt, and my hips feel like they're disjointed.

Wren is worse off. He's walking with a limp. We're paired up for another fight. Usually, it ends with him headlocking me or throwing me to the ground. But today, he's slower and less aggressive. In one series of attacks, I catch him off guard and have him in position to hurtle him. This should be an easy throw. But instead of going with the "flow," Wren grabs my right arm. I'm already in motion so I can't stop myself. I feel something tear in my shoulder as he flies past me. Pain stabs my arm, and I can't move it. I droop to the side, and there's no feeling. But as soon as I try to raise my arm, the pain returns in a fury.

"Sensei," I call. "Sensei!"

She comes over. "What's wrong?"

"M-my arm."

She tries to help me raise it, but I flinch.

She takes out a portical from her pockets, and says, "We need the medic." She disconnects and orders me, "Get out of the way."

I sit by a wall and watch the other students practice judo. Wren apologizes. "I'm real sorry. I don't know what happened."

"It's okay. It was an accident. It should be fine."

The medic is a woman of Malaysian descent named Minako, who looks a little older than the rest of us. She's carrying a medical kit, and I explain what happened. She checks my arm with her portical, which has extra sensors built in, conducting a real-time X-ray that displays on her screen. "Good part is no broken bones," she says, showing me my skeleton.

"Is it normal to have gaps there?" I ask.

"That's where your tendons and muscles are, which is what we're checking next."

She scans them several times. Sensei comes over.

"What's the prognosis?" she asks.

"Torn tendons on the rotator cuff. These palliative patches should expedite healing, and he should be all good in a week."

"That's too long."

"That's what he needs. No exercises or training. Just R and R." Minako puts her portical down, asks me to take off my shirt. I do. She wraps a cloth around my shoulder that hardens when she applies a special liquid. She injects the palliative and gives me six dosages I have to apply myself over the week. She closes up her kit, gives me a thumbs-up, and leaves.

Sensei looks down at me. "Tough luck, Cream."

"What do you mean?" I ask.

"A week is too long to miss. You're out. Go see the administrative office for your termination notice."

"W-wait. You mean I'm done with the training?" I can't believe it. After all I've suffered, it's going to end with me getting cut over an accident?

"Without your arm, you're worthless. And losing a week means you're behind everyone else."

"What am I supposed to do?"

"Wait for the next training cycle and try again."

Another two months of hell just to get back to this spot? What if I get hurt again? My sense of outrage overwhelms the pain I feel in my arm. "This is unfair."

"There's no such thing as fair. We're not a charity," Sensei says, and turns around.

In giving me her back, I feel the disdain everyone's felt for me my entire life. Her disrespect and indifference is unbearable. Custom dictates I should shut up, accept my fate, and try again. But I think about all the failures of my life, and I can't stand it.

"Sensei!" I call to her.

Sensei turns around. "I told you you're done!"

"I'm not done!" I shout back. "Not without a match."

"A match?"

"Three chances. If I throw you once, I stay."

"And after you fail?" She doesn't even doubt the outcome, which infuriates me more.

"I'll leave without protesting, knowing you weren't a very good teacher."

There's a glimmer of irritation. She lifts up her fingers and challenges me forward. The other students gather around, forming a human circle. Vultures coming in to sate their appetite for drama.

I know I have no chance. She'll probably aim for my arm, which is immobile. As soon as she applies pressure, I'll be paralyzed. And from the way her eyes are hawkishly focused on my shoulder, I know even if I had ten chances, I'd fail. Just like I failed the exam and pretty much everything else I've tried at in my life. If only my arm were good . . . Who am I kidding? Even if my shoulder weren't damaged, how could I compete with her?

We face off. I keep my distance, watching her for an opening.

"Are we dancing again, Cream?"

"My name is Makoto!" I shout at her.

She grins. "Sincere people are often the dumbest," she responds, mocking my name for its literal meaning, "sincerity." "You're not the exception, Cream. This dance is over."

She steps toward me, feints left, then goes for my right arm. I duck and leap for her feet, hoping to knock her down. She jumps up, avoiding my charge, her feet coming down on my back. She stomps down on my bad arm. I swear a knife went through it. For all purposes, the fight is done, and I've lost. But I suppress the pain and flip in place, grabbing her by the legs and bringing her down with me. She stumbles in surprise, but lands deftly. It was a cheap move on my part, but I had no other choice. She lands a foot in my face and another. I'm in too much pain to retaliate, and I know she's within her rights to beat me to death. But she starts laughing hard. Not the reaction I was expecting. Is she mocking me again?

"You've got spirit, Cream." She gets back on her feet and points at me. "Three days of R and R, and you're back on the field."

The other students are shocked. So am I. Sensei goes back to yelling at everyone like nothing happened. I'm relieved to find out I'm staying.

TO ACCELERATE MY RECOVERY, I'M TAKEN TO RAMDET HEADQUARTERS IN Dallas Tokai. It's a huge facility that resembles a corporation more than a security base. There are eight main buildings, with four devoted to maintenance of their various defensive craft. RAMDET has operations throughout the world wherever the Empire shares a border with the Nazis or Italians. Here, they have a complex of dormitories for staff members, and I'm given a studio about the size of my old apartment. The difference is, I have it all to myself.

I've been ordered to spend my recovery studying the history of the mecha and given a textbook to read on my portical. The *RAM-*

DET History of Mechanized Combat and Defensive Units is full of footage from history, charting the evolution of mechas.

It all began with a small tech company in the mid 1940s called Sono Industries, which was doing subsidiary contracts on tanks. One of their main scientists, Hiroshi Boshiro, had been studying German railway guns, but because they were limited by mobility, knew they were ineffective for actual combat. According to folklore, Boshiro was watching a military parade in Osaka when he saw a troupe of samurais followed by a tank brigade and came up with the idea of combining the defensive armor of a samurai suit with the firepower of a tank.

Boshiro was one of the most brilliant minds at Sono. He was also emotionally devastated after his son was killed by an American suicide attack. Boshiro was driven to get revenge and worked tirelessly to exact it. They have only static 2D images of the mechanical samurai-tank prototypes in black and white, which are surreal to see. The mechanical samurai tanks started off at about five meters tall and used treads for locomotion. I see some film footage of their first attempt at taking a step, which is a disaster. The mecha can't maintain its balance. It would take multiple rebuilds before they got the mecha walking.

That's also when Boshiro devised a formula to equalize weight distribution and its relationship to the energy required to take a single step, which he then put into the "gyration stabilizer." The GS is still considered one of the most important inventions of the Pacific War, allowing our forces to build mechas much taller.

I take a bathroom break. As I wash my hands, I see myself in the mirror for the first time in a long while. I've lost so much weight, I almost don't recognize the face in front of me. I never knew how pudgy I was until now, seeing my cheekbones pushing out. My belly, which previously was a brick of fat, actually looks like an assemblage of muscles. I'd seen the transition so incrementally, looking down at my body every morning, that I hadn't realized how significant it was until now.

I hop back in my bed, check my portical messages regularly since I've regained access. I know the chances of BEMA changing their mind are slim, but I'm awaiting word on if they've reconsidered my rejection based on Colonel Tachibana's request. I get stupidly giddy thinking about how I'd react if they did.

There's a knock on my door. I put on my trainers and open it. I'm surprised to see my medic, Minako. She's wearing a pink cap, denim overalls, and sequined shoes split into a hundred even pieces.

"I heard they sent you here," she says. "Let's go."

"Go where?" I ask.

"We'll show you around Dallas Tokai."

"But I have to study."

"You studying all night?"

"I guess I could use a break. But I'm supposed to finish the book before the three days are up."

"That's what Leiko told you, right?"

"Who?"

"Your Sensei," she clarifies.

"She gave the orders."

"Believe me when I tell you she'll be okay with you taking a night off. You have any other clothes?" she asks, peering at my training suit.

"Not with me."

"We'll have to buy something on the way."

"On the way where?"

"To the Bertoli," she answers. "It's the new discotheque in town."

We meet her boyfriend outside the base, where he's waiting for us in his car. "Izanagi," he introduces himself. "But everyone calls me Izzy. Min says you're a RAM?"

I take that to be abbreviated for RAMDET. "In training."

I get in the backseat, and Minako takes shotgun. The sun is out late for the summer evening but is slowly melting into the buildings beyond. Izzy drives us out of the parking lot.

"You RAMs get more action than we do," he says.

"What do you mean?"

"We guard the city, but we're never allowed to leave. They usually keep the Quiet Border clear of our forces to keep it strictly neutral. RAMs are technically civilian and have a deal with the Nazis, so y'all can enter Texarkana Fortress and escort trains through the border."

"Are you in the mecha corps?" I venture to ask.

"I am."

"What do you do?"

"I'm a navigator."

Navigators chart the paths and constantly check terrain to make sure it's suitable for the mecha to traverse. They have to monitor composition of the ground in case it's not strong enough to support the weight of a full mecha. There are at least five battles I can think of in which a minor navigational mistake cost the mecha corps victory. I know this thanks to my mom, who was also a navigator. Izzy has to be very smart to have that position.

"That's amazing," I say.

He shrugs as he drives. "Not really. I do nothing since we never go anywhere. See that cluster over there?" Right above the Ida Train Station, I see the towering figure of four Sentry-class mechas. They're bulkier, rounder, and more stalwart than the *Korosu* classes I saw during the fight a few months back. "The one on the left is the *Fuka*, which is where I serve. To be honest, I don't know if the legs work anymore."

"Izzy," Minako says reprovingly. "Peace is a good state to be in."

"I'm not complaining."

"It sounds like you are."

"Not like them Nazis are waiting around doing nothing. Texarkana Fortress is their hellish *Yomi* on earth."

They make jabs at each other, the typical needling couples engage in. I look out the window. Dallas isn't as shiny or electric as Los Angeles, but it's a huge city in its own right, especially the farther west away from the border we drive. It's not long before we arrive at the Ura-Hara Shopping District, which is ten streets full of clothing stores.

"What kind of clothes do you like?" Min asks.

I'm puzzled by the question as it's one I've never been asked before. I confess, "I've never been shopping for clothes before."

"Never?"

I search my memory and am forced to shake my head. "I've always worn school-issued attire."

"Just get him a z-cloak," Izzy suggests.

"Good idea. They're so convenient," Minako says.

Ten minutes later, she brings back clothing that looks like a regular cloak. But when I put it on, it fits snugly to the contour of my body. Minako inputs commands into her portical that change my z-cloak's visual appearance to resemble a silk shirt and black dress pants. She asks for my portical and sends me access codes for my z-cloak attribute interface. I scroll through, and can change the length of my sleeves (the z-cloak will make surfaces transparent), adjust material appearance to whatever I want from fleece to purple leather, and scale overall size, making it baggy or tight-fitting. The hood is detachable and can be used to switch between a jacket, hoodie, and turtleneck sweater.

"Best way to travel light," Minako says.

"How much do I owe you?"

Minako smiles. "Forget it. It's an honor to take you on your first shopping trip."

I bow to them both and thank them.

"You're too polite, kid," Izzy says, though I can tell both are pleased. That's when I notice he has a *shin guntō* sword with a special holster in the driver's seat. He notices my gaze. "Had this custom built at Albuquerque. Don't let the snobs fool you into thinking that only the Toyokawa swords are good. They mass-produce those. This is customized for me." It has the carvings of a shark on its hilt. Most of the officer swords from Toyokawa Naval Arsenal are standard-issue with no special designs.

"That sword has only one use," Minako states.

I find out what it is when we arrive at the Bertoli. The front door is crowded with hundreds of people, but Izzy takes us to the side and valets the car with the attendant. "VIP entrance," Minako explains. "Only for mecha corps members."

Sure enough, when the pale bouncer in a robot kimono sees Izzy's sword, he waves us through without a question.

Inside, there is a museum of older robots. I espy synthetic waitresses, gladiatorial machines from the seventies, and portical-driven humanoids that mimic historical figures like Mussolini and Rommel. There's even the hulking armor of a corgi prototype suit called ODIN that the engineers fit with machine guns and toe pistols.

The servers are dressed as sleek robots with silver makeup. The discotheque has multiple floors, and each is based on a different decade. We go to the sixties stage, which is full of older designs, gaudy lights, and restoration-era architecture. Our booth is among a hundred others with velvet seats. There's already a bottle of vodka waiting for us. "*Sake* never gets us drunk," Minako says. "Especially the hot kind."

Izzy pours vodka into his glass and Minako's. "You drinking?" he asks me.

I shake my head. He puts the bottle down. Minako and he

toast, then take the shot. He quickly pours another, and they take three shots straight.

Izzy doesn't handle it so well, and his face turns red. Minako orders pork skewers, which they bring along with wasabi-coated macadamias.

"Why'd you join the RAMs?" Izzy asks me.

I don't think there's any point in hiding the truth. "Because I want to be a mecha pilot."

"I wanted to be a pilot too, but my reflex sync scores weren't high enough."

"You should have spent more time practicing," Minako says.

"I was too busy chasing an elusive someone," Izzy objects, which makes Min simper. "Was worth it in the end. I have a cushy job. Plus, don't have to deal with Nazi biomechs."

"You've fought them?" I ask. Very little record of German bio-mechs is public.

"No. But I've seen combat footage. You ever see a biomech?"

"Just the stuff they've released."

"They're terrifying. Even before they attack, dozens of gnats swarm the mechas."

"What are gnats?" I ask.

"These black drones with rockets on 'em that wear their opponents down. They make this gnashing sound right before they attack, and it's like a fog of artificial bugs. That's just to get you nice and vulnerable, so the monster has you in a weak spot." He looks at me like he's going to make a point, then says, "I gotta use the bathroom," before stumbling away.

Min shakes her head. "At least he's a jovial drunk. I hate mean drunks."

"Why'd you join the RAMs?" I ask her.

She pours herself another drink and rolls the vodka around her cup. "Because I hated the army medical corps. There were too many dead to deal with." She takes a shot. "In the RAMs, I can actually help people instead of trying to stitch them back together so they can get killed or kill someone else."

"Were you in San Diego?"

"I was. Along with your Sensei, Leiko."

"She served?"

"As an engineer. A damn good one from what I understand. We all graduated VMI together." That's the Vancouver Military Institute.

"How did she go from the corps to the RAMs?"

"Her squadron was out on a mission in San Diego when they were ambushed. Some unidentified mecha fought them off the shore right before they were going to attack the George Washingtons. They were immobilized and ended up blocking a road. Their lead mecha destroyed them to clear the route. She lost everyone on board and barely escaped with her life. By the time she got out, the GWs had already broken through the wall."

"How'd she survive?"

"Colonel Yamaoka saved her. A lot of people in the USJ owe him their lives."

Colonel Noboru Yamaoka, the hero of the second San Diego Conflict, designed the brilliant Irvine Trap that decisively ended the George Washington revolt. It's still considered one of the most ingenious, and bloody, strategies ever implemented.

"She still doesn't talk about it," Minako continued. "I've heard from others that the GWs actually shot her while she was on the field but kept her alive to torture her. She struggled for days, trying her best to get away. When some of our soldiers finally found her, they tried to rescue her but were killed from mines the GWs had set up around her as bait. The—"

Izzy returns and has seven others with him who are from Izzy's battalion. Two of them transferred from Mongolia, and another, a man who has dyed his hair blue, introduces himself as Orwell. "I transferred from Fargo Station up north," he explains.

The rest came here directly from Vancouver Military Institute. The Vancouver graduates take a toast. "Longevity," they toast, "and booze."

"Mac here wants to be a mecha pilot!" Izzy says. "We should all put in a rec for him." He gives me a friendly elbow. "We like to spread the misery of the corps."

The others laugh and drink to that. They engage in familiar banter about Dallas, failed romances, and redundant military exercises.

Orwell, who served on the Fargo Wall, says, "The Nazis are like fleas. They play their loud operas all night just to annoy us. I don't think they ever sleep. At least here, Texarkana is far enough you don't have to deal directly with them."

"Orwell doesn't like Germans," Minako says to me.

"I don't trust 'em. Look how many there are in this club. Is this still the United States of *Japan*? Do you know they laugh at us for bowing whenever we see them? I don't bow to Nazis no more."

My eyes wander over to the German crowd, and I spot someone who looks familiar.

"Mac. You okay?" Minako asks.

I point at the blond-haired woman in a black dress. "I think I know her."

"Go say hi!" Minako says, then pushes me in her direction.

The closer I get, the less certain I am it's her. With the lights changing every few seconds and dancers swarming by, I get more nervous. When I'm almost next to her, I see that she's wearing lipstick and has cut her hair shorter, but it is Griselda. I'm ecstatic.

"Griselda!" I call out, still wanting to get auditory confirmation in case my eyes are deceiving me.

"What do you want?" she snaps.

I'm surprised by her response and hope it's because she doesn't realize who I am. "It's me. Mac."

She looks carefully at me. "Mac? You—you look so different." She immediately brightens and hugs me.

"It's the training," I explain. "We've been running a lot. If you still run in the mornings, I guarantee I can keep up."

"I bet you can. You've grown taller."

I realize that I'm taller than her now. "What are you doing here?" I ask her.

"I got transferred to Texarkana. But it's so dreary and bleak there, I couldn't stand it, so I'm studying in Dallas Tokai for a year."

"What are you studying?" Behind Griselda, I see Minako, with her thumbs up and a wide smile.

"USJ history," she replies. "It's shocking how much the Empire achieved in such a short time. Do you want a drink?" she asks.

"I, uh . . . Sure. Actually, I haven't had alcohol before."

"Why not?"

"There's just never been the right occasion."

She perks up. "Then we can break your beer virginity! But the beer here isn't as good as back home. Can you believe the Americans made drinking illegal?" Griselda asks.

"They did?"

"A long time ago. It was for, like, a decade. They thought drinking was 'immoral.'"

"That's strange."

"Tell me about it. People still wanted to drink, so they had to do it illegally. They had American yakuza who distributed the alcohol, and people literally died for beer. Can you think of a dumber thing to die for?"

"Unless the beer was really good?" I offer.

She laughs. "I guess there are some drinks worth dying for. Unfortunately, you won't find any here. I take it you're a RAM?"

"I am," I state.

I explain in brief about the past few months. She listens attentively and asks questions about this and that.

"You really think you're going to get the chance to pilot a mecha?" she asks.

The truth is I have no idea. But I tell her, "I'm going to keep on trying."

"At least you have a dream you're fighting for."

"Sometimes, I wonder if I'm wasting my time pursuing this. It's a long shot, and there are no guarantees this'll amount to anything."

"The Fuehrer had even less than you, and he became the ruler of Germany," Griselda tells me, which isn't exactly a comforting example to follow even though she seems moved by the comparison. "I hate people who give up. Most of my older relatives live lives of regret and make it miserable for everyone around them because they're so unhappy."

"Is it regret that they failed at something or that they never tried?"

"A combination, I think? If you gave it your best shot and failed, then it wasn't meant to be. I think I can live with that. You hungry?"

"Starving."

"Let's go eat!"

"Are you—are you here with anyone?"

Griselda grimaces. "I was. But he threw a fit, and I don't have the patience to deal with him tonight. C'mon—I'll take you to my new favorite bistro, and then we can have some *good* drinks afterward."

She goes to grab her jacket.

I want to greet Minako and Izzy before leaving.

They both give me jocular grins, and say, "Have fun."

"It's not like that."

"It never is until it is."

"I'll try to be back at the dorm before midnight," I say.

"There's no curfew," Minako replies, reminding me I'm not in training camp anymore.

Griselda comes back with her jacket, and I introduce them to her. They greet her warmly. All excerpt Orwell, who asks, "Are you German?"

"Half," she answers, with a bright smile.

"What are you thinking?" Orwell asks me angrily.

"Relax, Orwell," Izzy says.

But Orwell glowers, and says, "Do you know how many of our compatriots have died because of Nazis? Do you know what they do to their own people?"

"Nothing less than what the Empire does," Griselda snaps back.

"I wasn't talking to you," he snarls, and turns back to me. "You want to be a mecha pilot, but you're friends with a Nazi. That's not the way it works."

"Griselda's not like that. We're friends from high school."

"A Nazi's a Nazi. If you were thinking straight, you'd know how dishonorable this is."

"She's my friend," I affirm. "I don't care what nationality she is."

"Then you have no place in the mecha corps or as a RAM."

"That's not for you to say."

"It is. And I'll be sure to let everyone know that too."

"Stop it, Orwell!" Izzy and Minako yell.

"I hate Nazis," Orwell says. "Even seeing them makes me sick. You don't deal with them every day. You don't see the way they torture their prisoners along the wall."

I'm about to retort back, but Griselda puts her hand on my arm. "You've made your point. I suggest you shut up," Griselda firmly warns. "As a foreigner, I'll be patient, but I won't let you malign my people anymore."

"Your people? The Nazis are a cancer to—"

Griselda roundhouses Orwell in the face, knocking him to the floor. Immediately, his Vancouver classmates surround Griselda. "I told you to shut your mouth!" Griselda yells.

That's when several Germans appear, asking Griselda if she's okay. This enrages Orwell's classmates, who respond with fists. Fighting breaks out as Orwell gets to his feet, and shouts, "I piss on Hitler an—" But before he can finish, a barstool smashes him in the face.

Another of Orwell's goons charges Griselda. I rush to try to grab him from behind. Griselda hurls a fist, though the guy ducks just in time for her punch to hit me in the eye. "Mac! Are you okay?" she exclaims.

My right eye is in a lot of pain, and I realize I'm on the ground. "I—I, uh, think so."

Griselda helps me up. Izzy pulls us both away from the fray.

"You two need to get out of here, NOW!" he shouts, pointing at the exit as the fight intensifies.

I have to lean on Griselda because I can't see out of my right eye. We go down a floor into what is labeled the Digital Forest Dance Stage. It's almost pitch-black except for hundreds of neon lights that appear to be floating in midair. You can barely see the person in front of you, which is the point, as everyone's dancing without knowing who their partner is. Griselda grabs my hand and leads me through the crowd. Random strangers grope at my body, trying to make me dance with them, but Griselda pulls me through.

We make it down to the first floor when someone yells, "She's the one who started the whole thing!"

From my left eye, I see two men sprinting toward us. As soon as they get close, Griselda kicks the first one in the groin. A waitress is passing by, and Griselda grabs a bottle and batters it into the head of the second. Both are down on the floor as we continue to head for the entrance.

"You sure know how to make an exit," I tell her.

She grabs another beer bottle and tells me, "Put this against your eye."

The bottle is cold and wet. I press it onto my bulging eye. Griselda gives the waitress a wink and pays via her portical.

We get outside and grab a taxi.

"Where are we going?" I ask her.

She brushes dust off her shirt and says, "To eat, right?"

WE TAKE A CAB TO THE BISTRO. ON THE WAY, SHE'S TELLING ME ABOUT food, intentionally avoiding talking about the fight.

"My *mutter* loves eggplant with vinegar. She cooks eggplant a hundred different ways, and it tastes new every time. My *vater* loves blood sausages with apple sauce and garlic mashed potatoes. I introduced him to stinky tofu, and he loved it, but my *mutter* couldn't stand it."

"I can't stand stinky tofu either."

"It's the best!"

I try to think back on my own parents, but my memories are blurry. "I wish I remembered what my parents liked to eat."

"You don't remember?"

"I know my mom liked *basi digua*."

"What's that?"

"They're like sweet potatoes with caramelized sugar. There was other stuff, but I couldn't stand the smell of vinegar. I liked only the sweet food, especially pears. I couldn't peel a pear, and I'd have to wait for her to do it for me because I didn't like eating them with their skin on."

"Can you peel a pear now?"

I shake my head. "Either I chop it all up, or I cut my fingers."

We arrive at the Cunningham, a restaurant devoted to a multi-tude of cuisines, with each of the eating areas based on a different field in portical entertainment.

She pays for the cab via her portical as I have no money.

"I'm really sorry about what happened," I say, broaching the fight.

"I know you RAMs don't get a whole lot of money," she replies. "My treat."

"Sorry, I—I meant the fight."

She nods. "I know." She waves it off. "I get it all the time. I don't deny what the Nazis have done. Their actions are inhumane and evil. But that's not all of us. It's a group of lunatics who never should have been given positions of power. There are many who oppose them."

"There are?"

"Of course."

"Why don't they say something?"

"Things are changing in the German Americas. For many of us, we have no choice. We're born there and taught that Aryans are the superior beings. It's a slow transition, but this brutality can't last. I just can't stand the hypocrisy. Do you know how many the USJ killed in San Diego?"

The question reminds me of the one from the imperial exams last year. "A lot," I answer her.

"I'm sorry about your eye." She puts her hand on it. "What if our two sides get less friendly in the upcoming years?"

I'm saved from answering by the hostess, who says, "We have an opening for two in the Onmyoji section if you come with me right now."

We take off our shoes and are given slippers—servers take away our shoes and store them until the end of the meal.

Several waiters dressed as magic and divination specialists bow to welcome us. One says to me, "Your spiritual outcast looks foggy," while to Griselda he says, "There is much conflict and confusion in your path."

"So vague as to mean nothing," Griselda says to me, as we both take our seats.

I leave the food choices to her and go to use the bathroom. I stare in the mirror and see my eye has swollen. It looks like the entire side of my head has a bulbous mass popping out of it. I wonder about the question she asked: What if we do go to war with the Nazis? How would our friendship change? Even thinking about it gives me a headache as I can't bear the thought of our being on opposing sides. I wash my eye before heading back to our table.

One of the onmyoji brings out a covered plate on a tray. He uses his fingers, does a chant in Japanese, and suddenly, the plate cover floats away.

Griselda claps as they place the food on the table. She explains, "They dip the Wagyu beef in special panko and soy sauce, and they fry it for thirty seconds at one hundred eighty degrees." She cuts it open. "It's pink in the middle, just perfect. This miso soup uses this fresh aka dashi the chef makes every morning. The dashi stock here isn't the powder kind, but it's boiled with just the right amount of Katsuobushi, so the umami balance is spot on. *Itadakimasu!*"

She takes a bite. I do the same. The beef is very tender. When she asks how it is, I tell her, "I love it."

I've never had a miso soup that is this rich with flavor, especially with the dried tuna from the Katsuobushi. The tofu practically melts in my mouth. We eat in silence, relishing the meal. The onmyoji brings out two mugs full of beer.

"This is for lightweights," Griselda says. *"Kanpai!"*

"Prost!" I reply, as our cups clash.

I take a sip. It tastes bitter, and I don't like it at all. But when I look over, Griselda's drunk almost half her cup. I force myself to drink a quarter before I have to stop.

"How is it?"

"Good," I say.

I was expecting to be drunk with my first sip, but it doesn't have a noticeable impact. Griselda is already finished with her drink. "Don't let me pressure you, but, uh, hurry up."

Two mugs later, I'm too full to drink any more. I still don't feel anything until I stand up. I feel dizzy and stumble. Griselda catches me, laughing.

"I feel like the whole planet is spinning around me," I tell her.

"That's what I thought the first time too. Does beer put me in tune with the planet? But actually, it's because alcohol thins your blood and creates a distortion in your cupula."

"What?"

"Your reality is distorted because chemicals inside your ear are going crazy."

"Oh," I say, not sure what it means but accepting it.

She laughs, and says, "Let's get out of here. Something amazing I want to show you."

WE'RE TAKING THE CAB TO OUR NEXT DESTINATION WHEN I SEE A BRIGHT blue light shining up to the sky in a single beam.

"What is that?"

"It's from the memorial," Griselda says. "You've never been?"

"No. What kind of a memorial?"

"For Old Dallas and the radiation shield."

"From when we fought the Germans?"

"From when *you* fought them. We can stop by if you'd like."

"I don't want to go to a memorial tonight."

"Looking at thousands of gravestones isn't the way you want to spend your Friday night?"

"Not exactly a spirit lifter."

She laughs, and asks, "You think the spirits of the dead watch us?"

"I'd hope the dead would have better things to do."

"Like what?"

"Like thinking about how they'll get off the planet if they're still here," I reply.

The taxi comes to a stop. "This is the biggest night market in the USJ," she tells me.

It resembles a field of glowing mushrooms. Outdoor kiosks and shops are everywhere. Thousands of people are searching for bargains. Griselda points out some of the women dressed in mini-kimonos that are identical to the traditional clothing on top but cut short below. Merchants sell everything from old gun pieces to dead insects like cicadas and tiger moths. The smell of anti-mosquito incense oozes through the air. The shops spiral outward from the old subway station, and it is bigger than any night market I've visited.

"Can you believe they paid someone to design this?" she asks as she points at the old station's architecture. "It looks like a long bathroom hall. All the walls are tiled like a bathroom. Makes me want to pee!"

We glance over old fedoras, trinkets that hover when thrown into the air, and retro games. There are many dealers of cartridges from before portical games went purely kikkai. I spot *Bionic Commander*, which is about an IJA soldier with a mechanical leg thwarting a fringe group of American terrorists trying to resurrect Franklin Roosevelt. "That's one of my favorites too!" Griselda exclaims. "Did you stop FDR?"

"I did," I reply.

"Remember, you have to time the bazooka shot just right on the cockpit or you fall to your death?"

I remember that last sequence well. I check the price, and it's shockingly high. These older games have been going up in price, with all the new portical channels devoted to reviewing them (and in most cases, mocking them).

She suddenly asks, "What blood type are you?"

"I don't know. I've never checked."

"I bet you're a B blood type."

"What's B type mean?"

"Independent, goes their own way, flexible and afraid of being alone."

"What are you?"

"Type AB."

"What's that mean?" I ask.

"I'm a dreamer whose private life is precious to me, and I have a strong spirit."

"I think I prefer AB," I tell her.

"You don't get to choose. But it determines what kind of diseases affect you and what foods make you gain weight. The Fuehrer was a type A blood, and his vegetarian diet matched perfectly."

"Wait, so these blood differences actually make a difference in who we are?"

"Of course. They determine your entire physiology. Based in that and your reaction to the environment, you can get a good picture of what kind of person you'll generally be and who you match well with."

"What type do B blood types match with?" I ask her.

"AB," she says with a smile. "C'mon—let's go that way."

We both smell food as we approach the food vendors. There's a pork-belly taco shop that almost makes me ignore my full stomach. "There are so many things we have to try. When's the next time you have a day off?"

"This is the first time they've let me off, so I have no idea."

"Too bad we don't have second stomachs," Griselda says.

The burger and sriracha-flavored tater tots smell so good. "I wish."

We keep on walking until we arrive at a couple of apartments.

"This is my place," she says. I'm surprised, not having expected us to come to her home. "Want to come in?" she asks.

I'm taken aback by her invitation. "Uh, sure."

We ride the elevator up to the eleventh floor. Her apartment is a one-bedroom that I was expecting to be filled with German propaganda but is actually bare aside from some furniture I'm assuming came with the place.

"Where's your portical?" she asks.

I take it out. She puts both of ours into a metallic case and locks it.

"Is that a nullifier?" I ask.

She nods. "Don't want anyone listening in. Want some wine?"

"Sure."

She finds a bottle of red wine, pours out two glasses. I have a sip of mine, which is way too strong for me. She turns on the visual display on the wall and we flip through channels.

We land on a priest from one of the religious sects testifying that there is "a woman deeply in debt. She had almost nothing left except her faith. So she paid tithes to the gods, ten percent of all she had left. And through the blessings of the divine spirits, within five years, she was debt free again. Brothers and sisters, it is important that you give from the heart, not for rewards but because you are giving the gods their due."

"Those priests are richer than we are," Griselda says.

"What religions do you have in Germany?"

"We're officially atheists, but we have the Vatican the late Himmler built at Weweslberg. There are a lot of Celtic rituals, but it's mostly for the SS. It was gracious of your empire to allow the Christian God into the Shinto Pantheon."

"It wasn't enough for the George Washingtons," I reply.

"The GWs despise the NARA because the NARA doesn't believe in a second coming and they think that Malek isn't the daughter of God. The True Believers believe that Jesus isn't real. The *Realpolitik* think all religions are false and that for America to arise again, they have to embrace the world for what it is. There are a lot of different factions vying for power, and they all disagree with each other."

I honestly didn't know there were ideological differences between them. "What about you?"

"When I was ten, I was required to join the *Jungemadel*."

"What's that?"

"It means Young Maidens, and we all have to take an oath to the Fuehrer," Griselda replies.

"Do you remember the oath?"

She nods. "'In the presence of this blood banner, which represents our Fuehrer, I swear to devote all my energies and my strength to the savior of our country, Adolf Hitler. I am willing and ready to give up my life to carry out the mission he began, so help me God.'" She finishes her glass of wine and pours herself another.

I drink down my cup and think about our friendship. I wonder what it would be like if there was something more between us. The alcohol must be warping my mind as I don't think there's any way she would reciprocate, is there? She is smart, witty, and one of the toughest people I know. Then I think about what Orwell said, and it makes me even more upset.

"I accidentally saw a portical film my dad made the other day," Griselda says, snapping me out of my thoughts.

"What kind of film?" I ask.

"It was about a world where the media runs everything. People couldn't distinguish between reality and fiction because everything became a headline."

"Was it good?"

"It was funny and bizarre. The whole message was that censoring media is good for the health of the Reich."

I laugh, and tell her, "I've seen plenty of films like that on our side too. Did your dad make lots of films?"

She shakes her head. "He got into trouble, irritated one of his superiors, and got sent over to the East Coast in the German Americas to make nature films."

"Nature films?"

"He had to record the reproductive habits of animals." I look at her to see if she's serious. She bursts out laughing. "It sounds funny now, but he was so bitter about it," she says.

We finish off the bottle. I'm feeling dizzy so I lie down on her sofa. Griselda comes to me and squeezes next to me. She puts her fingers on my cheeks.

"Did you think about me after graduation?" she asks.

"I did," I reply. "Remember that time at the apartment?"

"Which one?"

"After—after Hideki."

"Yes."

"You said *sayonara*."

"That means 'good-bye,' right?"

"So does *jaa ne*, but *sayonara* is more final. You say it only if you know you're not going to see someone for a while. When you said *sayonara*, I thought it was the last time I'd see you . . . I'm glad it wasn't."

But she doesn't reply, and I realize she's fallen asleep. I hold her in my arms, and look at her. I wish I could stay like this long past the night. I make sure she's comfortable, snuggle my head into a softer spot on the sofa, and doze off.

WHEN I WAKE IN THE MORNING, SHE'S IN UNIFORM. THE RED SWASTIKA armband seems to put up a barrier between us.

"How you feeling?"

"I have a huge headache," I tell her, my brain feeling like an iron ball about to tip over.

"You're hungover. Drink lots of water. And eat something."

"You going somewhere?"

"Class. It was so nice to see you. But I probably shouldn't have brought you here."

"What do you mean?"

"Some of your fellow soldiers might misunderstand . . ."

"I don't care."

"You should."

"Can—can I see you again?"

"My portical number is still the same . . . The door locks automatically, so shut it behind you when you leave." She kisses me on the cheek. *"Jaa ne,"* she says, waves, and leaves.

I SNEAK BACK TO MY DORMITORY AND SLEEP MOST OF THE AFTERNOON. It's a restless, sweaty sleep that leaves me even more tired when I wake. A part of me hoped Griselda would be here when I opened my eyes. She obviously isn't. I check my portical, stupidly hoping she contacted me. She hasn't. I regularly refresh, hoping for messages from both Griselda and BEMA. I try to study, but my brain feels too clouded. I open my window, suck in the night air. I watch portical footage of the official mecha tournaments at BEMA among the cadets (something I've watched every year as long as I can remember). I get very excited when I see that Noriko is actually taking part as the cadets spar against one another. She defeats her opponents with ease.

There's a knock on my door. It's Minako, smiling. "She seemed like a nice gal. You stayed with her last night?"

I nod. "We watched some portical shows and went to sleep."

"You sly badger," she says.

"Nothing happened."

"So say the guilty. Can I show you something cool?"

"What is it?"

"You'll see."

I follow, realizing I'm not going to get any studying done. She leads me down two floors to a training room/dojo. As I enter, I realize too late that there are five others in there. One of them strikes me hard with a *Shinai* kendo stick. I stumble to my knees, scraping them against the wooden floors. Three more blows hit me in my back. I look to Minako, but she's turned away with a guilty expression. Approaching me is Orwell, the irascible soldier from last night.

He snarls at me, "You turned your back on us for a Nazi!" He elbows me in the upper cheek, and my eye starts bleeding again. "You want to serve the Empire, but you can't even think straight when it comes to your loyalties. Do you think we would ever allow anyone like you into our ranks?"

"The Germans are our allies," I remind him.

"The hell they are. They're waiting to attack us. The only reason they haven't is they know we'd wipe them clean with our mechas. They're looking for idiots like you they can trick into betraying the Empire. You think your Nazi friend is so innocent? What is she even doing in the USJ?"

I don't like his insinuation, and inform him, "She's been my friend since high school."

"Your friend?" he states, with a scoffing snort. "Where is your *friend* right now?"

I stay quiet.

"She humiliated me in front of everyone. You have a simple choice. Stand by your country. Or betray it for a Nazi."

"It's not that simple."

"Yes it is," Orwell states. Someone hands him what appears to be a branding iron with a swastika sign on it.

"You can't do that!" Minako yells.

"I'll leave his face alone. But I'll brand you so that every girl knows where your heart really belongs." The iron heats up automatically, and they take off my shirt. "Or, you tell me her address, and we let bygones be bygones. What'll it be?"

"Minako," I plead. "You can't let him."

She lowers her head. "I'm really sorry," she says, and looks miserable.

"Her hands are tied," Orwell tells me. "She's loyal to her boyfriend, which means she's not going to help you. Not if she doesn't want him to be reported to the MPs for the illegal trading he does on the side."

Minako glowers at him, but Orwell ignores her.

"I don't know her address," I state. "We didn't go back to her plac—"

"I'm going to count to five, and if I don't get an address . . ." He clicks his teeth together. Two of his friends grab my arms. "Five."

"Please—please don't," I beg him, struggling to break free. "I'm sorry on her behalf. I—"

"Four, three."

"Please, you can't do this. Y—"

"Two, one."

I feel pain on my stomach even stronger than when my skin burned off during the mecha attack at school. It lasts a few seconds, and I want to scream, but I restrain myself. I won't let them know I'm in pain. I grit my teeth, do my best not to show any weakness. The branding ends, and they let me fall to the floor.

Orwell puts his boots on my neck. "You're pathetic, Nazi lover." He spits on me, and I flinch when I feel it hit my neck. The saliva drips slowly down my back.

Two others spit on me too as they file out. Even though the branding hurts, it's the insult of the act that stings more.

Minako remains after they leave. "I'm so sorry," she says. "I—I—"

She cries. I tell myself she had no choice. She tries to give me patches to heal me, but I refuse them. "It's going to hurt the whole night," she warns.

I don't care, and I refuse to speak to her. I hate her and her friends. At least I stayed true to Griselda. At my stubborn silence, Minako gives up and leaves. I eventually pick myself up and go to my room. I take a hot shower, wipe my back. I peer down at the red swastika imprinted on the side of my stomach.

I get out of the shower and dry myself. I lie in bed, deeply upset. I can't sleep the whole night. I feel like I'm going to explode and wish there was some way I could have fought back. Orwell's sneering scorn makes me bristle. I have no idea what to do about the sign. It's a big red welt that I know is going to get me into a lot of trouble if I don't deal with it. Just a few more hours and back to training. I give up on sleep, try to read up on mechas. None of the words register. I exit and grab a taxi.

IT'S FOUR IN THE MORNING. I KNOW GRISELDA IS ASLEEP. BUT I KNOCK ON her door anyway, hoping not to annoy her. She looks through the peephole, sees it's me. "Mac?" She opens the door.

"I'm sorry to come here so late. I—I didn't know where else to go, and the guys from last night. They . . . th—" I fight back bitter tears, refusing to let my anger get the best of me.

She helps me in, puts her arm around me. Her hand gently presses my stomach, which causes me to wince.

"Are you okay?"

"I'll be fine," I answer. "They might be looking for you."

"I can handle them. What happened to you?"

"It's nothing."

She's not convinced, and she touches my stomach again. It stings. She lifts up my shirt before I can stop her and spots the swastika.

"They did this?" she asks grimly.

I don't answer her.

"Because of me?"

"No, no, they're assholes, and—"

I see Griselda's face become cold and mean. "We'll get them back."

"Even if we wanted to, there's no way we could find them in time. I have to report to my shuttle in three hours."

She eyes my branding. "You have to get that fixed."

"I will."

I'm surprised when I see her eyes get wet with tears. "I'm sorry," she offers, confusing me.

"You didn't do anything."

"Do you know how hard it is to be an Asian in the Third Reich?" she asks.

"I've heard stories."

"Being mixed like me is worse. Neither side accepts you. People are always questioning where my loyalties stand. At least you belong in the USJ. I don't even know where I can call my home," she says.

The USJ has always been my "home," so I'm struck when I realize even a sense of place remains elusive for her.

"My mom was a soldier serving near the Fargo Wall," she continues. "They were on a patrol when they came across a tent of civilians in the Quiet Border. She was ordered to fire on them. But she refused. Maybe it's because half of them were of Asian descent. She never told me."

"What happened to her?"

"Arrest and reeducation to wipe out any 'defects' in her mind. When mom finally came back home, she was a different person. There were times I swore she didn't recognize me. I'd ask her a question, and suddenly, she'd quote *Mein Kampf* and cry about how much she loved the Fuehrer." She lifts up my shirt, touches the swastika, bites her lower lip. "I can't ever say what I really feel. None of us can. But don't think all Germans believe the same thing."

"I know they don't."

She sighs, looks at my brand again. "I wish people weren't so cruel to each other . . . It's the world that forces us into this."

"Or human nature."

"Would you have done this to them?"

"Right now, yes and much worse."

She gives me a weak smile. "If anyone did that to me, I'd burn them alive."

"I guess that's an option," I say, surprised by the venom in her tone.

"Do you want some tea?" she asks, mainly to break the tension.

"Sure."

She sets the water to boil.

I realize I don't want to part from her. But I know I have to report back soon. I wish I didn't have to go.

"Mac," she says.

"Yeah."

"You should sleep."

"I can't."

She nods. "Dolphins only sleep with half their brain. The other half of their hemisphere stays awake and keeps them breathing and alive."

"I could use that in training tomorrow."

"I wish I could do that too. Did you know the new *Cat Odyssey* update got released? They added some cool features. Want to check them out?"

05

★ ★ ★

BY THE TIME I REPORT FOR MY SHUTTLE, FATIGUE HAS CAUGHT UP WITH me. I doze the whole trip back in both brain hemispheres.

When I arrive, everyone is doing judo practice. Sensei lets me ease in and has me running for the next four days I'm back. I have to lug my heavy backpack only for the last two. The palliatives do their work. On the final day, my arm feels like new. Normally, the training is torture. But I keep on thinking about Griselda, and somehow, the days seem more tolerable. The constant exercises help clear my mind, diffuse my rage at the memory of what Orwell and his friends did.

At the end of the week, they bring in physical armor.

"You want us to wear that?" Wren asks incredulously.

"Do you think I brought it here for you to look at?" Sensei asks, annoyed, which usually results in a long run.

I realize the armor weighs about the same as all the equipment we've been lugging around, and the training we've endured begins to make sense. There are only twenty-seven of us remaining. I knew Chieko was going to get through. But I'm glad Wren persisted as well.

There's also an old-timer we call Spider because he has tattoos of arachnids all over his arm. He's thirty-two, is of Australian descent, and is the oldest in our group. Nothing fazes him, and he's usually leading the pack.

Chieko asks him, "What you doing here, old man?"

"I served aboard the *Shirokuma* in the Arctic looking for U-boats. It was freezing, even with the heaters, and I was typing communications all the time, so I got something called repetitive stress disorder. Basically, it screws up your nerves since you repeat the same motion over and over. They discharged me because I was pretty much worthless, but civilian life was worse. I don't know how people go to an office for decades of their life. They had me overseeing traffic porticals in Melbourne. My boss was five years younger than me. He lorded over us, and I couldn't take it when he'd yell at us. So I punched him and got exiled to the USJ."

"That's why you're here?"

He stretches out his arm. "My hands are a lot better."

Spider usually leads all the runners, and today is no exception. Jogging in the armor is like carrying around a portable version of a sauna. The plates are heavy, and the heat amplifies the weight. It makes many of us short-tempered, and even the smallest annoyances cause us to snap at one another.

Sensei punishes us all if anyone falls behind on a fifteen-kilometer run. "Another three kilometers!" she'll yell. "Another!" if the person straggling behind doesn't catch up.

One day, it's the recruit we call Poet because he always spouts poems to us. He's falling way behind, and we've already accumulated ten extra kilometers.

"I swear on the USJ if you don't catch up, I'm going to kill you," Chieko yells at him. We all share her sentiment.

Poet feels bad, but he's sporting stomach woes from a case of food poisoning. Eventually, he can't hold it and craps in his pants. That at least makes him feel better, and he catches up, running on pace the rest of the way.

"What is that smell?" Sensei demands when we line up.

His answer isn't what poets aspire to, though there is something poetic about the climax.

THE POUNDING SOUND WAKES US UP. I RECOGNIZE THE SOUND OF A LIGHT mecha. It's a Crab class, a six-legged beast used by the RAMs for security. Each Crab fits five of us, and there are a total of five Crabs in the field. We're not allowed inside the first few days, but it hovers over us as motivation. No one slacks off that week, and everyone is doing their best during exercises.

I gaze over at the Crab every chance I get. I haven't studied its specs as closely as the bipedal mechas, but in many ways, it looks like one of our supertanks, only with six legs rather than tracks. In its stationary pose, the limbs are folded up, jointed at the shoulder (which has a flex-armored skirt), merus, leg, and tip just like a crab. Rather than claws, though, it has a 120mm cannon that can be swapped for other compatible armaments. There are also missile launchers to the side of the hull as well as two auxiliary gun turrets. While it doesn't have the bumpy spines of a crab, it has shocks to protect itself. Entry is from the cupola hatch, and there are detachable wheels on the limbs of the Crabs to ease transportation. If I'm correct, the circular orifice just above the missile launcher is an experimental heat gun that propels a concentrated laser to melt opposition. I don't know how powerful it is, but there's an Amitani logo, usually a sign of excellence. The Crabs are colored desert tan for camouflage, though I'm sure they come in different colors depending on location of deployment.

We're given company-issued porticals, and they have training tutorials on them ready for our perusal. The program details the basics of Crab control through a simulation. We're required to spend two hours every day practicing on the portical to prepare for actual driving. I steer, and the back four legs follow. I can take individual control of any leg at any time. But the automated kinematics are sufficient ninety-nine percent of the time.

"Then why do we need to learn how to use the rest of the legs?" Wren asks Sensei.

"Because winning battles is about that last one percent when you're under fire and some stray missiles blow up your automation. Fifteen kilometers, everyone, for asking such a stupid question!"

We would be angry at Wren if each of us hadn't at one point or another caused the whole company to run. The only thing is, the sun is blazing in all its glory, and I wish it would take a break. Amaterasu, don't you need sleep?

It's another week of baby steps as we switch among the roles. One day I'm pilot; the next, navigator; and after that, communications officer. Munitions requires making sure the cannons don't overheat, which doesn't happen often as they are self-regulating. Since the weapons are customizable, the majority of my work is selecting the best weapons before the battle based on intelligence reports. Engineering is the most difficult position and the one I struggle most with. It's still all simulated, and when we finally go aboard, we don't actually get to drive the Crab ourselves. It's one of Sensei's assistants who takes the controls as we watch. It's more spacious than I'd thought, looking at it from the outside, even though Spider complains, "I feel cramped in here."

When the Crab turns on, the first thing it does is uncurl its legs, raising the hull. The interior actually has an independent stabilizer to try to keep it steady despite the motion of the legs. When our instructor speeds up the Crab's motions, we're surprised at how fast it moves. It's almost like a roach scurrying at quick speeds. Maneuverability is where it excels, able to turn quickly, traversing uneven terrain with ease.

There are manual gauges, but those are for backup. Everything is overlaid on an interface from a portical display we wear over our eyes to obtain visuals from exterior sensors. That way, there's no direct opening, and the hull is technically impenetrable. There is an optional periscope for emergencies.

"A good pilot with good reconnaissance can single-handedly defeat a battalion of tanks," Sensei tells us. "It's been done twice in Afghanistan and once on the Quiet Border."

I gather from the constant simulation tests that Sensei and her assistants are determining where each of us is most adept. At the end of the week, we're split into groups of five, and I'm with Spider, Wren, and Botan, who still beats everyone at cards. Our final crew member is Olympia, who's of Mongolian descent, though I haven't interacted with her much. She's a very fast runner, which is why Sensei gave her "Olympia" as a nickname.

"Cream!" Sensei calls.

I hope for pilot but would be happy with navigator. Even munitions officer would be great.

"Communications," she says.

Communications? My job is to get orders and relay them. It's almost a redundant position because, technically, anyone else can do it.

"Is there a problem, Cream?" Sensei asks.

"I didn't join RAMDET to become a communications officer."

"You got a problem, quit."

Chieko and Spider both get pilot. Wren and Olympia are the gunners on my Crab, handling left/right-rear/front cannons as needed. Olympia will also cover engineering. Botan acts as navigator to check the terrain via sensors. I take over communications and assist everyone as needed.

When we're on board, I'm frustrated by my situation. I sit in my chair, check messages. There aren't any. Spider laughs at me.

"What?" I ask, irked by his levity.

"You realize what happens if a pilot gets hurt or misses their mission for whatever reason?"

"No."

"Someone has to take their spot. Navigator and munitions are too important to be reassigned. It's the communications officer who drives. Not saying you're going to get a chance with me piloting, but don't knock the position."

"Trying not to," I reply.

"Getting to be a pilot is more about politics than skill, man. If some high-ranking officer likes you, your chances are better than if you're the best pilot in the universe. If you want to get anywhere, you got to learn that part of the business."

"This isn't a business. We're soldiers."

"We're not soldiers. We're glorified security guards," Spider says. "Not trying to burst your bubble, but you got to be real with yourself."

Spider is a good pilot. The first steps on the Crab mecha feel very stable, and he has an intuitive knack for the controls. They've built up several obstacle courses a few kilometers from camp. The largest is an urban environment full of empty houses we have to pilot through. There are about fifty buildings in total. Many of them are hollow and could be easily knocked over. The whole purpose is not to.

The Crab mechas use a smaller Bradlium Particle Generator (BPG) for power and, like most mechas, have solar panels that are hidden under the armor and can be used in emergencies. I wait by my communications post for messages that don't come. The only thing that gives me motivation is that at night, anyone can pilot the Crab mecha for training purposes.

I take full advantage of that.

Spider agrees to be my "chaperone." "The weight takes some getting used to, and you can adjust sensitivity," Spider tells me. "Some people like it light and easy. I like it a little heavier."

I take the pilot's seat. It is fully adjustable and spins in all degrees. It even turns into an ejection pod if needed. I put on the goggles, try to fit the gloves and boots, which are tight but grow to my proportions once I'm in position. The goggles, using the visual data from the exterior of the mecha, make the walls of the bridge disappear. I am floating in the air. The interface is simplified compared to the bigger bipedal mechas. Motion can be controlled through a digitized wheel, tank controls, or directional pad, depending on preference. I select the directional pad, which shows arrow keys I command for motion.

"Take a few steps forward," Spider tells me. "Just put your hands out in front of you."

I do, causing the Crab to take steps. I increase speed and play with the acceleration. Depending on how I move my gloves, it will step in that direction. If I move both my arms left, then the crab will veer left. Sensors will automatically avoid collisions with any objects.

"Visuals can be deceiving, kid," Spider tells me. "All the pros rely on the GLS." The geographic location service. "No matter how good your eyes are, up in the bridge, you might measure size and distance wrong. That means death out there, or worse, civilian property damage. Nothing gets you kicked out faster than costing the RAMs extra money."

The GLS creates a 3D representation of the surrounding terrain and displays it interactively on a first-person grid. It's not perfect, and you still require a navigator to analyze best courses, but, because you can adjust the angles in real time, it's the most accurate way of judging the layout of the land. I have the option of overlaying the GLS on the actual view. Any discrepancies are relayed to the camera, and I can change focal length and aperture manually, though auto adjustments generally tend to work the best. The camera's metadata is automatically accounted for.

I crawl around the buildings several times. I get a feel for the independent elbow control between the leg and tip, as well as the ability to adjust the limb length, which causes an increase (or decrease) in speed. The neural interface has a one-to-one correspondence with the simulations. The biggest difference is that in sims, you don't feel resistance or the sudden twists and turns rocking your head. The internal stabilizer does a good job keeping it steady, and no matter how bumpy the ride, it tries to keep everything level. Even when I climb a hill at a forty-five-degree angle, the bridge rotates to stay straight. But that doesn't take away the g-force when I hit the acceleration and the massive Crab uses all six legs to sprint.

Two hours later, I'm still experimenting with different configurations when Spider says, "Let's call it a night, kid."

"I'm not tired."

"It's a marathon, not a sprint. Don't burn yourself out."

He's right. It's exhausting work to continually adjust controls as well as stay mentally focused. Even with all the training we've done, my legs and arms are fatigued. He leaves me on board. Against his advice, I practice until the sun rises.

IT'S A RACE. OUR FIVE CRABS STAND IN A LINE ON A FIELD. THE FINISH line is twelve kilometers ahead. "Losers run thirty kilometers," Sensei announces before we board. "Anyone who touches the mecha next to them is automatically disqualified."

"Who you betting on?" Wren asks Botan.

"Chieko," Botan replies. "Want to wager?"

Wren, Olympia, and I say, "Spider."

"This is on future wages," Botan reminds us.

"Don't make us lose money," Wren says to Spider.

"I put ten thousand yen on Chieko," Spider jokes in response.

"Oh c'mon!" Wren protests.

Sensei signals for the race to start. Spider moves his hands forward, accelerating our Crab. But Chieko has already taken the lead. Spider pushes the accelerator, shifting armor plates, adjusting individual lengths of the limbs, trying his best to catch up. But no matter what he does, Chieko just keeps on increasing her distance from the four other Crabs. Spider curses, pushes the accelerator even farther, doing quick hand motions. We decrease the gap for a bit.

"Our BPG is overheating," Botan warns him. "If we continue at this rate—"

Spider shuts the engine down. Ahead of us, Chieko has won.

"How was she so much faster than us?" Wren asks.

Spider appears baffled. "I have no idea." He turns to Botan. "Do you know?"

She shrugs with a facetious grin for victory. "No idea."

"How'd you know she'd win?"

"Intuition."

When we assemble on the ground, Sensei congratulates Chieko while the rest of us run thirty kilometers. I notice Spider holding his forearms, massaging them.

After the run, a bunch of us approach Chieko.

"How were you so much faster than the rest of us?"

"I manually controlled each of the legs," she replies. "And I used boosters."

"How'd you learn to do that?"

"In the sim."

"Can you teach us?"

"Of course," she replies.

Spider isn't in the group, so I go to look for him in case he's interested. He's back in our bunk and has wrapped his hands in ice packs.

"You okay?" I ask him.

He startles and initially tries to hide the ice packs. When he sees it's me, he says, "I'm good. My hands just ain't as good as they used to be." He opens his hands, flexes his fingers. "Our bodies can handle only so much, and then they just don't work anymore. I know you're eager to learn. You're young and excited, I get it. But there's a reason why you don't see many older mecha pilots. Take care of your health, kid, 'cause no one else will."

BACK ABOARD THE CRAB, EIGHT OF US STUFF OURSELVES INTO THE bridge. Chieko gives us a quick demonstration, turning off the manual inverse kinematics on the legs and controlling them directly. There's a lot more involved than the simple glove controls that we're used to, continually rotating, counter-rotating, and using boosters to increase distance and speed. It's much harder than any of us anticipated, though the speed edge makes sense since the manual structure is optimized in a way the automated one isn't.

What's surprising to me is that the controls remind me an awful lot of *Cat Odyssey*, which I point out to the group.

My comment elicits groans.

"Portical games are not like controlling mechas."

"I'm not saying it's identical, but they're similar," I state.

Chieko tells me, "You're right. I used to play *Cat Odyssey* all the time. Escape mode. That's how I figured this method out."

This surprises everyone.

"Rogue199 designed the controls for *Odyssey* and the mecha interfaces too, so it makes sense," I reply. It's not an exact match, but it's close enough. It makes sense too as the military and the gaming divisions are so closely connected. I realize portical games are a way of training a populace how to use weapons of war without their even being aware of it. "I didn't know you were into *Cat Odyssey*," I say.

"My ex-boyfriend and I played all the time. He sucked, though, which I have to admit, was a deal breaker."

"I'm learning how to play *Cat Odyssey* on my free time," Wren suddenly volunteers.

We all laugh.

I PRACTICE CHIEKO'S TECHNIQUE OVER THE NEXT TWO WEEKS. THE Crab's specialty is mobility, which is why they've gained favor over tanks. Tanks are limited in their ability to change direction. With the Crab, I can be going max speed in one direction, then do a one-eighty turn right away, just by changing the limb direction, which is easily done with the reversible joints.

"The one-eighty is tricky until you get the hang of it," Spider says on one of our evening training sessions. "The mistake most pilots make is that they slow down before they activate the reverse. You lose energy and time that way. Let me show you."

He pilots the mecha straight into a building and I swear we're going to crash. But just a second before we do, he swirls his arms around on the controls, and in a smooth motion, we're running the opposite way. The Crab legs, bending one direction, are now bending the other way. The bridge is still facing the same direction, but the visual interface in the goggles are pointing forward, so his actual position on the bridge is irrelevant. Eventually, the hull rotates to match but so casually for it not to be noticeable.

"How'd you do that?" I ask.

"It's all about anticipation and timing. You have to trigger the inverse kinematics at the right time. Try it slowly first."

I march the Crab forward and trigger the inverse. But rather than the fluid steps I'm hoping for, the Crab stalls and comes to a halt, the elbows locking in place. If not for the autostabilizers, I would have tumbled.

Spider laughs. "You'll get the hang of it. Things like this are important. I know the RAMs, and one of their most important functions is rescue ops. A good Crab pilot can get in and out before anyone even knows what hit them. My brother's a RAM out in the Russian Territories. He's always rescuing knuckleheads who get in trouble."

"Didn't know you had a brother."

"He's a knucklehead too. A damn good pilot. But he liked drinking too much, got into too many brawls. He joined the RAMs hoping he'd get another shot at entering one of the military academies."

Just like me. "How's he doing?"

"He's been at it seven years and still hasn't had his shot."

"Seven years?" I say, astounded and disappointed.

"He's wasting his time," Spider replies. "He believes if you have spirit, you can overcome all obstacles. But he doesn't get that sometimes, you can want something desperately and still fail."

"You want to get into one of the academies and become a pilot?"

"Hell no. I just want a decent-paying job that doesn't have me sitting at a desk all day. Plus, we get to travel all over the world. What about you, kid?"

"I want to get into BEMA."

He laughs, then sees my intent expression and apologizes. "You're serious?"

"Yes," I say, chagrined.

"You're a fast learner, but getting into BEMA is more than just skills."

"You said it needs politics."

Spider nods. "My brother is a good man. But he punched out a sergeant over beers. He's never going to get into the mecha corps."

He reminds me I've done worse. "I—I broke the arm of the lieutenant who was testing me for my exam."

"A lieutenant?" he asks. I explain what happened during my exam. "There you go," Spider says.

"You think I have no chance?"

Spider shakes his head. "Probably not. But you never know." His tone in that last part isn't convincing.

WE SPEND THE NEXT FEW WEEKS PRACTICING MOVEMENT. SENSEI teaches us how to use a leash program on our porticals to drive the Crab.

"This is useful in instances where the bridge may be inaccessible. The auxiliary portical can control the Crab, and if that's not damaged, the leash can be effectively used. The only problem is the interface is hard to use because it's a much smaller screen," she says.

Ironically, while others struggle, Chieko and I excel. The UI is a more complicated version of the one we played on *Cat Odyssey*. We even race via the porticals after hours, and though she beats me, I come in a few seconds behind her.

"Not bad," Chieko tells me.

When Sensei sees a few of us enjoying the controls, she warns us, "Don't treat this like a game. Right now you're relaxed, but under fire, everything changes."

Weapon tests are minimal, and we fire only blank shells from the Crab mechas. Even that's handled by munitions, and despite my hopes, we never get to try the heat gun. We do get personal pistol practice on the ranges, but it's nothing we haven't done in high school for the basic military training everyone gets their junior year.

Sensei shows us the self-destruct mechanism, which requires three layers of coding and approval from the entire crew. If they're not available, there are overrides, but they're to be used only in extreme situations.

"Technically, you can use the leash, set off the self-destruct, and control it from afar," Sensei says. "This is for extreme cases only, so you can use the Crab in a type of kamikaze run without having to sacrifice the people inside."

I get very little sleep, practicing on the Crab mecha every chance I get. The only other people I see out there at night are Chieko and Wren, who are both practicing as well. We often meet afterward and share notes. Wren has uncovered a trick where, "You can start on the wheels, build up acceleration, then jump, which'll give you a short burst."

"What good is that?" Chieko asks.

"What if you had to use the bathroom really badly and that minute makes all the difference?" Wren postulates.

"I do agree they need potty pots on board."

"You don't know how badly I had to pee yesterday," Wren confesses.

"Did not want to know that," I say.

"One of the guys farted during training, and we couldn't get the smell out of the Crab for an hour," Chieko says.

"I actually farted today, but no one noticed," Wren says.

"Thank you for sharing that," I tell him.

"Good night!" Chieko says.

Wren and I head for our barracks.

"It's finally graduation time," he says.

"What?"

"Did you forget what tomorrow is? Our training is done."

I can't believe it.

"We survived," he says, expressing my sentiment perfectly.

WE DO BASIC EXERCISES FOR THE FIRST HALF OF THE DAY. IN THE EVE-ning, we get called into the mess hall. Sensei is standing in front. There are barrels to either side of her. I wonder if we're going to have to haul those around all day for our parting exercise. Her arms are crossed behind her back.

"I've pushed all twenty-six of you hard. You may dislike me. Hell, you may hate me. But it's because I know what it takes to be a soldier and survive. I barely survived San Diego. I don't want any of you to suffer the way I did." I think back on Minako's story about Sensei's being kept alive as bait by the GWs. "The only way is preparation, and even that sometimes won't be enough. I've lost compatriots who were much worthier than I." There's a vulnerability in her voice that surprises all of us. "We have one training mission to go on, followed by a final mock battle between the Crab tanks. The weapons will be digitized, but you'll be aboard the Crabs for the fight. Think of it as a final exam before you officially graduate and complete your basic training. After that, you'll be deployed throughout the world. For my part, it was an honor to train all of you," she says, and bows to us.

It's a moving gesture, and everyone starts clapping.

She puts her hand up to belay us. "We'll have a chance for a bigger celebration following your official graduation ceremony. I've brought beers for everyone. Don't overdo it. Take tomorrow to rest. The day after, we'll head to Texarkana Fortress for the training mission. It's simple convoy duty. I don't anticipate any difficulties. For anyone traveling to the German Americas for the first time, do not be surprised by anything you see. Do not, and I repeat, do not apply your moral and ethical standards to them."

We've all heard the tales of how inhumanely the Nazis treat their people and the massive prison complexes they have—there's even one the size of a city—but I don't know much about what it's actually like living there. I try to imagine what Griselda's life must have been like in the Reich.

People start sharing beers. There's general cheer, singing, and joyous proclamations. There's actually real food. We've made it. I've made it. Wren gives me a warm hug, lifting me up. Everyone hugs one another. Botan gulps down beer like it was sugar water. Poet spouts bad haikus about the joy of endurance. Chieko arm wrestles anyone who challenges her and beats them handily. Spider reflects on the different beers he's enjoyed throughout the world. I wish Griselda were here so I could celebrate with her.

AFTER THE FESTIVITIES, I HEAD TO THE BARRACKS. I'M NOT TOO DRUNK, though I feel a light buzz after two cups of beer. It's breezy outside, and I try to identify some of the stars. I spot Chieko and Wren running off together, holding hands. All of us suspected they were interested in each other, but this is the first time I see it for certain. I'm happy for them.

The loose sketch of celestial bodies above resembles the constellation *Ohitsuji*, and another series of stars has to be *Ryouken*. I notice someone waiting for me. It's Sensei.

"You've been working hard," she says.

"I want to learn as much as I can."

"You've done a good job coming back from your injury."

As it's one of the first compliments I've heard from her, I'm delighted. "Thank you, Sensei. For everything."

"You have a solid future in the RAMs. This also came for you. I don't know the contents, but I'll be honest. I recommended you. I think you'd make a good officer. I don't know what their final decision was."

She hands me a portical with a sealed message. I enter my personal code, curious who it is. It's from BEMA.

I skip the opening salutations, speed past the notes about the request from Colonel Tachibana, and get to the point. "After a thorough reevaluation of your application, we have determined that we cannot offer you a place in the forthcoming class at BEMA."

I don't know if it's the alcohol or my shock, but I stumble. I have to lean against the wall to stabilize myself.

Sensei sees my expression, understands, and assures me, "You'll get other opportunities," putting her hand on my shoulder.

"Thank you," I weakly reply. My legs feel like they're going to give out under me.

"We'll talk more in the morning. Good night." She leaves, and I feel embarrassed she was present for my second rejection.

I sit on the ground and pick up dirt with my hands, letting it slide through my fingers. How stupid of me to think they would change their decision. It was naive to even entertain the idea that I could get into BEMA after how badly I did on the test. Spider was right. I don't have the right connections. I feel like that dirt, recycled and tossed back out.

MOST OF US SPEND THE NEXT DAY RESTING. BOTAN HAS EXPLOITED everyone's enthusiasm for the forthcoming graduation to wrangle together some Hanafuda card games. I spend most of the day feeling despondent. Our Crabs are being transported to the trains for our mission, so I can't lose myself in one of them. Even running does little to wipe away my feeling of dejection. I went through all of this training in the hopes of improving my chances for BEMA. Now that the door is shut again, I wonder what it was all for.

Another part of me goes into a state of denial. Maybe it was a mistake. Maybe they got me mixed up with someone else, and I was supposed to get accepted, but they sent the wrong message. I ask permission to check the portical again and read the letter from beginning to end ten times. No mistake.

I'm furious and want to meet the panel who made the decision, inquire of them directly even though I know it's pointless. I failed the test and got average grades. What else could I have expected? A few hours later, I'm running myself into mental knots that leave me weary. Meanwhile, Botan has won the first week's pay of everyone who played.

Everyone's too loud, and I feel aggravated by their complaints. Suddenly, Chieko punches me in the shoulder.

"What's that for?" I yell at her.

"I hate this moping. What the hell's wrong with you?" she demands.

"We should be celebrating, man!" Wren says.

"Don't tell me you lost all your money to her," Chieko says to me, pointing at Botan.

I don't know if I should tell them the truth and am about to. Spider's arrival seals my silence as I couldn't stand it if he knew he was right when he told me earlier that I had no chance. "Sorry, still a little hungover from last night," I lie.

"You barely drank!" Chieko yells, and laughs.

Spider says, "Best cure for a hangover is food. You get enough to eat?"

"I'm fine," I state. "Just need some sleep."

But when I get to my mat, all I can think about is the rejection.

06

★ ★ ★

EARLY NEXT MORNING, WE'RE GIVEN OUR RAMDET UNIFORMS. THEY AL-
ready have our measurements, so it's only a matter of making sure
the individual pieces aren't too tight or loose. They're similar to
army uniforms but are colored black, and our insignias clearly
mark us as nonmilitary. I put on the long-sleeve shirt, pants, and a
vest to provide nominal protection in case of turbulence on the
mecha. We're also given a RAMDET-issued portical to be used for
official business only, but I already see the others checking personal messages and reading news sites.

The Ida Train Station is heavily guarded. There is a mural of the
Emperor on the massive portical display in the main hall. The
domed ceiling is glass that also serves as a portical display and will
occasionally change to station updates. I see four Sentry mechas
through the glass towering above. Banners of the rising sun are
draped above many of the hub's gateways. Terminal 8 is a ribbed
hallway colored ivory, and there are thousands of people rushing
to the connecting subways. The speed trains on the border go

everywhere, from the technological wonders of Bogota to the underwater structures of Takeshi Ciudad.

We hop on board our train. We're in the fifth passenger car from the front. Half of us split off so that minimal crews remain in the four Crab tanks for emergencies. They're on their wheels and tied by hawsers to both sides of the train to provide convoy support. If anything does happen, it's easy for us to access the Crabs. A fifth Crab tank is positioned on the final flat car and acts as aft guard. The locomotive has cannons in its front in case of trouble. More than three-quarters of the train cars are cargo freights carrying shipment from the USJ. They were loaded earlier in the day, and I don't know what their contents are.

Inside our room, there's a portical display set to a military channel. The famed Colonel Yamaoka is actually visiting Dallas and giving an inspiring speech while conducting an inspection of the border.

"While we're disturbed by reports that the Nazis are stirring up trouble with the NARA, be assured that we're on top of every operation they're planning."

Before we can leave, we have to have our fingerprints scanned. Sensei gives the inspectors our identification. After confirming everything is in order, the train speeds out. Dallas Tokai is a blur, and within seven minutes, we've left the city borders.

Sensei informs us, "If all goes according to plan, we'll reach Texarkana Fortress without any problems. Our duty is minimal today, and we'll stay there overnight. Once we enter the Fortress, keep conversations to a minimum and assume everything you say will be recorded. Our official mission begins tomorrow. Our client, Sanshouo Enterprises, has asked us to escort their new shipment back to Tulsa first, then to the Bokujin Air Base at Wichita Falls. The first part of the trip to Tulsa leads us through a long stretch of the Quiet Border, which is why we've been asked to escort the train. All Crab tanks will be fully manned throughout the duration of the mission, and I'm sending you optional briefings if you want to know more about the region."

"What's the cargo?" Chieko asks.

"That is confidential information."

"Do *you* know what it is?"

"No."

According to the briefing, the terrain and climate in the Quiet Border have changed drastically in the last decade. We've engaged the Germans in battle multiple times in the zone. Each time, the destructive forces used have reshaped the geography. I look out the window. It's more like a desert now, with the long expanses of sand. The dust storms are blindingly strong. There are said to be the ruins of cities underneath. Ash fertilizes the seeds for more decimation.

"Do you believe in ghosts?" Poet asks us.

"Of course not," I laugh even though I get terrified just thinking about them.

"I've seen ghosts along the Quiet Border," he says.

"I eat ghosts for dinner," Chieko states, and everyone laughs.

"Where in the Quiet Border?" someone asks Poet.

"I've ridden the border trains twenty times and seen shadowy figures outside on half of those trips," Poet replies. "I'd blink, and they'd be gone."

I try to nap in my seat and block out anything Poet is saying. I'm susceptible to ghost stories and don't want to hear anything that'll scare me. Still, when he talks about the ghost train full of dead Nazi and USJ soldiers, killing everyone they see, it freaks me out. Outwardly, I act indifferent to it, but everyone is absorbed in the stories and urban legends they've inspired.

Truth is, I can sense they're as curious and wary of seeing the German side as I am. We've heard so many horror stories about the death camps and mountains of corpses that are still standing as warning against dissidence.

It isn't very far to the fortress, a little less than three hundred kilometers, but we're going slower because of our heavy load.

Spider and Botan talk with Sensei the whole way there. I overhear them converse about different teas from around the world.

I stare at the border, wondering how many dead are buried out here.

THE HOURS PASS SLOWLY. JUST WHEN I'M ABOUT TO ASK SENSEI HOW much longer it'll be, a voice over the speaker politely informs us, "We are entering the German Americas."

Texarkana Fortress has a wall extending as far as I can see. There's barbed wire nestled on top and mounted guns on guard posts. There are cages everywhere, connected like the skeleton of an enormous snake whose skin has rotted off. They're composed of rounded bars rising from the rusted-metal floors. They're filled with people, captives of all ethnicities and gender. They don't look at us. Most of them are bony, emaciated, covered in scars and sheaths of dirt. I spot a scuffle, captives fighting over breathing space. There must be thousands of prisoners trapped inside, the scorching sun causing their skin to peel and dehydrate like dried fruits. The stench of suffering is limited on the train but still jarring, with its essence of decay and inhumanity. Most of us look away, realizing not much separates us from them.

I ask Sensei, "What is this?"

"That's Goering's audience. Traitors, enemies, and anyone who displeases him gets sent here."

"For how long?"

"Till they die."

"What do they eat?"

"Each other."

Gauleiter Goering is one of the most popular officers in the Germanic Americas. He is the ideal Aryan, tall, blond, and photogenic. He also has an angelic voice that has made him a celebrity, even in the United States of Japan.

When he starts his nightly singing, it is broadcast over the entirety of the fortress and even in our train. His German sounds divine, and I could swear it's a religious hymn. Only, it's a love song to Hitler, and though I don't understand the words exactly, the primary lyrics are those of worship.

"He sings like this every night?" I ask.

"Every night I've visited," Sensei replies.

The voice is hypnotic, aside from the occasional "Fuehrer" that's thrown in. I want to ask Griselda what she thinks about the Gauleiter.

We pass a deep moat. Wren points at it, and tells us, "Alligators down there. Haven't seen them personally, but I've heard they're mutated to be three times their normal size. Shipped in from Florida."

"Alligator meat tastes pretty good if you fry it," Chieko says. "Key is how you season it before you dip it in the flour."

"You know what tastes good?" Wren asks. "Alligator and kimchee. I swear, it's the best combo ever."

"You think adding kimchee makes everything taste better," Chieko points out.

"It does, doesn't it?"

Rising above the city is the most enormous statue of Hitler I've seen. It almost blots out the sky and casts a shadow down on the tracks. The Fuehrer is not wearing his hat but is gazing toward the USJ. He has a pensive, almost meditational look, his eyes as fiery as the old footage we've seen of him. It's as though he sees beyond, wondering in disappointment what is keeping the Nazis from global dominance. How about mechas that are equally big, ready to bust Hitler's statue up into a billion pieces?

The depot is full of Reich flags and statues of naked men holding swords. They're carved by sculptors from the school of Josef Thorak, which was purportedly Hitler's favorite. Soldiers are clad in black uniforms with their swastika armbands that look like blood tattoos carved into charred flesh. The business workers get off first. The quad mechas are deployed from the rear trains. Spider leads our crew aboard the Crab to help transport their cargo off the train into a convoy truck. Several Nazi officials receive us. Sensei chats fluently with the merchants in German.

I coordinate with the other Crabs, but there's not much I need to communicate. This part of our mission is over pretty quickly. It's actually disappointing how little we have to perform.

We park our Crabs in specially designated spots adjacent to the tracks and exit.

The security wall reminds me of an ancient castle with the cobbled roads and stone fortifications. I'm so used to the bright neon of the USJ, it's a grim contrast. The adjacent square has a massive guillotine, which is surprising considering how antiquated it is as a method of execution. Almost everyone we see is a Caucasian soldier. I'm one of the few Asian people present, and the absence of other ethnicities is jarring. No matter where we go, the Hitler statue is visible.

We're stationed at a hotel next to the wall. Dinner is a somber set of bratwursts and sauerkraut. We don't cheer, don't talk, don't comment on our surroundings, as Sensei advised. Even without her warning, I don't think any of us are in the mood for it. I can't stop thinking about the people in those cages.

Wren and I share a room. He falls asleep as soon as he hits his bed and snores loud enough to wake the dead. I think his snore is a good charm against scrupulous ghosts as well.

I toss and turn. It takes me a while to drown him out, but I eventually fall asleep. It's only a few hours later when there's a loud banging on my door—our wake-up call. I feel like I need five more hours of sleep.

Spider and a few others are already at the train station, equipping our Crabs with the proper air filters when we arrive. A hundred or so people board the train. I don't know if they're civilians, military, or contractors like us. Our Crabs are still adjacent to the train.

"If anyone needs to use the bathroom, do it now," Sensei orders.

I go use the restroom. The first Asian I see on this side of the border is a janitor who is sweeping quietly and avoids my eyes. I wash my hands and exit. Just as I'm about to hop back on board the train, I see Sensei in a heated discussion with a Nazi officer.

"Makoto?"

I'm surprised that someone calls me by my name and turn. Behind me is a tall German with long blond hair and blue eyes. Oddly enough, I recognize him, but I'm not sure from where.

"You are Mac, aren't you?" he asks me.

"Yes. Do I know you?"

"I'm Dietrich. You ran with us one morning last year," he states. "Griselda is my cousin."

"Oh," I say, and laugh, embarrassed about the memory. That's when I notice the mark of a crimson panther, meaning he's military.

I wonder which branch.

"Have you seen Griselda recently? She transferred to Dallas a few months ago."

I don't know whether I should tell the truth or not. "We bumped into each other," I say.

"How was she?"

"Good, I think."

He stares at me pensively. "Perhaps I can show you around the fortress. You can return to Dallas tomorrow."

"I'm sorry, but I have a mission today."

"Lot of nasty NARA activity out there. Maybe you should skip this mission?"

Does he doubt my ability because I ran so poorly last year? "I appreciate your concern, but I've dealt with them before. I'll be fine," I reply to him, snappier than I intended.

He shifts his feet uncomfortably. "Be careful," he tells me.

I climb up to the top of the Crab but feel uneasy. Was he trying to tell me something? But this is just a convoy mission, and we're heading *away* from Texarkana.

Spider is adjusting his seat, running diagnostics across the Crab to make sure everything is in order. "You all ready for this?" he asks.

"No," Wren replies, echoing our fatigue.

"I know why you're not ready," Spider says in an insinuating tone we all know refers to Chieko.

He smiles abashedly. "I didn't see her last night. You can ask Cream."

"Switch to tread mode," Sensei orders us. "Once we enter the Border, no more audio communications unless it's an emergency. Everything will be encrypted through text that your communication officers will relay. We'll remain tied by hawsers to the train. It's 422 kilometers, and more than two-thirds will be through the Quiet Border. There hasn't been any reported activity along this way for the past year, so we're not expecting difficulties. But if there are, you've been trained to deal with it. Remember, our primary objective is to defend the train, not engage enemies. Over."

Spider deploys the treads on the knees of the Crab, bending them so we're close to the ground. The hawsers are still connecting us to the train, but we can detach at any time. Autopilot is engaged, and there's nothing we need to actively do throughout the duration of the trip, assuming all goes without a hitch. I look over at Botan's GLS, which charts the path from the fortress to Tulsa. There is no enemy presence detected. Spider leans back in his pilot's seat, and says, "Y'all gonna learn real soon that stealing minutes of sleep is vital to a prolonged career." He closes his eyes and dozes off.

Wren and Botan follow suit. I'm surprised Wren's snoring isn't heavy. Maybe it's the engine sound that blocks out the noise.

Olympia says, "I don't know how they can sleep."

"Me neither," I reply. "You ever been to Tulsa?"

"I'm from Tulsa. My parents used to work at a sawmill and helped design the machinery."

"They still live there?"

"The Nazis killed my dad during a sneak attack," she replies. "We used to have a border collie–lab mix, Beniko. She was such a smart dog, but she was barking all morning that day, and we couldn't get her to stop. I had no idea why until the Nazis came . . ."

"I'm sorry."

"So am I," she replies. "I was glad when we moved to Portland. My mom took a job testing for cosmetic companies. I remember she'd come home with different makeup on her face every day. She eventually remarried. I didn't get along with my stepdad, so he had me sent to military school."

"How was military school?"

"I hated every minute of it, but I didn't want to go back home, either. So I enlisted as soon as I graduated." She is lost in unspoken pain. "Nazis did this to us," she snaps. "I'll be glad for a chance at payback."

"I hope you get it, but not on this trip."

"The Nazis have been provoking our side for months. The only way to send them a message is through force." I can feel the hatred brimming up in her. I'd feel the same way in her shoes.

"What do you think would happen if we went to war?"

"We'd wipe them out, of course," she confidently declares, brooking no doubt.

I think we all share her confidence. The Germans have never been able to defeat our mechas without huge losses.

The minutes seep into each other the same way our speed makes the landscape of dry hills, occasional foliage, and cactus look like a painted blur in the desert. Nature is a whimsical sculptor, molding veins and wrinkles into the dry ground. I wonder how radioactive it is out there after all the fighting and use of nuclear arms. Fortunately, we have an atomic moratorium with the Germans, but the impact still hasn't fully faded. I had a teacher who served on the border and became sick from radiation poisoning he'd gotten more than ten years before. They were able to regenerate his organs, but if his tumors had advanced just a little more, our doctors wouldn't have been able to help him.

An hour passes, then two. My mind skips through a hundred flash memories even though I don't remember a single one when I try to consciously recall them.

Spider awakes and stretches his arm.

"Get a good nap?" Wren asks.

"Lovely dreams until I saw you," Spider says.

"That's what I was going to say," Wren retorts.

"You can't steal your senior's words. Anything happen while I was out?"

"All quiet on the Quiet Border," Botan, who woke up a few minutes before, replies after checking the scans.

We begin to see more rock formations and hints of a mountain.

They turn into a valley that looks like a colossal trench, a parted Red Sea of stone. Tracks wind right through the middle.

Spider explains, "This here is the Nazis attempt to dig a trench and protect themselves from us. They used seismic constructs to build it but never got to finish it."

"Why not?"

"Because we found out what they were doing and beat the hell out of them."

The formations remind me of the Grand Canyon as the path gets narrower. But there's something about it that feels unnatural. Is it my foreknowledge that the Germans were trying to reshape the planet, the way they tried building underwater cities that killed much of the sea life in the Mediterranean? Or is it that somehow, my brain senses the conscious patterning of humans versus millennia of randomized geographic evolution?

"Something isn't right here," Botan says.

"Do you have anything more concrete than that?" Spider asks.

"I'm getting strange heat blips on the scans that regularly vanish."

"Cream. Message the others and see if they're getting anything," Spider orders.

I relay the anomalous markings. Chieko is the first to reply, and she confirms them. Sensei's Crab does too.

"If there's an ambush here, we'll be sitting Crabs," Spider says. "Ask Sensei what she advises."

I message her the question. Sensei replies, "It could be radiation distortion affecting the sensors. Keep alert for now. I'll communicate with RAMDET for further orders."

Purely out of curiosity, I check her external output and am surprised I can read her messages. I shouldn't with its encryption, but I see what she's asking her bosses without much difficulty.

"We're detecting unusual activity. Recommend abort mission," she writes.

The response takes four minutes.

"Abort request denied. Cargo is precious to USJ. Essential that it be delivered on schedule."

"We're a training unit," Sensei protests. "They're not ready if there is a combat situation."

"At worst, they're American terrorists. Your RAMs can handle it."

"If there's an ambush, it will be difficult to repel considering our position," Sensei protests.

"The Crabs should be able to resist anything they fire at you."

"If this were an experienced crew, there'd be no concerns," Sensei writes back. "But they haven't formally graduated yet."

Two minutes later, the response returns, "Mission cannot be changed. Cargo too important. Discussion over."

I'm surprised RAMDET has revealed that we have valuable goods on board, especially with their weak encryption.

Sensei writes to us: "We proceed as planned. If any resistance encountered, you've been trained to handle it." No sign of weakness or doubt in her words.

But just as her message finishes, Botan's navigation panel triggers an alarm.

"There are four vehicles coming our way," Botan says.

I relay the message to Sensei, who confirms the visual.

"Disengage the hawsers and prepare for combat," she orders three of us, staying behind as well. The fifth Crab tank continues to escort the train, which goes on without us.

Spider disengages the hawsers, but as he does, I notice his reactions are stiff. He actually has to stop to massage his right arm as the controls get more intricate. Our split is bumpy as we skitter off our connection, and Spider doesn't use his right hand to complete the process.

If I didn't know better, I'd say he's in pain. The more he's pressing buttons, the more he's agitated. His right forearm looks like it's locking up. He notices me watching him. "It shouldn't be doing this. They gave me cortisone shots to relieve it."

"What's wrong?" Botan asks Spider.

"My right hand isn't in good shape."

"We're about to get into a fight, and your 'hand isn't in good shape?'"

"Relax. I can handle this."

Botan shakes her head. "Cream, can you pilot this thing?"

"Sit down," Spider orders her. "I got this."

Botan is unhappy, but when Spider moves us toward the enemy targets, she sits back at her console. The train speeds away. I see a familiar sight approaching us from both sides. They're four Javelins, the preferred vehicle of the NARA. Their cannons are aimed our way.

Sensei sends us text communications. "I'm assigning one target each. Your job is to dispose of the Javelin. These are pieces of junk compared to our Crabs. Their weapons will not harm you."

We're assigned the third one. Olympia gets the weapons lock.

"Use incendiaries," Spider says.

"I got it," Olympia replies. She looks over at Wren, who's securing his lock.

"Done," he confirms.

"Fire."

Olympia and Wren fire an incendiary shell from the side guns. Both shots hit the Javelin. But the Javelin appears unaffected, and it unleashes a devastating blast from its frontal cannon in response that knocks us several meters back. We're all rattled by the strength of the attack. The Javelin begins to charge us. We're not moving, though, as it gets closer.

"What are you waiting for?" Botan asks Spider.

"There's something wrong with the automated kinematics."

Olympia brings up the diagnostics. "They were busted in that attack. You'll have to go to manual mode. The—"

The Javelin fires again, this time at a closer distance. The Crab shakes violently, throwing us back even farther. Armor hasn't been breached, but our internal lights dim, and the shell has taken a bad blow.

Spider unstraps himself, and says, "Cream. Take the controls."

"You sure?"

"Get over here."

He jumps out of the way. I get into the seat. It's a bit large, but it automatically begins to mold itself to match my body before hardening. I put on the belt, gloves, and goggles. They adjust size for my proportions, but the gloves are wet, and I realize Spider was sweating. I clutch the manual controls to acclimate myself, then turn to the visual interface and use my gloves to control the tank with tactile motion.

The Javelin is taller than us but, I also remember, vulnerable to attacks that will upset its balance. Olympia and Wren are firing, but our artillery isn't making a big impact on it. I try to recollect how Chieko did her spring. Repeat motions for all six legs and when activating the far rear legs, use the boosters to add even more speed.

"What are you doing?" Spider asks, echoing everyone else's thoughts.

"Ramming it," I say, and feel clever for incorporating our "RAM" title. "Make sure you're all buckled in."

I watch the Javelin, wait for that moment Noriko did in our fight in Granada Hills before sprinting into the bipedal vehicle just as it got ready to fire. The Javelin fires again. This time, I use the controls to quickly get out of the way. I get the fourth leg to move before the second is finished and nearly cause us to tumble. Fortunately, I'm able to use the frontal legs to balance us. More important, we dodge the attack. The Javelin rotates its turret to our new position. I sprint toward it as fast as I can. It fires, and just as it does, I "ram" into it.

The Javelin moves its leg to compensate, bracing itself for impact. Our hit should have knocked it to the ground like last time. But that doesn't happen. We're both still standing. It looked much easier when Noriko was doing it. I overestimated the strength of the Crab and underestimated the sensitivity of the Javelin. I've also put us in major harm's way. It's sobering to realize that if I screw up here, my whole crew dies.

"Above us!" Botan yells.

The Javelin has its cannon aimed at us. Olympia and Wren both shoot artillery straight at it. It doesn't have much impact on its armor, but it causes the turret to rotate askew. The shell hits the ground rather than us. I use the front claws to separate us, moving away from it. About thirty meters from us, the other Crab, piloted by Chieko, is still fighting the Javelin.

"Check the kikkai for any connections coming out from the Javelins," I order.

"Why?"

"Just do it." I'm hoping that maybe one is a slave to the other and by destroying one, we can dismantle the pair.

Botan complies. "I'm not getting anything."

"Are you sure?"

"Yes, I'm sure," she snaps, annoyed that I'm questioning her. But how can that be?

Every Javelin must be different, so we can't disrupt the connection. We just have to use what's available to us.

"Spider. Can you ask Sensei how to use the heat gun?"

"I know how to use it," Wren says. "At least I practiced using it in the sim with Chieko. It's powerful, but it'll drain the energy from the tank for six seconds, and we won't be able to move. It also takes us about thirty seconds to recharge after each attack."

"So if we miss—"

"We'll be vulnerable."

If I sprint toward the Javelin again, lock ourselves in, and fire, it should do the trick. "Charge it up," I state.

"Engaging."

Immediately, there is a loud buzz, and the entire cockpit warms with activity.

"Twenty-eight seconds," Wren informs us.

Botan says, "My scans say there's a patch in the hull that's eighteen percent thinner than the rest. I'd suggest Olympia fire first, soften it up, and Wren, you shoot the heat gun after that."

"On it," Olympia says, while Wren jumps in with, *"Yōkai!"*

The next twenty-five seconds might determine whether we live or die. Hard not to think about as I articulate each leg individually, the joints rotated and counter-rotated to make sure the Crab sprints without falling. The motion is rapid, and I'm using all my fingers to mimic the leg motions I require on the interface. The Javelin moves away from us, knowing if it's too close, its cannon is worthless. Seventeen seconds. I do a quick scan of the other side, see that Sensei is still fighting off her Javelin. Chieko's Crab is running circles around her target. Our Javelin fires at us. I rapidly sprint out of the way. This Crab is fast! Ten seconds before the heat cannon is ready, I begin my charge toward the Javelin. It tries to elude us, but we're way too quick as I ram into the Javelin and wrap my front legs around its limbs.

"Olympia, shoot everything we got," I state. "Wren, it's all you after that."

Olympia unloads a volley of gunfire that dents the armor and pierces it. Just as she finishes, Wren fires the heat gun.

There's no recoil, rather a sudden searing sensation all around us. After the gun emits its rays, the whole cockpit cools down and silence overtakes the previous cacophony. I try to look out through the goggles, but power is off. Six seconds to see if we succeeded. I flex my fingers, curl them, waiting. Four, three, two, one. The energy from the BPG surges back through the Crab tank. Visuals flood into the goggles. There is a hole through the Javelin's hull, an empty space with heated edges that are still red. I use magnification to look through the opening. There's nothing inside. I'm not sure if the heat gun incinerated the pilot, or there wasn't one to begin with. I push us away from the Javelin The Javelin falls over without anyone to keep it balanced on its feet.

"It worked?" Wren asks.

"It worked!" Botan and Olympia both yell.

We actually beat it!

"Nice piloting!" he shouts.

"Nice shot!" I shout back.

Spider is grinning from his seat. "C'mon, kids," he says. "The battle ain't over yet."

"How's Chieko doing?" Wren asks.

Botan runs to her console. "She's fine."

Outside, Chieko's Crab moves nimbly. She doesn't deploy the heat gun. Rather, she snipes at the Javelin. The Javelin responds with a blast, but the Crab is too quick, gets around to the other side, and fires at the Javelin's leg joints, which are badly damaged. A few more blasts, and its knee buckles, causing it to crumble in place. It's a far more elegant strategy than the one I used, and I admire the way she uses the Crab's capabilities in the optimal manner, contrasting with my brute-force attack risking it all.

Across from us, the remaining two Javelins have also been destroyed. We all get up and into a big group hug. It's our first battle, and it's a victory.

"Great job," Spider tells me.

"Thanks," I reply. "You helped me to train all those off-hours."

"It's all you."

I start to take off the gloves and goggles to hand back to him.

He refuses. "You're the pilot," he says.

"It's your seat."

"You earned this. Besides, I'm hurt. Anything else comes up, we'd have to switch places again."

"But—" I'm about to object.

"I'm not debating this."

I bow. "Thank you."

"Don't thank me. Just get our asses back in one piece."

I take my seat again, but I feel jumpy. It must be the adrenaline. I loved the intensity of that moment, almost long for it again. I wish there were more Javelins to fight, which doesn't make sense. Those things could have killed us. But I feel supremely confident in our ability to take them down. This isn't like a game, where the consequences are digitized. I'm puzzled by my reaction as it's similar to the one I had during my first encounter and wonder if it's abnormal to crave danger.

We have an incoming message. Spider reads it quickly.

"The train is reporting an obstruction blocking their path eighteen kilometers ahead of us. We're to help clear the path and deal with any interference."

I've never been so ecstatic to hear bad news.

07

★ ★ ★

I ACCELERATE AS FAST AS I CAN.

Olympia asks, "Any of you know about the NARA?"

"All them terrorists are the same, savages who want to destroy the Empire," Wren states.

"I've heard the separate factions hate each other as much as they hate us," I say, remembering what Griselda told me.

"Aren't they all on the same side?" Wren asks.

Olympia shakes her head. "The NARA have a quack two-bit charlatan as a prophet who claims all other sects are false. He used to sell porticals in Anaheim until he had a vision that told him our world is false and there's another reality where the Americans won the war."

"That sounds ridiculous."

"Tell that to his followers. He has them believing that in this other world, the Americans live in prosperity and complete equality. After winning the Pacific War, they decided to reform and institute changes that brought about the wealthiest and happiest period in humanity's history."

"Sounds nice," Spider says.

"Americans locked my grandparents in a prison camp during the war because they were Mongolians and all Asians were suspected of espionage for the Empire," Olympia says. "Equality wasn't on their agenda."

"Victory has a way of blunting swords," Spider offers.

"Or sharpening them," Olympia retorts.

"Even if it were true that's there another reality, what are they after here?" Wren wants to know.

"They hope to plunge the Empire into war against the Nazis, so we devastate each other. Then they'll take over."

"How do you know so much?" Wren asks.

"One of my jobs when I enlisted was studying these fanatics," Olympia explains.

"This is really strange," Botan interjects. "I don't think the Javelins had human pilots."

"Why not?" I ask.

"There would be remains to indicate identity. Traces of blood, organs, and teeth. But the scans don't register anything."

"Maybe they melted from the heat gun," Wren says.

"Even then, there should be some trace. I think those Javelins were controlled by a portical AI inside of it."

"So what if they were?"

"Cream," Spider interrupts us. "Sensei says there are rocks blocking the rail." He reads the new message. "We need to help her move them. She—wait. The message stopped midline . . . I'm trying to send her a message back, but it won't send."

"Maybe she took damage and can't relay messages?"

"Could be."

But something feels wrong. I think Botan senses it too as she approaches the communications console. "All our encrypted messages are being jammed," she states.

"By who?" I ask.

"I don't know." She heads back to the navigational sensors. "Everything's clear here. Maybe we should break silence and switch to audio communicators," Botan suggests.

Ahead, I see the pile of rocks blocking the tracks. The train is fully braked. Sensei takes her Crab forward to investigate.

We start moving toward them when her quad mecha explodes. Before I can turn to the sensors, something hits us, and we're flipping through the air. I can feel the heat on my arms, smell the melted armor plates. The motion is rapid, and I clutch my seat. I look over, see Olympia and Spider falling out of their seats as we flip upside down. When the Crab mecha hits the ground, both smash their heads on the ceiling, which is now the floor. A quarter of the Crab mecha is gone, Botan with them. Olympia and Spider look like they've broken their necks. Neither are breathing. I'm hanging from my seat's buckle, which is now on top. Wren's leg is crushed under a plank, and he has passed out.

"Are you there? What is your condition? Over. Mac. Spider. Wren! Are you there?"

It's Chieko, shouting over the audio communicator, forgoing the encryption.

The world seems to be spinning. My ears are ringing, and I want to loosen my belt. But then, the high-school examination comes to mind. I was under simulated attack near Dallas back then too. What was my first prerogative?

"Chieko," I respond to her over the communicator.

We still haven't traveled far. Is it closer to Texarkana Fortress, or Dallas at this point? Is it even safe to go back to the fortress?

"Mac!" she calls back. "What happened?"

"You need to head back to Dallas ASAP, inform them of the situation, and get backup."

"Is—is Wren okay?" she asks.

I look down at him but can't tell whether he's breathing. "His leg got crushed, and he passed out, but he's alive," I tell her, wanting to believe my words even though I'm not sure they're true.

"Promise me you'll keep him alive."

"I don't know if I can do that."

"Promise me you'll find a way," she insists.

"I—I promise."

"I'll bring help. Survive until then," she orders me.

I unbuckle myself, grip the seat bars, and let myself down. I check Olympia and Spider, to see whether they have a pulse. Spider's neck is skewed at an irregular angle. Olympia is facedown in a pool of blood. I have a hard time breathing when I realize they're dead. Just like that. I can't believe it.

Is there anything we could have done differently? There was no warning, no indication of a projectile.

I feel numb, look toward Wren. Everything below his waist is crushed. The plank is way too heavy for me to lift. But he's somehow breathing.

"Wren!" I call. "Wren!" But he doesn't answer.

It's okay. At least he's still alive.

To the right, where Botan's navigation console had been, is a big, gaping hole. I can see that two of the Crab's legs have been incinerated.

I don't want to stay inside with the corpses of Olympia and Spider. I shut both their eyes and stumble out.

Then wish I hadn't.

There is something like a shadowy goliath blotting out the sun. It's taller than most mechas I've seen and at least twice the size of the biomechs in my simulation test. The metal plates seem alive, black undulations forming its armor. Strips of the living skin assemble together, forming layers that pile one on top of another. It's already a behemoth, but as the monstrous armor connects, its organic shape becomes even more enormous. It appears to have a purple dorsal fin slithering down its back. I'm certain this is a Nazi biomech, a monster made out of tumors and decades of genetic manipulation. But how? Does this mean the NARA is working with the Nazis? The plates on the biomech are ebony but gleam on their bloody underside, as though fueled by hate. I never knew they were so big. It's making a strange sound, like a mix of violent bees and an animal splashing desperately in the water so it won't drown. The body is pulsating with fluids, and every part is beating. I'm afraid to look in its direction. I try to think about what options I have available, but I'm certain anything I do will lead to my death. My legs are shaking. It's not just the hot weather causing me to sweat.

They've attacked twice. First time must have been an attempt to assess our strength. This is the real attack. I visually check the train. It hasn't been damaged. It'd be safe to assume they're after the cargo. But what's so valuable about it?

That's irrelevant. I don't care if they get it. How do I make my legs move? Maybe I can sprint to the train and hide underneath? But the most likely result is that I'll be shot as soon as I emerge. The ground shakes as the biomech takes a step; then comes a deafening shriek as something fires from an orifice that opens and seals right back up. I hear another explosion on the far side of the train. My ears sting like someone's put a drill inside them. *Please don't be Chieko.*

I force myself back into the Crab. See the two dead bodies again. I wish it were a nightmare and I could wake myself up. But this is all too real. The tremors begin again as the biomech moves. The Crab is insulated against thermal scans, but half of it is open now, so they could potentially spot me down here. The piloting controls appear to be functional. I try not to look at Spider again. It was just a few days before when he was helping me practice. I'm shocked to realize I don't know either of their real names.

Don't think about that now! What are my options?

It chills me to realize I will die no matter what I do. The only way for me now is to cause as much damage as I can before I get killed. It's for my friends who've died.

I'll have to drive it upside down. But I need to restore auxiliary power before I can set off the self-destruct. And the only way I'm going to be able to move this thing without getting flung all over the place is to strap myself into the seats, which are now above me. I flick on the BPG manually with the emergency switch. Just as I'm about to get into my seat, several NARA jump into the Crab.

"Get down from there!" they order, guns pointed at me. "Put your hands up!"

I comply.

"What should we do about this one?" the NARA member asks about Wren.

"Shoot him."

"No! No!" I yell. "Please, he—"

I feel something club me in the cheek. I drop, hear a gun blast. Wren's dead. I will be too. I don't feel anger. Only pity that our lives were wasted for a reason we'll never know.

MY THIRST WAKES ME. MY THROAT IS DRY, AND I TRY TO SWALLOW WHAT little spit I have in my mouth. I'm sitting on the ground, arms restrained. The sun must be setting as the canyon walls are stained in a lurid orange.

"You're finally up."

It's Botan next to me, arms tied up.

"Where are we?" I ask her.

"The NARA have taken us captive."

"How—how are you alive?"

She turns her head, and I see that the side of her face away from me is badly burned. "We were moving along. I felt the Crab shake. Then I was outside, hot metal on my face."

"Shut up!" one of the NARA yells.

There are about twenty of us in a row, and ahead of us, I see about a dozen of what I presume are NARA members holding guns. They're dressed in clothes that would make them indistinguishable from a USJ citizen if we were in another place. I don't see Nazi officials among them, but the biomech looms above us.

The NARA have gathered the survivors in front of the train, and I see several bodies in a pile, stripped of clothes. A squat man with a puffy tower of hair and black grease painted under his eyes addresses us. He scratches his teeth with his thumbnail and has huge rectangular glasses that are shaded pink.

"You think you're all Japanese? You're wrong. You're Americans, like me. You want proof? Your train was blaring messages about how critical the cargo on board was. No encryption. Too sloppy to be credible. But I was curious what you were stowing." He lifts his hand up. A woman brings him a box. He grabs what's inside and pulls it out. "Goose feathers. Very chic for comfy pillows. That's your cargo. You all were bait. What for? It doesn't matter. That up there"—signaling toward the biomech—"will crush anything your military can send."

Is he right? Were we just bait? But for what? Sensei asked multiple times to retreat, but her superiors insisted we stick with the mission. Did they know?

"You might be wondering why I'm here. It's because this is a special opportunity for me to get to know all of you personally. You have no idea the cultural heritage you've lost! Our prophet has told us what this world is meant to be, a place where we have true freedom and equality!" he exclaims, ejaculating spit out of his mouth. His face reddens, fists swinging around him. "None of you have seen the true face of the Empire. Stop being mutts, wagging your tail for your overlords as long as you're content. I've seen first-hand the things the Empire does. They've killed thousands of my fellow Americans. I was like you, a loyal citizen with a loyal Japanese name. But no longer. I've retaken an American name now. Clarence."

Clarence twirls in place, lifts his hands up to the air as though addressing a celestial being.

"Because I'm charitable," Clarence continues, "because my God teaches forgiveness, I will give all of you a chance. Join me and retake your heritage as an American, or go to hell. You first."

I can't see the person he's looking at, but two NARA members hold rifles at their head.

"What'll it be?"

"I am a loyal servant of the Emperor!" a woman shouts.

"Congratulations."

There is a loud gunshot.

"You idiots!" Clarence yells. "Don't shoot them before you take off their clothes or you'll get blood all over them. See, it's a mess, and we can't use her clothes anymore. Take this man. He looks like he has good sense. What'll it be?"

"Please don't kill me. Please . . ."

"So that means you'll join us?"

"I'll do anything to live."

"See how easy it is?" Clarence lifts the man, puts his arm around him. "You just need to say one thing for me out loud."

"What?"

"Say you renounce the Empire," he states. "Then spit on the ground. Simple, right?"

"But, but if—"

"It's very simple. Renounce the Empire in front of your compatriots. We have one of your porticals recording your renunciation to make it public and official. Up there on top of the train. Smile for Cain!"

"If I did that and it got out, they'd put my family in prison."

"That's a tough dilemma," Clarence says. "Strip him."

"No, wait, please. I have money, I have—"

They take off his clothes, and when he's butt naked, Clarence personally stabs him in the throat with his knife. Blood splatters over Clarence's face. He asks for a handkerchief. "I hate blood that smells like onions," he comments. "Too many onions aren't good for your health. Garlic, though, is good. It just makes you smell like garlic all the time."

His running commentary and the way he revels in each of the ensuing eight executions makes the macabre situation even more sinister. The way he tantalizes the victims with the hope of egress, then pulls it away, feels so much like a travesty, I can't believe this is actually happening.

"I renounce the Empire," one man yells, spitting on the ground. "I want to reclaim my American heritage!"

I think all of us empathize with his desperation and betrayal, just as we despise him for it.

"Good," Clarence approves. "Now that you're one of us, brother, you have a simple task." He gestures to the next person in line. "Kill your neighbor."

"But—but what if he wants to be American?"

"I don't like the way he looks," Clarence states. He gives an embarrassed shrug. "Sorry, I'm superficial!" Clarence hands the man a knife. "Poke him in the eye, or the mouth. Whatever you please."

"I—I . . . I've never . . . I can't."

"This is now your country, sweet land of liberty. Of thee, we will sing. It's the land where our ancestors died. And you must kill to honor them. Right?"

"I'm an—an accountant. I wasn't even supposed to be on this train. I have a daughter who's only eight months old. Please, sir. Pl—"

"Daughter? I had a daughter once. Two actually. I don't want to see your daughter bereaved. Kill your neighbor, and I'll let you go home."

"W-what?"

"You're an accountant. Eye for eye, one life equals another, right? Numbers make sense to you. Kill him."

The accountant shakes, pissing in his pants.

Clarence laughs. "It's not all that bad. Believe me. I'd love to counsel you and walk you through this, but I don't have all day. I'll give you thirty seconds to decide how badly you want to see your daughter."

"I have a son!" the male next to the accountant barks. "I would never be able to look him in the eye if I betrayed the Emperor."

"You wouldn't be able to look him in the eye even if you didn't since you'd be dead," Clarence dryly remarks.

"At least my honor will be intact!"

"Honor's overrated when you're dead. Believe me. I have lots of honorable friends who are ant food," Clarence says. "Accountant. Fifteen seconds."

The accountant fumbles with the knife, delaying, trying to eke out minutes from seconds. But the seconds pass too quickly. His hands shake as he points the blade at his neighbor. He plunges the knife into the man's cheek, but aims it too high. The knife hits the cheekbone and deflects off. Most of us look away as the accountant does his best to kill the man, sobbing and screaming as he does. It is a grueling death.

I play with my shackles, see if there's any way to break free. There are NARA members with guns on top of the train and in the perimeter. Even if I tried to escape, they'd just shoot me.

When the accountant finishes, Clarence grabs him by the

shoulders. "You did a brave thing. You hear me? You showed your love for your daughter." Clarence wipes the blood off the accountant's face. "You will appreciate your daughter in a way you never did before. You took a life for her. Now, you know what drives me, what drives all of us. Bring the bike."

The NARA bring out an old bicycle and give it to him.

"Ride southwest for half a day and you'll reach Dallas Tokai," Clarence says. "I salute you for embracing your inner savage."

The accountant can't believe he's actually being allowed to leave. He begins to pedal away, but as he does, he laughs maniacally, falling over. I think he's lost his mind from shock. He gets back on and continues to ride.

"Now that's honor. An office worker kills for his daughter. Don't scoff at him. What do you all kill for?" Clarence posits, and wags his finger at us. "He has been liberated in a way none of you will fathom unless you follow in his footsteps. Now, what'll it be? Renounce, or die?"

I'm convinced Clarence will let the accountant get far enough so that he believes he's free before sniping him in the back. But as his silhouette gets tinier, I realize, they're really letting him go.

It's almost our turn. I think about my parents. Did they know when their moment had arrived?

"I'm scared of dying," I whisper to Botan.

"Don't be scared. I'm happy to die," Botan replies.

"Happy?"

"Life's a gamble. You win until you don't. Then it's shutout time. See you in the next life."

The two guards strip Botan of her clothing. I can't bear to look in her direction.

"You don't know anything about being American," Botan defiantly declares to Clarence. "Don't dirty their name by saying you represent them."

"You're so moral and righteous. I love it. It used to be a grand old flag, and now it's just a dirty disgusting rag. You all began it by murdering my friends."

"I have no idea what you're talking about. I didn't kill anyone."

"Just because the right hand doesn't know what the left hand does doesn't mean they're not from the same body."

"What the hell does that mean?"

"You'll find out what the *hell* that means soon."

He takes a pistol out of his belt and shoots Botan in the head.

They remove my restraint, take off all my clothes. I can't believe I was just talking to Botan a minute ago.

Clarence points at her corpse, and asks, "She was your friend, right? I guess there's no point in asking if you'll join. I respect that."

He lifts his pistol to my head, and the barrel burns me, but then he stops.

"Why do you have that?" he asks, examining my belly.

I peer down and see the swastika. "What's it to you?"

"Are you working for the Germans?"

"I'm a RAM."

Clarence tilts his head, confused. "I realize you're a male sheep. But does that mean you're an undercover agent for the Nazis?"

"I'm n—"

There is a huge explosion, and something begins firing on the biomech. The NARA members race toward their Javelins.

Clarence grins at me, and says, "Tadao."

Beyond the train, on the other side of the canyon, I spot Chieko's Crab tank. It's followed by the stomping of three enormous Sentry mechas, matching strength and size with the biomech.

Why couldn't they have come just a few minutes earlier?

I go to Botan's body, try to turn her around. Part of her brain spills out through the opening in her head, and blood is everywhere. I try to clean her face, give her some final form of dignity, but I'm only making it worse, as the blood smears everywhere.

I'm so sorry, Botan. I'm so damn sorry. I shouldn't be alive. I should be dead. Now I have only one reason to live. To get revenge for you all: Spider, Sensei, Wren, Botan, Olympia, and all the other RAMs.

"We are a pacification force from the United States of Japan," a woman's voice booms from the Sentry mecha. "Drop your weapons, and you will be taken alive. Resist, and you will be forcibly pacified."

The Sentry mechas have the toughest armor in the corps and move forward to fight the biomech. I put my clothes back on. An unnatural sound emanates from the Nazi monstrosity. Something resembling a black fog fumes out from its arms, and I realize these are the "gnats" I'd heard about, insectoid-shaped cannons with propellers. There are hundreds of them that swarm our Sentry mechas. The big mechas have a ball of a torso, bulky arms designed to withstand an array of armaments. When the gnats surround them, they charge their fists with electric volts and swat them away with ease. Even their attacks do minimal damage to the Sentry mechas.

The NARA quickly get their forces into position. They're led by one of the most unusual mechas I've ever seen. It's an ostentatious robot, painted red, white, and blue with stars on its head. It moves almost like a wingless vulture and has a longer neck than other mechas I've seen, hunching as it walks, indicating a possible problem with the autobalance, unless, for an indiscernible reason, this is by design. It's the helmet that gives the mecha its aviary features, a beaklike protrusion attached to the front. I can't determine its strength from an initial glance because it's probably scavenged from multiple mechas and fused by the NARA creed that drips in the colors of their old flag. On its side, there are the letters, FDR, which I presume is its name as well as a tribute to the last ruler of the old America. The *FDR* is a quarter of the height of the biomech and leads the party of twenty Javelins to fight our Sentry mechas.

The first five Javelins are no match for our forces. One Sentry mecha punches a Javelin in its cannon, crushing it and causing the whole hull to collapse. The other Sentry mechas pummel the Javelins, not even bothering to unleash their arsenal. The shells the Javelins fire don't make a dent on the armor. They seem to be even less effective than the gnats. After the initial assault fails, the Javelins withdraw. The FDR launches three gaudily painted missiles at the Sentry mechas. They use their shields to block most of the blast, and the explosion from one missile hitting the shield actually hurts a Javelin.

The FDR sidles next to the biomech, waiting for the bigger beast to handle the hard work so it can eventually feast on metal carrion.

I don't think the biomech will fare any better, but I need to have an escape strategy in place. I think about rushing back to my Crab, but I don't know if the auxiliary generators gave it enough juice so that it can still drive. I don't need to ponder too long, as Chieko's Crab finds me. A ladder drops, and I climb in.

I'm so glad to see her and Poet. The other two aren't there, and I wonder if she dropped them off.

"Where's Wren?" is the first thing she asks me. I can't see her eyes underneath her goggles, but her lips are anxiously pinched together.

It slowly comes back to me, the moment right before the NARA knocked me unconscious. Chieko sees me hesitating, and demands again, "Where is he?"

"I'm sorry."

"Sorry for what?"

"We—we were aboard, and I was trying to escape, but the NARA got in and they . . . they shot him."

"Where's your Crab?" she asks.

MECHA SAMURAI EMPIRE 185

I point in the general direction. Navigation finds the exact spot. We speed toward it. Poet is at communications, and I ask, "How long did it take to get to Dallas?"

"We actually didn't go to Dallas," Poet replies. "We met the Sentry mechas halfway there."

"What were they doing there?"

"I think they were waiting for us."

Clarence had said there were only goose feathers on the train. That, combined with the Sentry mechas already waiting, and I feel convinced he was right that we were bait. But for what? The biomech?

That idea gives birth to a small, cold fury that begins to swell inside of me.

Poet taps me, hands me a towel. I wonder why, until I see him looking at my hands. They're covered with Botan's dried blood. He's about to pour some water from the rations, but I decline. "Hygiene is important," Poet reminds me.

"Not right now," I tell him. "Why is it only you two?"

"The other three got in the Sentry. She came back for Wren, assuming the Sentry mechas would be too busy fighting to rescue him."

"And you?"

"I can't write poems about today if I'm not here to witness the ending."

I don't know if he's brave or out of his mind. Maybe poetry requires a little bit of both.

Our Crab isn't far, and when Chieko gets there, she takes off her gear.

"I don't advise you go out there," Poet says to her. "I can't pilot this if something happens to you."

But if she hears him, she doesn't acknowledge it. She rushes for the hatch. I follow her as she climbs up the ladder and scrambles inside the Crab.

I'm about to enter as well when I hear a loud crunching noise. Just past the train, the biomech has engaged our Sentry forces by charging straight into them. The ebony monster runs like it's possessed and grapples the first Sentry in its way. The finlike structure seems to be giving it balance and the ability to move more quickly. The biomech pulls at the head of the Sentry, using its fusion dagger to sunder the connections to the body. The wire starts to split apart, sparks still charged while flopping like noodles. But the head doesn't fully detach, even with the BPG tubes cut. The organic material on the biomech's surface is amorphous, fluctuating and flexing like muscles. It's almost as though its skin has an intelligence of its own, reacting to the tectonic shifts of the structure underneath. This is in contrast to the shiny armor of the Sentry mecha and the multiple lights flickering on and off. The animalistic intensity of the biomech seems to be overwhelming the samurai's patient and careful approach. The Nazi monster kicks the Sentry in its belly, which causes the rotund shell to cave inward in the shape of a foot. The biomech pounds on the mecha repeatedly, while the two Sentries circle around to try to flank it and not hurt their fellow mecha.

That's when the biomech tears the head off the Sentry it has in its grip. I'm shocked, and so are the two other mechas as they both come to a complete stop. These Sentry mechas are defensive stalwarts, and from what I've studied, not a single one has been lost in battle. Until now.

The biomech tosses the Sentry's head, makes a fist, then punches straight into the orifice where the head used to be, destroying everything from the neck down. Whoever the crew was, they're dead now. The Sentry's autobalance keeps it standing as the biomech moves to confront the remaining two mechas. The gnats deluge the opening, presumably to target any possible survivors.

I can't believe how quickly the biomech disposed of our mecha. The second Sentry raises both its arms. Its hands rotate away from the wrists, leaving an opening in the forearm where two cannons emerge. It fires multiple acidic shells. (I recall acidic incinerators were effective in the past.) But there is no effect on the biomech. It looks like the Germans have found a way to defend against it. The Sentry changes to regular shells, letting loose a deadly shower. The biomech's chest gets perforated, and it stumbles. The two mechas sense weakness and close in.

I climb into the Crab and see Chieko with Wren. Wren has two bullet holes in his head and isn't breathing. Chieko is holding him. She does not cry, but her eyes are consumed by rage. I look to Spider and Olympia, necks still twisted all wrong. Damn.

"You didn't keep your promise," she says to me.

"I did my best."

"You're still alive!" she shouts. "You saved your own ass, but let him die."

"It's not like that. I tried. I really tried."

"Then why is everyone dead but *you*?"

"Chieko."

"Don't say my name!" She holds Wren's corpse more closely. "You ordered me to leave! I should have stayed and helped."

"You would have been killed like everyone else," I reply.

"You think I care about death?" she yells. "You think I'm afraid for my life? The reason I left was because I trusted you and I believed leaving would save more lives."

"So did I."

"You were wrong."

I can't deny it. "The biomech is—"

"I don't give a damn about the biomech!"

"It just destroyed a Sentry!"

That startles her, but her anger quickly overtakes her. "I don't care if I die here. At least I'll die with dignity and not abandon my friends."

"I didn't abandon them. You didn't see what happened."

"I've seen enough," she scoffs.

"What was I supposed to do? We were ambushed."

"The least you could do was try to avenge them!" she exclaims.

"I'll make the person responsible for this pay," I tell her.

"Will you?" she asks, a bitter and taunting tone in her voice.

"Look at our tank!" I reply. "I was trying to power it back up when the NARA took us away."

"It looks fine to me."

I glance over at the console. The auxiliary generator must have gotten the BPG working again. There's power humming through the Crab.

"Chieko! Cream! We have trouble," Poet warns us through the communicator.

I check outside the opening. The FDR is heading our way. Past him, the biomech is fighting both Sentry mechas in fierce hand-to-hand combat. There are orifices all over the biomech from our mecha attacks, but those holes are regenerating. Every time there's a heavy blow, the ground trembles. On the back shoulder of one Sentry, I spot a name: *Fuka*. I wonder if Izzy and Orwell are inside.

"The NARA mecha is coming our way," I tell Chieko.

"They're the ones who shot him?" Chieko asks me.

"Yes."

She stands up, marches back to her Crab. I'm about to follow her, but she angrily warns me, "Don't come into my mecha."

I get off the ladder. Just as she's about to enter the hatch, the FDR aims its cannon and fires a missile. The FDR must have an interchangeable system that swaps between shells and missiles. It's propelled directly from the gun and foldout fins open up, its engine igniting. The missile hits just as Chieko closes the hatch. I can't tell the extent of the damage from below, so I rush back into my Crab and message Poet.

"Are you okay?" I ask him.

"I'm fine, thanks for asking," the familiar voice of Clarence gleefully replies back. "Normally, this is the part where I'd tell you you're hopelessly outgunned, but I don't advise you surrender as I'll kill you if you do."

Chieko's Crab isn't moving.

It'll be too difficult to pilot the Crab upside down. I grab the tank's portical and turn on the remote control to relay navigation and weapons into the interface. It's not as intuitive or easy to control, but I have no choice. I check if I can connect with Chieko's Crab for a more secure way to communicate. I don't get a link with her tank, but a connection is made to a different one. I do a visual search and realize it's the fifth Crab tank, which was hawsered to the last car in the train and has no one on board.

Can I take remote control of that crab? Has it been damaged? All I see on my portical are weapon controls for the fifth crab. That might be enough. There's also the self-destruct sequence. The tank is still wired in with the train. Blowing it up could potentially set off a chain reaction, destroying the entire thing. Is that a smart thing to do considering our primary mission was to protect the train?

Chieko's tank still isn't moving. Did she get hurt? The FDR is getting closer. According to the navigation, the Javelins are splayed around the train.

I take a deep, long breath. I look at Spider, Olympia, and Wren.

My rage calms me. Everything slows.

I input the overrides to trigger the self-destruct in the fifth tank. It's almost instantaneous, causing an implosion in the Bradlium Particle Generator that blows up the Crab from within. The shells inside exacerbate the blast. The rear part of the train follows suit as the cars begin to explode like a trail of fiery dominos. Their interconnectedness makes the devastation far worse. Goose feathers are everywhere, mixing with the debris and train parts raining down.

The explosion rattles the FDR, destroys four neighboring Javelins, and damages five others. This is my moment to pounce. At least I hope. I have only four legs, but even if I had six, I don't know if I could pilot this thing inverted.

"Very naughty thing you did there!" Clarence declares.

"You're next," I reply to him, no longer caring who hears us.

"I've heard those exact same words, oh, twenty-eight times. Sorry, twenty-nine. Well played, friend. Didn't know you had that trick up your arse. But you would have been better served if you'd waited until I was closer to the train so you could have actually damaged me."

"Are you always this annoying?" I ask him.

Clarence laughs in a coarse tone. "To my enemies, I am the eternal bedbug."

I place commands into the portical so that my Crab's legs are rotating. I rotate them backward so that instead of pointing upward like the legs on a dead roach, they've swung downward. They make contact with the ground, and I cautiously lift the hull. It rises, and the balance is maintained. I take a step forward, then another. It's confusing doing everything in reverse, but at least I know it'll work.

The FDR fires four missiles at me.

I accelerate toward the other side of the train. Manually controlling each step on the portical is laborious, but I have no choice, as it looks like the missiles are following me. I clamber through the train debris, hoping the armor will shield me from the fire even with the hole in my side. Smoke seeps into the opening, and the interior gets flooded. I cough involuntarily, and my nostrils smell of ash. The first missile hits the remains of a car next to me. I keep on moving, and the missiles lose my signature in the destroyed train. Unfortunately, I'm also essentially blind as my scans have gone haywire and the visual feed is fire and smoke.

I cough again and search for a gas mask. If I hide in here too long, my lungs will be poisoned.

Clarence asks me, "You think you can hide in there forever?"

No. But if he keeps on talking, I may be able to calculate his location through a triangulation process based on the source of his communication signal.

"I once hid from imperial soldiers like you did," he continues. "Hoping they'd forget me. Some did, but your assassin, Bloody Mary, didn't. My family paid the price for my foolishness."

I have his location, which is just ahead of me. If I jump out now, I should be able to catch him off guard. I pop out through the smoke, but he's not there. He's several meters ahead of me, cannon fixed, which he fires. The blast rips another hole in the hull.

Clarence laughs. "It's not that easy," he says, and continues taunting me. I ignore him.

Speed is the Crab's strength, but right now I don't have much of it. I have only one option left to me. I race toward the FDR. Before it can fully block me, I crash into it, seizing its hips with my claws. I want to unleash artillery, but it takes me a few clicks before I find a way to fire on the portical. It's not functioning. That last blast must have screwed up the wiring. I take a measured breath and activate the self-destruct, but that fails as well. I repeat the self-destruct command and this time it appears to execute successfully. But it doesn't trigger the BPG.

I release his hip and start pounding on the FDR's side with my legs. The FDR has an arm guard it raises to deflect the attack. We exchange fists, but his mecha is much stronger than my Crab. He pushes me away, then lifts his foot and stomps me from above. My legs buckle, causing the Crab to be pressed flat on the ground.

"This fight is making me hungry for crab," Clarence says, as his mecha batters my side. "They used to have a place in Los Angeles, great Alaskan King crab legs with their special Cajun sauce. It'd give me diarrhea, but it was worth it. I almost wish I could go back to L.A. just so I can have some again." He grabs one of my legs, then hammers on it with an actual hammer. I look toward Chieko's Crab tank, but it's still not moving. The FDR yanks my fourth leg out, and Clarence asks, "You think it's worth the risk to try to go back and eat there?"

I close my eyes, breathe in through my nose. I am ready for death. But I won't die without taking him with me.

I check the diagnostics on the heat gun. There's just enough power in the tank to shoot once. But I don't know if that's enough. Can Chieko's tank help? I don't know her condition, so I go to the communicator and send a message. There's no reply from Poet. I sync with her Crab's portical, and, as with the last tank, I can't take over her movement. But I have access to her weapons. I search for the heat gun, find it, and aim at the FDR.

"Even if you beat me, our mechas will destroy you," I reply to him for the first time.

"You don't see the battle?"

"What are you talking about?" I ask him as I furtively aim at the FDR's back.

"You don't realize the balance of power has shifted."

"Actually, I do."

The heat cannon fires from Chieko's Crab tank. The FDR detects the discharge and attempts to withdraw. I use that moment to prop my Crab back up and clutch his foot. He's stuck in place, and when the wave hits him, it blows away half the FDR's head as well as its right arm. At the same time, I rotate my Crab's heat gun, aim it toward the center of the FDR's chest, and fire. My tank shuts down, completely enervated. The visual feed is dead. I rush to the opening in the tank and look at the FDR. There's now a hole through its center, power draining out. From the back, Clarence ejects out of the FDR. He's missing his arm and is leaking blood.

Minimal power returns to the Crab, but when I try to move, I realize I'm tangled with the FDR. He's locked us together. The scanners pick up an unusual surge from the American mecha. I try to detect the source, but the portical can't figure it out. But it does relay a countdown.

A self-destruct on the FDR.

I look over at Spider, Olympia, and Wren one last time. I should die here with them. But Clarence is still alive. I climb out of the hole, clamber down one of the Crab's legs, and jump down. I run as fast as I can. Clarence gets picked up by a Javelin, which drops a ladder for him. He climbs up, and the Javelin moves quickly to a safe distance. Behind me, the self-destruct activates and blows up both vehicles. The shock wave hurtles me several meters away, and I eat dirt, rocks scraping against my face until everything goes black.

IT'S A LONG STRUGGLE BACK TO CONSCIOUSNESS. BUT THE DISCORDANT clash of chemical plates grating against an unnatural bone structure wakes me. I look up and see the biomech looming over me. It is holding the heads of the two Sentry mechas it fought, one of which is the *Fuka*. I try to stand, but my feet aren't working. I pull backward, even though I know it's hopeless. I can't believe it destroyed all three Sentry mechas. That shock overwhelms even my fear of death. I have no chance.

At the same time, I've suffered what feels like ten near deaths in the last few hours. I didn't get Clarence, but I destroyed his mecha. If this is it, I accept the end. I did my best, and I failed.

The biomech's skin looks reptilian in some parts and insectoid in others, the heavily segmented darkness that pulses with red tissue occasionally visible. If it takes a step forward and stomps me, I'd die a painful, but quick, death. The face is hard to decipher, the nose morphing into a chin and a visorlike slab where its eyes would be. I glance over at the *Fuka* and wonder what this portends for the Empire.

I don't try to flee anymore. I sit upright, posed for the type of *harakiri* I've seen in the games depicting old times.

But the monster doesn't fire. I know it sees me. Is it trying to make it worse by teasing me with the hope of escape? I won't run, not when it's so obvious I have no chance. Better to die here with dignity. My wait doesn't last long as the biomech does the one thing I never expected it to do. It turns around and begins moving away.

What in the world just happened? How am I still alive?

I stand even though my legs are shaking. I do my best to calm my nerves.

I rush to Chieko's Crab, climb the ladder, then bang on the hatch. There's no answer. I twist it open and climb in. Poet is holding a dagger.

"Cream!" he shouts in relief.

"Where's Chieko?"

He points to the corner. Chieko is lying there, badly hurt and unconscious.

"The missile attack knocked her out," Poet says.

"Why didn't you reply to my messages?"

"I had to play dead in case you didn't make it," Poet replies.

"Why didn't you try to escape?"

"I never got good enough to pilot this thing by myself."

He looks like a different person, and there's something about the fear in his eyes that I empathize with. I put on the goggles, gloves, take the seat, which calibrates around me. I consolidate the navigation back to the pilot's interface and chart the coordinates for Dallas. The Crab is in good shape. Auto-kinematics for now as my hands are too tired otherwise.

What remains of the train is still on fire. I speed past it, climb up the hills to the side of the tracks. The remains of three massive mechas have toppled over, all of them missing their heads.

"I'm getting a message," Poet says.

"From the Germans?"

"It's from a mecha survivor. I'll send you the coordinates."

It's not far from our current location. I make my way around the leg of one of the fallen mechas, see how the armor has been torn away. The bottom half of the *haramaki-dō* has been shredded, and all the internal circuitry is exposed.

There are two survivors on the surface. I approach quickly, drop the ladder. They board. One of them is Orwell, the bastard who branded me with the swastika symbol. The other is a major; her arm is in a makeshift sling and looks broken. Both of their faces are covered with dirt and blood.

"Who are you?" the major asks. Like many mecha pilots, her hair is cut very short, and her brows are shaved. She is calm and seems expressionless as she talks.

"Excuse me?"

"What's your name?"

I almost answer Cream as it's been my designation for so long. "Makoto Fujimoto, ma'am," I reply.

"I'm Mori Aramata," Poet answers in turn, which surprises me, only because I hadn't known his real name.

"Stand to address the major," Orwell commands both of us.

If Orwell recognizes me from before, he doesn't indicate as

much. Then again, I have these huge goggles on my face. My initial sense of animosity alleviates as I realize that the swastika he branded me with got me the momentary distraction that serendipitously saved my life. There is an irony that I'm saving his life in return without his being aware of how he saved mine.

"Forget ceremony. Thank you for rescuing us. I'm Etsuko Mizukami," the major says. "That's Orwell. We need to return to Dallas and inform them of what's happened here."

I don't need her urging. I'm already rushing away. But as I do, I have to ask her: "Did you know our train was going to be attacked?"

"It's not your place to question the major!" Orwell snaps.

"It's fine," the major says to Orwell. "You're not part of the corps. And you want an answer. I would too. The truth is, we weren't sure, but we were anticipating an attack."

"Why?"

"We'd heard rumors about a new type of German biomech, and we wanted to see it ourselves. We had no idea how powerful it was or that we'd lose control of the situation."

"We're RAMDET trainees, ma'am," I remind her. "We weren't soldiers."

"That's what made you a more attractive target."

So they did know, and we were sacrificed in their pursuit of data. I want to throw them both off, but, I realize, they're just following orders too.

It's all flatland as far as I can see. The terrain is optimal for escape but provides no cover of any sort. I get only five kilometers away before something pops up in my rear scans. From the size and speed, I assume they're Javelins.

"Everything okay?" the major asks.

"There are a couple of Javelins in pursuit," I reply.

"It's dishonorable for a soldier to run from a battle," Orwell states.

"Good thing I'm not a soldier," I reply, incredulous that he has the nerve to talk to me about honor.

"What'd you say?"

"You heard me. You have no right to talk to me about honor, not after what you did to me. You have an issue, you can get the hell off."

"Do I know you?"

"You probably don't even remember since you and your buddies attacked me in the middle of the night like the cowards you are."

"Get up," Orwell orders.

I do, take off my goggles. His eyes widen. "If I hadn't seen so many people die today, I'd kick your ass off," I tell him. "Sit down and shut up, or I swear, I will throw you out."

"Orwell!" the major shouts. "Do you know how to drive this Crab mecha?"

"No, ma'am."

"Then sit down and remain quiet. Our lives are in Makoto-san's hands."

Orwell reluctantly complies.

"Forgive us," the major apologizes, and I realize by her bow she doesn't just mean Orwell's words.

I take my seat again, put on my goggles. The Javelins shouldn't be able to match our speed. But the three indicators on my scans are catching up fast. They are relentless in their pursuit, but they're still not fast enough for the Crab—which might explain why they're firing surface-to-surface missiles (SSM) at us.

There's no way I'm going to dodge them, and the electronic countermeasures aren't very effective. I aim the cannons at the SSMs, try to auto-aim. I get locks and fire. The first volley of three missiles gets destroyed. But the fourth one eludes my defensive shots and is about to hit. I release a chaff cluster, hoping it'll muddle the last missile. Fortunately, it does, and the missile explodes in the ground instead of the tank. At that moment, the front leg hits a big boulder, causing the Crab's motion to stutter. Autobalance fixes the step, and I turn back to driving, but I know why the position of pilot and gunnery are normally split apart. It's hard to attack and drive at the same time.

I can't determine how many missiles they have left. But if they have a lot more, it's going to be tough to fend them off. Their combined forces strafe me. Though the plain makes it easy to run, I also don't have any protection. I have to run in a zigzag pattern so that I'm not too easy a target for their cannons. But that also slows us down.

I check navigation and scour the vicinity for somewhere I can either hide or take cover. I'm also piloting while checking the status of our rear armoring to make sure it doesn't get too weak, firing shots whenever I can. I jump through the maps, but I need help.

"Poet. Can you go to nav and find some hills for me?"

"Our nav is busted."

"I can help," the major says, and uses the emergency periscope. "You think we can't outrun them?"

She already knows what I'm thinking. "No," I answer.

A minute later, she says, "About eight kilometers west of here, there's a patch that looks like it might work."

I change course and race toward it.

"Why are you in such a hurry to leave?" a voice says over the communicator. It's Clarence again.

"I didn't want to overstay my welcome," I reply.

"You can't leave without paying the bill. Do you know how long I spent putting the FDR together?" Clarence asks. "Three years.

Scavenged, pirated, and stole parts from thirty mecha to get my beauty together. And you just destroyed him. What an ungrateful guest you are."

The hills the major found provide cover and, more important, a space where I can fight without being surrounded by all three. Also, they can't snipe at me from afar. Right as I arrive, the mechas I mistakenly thought were Javelins are on me. They're actually American mechas, each wielding a different weapon. The one with the painted name of Fillmore holds up a gigantic chain saw. Another called the Belmont has a charged whip. The third of the bunch, which has the name of Spencer marked in blue, has a hooked claw that it fires. Like the FDR, they're chimera mechas, clumped together over time from different units so that there isn't any design unity. There are many strange protrusions from parts that just don't fit but were put into place solely for functionality.

The Fillmore attacks first, lifting its chain saw. Just as the chain saw is about to cut into my shoulder, I lift my arm up, timing it to grab and deflect the Fillmore's wrist. It tries to attack again, but I block its arm, then use the natural momentum to pull it into the Belmont. The Belmont tries to parry with its whip, but the chain saw rips through it to the chest plate. I scurry around the Fillmore and give it a little bump on its feet, causing it to fall even more and assault the Belmont.

"Naughty naughty," I hear from Clarence.

Just then, the Spencer fires its hooked claw onto one of my legs. It pulls, causing that leg to straighten and the whole tank to crash forward. I have no choice but to release that limb, separating it from the body. With five legs, I recover my pose and rush toward the Spencer. The Fillmore has removed the chain saw from the Belmont's chest. It tries to attack me, but I make what I realize is a foolhardy move and jump onto the Spencer's leg. I doubt it can support our weight, but I use the speed to wrap around the Spencer's back and use it as a shield against the chain saw. The Fillmore leaps to the side and is about to attack me. I release my hold on the Spencer and actually allow myself to fall backward. We're strapped into our seats, and before the hull can crash into the ground, I flip the legs so they catch us upside down. The chain saw slams into the Spencer's side, carving a huge gap into it.

I will not die today. Not at their hands. Not after surviving the biomech and every adversity the world could throw at me. My rage, my stubborn insistence on victory, is doing something to my senses. It's almost like time has slowed down. The NARA are pantomiming their moves, and I know what they're going to do before they do it.

The Fillmore causes more destruction for his companions than for us because I can anticipate its actions. With its companions more or less debilitated, I know it's time to dispose of the Fillmore. But just as I'm about to engage the Fillmore, the Belmont and Spencer attack it in savage, close-quarter combat. They are frustrated that their attacks are hitting one another rather than me and have turned on one another.

It's time to make our escape. But not without a finishing blow. I have to keep my word to Chieko.

I move the Crab to a safe distance, flip the bridge back to its normal angle, then aim the heat gun. I carefully set up the projection so that it'll hit all three in a row. I fire, and the tank shuts down for a few seconds. When the energy returns, I see that all three chimeras have stopped moving, massive damage impairing them. I get ready to fire again, but one of the mechas explodes, blowing up the other two as well.

"That was magnificent," Major Mizukami tells me. "And efficient."

"Thank you," I say to her. I plot the course to Dallas again. I am relieved that I could avenge Wren. But I don't let my guard down until we reach Dallas.

Fortunately, it's an uneventful trek back. None of us talk. I check my aft cameras continually, afraid the NARA will send another force.

They don't.

The hours feel like one long minute stretched into repetition. I feel the Crab's every step, sense every shift in the terrain. I've become one with it, and even though we have only five legs, I push us faster than what we were doing earlier with six legs.

As soon as I see the wall surrounding Dallas Tokai, I slow the Crab. Exhaustion and relief take over. But it's short-lived as another part of me can't believe we're safe. I'm convinced the German biomech will come after us. Why else did the biomech let me go? Maybe this is part of their trap too. Poet communicates with Dallas, and the major identifies herself, asking for medical support. Rear cameras still don't register any enemies. I try not to think about all the dead bodies or that it's Botan's dried blood on my hands.

I startle when the major puts her hand on my shoulder.

"Well done," she tells me. "You can power down."

Outside, a relief unit is coming to meet us. I check the visual feed to make sure they're imperial forces. Even though they're wearing our uniforms, I can't be sure they aren't just disguised as our troops. The major doesn't seem troubled and exits.

Poet says, "I'm going to write one helluva poem about today," before hurrying out.

Orwell waits for me. I await some smart-ass crack and will punch him in the face if he makes one. Instead, he bows to me.

The unexpected gesture doesn't erase the brand. But I signal for him to exit first. He climbs out. I rush back to the scans and check again. No biomechs, no NARA vehicles. I should head down. But I'm afraid of leaving the safety of the tank. Not even our own mechas can protect us against that Nazi goliath. I strap myself back into my seat, shaking. I want to run away in the Crab as far as possible.

Medics climb in, spot Chieko, and carry her out.

"Fujimoto-san," a soldier says. "We have an ambulance waiting for you."

I remember Spider, Sensei, and Wren, all dead. Nothing seems real. I hate this feeling.

"He's in shock," I hear someone say. "We'll be applying a sedative. You'll feel a sharp prick, and—"

I should be dead, not them.

08

★ ★ ★

A DR. TAKEYAMA DOES A QUICK CHECK ON ME, RUNNING HER MEDICAL diagnostic. She examines my eyes, checks inside my mouth, performs a live X-ray over my body that shows up on her portical display. She asks how I'm feeling.

"I'm alive," I answer her.

"You have muscle damage and minor burns that should heal quickly. I'm ordering a special gel bath for you. There was also a burn mark the Nazis left on you. I had it removed. You stay in the bath for eight hours every day for the next four days, and you'll be all better."

After Dr. Takeyama leaves, a string of officers come by with questions about what happened during my mission, what I witnessed, how I survived. I try to answer, but I abhor the attempt to recall details. Anything I'm unclear on, they ask over and over, trying to ascertain whether I missed anything. They're mostly respectful and polite, but I don't have the appetite for it.

It's the official from RAMDET who really irks me by asking,

"Who authorized you to self-destruct the Crab tank that led to the destruction of the train?"

I glower at the older man, who looks like an office clerk wearing a suit and oval glasses. "Who authorized putting our lives at risk so the army could draw out the biomech?" I ask back. "There wasn't even anything on the train. Sensei tried to abort the mission, but you insisted the cargo was important even though you knew we were bait. All my friends are dead because of it. Don't talk to me about the stupid train. I'd blow it up again if I could!"

He is stunned. "E-everything you said is unsubstantiated," he stutters.

"Then why are you bothering to ask me?"

I'd sock him and all his colleagues if I weren't stuck naked in this gel.

The next day, they send another RAMDET official. I expect more dumb questions, but instead, he asks me, "Are you excited about graduation?"

I'd completely forgotten about it. The idea of even going through with it feels like a farce. In our class, only three of us are alive. Are we supposed to celebrate? The official rambles awkwardly when I don't answer, telling me how happy I should be about future opportunities. "You'll get to drive your own vehicle for sure," he informs me.

I wish he'd disappear.

But that gets me thinking about the future. The idea of being a full-fledged RAM seems ridiculous now. Spider was right. We're just a glorified security force. We shouldn't have been out there in the first place. I can't get over the fact that we were sent out as bait. My life was that meaningless to them.

As I float in the vat of regenerative gels, I realize this stupid dream of wanting to be a mecha pilot is the root of my problems. That dream has brought me only suffering, ridicule, and misery.

RAMDET exploited my desire, knowing that I'd do almost any-thing if it got me into a mecha. I've wasted so much of my life in pursuit of something that is clearly beyond my grasp.

RAMDET officials keep on wanting a better account of what happened. They even send an accountant to explain the cost of my actions, going over every bill and the expense of intentionally de-stroying the train.

"What is it you hoped to achieve by doing this?" the woman asks.

"I told you, I wanted to destroy as many of the terrorists as I could."

"Our cost-ratio analysis indicates you would have been better off trying to flee, considering so few of them were destroyed. I can go over the numbers with you."

"I don't want to go over the numbers," I tell her.

"You don't have anywhere else to be anyway, and as long as you're in the hospital, you're on the clock."

She uses her portical to calculate, telling me the cost of the Crab tanks, artillery shells, fuel, human resources, train parts, and more. It's the way she taps on her portical screen as she inputs the numbers that gets on my nerves.

"Everything we do is about money?" I ask her.

"This is a business, not a vanity project," she replies in confir-mation.

I'm going to quit RAMDET as soon as my body recovers.

THEY HAVE A PORTICAL FOR PATIENTS TO HELP PASS THE TIME. I AVOID reading the news. I have very few personal messages. I try to dis-tract myself flitting through the streets of *Cat Odyssey*, but its digi-tized world seems too fake to give me solace.

The gel treatment is like being in a warm tub except it isn't as hot and there are other gelatinous chemicals in there that make my skin tingle. I'm required to stay in it all day to recover.

This means I can't attend the official funeral. It's a national ceremony presided over by Shinto priests, with most of the city's key officials attending. Even the new governor will come to mourn the dead. Representatives from the Imperial Japanese Headquarters (aka Tokyo Command) are coming in droves. War Minister Kotohito has issued a special message honoring those who were killed in the *kogun*, though there's no mention of RAMs like me outside of the Imperial Army. I watch part of the proceedings on my portical. I've seen national funerals before. But now it's different because I was at the battle.

"How long must we allow their tyranny to endure?" Colonel Yamaoka asks in a speech similar to the one I heard him give on the train trip to Texarkana. "This was a brazen attack on civilians, and our brave soldiers in the mecha corps had to pay the price."

I overhear the nurses discussing if war with the Nazis is inevitable. I wonder how Chieko and Poet are doing. I try to listen to music on the portical. Depressing choral music chanting about the end of the world appeals to me.

The gel treatment has the side effect of helping me to sleep soundly. I don't get the nightmares I've heard mar the sleep of many veterans, reliving their experiences in a nocturnal display that feels as vivid as the actual event.

What bothers me is when I see people, I imagine them with bullets in their heads, their insides flipped out, their skin and tissue burned. It's like they're the NARA's walking corpses, regenerating with every cycle. They cling to trivialities to help themselves endure, but human life isn't special. It's a biological process that can be terminated all too easily.

I have to keep my mind diverted. I try not to rethink the battle, what mistakes I made, how we could have avoided losing almost everyone. I go through emotional swings, angry at Sensei for not having defied orders and retreating, at Spider for having gotten hurt and not being in the pilot's seat, at myself for not navigating more carefully right before we were attacked. I scrub my hands incessantly, but they feel like they're still covered with blood. My skin gets dry and peels off my fingers. I miss Hideki and all my fellow RAMs.

ON THE LAST DAY OF MY TREATMENT, I HEAR A KNOCK. I'M SURPRISED TO see Chieko. She's pale, has lost weight, and there's a deadness in her eyes I can relate to.

"How you doing?" she asks.

"Been better. You?"

She sighs. "I, uh . . . I was out of line, uh, back, back on the field." I can see how much pain the memory brings her.

"No you weren't." I want to apologize to her for everything, but I don't have the right. Her words still sting and the enormity of my mistake weighs on me. "I—I shouldn't have told you to leave."

"I chose to go. I can't blame my decision on you." She looks at me. I have a hard time meeting her gaze. "Besides, it wasn't you who attacked us. It was the Nazis and the NARA."

I do my best to control the surge of emotion that overwhelms me, and I'm grateful to her for her generous words. "Thank you," I tell her. "I know it doesn't mean much, but I got the NARA members who did this."

"I heard," she replies, and I see her blink back tears. "I didn't see you at the funeral."

"They wouldn't let me go. You went?" I ask her.

She nods. "I met Wren's parents. They kept on asking me how he passed. I didn't know what to tell them."

"Our superiors knew."

"Knew what?"

I tell her the major's confession that the whole operation was a trap for the German biomech and how RAMDET collaborated with them on it.

Chieko shakes her head. "How could they be so stupid?"

"They didn't know how powerful the biomech was."

"Heads should roll for this."

"I don't know if they will."

"What are you going to do next?" she asks.

"I'm quitting RAMDET."

She doesn't question why I'm quitting. Instead, she says, "I've fought so hard to be a pilot. I'll try to continue on."

"You're the best pilot they have."

"Thanks," she says.

It's by no means an absolution.

I don't think that's ever possible.

But her forgiveness releases part of the guilt that's been bearing down on me.

MY VAT TREATMENT IS DONE AND I'M TO BE RELEASED IN THE MORNING.
I'm writing my letter of resignation when a military officer enters my room. I prepare myself for a flurry of questions, but the visitor says, "You've been summoned for a meeting."

His name tag reads UGAKI and he's from the army, based on his uniform and markings. "Summoned by who?"

"Colonel Yamaoka."

He can't be talking about the war hero, can he? "*The* Colonel Yamaoka?" I have to confirm.

"Yes."

"W-what's he want?" I stammer because I have no idea why he'd want to talk to me.

"He'll inform you when he sees you. Are you ready?"

"Um, yes."

I'M DRIVEN TO THE NOGI MARESUKE OPERA CENTER, WHICH IS IN THE middle of a massive artificial lake. Ugaki accompanies me across the southern bridge. The main lobby has a huge marble statue of the famous general and a *Kanshi* poem he wrote right after the Russo-Japanese War in 1905, lamenting the death of the soldiers under him.

The workers are dressed in fancy red robes, and there are clay statues inspired by the opera, *The Delusion of Butterfly-san*. It's directed by Hideki Inouye, who pulled off the amazing *Water Geisha* a few years back.

We walk up the stairs to the second floor and head for an opera box. One of the attendants at the door informs us, "Sorry, there's no entry before the intermission."

"He's a guest of Colonel Yamaoka," my escorting officer states.

The attendant becomes noticeably embarrassed. "Excuse me, sir. Please enter."

Ugaki does not join us. I enter the box, and there are twelve people present. They are all wearing kabuki masks. There is no seat for me, and I stand in the back. All of them have cuff links with insignia marking them as military.

I watch the show. It's a dazzling spectacle with the two-stage format, most of the activity happening in the central area. Dancers run along the glass bridge to the islets in the audience and side characters provide a contrast. It appears to be a Buddhist wedding, though the main character, Butterfly-san, is inexplicably pining for a boorish "Yankee" soldier. Paper petals are falling like snow, and the stage splits into many colored partitions. She haughtily rejects Japanese suitors, which seems preposterous considering the

Yankee officer is a stranger who openly admits to his consul friend that he's interested in only a casual liaison. The *delusion* part of the title makes sense. The only thing that makes the opera bearable is the beautiful music and outlandish visuals. Lights are creating smoky flower mirages all around us.

When the intermission arrives, one of the masked people stands up and calls me over. I go and take his seat. The person across from me removes his mask. It's Colonel Yamaoka, ethnically Japanese, with the commanding look of a war hero. I stand to bow to him, and he says, "The original version of this opera was a scathing indictment of Western colonization."

"Sir?"

"The Yankee sailor seduces a young Japanese girl and claims to marry her for nine hundred ninety-nine years but breaks her heart by leaving. She longs for him, rejecting everything Japanese, giving up her family and her country for his sake. When he returns three years later, he's remarried an American woman and they coldly take her child away from her. Butterfly kills herself."

"It sounds aggravating," I tell him, my tone making clear I'm understating my irritation.

"That's why it's been updated. Now, when Butterfly realizes she's been duped, she takes her hara-kiri knife, kills the Yankee's entourage: the consul and his new wife. She beats her husband close to death but keeps him alive so he can work to provide a living for them. But not before she takes his manhood so he can't cheat again. Butterfly lives in luxury, and her son has a good life. I greatly respect our Italian allies, but this play has so many stereotypes about our people, even in its updated form, it makes me cringe. There are those in the Empire who want it banned, but I think it's an important reminder of how poorly imperial citizens and our culture were portrayed in Western media before the war."

A discussion of opera is the last thing I was expecting. I feel ignorant because I know so little.

"I heard about what you did out there," the colonel continues. "Major Mizukami spoke very highly of you. She was a very picky officer. Very impressive that you caught her attention."

"Thank you, sir," I reply, though I notice he refers to her in the past tense. "What do you mean, *was*?"

"Shortly after writing her last testament and her death poem, she committed *jigai*. Would you like to hear her *tanka*?" The summation of a life in exactly thirty-one syllables.

I'm shaken to hear the news that she carried out the ceremony of putting a knife through her throat. "Respectfully, no, sir. I thought this kind of ritual suicide was outlawed?"

"It is," he laments. "That's why I think about the old *Butterfly* and its misunderstood glorification of suicide. Soldiers can learn from their mistakes. What they gain in experience is invaluable to help us avoid repeating similar errors, which was why ritual suicide was outlawed in the USJ. But the major couldn't bear the thought of living when those dearest to her were dead."

I rustle uncomfortably in my seat, relating all too well. "I can understand," I state, but do I? Did she possibly feel responsible for what happened to the RAMs and was she driven by that guilt as well?

"She gave a very interesting report about the strength of their new biomech and their collaboration with the terrorist group, the NARA, with whom you've dealt before," the colonel says.

"Yes, sir. Back in school, they carried out an attack. Are we going to war with the Nazis?" I ask him, but it's more an angry plea for confirmation as I want to destroy them.

"The Germans are denying involvement, saying it's a rogue element working with the NARA who carried out the attack. They're even offering to help us."

"You can't believe them."

The colonel gazes sternly at me. "Do you have proof otherwise?"

"But at the funeral—"

"I said what I needed to, just as you did what you had to so that you could destroy your enemies. We should respond decisively, show them we mean business. But that's the governor's decision, not mine."

"You would respond differently?"

"It only takes one bad decision for an empire to fall," the colonel says.

I know I should probably be discreet, but I've lost the desire to give face to whichever idiot planned this whole debacle. "Whoever set us up got almost all of us killed. We were sacrificed, but it didn't even work. All my friends died for nothing."

"I know what's going through your mind."

"Respectfully, sir, I don't even know what's going through my mind."

Yamaoka laughs but in an empathetic way. "I appreciate your honesty. That plan was the brainchild of an inexperienced general who has been duly punished for his disgraceful part in this. He never should have been listened to in the first place, but his plan was accepted out of respect for his position as part of the governor's personal coterie."

The idea outrages me, but before I can lash out, I realize I'm just as culpable. "I think all of us made bad decisions out there."

"You took the extreme measures necessary to win," the colonel says. "You were willing to put aside weaker convictions to achieve the ultimate goal."

"That's a very positive spin on what happened."

"How would you describe it?"

"I survived," I reply.

Yamaoka grins. "That's what war is. The boldness of the NARA is worrisome. They've been upping their attacks, and it's clear they are pursuing a grander agenda."

"They want to incite us against the Nazis so we'd take them out," I say.

"Which is why we have to be careful before we attack the Germans. The GWs were a passionate but limited enemy. The NARA are much more insidious. They scheme and scheme, and their perverted religion galvanizes them. But we're limited in what we can do because of their connection with the Nazis. The USJ needs change. Are you one of the soldiers I can count on?"

"Of course, sir," I answer. "But I'm not a soldier."

"I saw the results of your high-school sim exam. You put your testing officer in a cast," the colonel says.

I'm surprised he's checked up on me. "Yes, sir."

"You should already be at BEMA."

"Thank you, sir. But I failed the exam."

"What are you going to do next?"

"I'm quitting RAMDET."

"Why?"

I take a deep breath.

The colonel watches me and waits for me to speak.

I am unable to articulate my grief. I search for words, but all I can muster is, "Too many people died."

"I lost many who were dear to me during the San Diego Conflict," he says with a tenderness that catches me off guard. I had no idea that he'd lost anyone during San Diego. "I was so angry, I too wanted to quit," he continues. "But I channeled my fury into making those who caused their deaths suffer. Would you like a chance at avenging the death of your compatriots?"

"I already got the NARA leader who killed them."

"I mean the forces behind the NARA."

I'd never thought it possible. But now that the idea's entered my head, there's nothing I want more. "Of course, sir," I reply.

"You'll get it."

"How, sir?"

"I've put in a formal recommendation for you," he says. "Together with Major Mizukami's praise and Colonel Tachibana's request for a third review of your results, you'll be gratified to know that you've been accepted as a special appointee."

"Special appointee, sir?"

"Into Berkeley Military Academy. You're joining the next class at BEMA."

I look at him, not sure if I'm hearing correctly.

"I was rejected twice," I inform him, just in case he didn't know that I tried reapplying.

"That had more to do with the lieutenant whose arm you broke. He opposed your acceptance on both attempts."

"I suspected, sir," I admit sheepishly.

"A formal evaluation has turned up several questionable lapses in judgment on his part. He's been transferred to the South Pole. The latest review of your examination, in conjunction with your combat experience, has indicated he was wrong in his opposition. The rejection has been overturned."

"*Arigatou gozaimasu,*" I say to him in Japanese to signify how grateful I am.

"It is regretful that you weren't accepted because of a personal bias," the colonel says. "But I'm glad the matter has been rectified."

As grateful as I am, I am wary as well. If he's getting me this appointment, he'll want something in return. We're all pawns. I just want to have some say on the conditions and the parameters.

"Apologies for asking, sir, but why help me?" I ask him, wanting to be clear.

The colonel nods. "Fair question. There are troubling times coming, and we need as many good officers as we can get. Finding a good mecha pilot is difficult. It's clear you're skilled, and I'm facilitating what you should have gotten in the first place. But there's also trouble brewing internally. BEMA is developing a new prototype mecha. The Germans have understandably taken a keen interest in it. I want you to be my eyes and ears there. Are you comfortable with that?"

"I—I think so, sir."

"It is true that we have enemies on our borders. But the only reason they've been so active is because of infighting and weakness in our leadership that has exposed our vulnerabilities. Our battles in San Diego were devastating. You know that better than anyone," he says, aware of the death of my parents in the conflict. "But so has the witch hunt carried out by the new governor against our intelligence community that has left it in tatters. How can we be prepared to fight when we blind ourselves? Our enemies have been emboldened. Especially a war hero among the Germans they call the Marshal. He is a charismatic leader who aspires to changing the Reich and is rattling the Nazi High Command, but we don't know what he's after. I believe he is most likely the rogue element they're afraid of. For good reason. He's won every battle he's fought. But we must put our own house in order before we can rule over others."

"I agree, sir."

"Good. Then it's settled."

Am I really getting into BEMA? Does that mean I'll get to be an official mecha pilot? I can't believe it. But I also think about Chieko and where she's going. I know Poet is staying on as a RAM, but Chieko has always wanted to be a pilot. "Forgive me if I impose upon your generosity, but there is something I'd like to request."

"What is it?"

"One of the other survivors, Chieko, is a very good pilot, and I believe she would make a good addition to the Academy as well."

"It's not that easy to get an appointment."

"I understand, sir. But I—" Do I really want to say this? I think about the battlefield again. "I can't accept the appointment unless she comes too. We spilled blood together out there, and I wouldn't feel right joining BEMA without her."

Yamaoka stares at me for a long time. I wonder if I've just blown my opportunity to get into BEMA, but I'm surprised to realize that I don't care.

The colonel grins when he sees the resolution in me. "I appreciate loyalty. I can't make any guarantees, but I'll have someone look into it."

"Thank you, sir."

"The new class doesn't start until next March," the colonel says. "Take the next few months off. As a BEMA student, you have free flights to anywhere in the Empire. You'll also have a small stipend, which, with your military discounts, should pay for accommodations and food. Go travel the Empire."

He puts his mask back on. Ugaki escorts me out.

I'm really going to get to be a BEMA cadet?

"Can I watch the rest of the opera?" I ask Ugaki.

"The colonel has already arranged special seating for you."

I'm taken to the front row, where I can see the orchestra as well as the faces of the performers up close. The elaborate costumes change multiple times during each song. When Butterfly begins to take revenge on those who wronged her, I feel immense satisfaction. I think of my fellow RAMs again and miss them.

I swear I will avenge you all.

BERKELEY

★

1996
SPRING

09

★ ★ ★

THIS IS THE FIRST TIME I CAN REMEMBER FEELING SO HOPEFUL.

From the moment I arrive at Yamaguchi Airport in Oakland, I feel a pervasive energy in everyone around me. Uniformed soldiers from the various branches are everywhere, going about their duties. The latest mechas guard the military installations. They have modern designs, sleek and curved for stealth purposes. I've heard they have access to weapons most civilians have never even heard of. Several dozen jet fighters are parked alongside some of the jumbo transports in case of emergencies, though the majority of our jets are at the Northern Air Base, about eighty kilometers from here. A week before arriving, BEMA sent my cadet uniform. I'm wearing it now, a single-breasted olive jacket with a white shirt outside the tunic collar. I won't get my *shin guntō* until later, though I remember Izzy's advice about the Toyokawa blades.

As a BEMA student, I get the special insignia of a bear. It's the symbol of the old state of California in the days before the Empire, the last grizzly bear in captivity. The military governor who took control after our victory, Yumiko Osame, thought it an appropriate symbol since California was one of the last states to fall.

Everywhere I go, civilians bow as a sign of respect to the uniform. Even when I grab a taxi, I get ushered to the front of the line, and the cab driver insists, "No charge."

The San Francisco Bay is a glorious sight, a great body of water surrounded by the city beyond. The Statue of Liberation, built to commemorate all the prisoners who were rescued by the IJA after the Great Pacific War, stands ninety-four meters tall. It's made in the image of the empress, holding the *Kusanagi* sword and a lantern.

There are a huge number of navy ships from our fleet based out of the Alameda Naval Yards. Much of San Francisco itself is testing grounds for mecha combat, and the buildings serve as props for our mecha pilots to train with. The population has been growing for the past decade, with about 350,000 in the city itself. The military presence has been expanding, but so has the weapons industry, with many of the top companies relocating here in the past decade because of the conflict in San Diego. The USJ Railway runs the underground subway system that goes below the bay and connects the south, east, and north bays with the city. From what I understand, Berkeley used to be smaller, but after the war, it absorbed its neighboring cities. The academy used to be called UC Berkeley, and the city itself was named after a British philosopher, George Berkeley.

I'm given a room on the fourth floor of the dormitory referred to as Unit 2. It's a spacious room with a comfortable mat. There's heating, though no air conditioner as the weather is generally cold to begin with. I only have an aluminum suitcase, which is stuffed with junk I don't bother to unpack. I charge my portical and look at the display screen on the wall. There's a welcoming message and a reminder that the superintendent's orientation speech is tomorrow morning. There's a knock on my door. I answer and see a student with choppy green hair and matching green eyes. She bows and asks excitedly, "You're Makoto Fujimoto?"

"Yes."

"I'm Tabitha Uoya," she introduces herself, giving her English nickname. "Welcome to your room! I'm the floor leader, so if you have any questions or problems, let me know." She has three stripes on her lapel, marking her as a junior.

"Thank you," I reply to her.

"Cafeteria is open until nine. Lights out at ten. We have optional exercises at five a.m., breakfast at six, and stretching at seven. Classes start at eight. We have a weekend trip with your floor mates every two weeks. We'll be going up to Vallejo this weekend to visit the aquarium and also my favorite fried-chicken restaurant. Hope you'll join." She clicks her portical, and concludes with, "Call me if you have any questions about anything."

My neighboring dorm room is empty, and I ask her who's moving in. She answers, "It's reserved for a late entry who should be arriving sometime this week."

Behind her, I see a familiar face.

"Noriko?" I'm so happy to see her and put out my hand to shake hers.

She gives me a warm hug. "I knew you'd make it here," she confidently states.

"I have to thank your parents. They really put in a good word for me."

"They told me to pass on their felicitations. RAMs got you into shape."

I laugh. She looks mostly how I remember her, though taller, with braided hair and much bigger muscles. She has two stripes but also other honorary marks I don't recognize, more than any other cadet I've seen. "It's been a wild year."

"I've heard," she says. "How are you liking BEMA so far?"

"I just got here."

"Have you seen the campus?"

"Not yet."

"Let me show you around."

We take the elevator down to the Channing Street exit. In the lobby, I see Chieko carrying four boxes. "Chieko!" I call.

"Cream!" she yells back. She's also bulked up, is sporting a new tan, and has grown her hair longer since I saw her a few months back.

"It's Mac here, if that's okay," I correct her abashedly.

"Sorry! Uh, habit."

"Cream?" Noriko asks.

"My nickname in RAMDET," I confess, and explain.

"Don't let anyone else know or you'll never be able to live that down," Noriko cautions me.

"*Sorry!*" Chieko exclaims.

"Please do not accidentally call me that in front of the other cadets," I plead, which makes them laugh.

"I'm Noriko," she introduces herself. "Friends call me Nori."

"Chieko," and they shake hands.

"We went to high school together," I explain to Chieko. And in reverse, "Chieko was a RAM with me."

"Excellent. We need more experienced mecha cadets. I was about to give Mac a tour. Want to join us?" she asks Chieko.

"Sure," she replies. "Let me just drop these off."

NORIKO GUIDES US TO TELEGRAPH AVENUE, WHICH IS THE MAIN STREET for the academy. It's filled with shops tailored toward cadets and local researchers. There are stores for everything, from military accessories to portical games and even spare parts for electric pets. There are shops that sell fruit tea, ginseng tea, and even specially grown tea from the *Regno d'Italia* in their part of the drained Mediterranean. There's an unusual assortment of cafés and restaurants, including four I spot with different *kaiseki*-style courses at bargain prices and the newly popular *Neo Kobe* pizzas that have even become widespread in the German Americas. Noriko points out a conclave of ethnic restaurants, and says, "That place has cheap, tasty food that'll give your stomach runs for a week."

"Sounds dangerous."

"I've heard we should try the unagi kimchee fried rice with bacon curry poutine," Chieko says.

"It's a rite of passage among the mecha cadets to be able to finish the whole set and go the entire day without using the bathroom," Noriko replies.

"That doesn't sound fun."

"It isn't," she says, with a prescience that makes Chieko and me laugh hard.

"You've been traveling the past couple of months?" Noriko asks us.

I nod. "Went all over the place. The free flights cadets get are amazing."

"Totally agree. Where all did you go?" she asks.

"Anywhere and everywhere. Loved Venice. The canals are all lit up, and they have those hovering lanterns everywhere. After the sun sets, it was like we were floating through an island of lights."

"Venice was nice, but I was blown away by the aerial coliseum in Rome," Chieko says. "Those gladiatorial matches ware amazing and the genetic modifications the fighters got were unbelievable. It's like they were dancing, not actually trying to beat each other."

Noriko points at a crowded restaurant we're passing. "That place's *mimiga* is the best. It's not as good as the pickled pig ear I've had in Okinawa, but it's as close as I've gotten to an authentic *meibetsu*. I go there all the time."

"I'm not a big fan of pickled pig ear," Chieko states.

"This place will make you a believer. Did you both visit the main island?"

"Of course," I reply.

Chieko nods as well. "It felt like I was in the future. Tokyo has that shopping district where there's the underground area, the ground level, and the upper tier with bridges connecting thirty skyscrapers. The portical games they had there were amazing."

There's a bunch of *tachi-kui* restaurants that smell delicious though the terrible scent from a stand serving up fermented *nattō* makes my nose scrunch up.

Chieko sees my expression, and says, "I love a good *nattō*."

"I don't know you well, but I have a feeling we're going to get along," Noriko says. She lifts up a fist, and they fist-bump each other.

We cross Bancroft Way and enter the campus by passing under the massive Shimonoseki Gate. It's an arcade of fifty-six crimson *toriis* with the names of famous generals printed on them. Families of students are visiting, taking photos, some indicating to their younger children that attending here is what they should aspire to.

"The biggest decision you need to make is which 'circle' to rush for," Noriko says, as soon as we pass the gates. There are tables full of cadets, recruiting people to different circles divided by interest. These include regional groups, film lovers, sports clubs, portical-games hobbyists, and a popular book club called GACCOH, which is based out of Kyoto but has spread throughout the Empire. "It shouldn't be too hard for you to choose, since as mecha cadets, you're automatically given entry into the most prestigious circle at BEMA."

"What's that?"

"The Tadakatsu Circle," she says, and I assume it's named after the famous samurai under Ieyasu. Nori points to her badge of twelve long spears crossing one another. "One of the first things you'll both have to do is take a sim competition. That'll determine which group you fall in and whether you get to fight in the official tournaments or not."

"I thought the sim competition was only for sophomores?" Chieko asks.

"They changed it last year, so it starts with freshmen," Noriko explains. "If you get through the first couple of rounds at Emeryville Stadium, you'll duel it out on actual mechas."

"I saw you fighting on my portical last year," I recall.

"They broadcast the final rounds of the competition," she confirms.

"You won, right?"

Noriko nods. "It was tough, though. Lots of amazing competitors. A couple mistimed swings and it could have gone the other way."

I congratulate her and marvel at how good she must have been to defeat the other cadets.

"How many students are here in total?" Chieko asks.

"The freshmen class for the military academy is about six hundred to seven hundred new students per year, and only thirty-two of those are accepted for the mecha course. That equates to about three thousand military cadets. The civilian side of BEMA has almost twice that every year."

"What's the civilian side?"

"Diplomatic corps, engineering, international affairs, anything that doesn't fall strictly under military supervision but is connected to governmental work. So that's about nine thousand students total at BEMA when we're in full session. There are also support staff, administration, international exchange students, and researchers. I think the researchers outnumber cadets."

"What are they researching?"

She points to a building made entirely of glass, but the windows are tinted so we can't see inside. "That's biological studies, and I've heard they experiment on animals in there. Lot of the mecha testing and research is south of here in Emeryville. You'll spend more time there after your mecha training classes officially begin. You'll also get more practice this year than normal since most of the senior class is away for official field training."

"Where's their field training?" Chieko wonders.

"Mainly the Quiet Border and East Moscow," Noriko replies.

Chieko is surprised. "East Moscow? That's dangerous for cadets, isn't it?"

"Things are tense, but they get good experience on the Nihonzarus mechas." Those are our special winter-class mechas, built specifically for Russian terrain and weather. "I've read the specs, and piloting them is a completely different experience because they move so fast through the snow, kind of like snow monkeys. The winter is a nightmare. Your spit will freeze before it hits the ground. The—" Her portical rings. She checks her display screen, and says, "I got to take this," before stepping away.

Chieko asks me, "You doing okay?"

"Yeah, I'm 'okay,'" I reply as it's such a relative term. "How are you?"

"I'm managing." She grabs her arm and her eyes drift to another place. "Sometimes, I wake up and forget it all happened. And then it hits me again that it did and . . . I . . . I actually didn't travel as much as I wanted to. Every time I started enjoying it, I thought of the others . . ."

"I kept on moving so I wouldn't have to think about what happened," I confess. It worked only half the time.

"I heard you helped make this"—pointing to BEMA—"happen. It was one helluva surprise. I thought they'd made a mistake and asked them to confirm they got my name right."

"They wouldn't have accepted you if you didn't earn it," I tell her.

"Thank you."

"Don't thank me. You're an amazing pilot."

"I wish Wren were here."

"I wish all of them were."

Noriko returns and appears disconcerted. We ask her if everything is "okay" and she explains, "Things have been so tense since that attack outside Dallas Tokai. The Nazis are rounding up any of their citizens with family ties to the USJ and detaining them for questioning. A lot of them have just disappeared."

"You have family in Germany?"

"My aunt works at the South African embassy, and we haven't heard from her in three weeks. My mom is trying to find out where she is." Noriko straightens her uniform, wanting to change the topic. "Let me show you the cat garden."

"What's that?"

We find out five minutes later. It's a garden filled with cat statues. A massive monument of one licking its paw is the centerpiece. There are hundreds of cats wandering the grounds, mostly indifferent to our presence, although a few make friendly overtures to Noriko. "It's a celebration of cats by K. Yi," Noriko says, petting the striped one that sidles next to her.

There's a cat mecha statue built in Takaoka that looks both deadly and absurdly cute.

"Would you drive that if it were real?" I ask the two.

"Depends on the arsenal and armor," Noriko replies.

Chieko answers, "I'm more of a dog person."

"I read somewhere they were doing tests with cat and dog minds to drive simulated mechas, but they couldn't get them to work," Noriko says. "The problem was they were simulating bipedal mechas. Soon as they switched them to quadruped mechas, they were even better than human pilots." Noriko lifts one of the cats and says, "It'd be fun if this were my copilot."

We both laugh and move away from the garden. Noriko points out various buildings and recounts some of the urban legends behind them, stories of famous officers in the USJ and the feats they accomplished when they attended. The air is fresh and smells of trees like the London planes, coast redwoods, and copper beeches that are all over campus.

We climb the steps in front of the big campanile at the middle of campus. They've built three neighboring columns, which help support the enormous cannon underneath the big clock. I look in the direction the cannon points and see the university and the bay beyond. It's a spectacular view, and I still can't believe I'm here as a student. It's always been my dream. But after I got rejected that second time, I thought I'd never get the chance.

"Nice view, isn't it?" Noriko asks me.

"Unbelievable."

She points out several important buildings, like the Masuyo Yoshida Pavilion, named after the famous officer who liberated many of the Japanese-American prison camps.

"Berkeley's one of the best cities in the world. You're both going to have a great time here," Noriko tells us. "The other cadets have been asking about you two."

"Have they?"

"You survived the German biomech, saved the life of two mecha officers, and defeated the American terrorists in the Quiet Border. That's tough business."

Chieko and I shuffle awkwardly at the praise. Noriko doesn't press us for details.

Instead, she asks, "What are you two doing for dinner? They have a new place that imports soy sauce from Shodo-shima, and they have the *best* soy sauce ice cream. Put it on your waffle and you're set. C'mon, my treat."

THE DINNER IS WONDERFUL. I STUFF MYSELF AND GET BACK TO MY ROOM thirty minutes before lights out. The bed seems very welcoming, so I take off my uniform and lie down. I think about Griselda. I've tried calling her several times, but haven't been able to get any messages through. The political situation with the Nazis has gotten markedly worse since the incident at the Quiet Border, and I'm not surprised that my communications haven't reached her.

I want to tell her about all that's happened, how I have finally achieved my dream. I want to tell her that I'm *here*, really here at BEMA.

What gnaws at me is that instead of joy, there's a gaping hollow that's tearing me up inside. I can't separate the idea that all those who passed away paid the price so I could get this opportunity. That's too high a cost just so I could get a chance to pilot mechas. I play the logic game with myself, tell myself, *You're here to avenge them.* Then another part asks, *How are you going to get revenge?* Attack the NARA again? But I already got the FDR. Find the bio-mech who did this? Don't be ridiculous and dishonor their memories by trying to play "hero" when you're anything but.

Guilt and anger always start out specific before spreading like a voracious contagion through every part of me.

I move my additional pillow from my left flank to the right one. I think about mecha piloting minutiae, rearrange the schematics I studied during my break to come up with new designs. It usually helps me sleep. But not always. In my recent travels, I met veterans who alleviated their woes with games, alcohol, and companionship. While I understood them, I'm conflicted about trying to dull the pain like that. What I'm suffering doesn't compare to those who died. I juggle random accusations at myself, wrestle pointlessly with a remorse that never abates, and eventually nod off to the hum of exhausted self-loathing.

THIS YEAR'S FRESHMEN CLASS HAS A TOTAL OF 698 STUDENTS FROM all the various disciplines. We're in the Satoshi Ide Hall, named after the famous admiral from the class of 1961 who defeated a fleet of Nazi Super U-boats off Argentina.

Superintendent Tobo, who's been in charge of BEMA for the past eight years, gives us a gift from the Emperor. It is two books with specially embroidered covers. The first is by the military strategist Yamaga Soko, while the other is by Miyake Kanran, who cofounded the Mito school of nationalist learning. It has the Emperor's personal seal on the cover. We receive them with two hands, bowing as though we were receiving a gift directly from the Emperor.

"The Empire relies on your courage, bravery, and ability to defend against its enemies, both external and internal," Tobo-san proclaims. "We face graver threats than we've ever seen. There's a reason you were chosen to be here above everyone else, and that's because—"

I can see the excitement in the other first-year students. They're stirred by her speech, as I should be. I'd like to think it's all about glory, even courage, and lots of training. But I know luck plays a bigger role than anyone would like to admit.

As the superintendent evokes memories of the American's last stand in Canada during the Great Pacific War, she reminds us how the early mechas were mainly statues symbolic of the Emperor. It was the terrified Americans and Canadians who believed they were actually walking giants and spread stories of that nature that convinced the IJA to develop them further. The engineer I studied about while I was a RAM, Hiroshi Boshiro, would see his "gyration stabilizer" put to good use as the victory over the Americans quickly led to a precarious situation with the Nazis. The Germans felt they deserved more territory in the Americas for defeating the "bigger American force" on the East Coast. No way were we going to give them anything, and the second generation of mechas were there to ensure it. They were still limited, requiring vast collections of energy and infantry to defend them. It would be a continual headache until the development of the Bradlium Particle Generator (BPG), using minerals harvested from meteors and, later, asteroids, which would change the situation.

I'm recollecting the intricacies of mecha politics when I realize the speech is over and the superintendent is personally shaking all our hands, welcoming us to BEMA.

Her hand is surprisingly cold. I expect her to pass by without a word, but she says, "I've heard much about your feats on the Quiet Border. I hope you will impart your experiences to the other cadets."

I'm stunned she knows who I am. "Thank you, ma'am," I mutter.

She nods and moves to the next student. She only says, "Welcome," to the others. I know it's shallow, but, at least momentarily, I beam.

THAT JOY QUICKLY EVAPORATES WHEN I GET OUTSIDE THE HALL AND SEE the Tokko agent who interrogated me after Hideki's death, Akiko Tsukino. She waves me over, and I bow to her, wondering what I've done so wrong that she would personally come to BEMA. I get nervous seeing that her expression is ominously blank. It's obvious she's not here to congratulate me. We walk to an adjacent corridor. Curiously, someone is playing on a portical behind her, though she seems indifferent to his presence.

"You've spent the past few months traveling," she says with an authority indicating she knows everything I've done.

"Yes, ma'am."

"How was Keijo?" she asks.

"It was—it was good," I reply, remembering my time in Korea. "There was a protest going on against the governor. She's been swayed by some strange cult figure, but I couldn't figure it all out because it was too confusing."

"Gods and goddesses are excuses for defective ideologies. The Emperor is generous in allowing the regional deities to enter the Shinto pantheon. But there are too many traitors who exploit that generosity and use it to kindle treason."

"That's unfortunate. Keijo is a beautiful city. I wish I could have seen it without all the protests."

"Did you know in the Korean language, Keijo is called Kyongsong, and the original name for the city was Seoul, before they joined the Empire in 1910?"

"I didn't. We never spoke in the local dialect."

"How many languages can you speak?" she asks.

"English and Japanese." I wonder how many she can speak.

"No German?"

"No German, ma'am," I answer.

"You have German friends, though. One you've tried calling on multiple occasions."

"You mean Griselda?" I ask. Agent Tsukino remains silent. "She's been my friend since high school."

"I know." She looks at me. "You've done well for yourself. Entry to BEMA as a mecha cadet is only for the elite."

"Th-thank you, ma'am."

"Don't risk your career for a friendship with a Nazi," she warns me.

"She's not a Nazi," I instinctively reply. "Or she is, but she's different. She didn't have a choice about joining the party."

"Everyone has a choice. I've heard your conversations with her. Mostly vacuous, but if there was even the slightest suspicion regarding your intentions, you'd have lost everything you fought for."

"I would never help the Nazis."

"Desire has a way of clouding judgment," Agent Tsukino replies.

"I haven't spoken to Griselda in months."

"Better to keep it that way instead of repeatedly trying to call her. Her situation may be more complicated than you realize."

"What do you mean by that?" I ask, alarmed that something has happened.

"I mean all the citizens in the German Americas are in a precarious situation with the recent state of affairs," she says, making her statement more general in nature. "Don't make it worse for her."

"Did you come all the way here to warn me about that?"

Her eyes are grim. "I thought I'd check in on you. I also want to introduce you to a fellow cadet who's starting this year."

The last part catches me off guard. Who would she want to introduce me to?

She gestures to the student behind her, who is absorbed in his portical. He looks like a kid and has long black hair covering his face.

"Kujira," she says. "Say hi."

Kujira? Like the famous pilot?

He doesn't look up, sucked into his game.

"Kujira!" Agent Tsukino snaps. "Kujira!"

He finally comes over.

"Maybe you can show him around," she suggests to me. "Say hi, Kujira."

He raises his hand for a second before getting back to his game.

His rudeness, paired with the agent's warning, annoys me.

"I'm still familiarizing myself with Berkeley," I reply, wanting to politely decline.

Either she doesn't catch the hint, or she ignores it. "You can do it together. He'll be your dorm neighbor."

So that's who the empty room is for.

"What's with his name?" I ask.

"You got a problem with my name?" he looks up and asks.

"Kujira is the greatest mecha pilot in our history," I say to him.

"Second greatest," he corrects me.

"Who's the first?"

"Me."

I laugh at his preposterous confidence.

"Your delusion makes you think you have the right to use her name?" I demand, irked by the fact that he seems serious about his claim.

He pulls aside his hair, and, for a second, I see a scar across his forehead before it's covered back up. "I didn't realize her name was your property."

He leaves the corridor with his portical game.

Agent Akiko Tsukino explains to me, "Kujira was his mother. The name passed on."

It takes me a second to fully grasp what she just said. "I didn't know she had a son."

"He's one of the best pilots I've seen."

"But he's—he's my age."

"He's piloted mechas his entire life," she explains. "The problem is, he's better driving one of those big robots than he is dealing with people. Even if he won't admit it, he needs friends."

I don't know if it's proper for me to ask, but I have to know. "How are you involved?"

I expect her to snap back that it's none of my business. But instead she says, "He saved my life once."

"A few minutes ago, you were warning me against being friends with a German. And now you're asking me to become friends with Kujira? You sure you trust my taste in friendships?"

"Who we choose to befriend symbolizes the strange dichotomy of our world. We're all snails living on the razor's edge. Good day, Makoto Fujimoto."

She leaves the corridor. I follow a minute later to ask her another question, but she's nowhere in sight.

THE PORTICAL LISTS OUR DAILY SCHEDULE. EVERY MONDAY TO FRIDAY, we have classes from eight to five, with a break from noon to twelve fifty for lunch. Most of our classes are fifty minutes, giving us ten minutes to get to our next class. The *kenjutsu* class (the study of art of swordsmanship) is ninety minutes every weekday and is our final session before breaking for the evening. On Saturdays, the *kenjutsu* class is three hours and we can also take two electives of our choice. We can switch electives up every month so I'll probably check out *gagaku* (music) and *kagaku* (Japanese poetry). Sundays are marked as our day off and will be consumed by homework. Lights out at ten. As this itinerary is for first-year students, I will share most of my classes with Chieko and Kujira.

First class of the day is Battle Theory. Professor Onodera, who served in Afghanistan during one of our proxy wars, teaches the class. He doesn't bother with introductions and dives into the lessons. "Courage, coupled with stupidity, is worse than foolhardiness. We are the best army in the world not because of our bravery but because we couple courage with intelligence. The IJA can trace its philosophical roots to a Prussian officer, Major Jakob Meckel. He was an idiot and nearly destroyed the IJA with his idiocy. He believed tactics weren't as important as *élan*. His theories did help us in the short run. But, as we found out in the Nomonhan Incident, all the spirit in the world didn't help us against the Soviets in 1939. It was a catastrophic defeat. What's worse is that so many of those who died did so because of a stupid regulation that first aid couldn't be applied to fellow soldiers without direct orders from an officer. Countless soldiers needlessly hemorrhaged to death. Because of our defeat there, our forces were very reluctant to engage them when the Germans asked for our aid against the Soviets during Operation Barbarossa. If the Germans hadn't taken Moscow, we most likely would have driven into Southeast Asia. Who knows how the war would have gone if we'd taken that course.

"We had to adapt," Professor Onodera continues. "The mecha didn't become a focal part of our forces until after the Great Pacific War, so all the courage in the world was useless when our forces rushed like fools into streams of gunfire, believing their 'spirit' could save them. Fifty cowardly soldiers who are trained to point and fire a rifle are worth more than three hundred brave soldiers without guns. Army staff issued a directive after our defeat in Nomonhan, ordering research for a supertank to be used on the Manchurian Plains. They built a hundred-ton prototype, but the technology couldn't support the weight. So they went back to relying on 'spirit' again.

"The key to battle is to dispel your illusions about what helps win wars. Spirit counts. But logistics, which many would consider boring, are the key. Your ability to understand how technology changes the political landscape is vital as well. In 1888, the Army Inspector of the time, General Yamagata, understood Asia would become the focus of the western forces. Do you know how he knew that?" He looks at all of us rhetorically, expecting no one to know. No one does except Chieko, who raises her hand.

The professor points at her. Chieko stands, and answers, "General Yamagata was referring to the construction of the Panama Canal, the Canadian-Pacific Railroad, and the Trans-Siberian Railway."

"So not every one of you in here is an idiot. Those three monumental efforts meant access to Asia would become easier than it ever had been. Do you know what the national disease during the Meiji Period was and its relationship to the rations that were provided?"

"Beriberi was the national disease," Chieko replies. "The imperial doctors introduced a rice mixed with barley to reduce beriberi rates among soldiers, but the perception was that mixed rice was prison food, so it was not utilized as much as it should have been."

"Very good. And very dumb of them. Do you also know why our officers decided to change uniforms from white trousers to khaki ones?"

"During the Boxer Rebellion, all the blood staining our soldier's uniforms lowered morale. Bloodstains on khaki aren't as visible," Chieko replies.

I had no idea about any of this. It's fascinating to realize how integral our food menu is to our health, as well as the psychological effect even the color of a uniform can have on a soldier. Seems obvious when pointed out to us, but battle theory is much more practical than I'd anticipated. I feel like I'm back in high school again, generally ignorant about pretty much everything.

"You will meet some of our scholars who will attempt to assuage, even reduce the reported number of casualties during war. It's not because they believe it. It's because they want to camouflage the horrors of war with the mental equivalent of khaki uniforms. But make no mistake. War is horrible. Many civilians are killed. Soldiers, who in peacetime would be afraid to kill a fly, will butcher unarmed people. The better you understand that, the better officer and soldier you'll be. There is a human cost, a psychological toll, and those who try to mask that are worse than cowards. They're liars."

As he continues, I think again about the Quiet Border. I look over at Chieko. She too has a pained expression on her face. Is she also thinking about the battle? She spots me looking at her, and I realize she must see her emotions reflected in me because there's a calm that washes over her. We both take solace knowing we survived together.

JAPANESE LITERATURE AND RHETORIC IS MOSTLY A READING CLASS. WE get assigned the works of classic authors like Shirow, Kishiro, Fujii, Mishima, Gunpei, Anno, Miyazaki, and others. "Get your head out of the portical games and read more," are the professor's first words, which sums up our entire class. The cadets get excited when they hear one of the authors who's also a professor, Kojima, might visit to give a talk. He is clearly a class favorite as his works are so compelling, mixing war drama and interesting characters with existential questions about reality in epics that have become very popular throughout the Empire.

Right before lunch, we have physical-training exercises. We have a martinet for an instructor who yells so loud, I think he hurts his own ears. Fortunately, his routines are only an hour long, which is nothing compared to what we had to do as RAMs. Math (my worst subject), calligraphy (my handwriting has always been sloppy at best), military history (I get all the names mixed up and can't tell which officer did what), and chemistry (my second worst subject and a class where I space out the moment the professor begins to speak science jargon) follow.

Promising first day.

Right before our last class, Noriko catches up with the two of us. "How you both doing?"

"Tired," I reply.

"Exhilarated," Chieko answers at the same time.

Noriko laughs at our contrasting responses. "What's next?"

"*Kenjutsu.*"

"It's probably one of the most important classes you'll take," Noriko tells us. "You'll learn all the fundamentals of sword art, which'll be key for you as mecha pilots. There isn't a better instructor anywhere in the Empire than Professor Sugiyama. She used to be an imperial *mekiki.*"

Mekikis are experts at judging swords, but many are also the top blade fighters in the world. To be an imperial *mekiki* is an extraordinary honor.

I keep Noriko's words in mind when we enter the dojo-styled classroom. Professor Sugiyama is a middle-aged woman with blond hair and is 180 centimeters tall. Her eyes are covered by a white bandanna with the red rising sun in the middle. She is holding a *bokutou,* though her wooden sword looks more robust than the ones I've normally seen.

"You all want to be mecha pilots," the professor says. "But do any of you know how to fight without a robot? If not, you have no business in a mecha. In my class, you'll learn all the different *ryus,* from the *Koto-eiri* school of swordsmanship, to *Aisaka, Shinto, Shinkage,* and *Nen.* Your katana will be an extension of your will, and you will learn how wielding a sword is much like wielding a mecha. If you become one with it, you will be invincible. The Western countries lived by the sword until they met the Empire, where they quickly learned that no one can outclass a samurai with a sword. Rather than soporific introductions that don't mean anything, I will learn who all of you are by the way you fight. I want everyone to grab a *bokutou* and attack me. There is no shame in defeat, and you will be defeated. It's how you fight that interests me. Who wants to go first?"

The first ten students are defeated immediately, the *bokutou* flying out of their hands. It's Chieko's turn. She moves in slowly. I notice Sugiyama does not attack. Chieko's posture is impeccably poised yet loose and serene. There isn't any tension in her, the way I sense in the students who want to attack. Sugiyama just waits, listening to the footsteps of her opponents, gauging their breath, and maybe even being able to extract their state of mind from their agitated motion. Chieko takes her time attacking. When she does, her blow is quick and powerful. But Sugiyama anticipates this and parries the attack easily, about to sweep her off her feet. Chieko was hoping for this and grips the professor by her right arm, getting in close for another attack. It's a wrestler's feint. Just as she's about to flip her, the professor sidesteps Chieko entirely, knocking her back with the *bokutou* and causing her to stumble. Chieko loses, but it's the first time we see the professor nod approvingly. "Interesting," she notes.

The remaining students fall much faster. It's finally my turn. I hold my wooden sword, but knowing she won't attack, I remain still. I even try to hold my breath, but that lasts only a minute before I'm gasping for air. I take a lot more breaths before she takes a step forward. I take a corresponding step back. She takes another step, I repeat my step back, wanting to keep my distance. We continue this stepping game until I've moved her around so that her back is against the wall. This is her contest, her rules, her plan, so I have to mix it up a little to stand a chance. Last time I did this in practice was with Sensei almost a year ago, and she had me on my back. Not this time. Sugiyama will most likely expect me to attack right now. I begin to sprint, but not toward her. Rather adjacent to her. She moves in, and as she does, I strike. She blocks, and I know she's going to try to do a counterattack with a turn or a slicing attack, using an evasive turn on her knee. But before she does, I withdraw again. Let her think I'm scared or supercautious. I do this two more times. On the third, I pretend to withdraw. She overcompensates by stepping in closer. I do a spin around her and her back is vulnerable to my attack. I swing down, but as I do, her back foot catches my neck and knocks me against the wall. She turns around, wooden sword about to hit me in the neck. I duck, and the *bokutou* hits the wall. I strike her leg, and just as I'm about to swing again, she kicks me hard in the head.

When I wake up, my head is in a daze.

"How many fingers do you see?" Professor Sugiyama asks.

I look up and reply, "Three."

She nods. "I'm impressed. No student has ever hit me on their first try."

"It didn't do much good. You still gave me a whooping." I look around, but the dojo is empty. "Where is everyone?"

"Class ended thirty minutes ago."

"I was out the whole time?"

She nods and lifts up an unsheathed katana. "There are several schools of thought when it comes to the forging of swords," she says. "Some believe in the *sam-mai*, a 'three-plate style' where you wedge a plate of steel between two iron plates with steel along the edges. It's adulterated, but cheaper and quicker to create. The more pure form would be the *tsukuri* style, which only uses pure steel."

"Which do you prefer?" I ask.

"*Tsukuri*, of course. You are steel, Makoto, even when you pretend not to be."

She puts on her sandals and leaves.

THEY DON'T TAKE ROLL CALL, AND I HAVEN'T SEEN KUJIRA THE WHOLE day. It's possible he has a completely different schedule from mine, but I still stop by his dorm room before dinner. I knock, but there's no answer. I hear some noises from within, though. The door isn't locked so I enter. He's in his room, playing portical games.

"Hi, Kujira," I say. "You feeling sick?"

He doesn't answer. I don't know if he even heard me.

I want to see what kind of game he's playing. Is it a new type of simulation or strategy game? I can understand being addicted to a compelling narrative, wanting to know what happens to the characters. Or maybe it's some type of new mecha simulation? I missed quite a few classes in high school doing the same.

I peek at his portical screen and am disappointed to see a bunch of brightly colored hexagons. *Rokkakkei* is one of those mindless games that requires you to match hues in combos that cause layers to vanish. That results in more crystalloid hexagons appearing, forming an even more labyrinthine maze. This is all against the backdrop of cheesy music and cute pets cheering players on.

"You can't be serious," I say to him. "This is what you've been playing this whole time?"

He hits pause. "Why are you here?"

"Did you go to class today?"

"What's it to you?"

"I just wanted to make sure you were 'okay.'" There's that word again. Odd how often it comes up throughout the day. Why are so many of us so concerned with being "okay"?

"I saw the class list, and they all looked boring," Kujira informs me. "So I decided not to go."

It's not the answer I was expecting, mainly because tedium is the last reaction I'd thought anyone would feel on the first day of class.

When I think about it, it pisses me off.

"So you're too good for BEMA?" I ask him.

"Absolutely. I don't want to be here. It's a waste of my time. Sooner I'm done here, happier I'll be."

"What's with the hostility?"

"Did I touch a nerve? So sorry, *sir*. Would you like an apology? *Sumimasen*," he says in a mocking tone.

"You don't have to give me an attitude."

"You already got your congratulations from the superintendent. What more do you want?"

"If you're so unhappy here, why don't you quit?"

"I tried. But Akiko insists I give it a try. Says I can learn a thing or two 'bout piloting here. Doubt it. But she has a way of being very persuasive. Any other questions? I'm busy."

He's back at his game again.

AT DINNER, I'M MORE ANNOYED THAN I SHOULD BE. NORIKO AND CHIEKO have grabbed bento boxes. I poke at my *ika* and *kani* rolls. There's some type of Spanish casserole they've included that smells good. But I've lost my appetite.

"The worst sushi in the main island is still better than the best ones in the USJ," Noriko says.

"Sushi snob," Chieko replies to her.

"I'm not a snob if it's true. It doesn't take a connoisseur to appreciate good sushi."

"What do you think?" Chieko asks me.

"Food is food," I mutter, indifferent to the debate.

But seeing the raw fish makes me feel ill. I don't want to seem thin-skinned, but I can't stand the sight of uncooked flesh and the way it reminds me of a person with their skin peeled away.

"What's wrong with you?"

I complain to them about Kujira.

Noriko laughs at me. "You'll get a chance to show him up in three weeks."

"You mean the mecha competition?"

"Yep. That's how the instructors will know your skill level."

"What it's like?"

"It's tournament style and runs the whole week, depending on how long you last. The top group in the Tadakatsus are the Five Tigers. I'm second of five. We've lost three members because they were in the senior class. That means we'll be recruiting the top three cadets from next week's tournament. I expect both of you to make it. And I'm sure you'll meet Kujira on the way there. Teach him some humility," Noriko says. "If either of you wins, you'll face me."

From that moment on, all I think about is the competition.

I can't deny a part of it is a desire to fight against Kujira, the son of the legendary mecha pilot. But I know most legends don't live up to the rep. It's primarily a desire to redeem myself. Last time I was part of a test, it was back in high school, and I failed miserably. I won't let that happen again. I have way more experience than almost anyone here. I have to dominate to honor those who passed away and show that their sacrifice had meaning.

10

★ ★ ★

THE FIRST THREE WEEKS OF CLASS ARE INFORMATIVE, AND MY FAVORITE by far is *kenjutsu*. I enjoy learning all the different stances. The techniques are split up into *kiri* (cutting) and *tsuki* (thrusting), used in conjunction with defensive moves, of which there are countless varieties. Professor Sugiyama emphasizes the importance of *iatjutsu*, the moment when you first draw your sword.

We practice the *iaijutsu* by squatting with our *bokutou* sheathed. She rings a bell, which is our cue to draw. I stand, attack, put the sword back into the sheath, and squat back down. We do this a hundred times a day, which causes my thighs to feel like bricks.

It's not so much the act itself, she tells us. Rather precipitating the strike, choosing the right moment and position from which to launch.

"Most duels are over before they begin," Professor Sugiyama pounds into us. "Even with the most skilled sword wielders, you have to know what they're going to do. If you can anticipate that, you'll most definitely catch them off guard. All it takes is a short lapse to be defeated. There is no second place in a fight to the death."

I absorb her lessons, considering how best to incorporate them into our battles.

"Styles have evolved since the end of the war," she informs us. "What I teach is different from what you'd learn in Tokyo, Los Angeles, or even at a local dojo. There is no single right way. It's not a method to be repeated like a factory line. *Kenjutsu* is an art you develop for the duration of your life."

As we learn the fundamentals, I notice the subtle way the sword stops being a weapon external to myself, and more, an extension of my arm. The parts about the importance of breathing and mental balance are harder to grasp when I think about them but come as a by-product of practice.

The Sunday before the tournament swings around, most of our floor goes on a field trip north to Davis. I opt to stay and practice in the dojo after our morning run. Noriko and Chieko join me. We spar the whole day with our *bokutou*.

"Is there anything you can tell us about the simulation?" I ask Noriko.

She shakes her head. "The instructions are intentionally kept vague so that everyone can start at the same level. They'll go over the instructions with you tomorrow, and you can practice before the battle begins."

Noriko shows us some of the more advanced *kenjutsu* moves, the main one being a whiplike motion with the sword called the *kisagake*. "If you master this move, you can channel it into sixteen different cuts." Just as she starts showing us one of the defensive parries, she receives a call and leaves the dojo.

Chieko grins at me. "Didn't realize you were so competitive."

I explain to her about my first test and how Noriko helped me. "I don't want to screw up like last time."

"It's just a test," Chieko reminds me. "It doesn't matter how you do. You're not less of a mecha pilot if you lose."

"It doesn't make me less of a mecha pilot if I win."

"'Once you resort to violence, both sides lose.'"

I grin. "Spare me that Zen crap. Those monks never had to see anyone close to them get killed."

"That wasn't a monk who said it. It was Wren." She raises her *bokutou* to me.

I'm embarrassed by my presumption. "Are you challenging me?" I ask her.

"Isn't it obvious?"

As soon as I raise my *bokutou*, she charges. Her attack is furious, and it takes all my strength just to block her as there is anger in every blow. The unrelenting strikes result in my own sword's being knocked out of my hand and me stumbling to the ground. She places her *bokutou* against my neck. "Do you yield?"

"I yield."

Chieko gives me a hand up. "You won't win as long as I'm in your way."

I laugh. "Like I said, I yield. I'd be glad to lose to you as long as it's not to Kujira."

"If he gets in my way, I'll destroy him." She runs her fingers along the side of the *bokutou*. "I don't fight for victory. I fight for the memory of all those we've lost."

Just as I'm about to tell her I feel the same, Noriko returns. She looks numb.

Before we can ask, she tells us, "The Nazis murdered my aunt." There's a mix of rage and sorrow in her eyes. "I—I have to leave. I'm flying to Los Angeles to see my parents."

"Is there anything we can do for you?"

She shakes her head. "Just do well this week." She turns around and exits.

We spend the rest of the evening practicing at full force, promising each other, "We'll take the number-one and -two spots for Noriko."

THE SUBWAY TO EMERYVILLE IS ONLY TWO STOPS AWAY FROM CAMPUS. We ride the Berkeley Army Rapid Transit (BART) to the Powell Street exit. Only authorized military personnel are permitted direct access to the Coliseum as all civilians have to go through one of the other exits. Our IDs get us through the gate, and when we take the escalator up, we're already inside the Coliseum.

There are thirty-two of us who will fight in the five-round tournament. The first three rounds will be in simulation. We'll actually suit up in a Gladiator-class mecha for the final round and championship. I'm relieved Chieko is on the opposite bracket from mine, so we'll face each other only at the championship. I'm disappointed to learn Kujira is in the other division. I have no doubt Chieko'll make quick work of him, though I had been hoping to do the honors.

The Coliseum has an indoor stadium with a retractable ceiling. Huge display screens are visible for anyone who wants to watch the simulation sequences. Thirty-two pods with the sim consoles are in the field. There's a small crowd, mostly professors and curious officers. I remember Noriko telling us that crowds will come out for the finals and championship at the end of the week, when we bust out the real mechas.

As official observer and judge, we have Misato Hirono, a former member of the Imperial Guard who retired from her position by the Emperor's side. She was invited to stay in Berkeley as a military consultant several years ago and oversees the matches as the official judge. She is in her ceremonial uniform with eighteen golden buttons, the crimson coat with golden lacing, waist sash, and a red shako. She also has on a cape marking her former membership in the honored Imperial Guard, as well as her specially embroidered sword, the *shin guntō,* and her sash, the *sennibari.* She greets us in an underground conference room, gives us a word of encouragement, and goes over the basic rules. Disable the enemy or fight until one side surrenders. As it's not likely anyone will surrender, it's a match until only one mecha remains standing. There's an optional tutorial we're encouraged to use once we acclimate ourselves to the simulation.

Our matches will start in an hour.

We're escorted to the field by eight officials. Before we get inside the spherical pods, we're required to wash our hands in ritual water and cleanse our mouths too, spitting into a ceremonial spittoon.

I put on the tactile suit, gloves, and goggles, which are akin to what I wore on the Crab. I enter the pod and adjust the seat to match my body. Once the belts are strapped, we do the calibration for my weight, depth of field, and strength, which is further divided into grip, speed, and flexibility. The controls are intuitive, different from the high-school test because it's much easier to move and isn't anywhere as heavy. Bipedal motion is also simpler to drive in contrast to controlling the multiple limbs on the quad mecha and Crab tank.

The one difficulty is that it's tight and damp inside, making it hard to breathe.

"Are you ready?" we're asked individually.

"Yes, sir," is my reply.

They're making it extra hot, and I recall reading somewhere that this is one of their initial tests. They want to know whether we can handle the duress of a tight space. If anyone has any trace of claustrophobia, they need to disqualify them now, before they've invested all the time and training only to find out they're unable to handle it.

I'm given the option of using my name or going with a nickname for the fights. I stick with Mac. My first-round opponent is someone named Jotaro.

We get the choice of any melee weapon, though no guns are allowed, as that would defeat the purpose of the matches. I pick the electric sword and, as my subweapon, the shorter *wakizashi* blade. I go through the tutorial, but it's very basic, intended for cadets who've never piloted a mecha. I run around the virtual stadium, practicing with my sword. The simulation movements correspond to my own, and the controls are similar to *Cat Odyssey*, even if the mecha is bipedal. It's easy to wield the sword, use it like I did in *kenjutsu* class, thanks to all that gaming practice before. Honestly, I struggle more with the heat than the program. My whole suit is getting wet from perspiration, and finger movement is awkward because my hands are moist. I want to open the door, but they're also checking how long we can endure. Situations like this won't be uncommon aboard a full-sized mecha. Even though they have climate control inside, those are the first systems to get cut if there's a power drain.

I'll be in the first round of fights. Judge Misato Hirono gives an opening speech to all attendees, but I'm too busy testing to pay attention.

My bell rings as soon as the speech finishes. A new visual feed begins, and I'm inside the same round stadium, only with my opponent on the other side. The Gladiator-class mechas are about a third the size of the military ones. They're usually heavily customized for individual fighters, many wearing trophies from past victories to distinguish themselves. But for the purposes of the tournament, they want the mechas to be equal, so all of them have the standard factory look of an enormous samurai. We are allowed to change the colors of our armor in simulation mode. I opt for a dark blue.

My opponent, Jotaro, has kept the default gray skinning. We bow to each other as is customary.

From the beginning, I almost feel bad for my opponent. Jotaro is grappling with the controls, struggling with movement, and actually falls to his knees twice while trying to stand straight from his bow. He has never done this before, or if he has, isn't familiar with the interface. I'm still careful just in case he's faking it and might suddenly ambush me. But the closer I get, the more I'm convinced that he really doesn't know what he's doing.

I don't want him to lose too much face, so that when we begin our fight, I take it easy on him. I remember the humiliation of losing and don't want it to sting for him as this performance will be one of the first impressions the other cadets have of him. But he makes it tough not to make it too obvious that I'm drawing out the match for his sake. He tries to hit me a few times, but he telegraphs his attacks, making them easy to dodge. I let him get one hit in, but then strike him from below and uppercut his jaw. A fist to his breastplate follows, causing Jotaro's mecha to flinch back. I unsheathe my electric sword, and in a move that I'm sure will make Professor Sugiyama proud, carry out an almost flawless execution of *iaijutsu*. I plunge the blade into my opponent's chest generator, which splits apart like glass, withdraw, and resheathe the sword.

The motion fluidly mimics what I've practiced the past week. I turn around and walk away. The mecha across from me blows up and crumbles to the ground. I turn back, surprised that it actually worked and that I also had the chance to imitate the cool poses from my favorite portical-game mecha pilots. When I emerge from the simulation console, I'm giddy. I'd like to say it was the victory, but it just feels nice to get out of the scorching pod.

I immediately get a summons from Judge Misato Hirono. I don't know what she's going to say, but I'm hopeful she will praise my finishing move.

I walk up to the royal box seats. She is surrounded by several military officials, all of whom are carefully watching the fights on the big portical display screens. Judge Hirono looks sternly at me, and barks, "Why did you take so long to defeat your opponent when you were clearly superior in skill?"

I'm surprised by her harsh tone. "I'm sorry, ma'am. I didn't want him to lose face."

"And in the process, made him lose even more face. Mercy in the battlefield endangers the lives of all your compatriots. Do you think the enemy cares about face?"

"N-no, ma'am."

"It was idiotic and small-minded of you. If you defeated him quickly, he would at least know he has much more to train. But by stretching it out like this, you've done everyone a disservice. You pull this kind of stunt again, and that will result in an automatic disqualification."

"Forgive me, ma'am."

I am dismissed.

I feel deflated. It's not the attention I was hoping to get from the Imperial Guard. It feels unfair that I'm being punished for wanting to give my opponent face.

Although I'm done for the day, I want to see how the other cadets do and find out who my next opponent will be. Plus, classes are on hold for all participating mecha cadets this week. I go to where most of the other students are seated.

Chieko is about to start her fight, and her mecha readies itself on the big screen. There are cameras of the pilots' faces as well as audio feed.

Her weapon of choice is the *manriki-gusari*, literally meaning the ten thousand power chain. She has the two ends of the chain wrapped around her wrists. Her adversary is wielding a spear and begins his attack with a forceful thrust. Chieko dodges the attack, then hurtles her chain around the pole of the spear. She tugs, snatching it out of his hand. Without stopping, she twirls the *manriki* around the other mecha's shoulder. She pulls the chain away, causing the entire shoulder pivot to detach and the arm to fall out. This in itself should ensure her victory, but she gets in close and puts the mecha into a choke hold. Her wrestling move leaves her adversary helpless.

I'd thought earlier no one would surrender. Her opponent does.

When she comes out of her pod, I rush down to the field and congratulate her. Chieko shrugs. "Nothing to it. You did a nice job out there too. That last strike was beautiful."

I appreciate her words, especially coming after the Imperial Guard's rebuke.

"Remember, number one and number two," she says.

IT'S INTERESTING TO SEE HOW OUR FIGHTING STYLES MATCH OUR PER-sonalities. In the two matches I've seen, Chieko gets in nice and personal before causing mass destruction. I like to experiment, try out new things, but overall stay conservative. My second opponent lasts a little longer than my first, but not by much.

I'm curious how Kujira fights. A part of me wonders if he'll even show up, and I'm relieved when I see him suited and ready. Like me, he chooses the electric sword. I hear a few in the audience question his name designation.

Kujira's fighting style is loose, unlike any of the other combat poses I've seen. His opponent, with the nickname of Pyrrhus, wears purple armor. He's swinging a huge club in front of himself erratically, trying to bash Kujira. What's odd is that through the audio hooked into their cockpits, Kujira's opponent is breathing hard, guttural gasps, spitting out with every swing. But on Kujira's side, it sounds like he's chewing on food. It's a very loud chewing as he savors each bite, making sure his tongue claps with his palate.

Pyrrhus is getting annoyed by the sound, and actually demands, "Stop eating."

But Kujira chews even louder. This infuriates Pyrrhus, who charges in to attack. Somehow, Kujira's mecha punches him in the face, twists around him, then plunges the electric sword into the orifice between his neck and his back, which he then sunders in half. Pyrrhus's mecha suffers a total collapse as the back plating is ripped apart.

Kujira emerges from the pod, eating a sausage. His opponent angrily accosts him, upset about the perceived disrespect. The guards have to separate the two. If this bothers Kujira, he doesn't show it. He finishes his sausage and takes out his portical. He plays what I assume is that hexagonal coloring game.

I guess he's feeling pretty confident.

THE CLIMATE CONTROL INSIDE THE POD WORKS IN THE THIRD ROUND, SO we don't have to fight the temperature as well as our enemies. Most of the matches last under a minute, similar to the actual sword fights samurai engaged in. The matches that last the longest are between those with very little experience, as both opponents struggle to control their mechas. The last match of the day is like that. Both cadets are having trouble piloting their mechas. Both start pummeling each other. It's a brutal clash, made worse because neither of them knows what they're doing.

I'd like to say my third-round match gave me more trouble than the first two. Lesa Gozen, named after the historical warrior, does walk comfortably and properly wields her *naginata*. She tries to use the length of the spear to keep me at a distance. Unfortunately for her, I'm too fast, and before she can pierce me, I've used my sword to lop off her arm at her elbow. She tries to block me with her other arm, but I plunge my shorter *wakizashi* blade into her mecha's visor, where her cockpit lies. I like the feel of the short sword because I can use it in tight spaces, really drive it in to cause maximum damage. As is standard function, the moment of impact in the helmet causes the cockpit to automatically drop into the stomach. I've anticipated this and use my sword to cut into her belly. Match over.

I think Chieko's opponent, Soda, is even less competent than her second-round enemy. He chooses a light pink for his mecha, his weapon is a halberd, and he starts by taunting Chieko with, "Prepare to get a spanking."

Chieko shows no reaction on the screen except for an amused twitch of her brow.

As soon as the bell rings, Soda tries to strike Chieko with an awkward twirl. Chieko brushes the halberd aside, bends low, and grabs Soda by the waist, taking them both down to the ground. She wraps her chain around his hips and squeezes. He's paralyzed, and she starts smashing his leg socket. After destroying it, she rapidly punches his gut, puncturing it and destroying the BPG. She then dismantles his helmet, smashes the arm sockets, and leaves Soda's digitized figure exposed to the world. He's like a dead puppet, completely beaten and flopping around. She stomps down on his face with her boot. The match ends in a total victory.

She says for everyone to hear, "Don't talk smack to me if you can't back it up."

THE PRELIMINARIES END WEDNESDAY AFTERNOON WITH THE TWO OF US advancing. Tomorrow will be the finals and combat in an actual mecha. I'll face off against a cadet named Honda. Chieko will battle Kujira.

I meet up with Chieko for dinner. Chieko also invites her friend, Ella, who's in the Information Welfare and Propaganda Division. She is a "mecha aficionado" and knows all the cadets.

"So exciting!" Ella exclaims. "I can't wait for tomorrow!"

"You're going to be there?"

"Everyone in Berkeley will be there," Ella says.

"Really?" I confirm with her. "It's just a tournament for first-year students."

"Exactly. We get to see you pilots in action before you become big hotshots. My treat tonight, to congratulate both of you for getting to the finals."

She takes us to an Indian restaurant. I order salmon tikka masala, Chieko gets goat curry, and Ella picks baby shark curry.

"You want chopsticks?" Ella asks me.

"Fork, please."

"Fork?"

"I don't like using chopsticks," I tell her. I've always found them a struggle to use since I was a kid. Other students find it a source of amusement since almost everyone in the Empire uses chopsticks and only foreigners prefer forks.

"And you're left-handed," Ella says when she sees me pick up the fork with my left hand.

"Does that mean anything?"

"Southpaws are harder for most orthodox fighters to match up against," she explains.

"I guess I need to practice simming against a leftie," Chieko says. "You were going to sneak that up on me?"

"Oh no. Sorry if I revealed a secret!" Ella exclaims.

I laugh, as does Chieko. "I still need to win," I state. "Do either of you know about Honda?"

Chieko shakes her head. Ella says, "From what I've heard, he grew up in the Philippines and is one heckuva pilot. He used to be an enlisted soldier who drove tanks in Asia. He served with Kazu."

"Who's Kazu?"

Ella seems shocked. "He's the best pilot in the junior class. He won the tournament two years ago and is captain of the Five Tigers."

"Never heard of him."

"You will. He was enlisted with Honda before he transferred here. He represented BEMA against Tokyo and was only the second fighter to beat one of their pilots. It was a big deal around here. I'll introduce you tomorrow. If you join Nori in the Five Tigers, he'll be your sempai. People will be expecting both of you to win your Tokyo matches this year too, so that'll make it three years in a row."

"We won last year too?" Chieko asks.

"Yep. Nori sealed the deal."

So Honda is friends with the cadet considered the best fighter here *and* he has field experience? That's good to know beforehand as the first three matches were relatively easy. I've only seen one of Honda's fights. It was a relatively straightforward battle, and nothing caught my attention. I'll watch the collected footage later tonight.

"If we get through tomorrow, we're guaranteed the number-one and number-two spots," Chieko says. "So don't blow it."

"I won't," I reply. "Have you heard from Nori?"

Chieko shakes her head. "You?"

"No."

Ella takes a bite of her food, and says, "Things are going bad for the Nazis in South Africa. The African Resistance is fierce, and they've already taken back key territories. The Nazis really freaked out after their big Rommel statue got obliterated. They think anyone who isn't one of their Aryan supermen is subhuman, so the string of defeats is a huge shock to them. Many in the USJ, including Nori and her parents, have been lobbying that we support them more."

"With armed forces?"

She nods. "We've been providing supplies where we can. So far, it's all unofficial, but that's why the Nazis have been 'accidentally' harming our embassy workers. It's despicable."

"It's our duty to rid the world of Nazis," Chieko says. "My paternal grandparents were from Czechoslovakia. They had to flee when the Nazis took over. They had distant cousins in Seattle before it became Taiko City, so they were able to emigrate here and start a new life. But most of our relatives were sent to death camps and never heard from again."

"I'm so sorry," Ella says.

"So am I," Chieko replies. "The Nazis took away my family, and then they worked with the NARA terrorists to kill my friends. I will do my best to destroy them."

The ferocity in her eyes is blazing, and I think about people like Griselda, who are against Nazi rule but are also hated by our side for growing up there.

Ella looks at me, and asks, "What's wrong?"

"My food smells like crap," I answer. "Literally."

That causes both of them to chuckle. "You want some of mine?"

"I'll get snacks later."

ELLA HEADS HOME, AND I GO BACK TO CHIEKO'S DORM. THERE, SHE turns on the display screen of her portical and puts up footage from the matches, focusing on Honda. Honda is a big guy with bushy eyebrows that are very animated as he fights. He moves around a lot, and his weapon of choice is a whip and dagger. I notice that he stays back for his fights, deflecting with a whip, then does a sudden charge move where he unleashes a flurry of blows using his dagger. I rewind so I can watch his rush attack.

"You're seeing what I'm seeing?" Chieko asks.

"What are you seeing?"

"He takes exactly four steps before his dagger starts flying," she says.

"Actually, I was just noticing how much his brows twitch right before he attacks."

"Well, that too."

I watch again, and she's right. There are exactly four steps.

"Since you know that, now you have no excuse to lose," Chieko tells me.

I nod gratefully.

"You going to be okay with Kujira?" I ask her as I'm about to leave.

Chieko acknowledges, "He's good. But I'll be fine. Just make sure you take care of Honda."

I WATCH HONDA'S FIGHTS AGAIN. IT'S CLEAR HE'S A MUCH BETTER fighter than my previous three combatants. Plus he has tank experience. I've got to assume that he's also watched my previous fights.

I get up, pace back and forth in my dorm room. Tomorrow will be the first time I get to pilot an actual bipedal mecha. I don't know how many people will be watching, but I think back to my childhood, playing with the mecha toys my father crafted for me and the *jimbaoris* I'd dress them in. I'm still angry that my adoptive father forced me to sell all those toys to a neighbor for only a few yen after I moved in with them.

Save that anger for tomorrow, I tell myself.

I have a hard time sleeping.

IN THE MORNING, CHIEKO ISN'T IN HER ROOM, SO I HEAD TO EMERYVILLE without her. There's a small café in the underground center where I eat a breakfast of garlic-flavored bacon, miso soup, and two rolls of cucumbers. The rolls don't taste very good so I replace that with a curry croissant baked specially by a pastry chef from Shizuoka. I check the time. My fight is at three, so I have a few hours to practice.

I ride up the escalator into the stadium and am stunned. There must be over twenty thousand people present. Where did they all come from? Are they here to see Chieko and me fight? There are only our two matches scheduled for the day, and they're not until later.

I spot a male cadet who resembles the portical footage I saw of Honda last night. He's stout, taller than me by a few centimeters, and has those bushy brows. He's holding a young girl in his arms who I assume to be his daughter. The woman next to him must be his wife and the small boy next to them, their son. They have their heads bowed in front of a shrine to the Emperor, and they're praying to him for his blessing. I overhear his wife saying, "We've struggled so hard to get this opportunity. Please help us in our struggle and help my husband be victorious against his opponent today."

Honda's son opens his eyes, looks around, and peeks at me. I stare at him and swear it's a reflection of me when I was younger. He smiles. I feel embarrassed because I'm the subject of their prayer and my objective is to defeat his father in combat today.

I'm ushered to the locker room by officials who get me into my gear, then to the Gladiator-class mecha. It looks exactly like my digital one, even down to the colors I selected. The crew checks the equipment and safety belt, making sure I feel comfortable in my seat. They run stress tests on my straps, confirm my helmet is secure and that I'm properly buffered in case of damage.

"Has anyone been seriously injured in one of these fights?" I ask.

"All the time," is the reply I get.

Wonderful.

They make me try out each of the controls. I'm surprised they feel almost identical to the simulation. They've matched the weight and movement so that a minute in, my brain can't distinguish between the two. Once the basic walk cycle is complete, they do a few more tests on the armor and my link to the cockpit. After diagnostics confirm everything is optimal, they give their approval for me to try it out on my own. I'm advised to monitor the gauges and make sure nothing gets out of sync.

The final four cadets will have the early part of the morning to test their mechas in partitioned pens adjacent to the main stadium. I get accustomed to using the electric sword, bandying it about in combat poses and making sure there isn't anything I'm not prepared for.

They've given us "dummies," big piles of metal we can attack to get used to striking with our weapons. The first time I hit one of the dummies, there's a jolt to my arm, and I feel the reverberations all along my body. That experience was partly mimicked in the simulation, but nothing as strong as this. I do it multiple times to get accustomed to it. As we're separated from one another, we can't see what the others are practicing, but the audience can through the cameras in each pen. At first, I'm self-conscious about doing something wrong in front of thousands of people. But after a few minutes, I forget they're even watching. Time passes quickly as I practice harder. We're ordered to come out and eat lunch at noon. I spot Chieko, and she looks pale.

"You sleep well?" I ask her.

She shakes her head. "That dinner gave me runs all night. My stomach still feels bad."

"You should drink green tea. It always helps me when I get stomachaches."

We find some and finish our lunch—light salads and a mixed fruit drink to provide energy. We're asked to use the restroom, as we won't get the chance to exit our mechas for the next few hours.

Once we're back in our suits, we're given a final chance to practice and go over the tutorials.

In the main stadium, they have BEMA's marching band of two hundred students doing an elaborate show. It's entertaining, as the groups weave in and out of complex human patterns that morph from animal to vehicle and back. Eighteen jet-packed cheerleaders fly through the air, making smoke trails and writing Japanese characters in the air. I wonder if more people are here for the band than for us.

A teenage girl from Berkeley High sings a beautiful rendition of the "Star Spangled Sun." Shinto priests spread salt on the earthen battleground, an act of ritual purification borrowed decades ago from sumo wrestling.

For the final round, they bring in an Italian referee—whenever they want the semblance of neutrality, someone is brought in from the *Regno d'Italia*. It's a formality because there's not much the referee normally does other than enforce boundaries and call the match when it looks like one side might actually be in physical danger. They do possess the ability to deactivate either mecha for any reason. The ref is a portly gentlemen with a curled mustache who bows to the four of us. He then runs into the yellow referee mecha that is about eight meters taller than our own. He carries out an inspection of the field and another examination of our mechas to make sure all is fair. Once he deems us ready, Honda and I are asked to move into separate waiting areas.

Chieko and Kujira are up for the first half of the finals.

Kujira chooses a *yari* spear, unlike the electric sword he chose in the first three rounds. Is this to fend off Chieko's style as she likes to get in close?

The bell rings, and the ref moves away from the center of the stadium. The crowds go wild, cheering loudly. Audience members pick sides, many chanting for Chieko.

From the beginning of the match, Kujira keeps a distance. Anytime Chieko tries to make a move, he wards her off. He tries to stab his spear her way, but she easily blocks, using her chains. She does try to wrest the spear away from him, but he counters with a twirl and a jab, using his subweapon, a type of *tantō*. The dagger unwinds the chain before it can fully grip. Just as she is about to recover, Kujira strikes. She has to step back, and he follows up with a spurt of thrusts so she is not able to get into her fighting comfort zone. It's not a big leap to assume he's aware of her tactics and that he's been keeping tabs on her fighting style. I'm surprised that he noticed anything beyond his portical game.

Chieko's trying to find an opening, and Kujira is focused on pushing her back. This continues for two minutes. Chieko's face betrays her frustration, and she snarls with every spear attack. Kujira is chewing on a sausage, casually using his controls while eating. His seeming apathy is infuriating. I want to go down into the stadium and slap the hot dog out of his mouth.

That's when I notice Chieko's mecha is getting pushed toward the south end of the stadium, her back nearly against the wall. There's almost nowhere for her to go. She tries to avoid being cornered, but anytime she does, Kujira attacks. His attack intensifies as he stabs faster. The spear thrusts increase. Chieko is able to defend herself because she's so good with the chain. But it appears like he's effectively wearing her down. Just when the match seems over, Chieko grabs the spear that's about to stab her in the neck.

She steps quickly forward and hurls the chain at Kujira's arm. It wraps around his mecha's elbow. She tugs hard, causing him to stumble forward. Chieko goes in for a killing move, wrapping her arms around his shoulders. The sudden motion causes Kujira's sausage to drop from his mouth.

The reversal causes the audience to cheer wildly. Chieko has the advantage.

But the joy is momentary, as Kujira turns around, back to the wall, and crashes against it. Chieko is pinned between the stadium and Kujira's back. Kujira takes out his *tantō* and thrusts it into her wrist. In the close proximity, she is unable to avoid the dagger, and we hear the blade slash the wires that connect the wrist to the forearm. This causes the mecha's fingers to go dead and she loses her grip on the chain. Chieko, weaponless, wraps her leg around his and tries to take them to the floor. Kujira almost falls. But he uses the pole end of his spear to strike Chieko's knee. The patella plating snaps off, exposing wires and circuitry. He slices them with his dagger. Just as he's about to go for the other leg, Chieko headbutts Kujira's mecha. Glasgow's kiss causes a huge crack in both their helmets. But the next attempt is blocked by an arm guard, and Kujira extracts himself with a forceful push. He stands above her, and Chieko is immobilized by the loss of her right leg. He points the spear at her neck, and asks, "Do you yield?"

"Never," Chieko replies.

He's about to stomp her face, but she raises her one good arm to catch his foot. She pushes, causing him to tumble back. She crawls toward the chain and hurtles it at Kujira's mecha. Kujira rolls out of the way and lifts himself up. Chieko starts pulling at her broken arm until it detaches, then uses it as a crutch to stand up.

Kujira stands in front of her, and Chieko is holding up her subweapon, the *wakizashi*. She'll fight him till their destruction makes the fight impossible. Kujira grins inside his cockpit. His mecha bows to hers. He then powers down his machine.

We hear the ref inquire, "What are you doing?"

"I'm out of sausages, and I'm starving," Kujira answers.

"Get back inside and finish the match."

"The match is done."

"If you leave now, you forfeit."

"Fine. Bye."

Out on the stadium floor, we all see the tiny figure of Kujira emerge from his mecha and run toward the stands in search of something to eat.

I MEET CHIEKO OUTSIDE HER LOCKER ROOM. I EXPECT HER TO BE DE-jected, but she's very upbeat. "Damn, that was fun," she says. "These bipedal mechas are a hundred times better to drive than the Crab tanks."

"You're not upset?"

"Why would I be? That was one helluva fight. Kujira has skills," Chieko states. "C'mon," she says, and leads me away from the locker.

We find Kujira next to a hot-dog stand, eating a turkey dog and drinking a Hokkaido Pearl Milk Tea. She raises up her fist. Kujira bumps it, but accidentally spills ketchup, relish, and mustard on himself.

"Good fight," she says.

"You almost got me into a Nelson hold."

"It would have been over for you if I had," Chieko replies.

"I could have reversed you."

"I don't think so."

"Do you know each other?" I ask them as I've never yet seen Kujira attend class.

Chieko shakes her head. "We just met out there. But I've never been in a fight like that. That was awesome."

"Yeah, that was fun," Kujira concedes.

"It's your turn to fight," Chieko reminds me.

"Who won?" I ask them, not sure since technically there was no victory.

Kujira shrugs. "Who cares?"

ALTHOUGH THE OFFICIAL HAD THREATENED KUJIRA WITH A FORFEITURE, Judge Misato Hirono rules in his favor, and he will proceed to the finals. It's up to me to meet him there.

Two officers are giving public commentary on our fight for audiences watching on porticals. I listen to them briefly but regret it when I hear them call Honda "the overwhelming favorite and the crowd's choice." There's a moment when the footage cuts to Honda's family, and they cheer him on. I presume the older couple talking for a bit on the display screen are his parents.

I am envious, wishing I had a family.

As I enter the stadium, I see the tens of thousands of people directly rather than through the portical display. Adrenaline rushes through me, and a smile involuntarily breaks out. I can't see anyone specific in the crowd, but it doesn't matter as I've never felt this much excitement. Although I hear a few people yell my name, the overwhelming majority are cheering for Honda.

I'm calmer than I expected to be. If this were the past, I would probably have been trembling. But I block it all out as I know this is for honor, not life and death. This'll be a different kind of fight as I'm piloting an actual mecha versus the simulation. Plus, this is someone with a whole lot more experience than the cadets in the previous rounds. I know he has the support of the crowd and his family on his side. He's fighting as much for them as he is for himself.

I wonder who I'm fighting for. The only people I can think of are dead.

We make our way to the center.

"Let's keep it clean," our ref tells us, and signals for us to bow to each other, which we do. "Fight!" the ref yells as the match starts.

"You should be wearing a helmet when you fight me," Honda says over the communicator.

"I am wearing a helmet," I say, noticing he's opted for the two daggers again.

"I mean a thicker one," he taunts me.

Honda uses his mecha to jump from side to side. He's quick, using his dexterity to hop about. It appears much faster with him in front of me rather than watching it on a screen. Suddenly, he charges, almost catching me off guard. He makes several quick jabs with his dagger, any of which could penetrate my armor. I'm able to block them, but if I'd hesitated even a second, the battle would have been over. I do see an opportunity to strike and lunge with my sword. He deftly avoids it by stepping to the side, then gets in a kick, knocking me back. I put both my arms up to block his flurry of attacks. He bounces away, his footwork better than any I've seen. He's sprightly, constantly in motion. I didn't realize a mecha could be so fast, as I've always thought of them as bulkier and tanklike. But it's clear that with the right pilot, they can move like a martial artist.

I think back to my training with Sensei and recall the defensive techniques she taught us. What can I use here? How to prepare a counterattack?

Before I can devise a plan, he accelerates at me with a speed that catches me off guard.

Criminy, he's fast.

He gets a blow into my shoulder, rupturing the wires. A second fist strikes me in the opposite shoulder. The rush attack is unceasing, and even when I block one attack, his other hand knocks me back. I lose my sword and can't seem to find a way out. A final blow hammers me in the chest, and I feel my mecha fall backward. I crash into the ground, and my spine takes a heavy jolt. I check the sensors. Legs and arms are still functional, but there is major damage to the chest. The red blips make it clear if I take any more hits there, the generator will give out, meaning no more power. The match will be over then. The crowd explodes in awe at Honda's move.

Because it appears I have been badly damaged, the ref pulls Honda back and sends a message to me.

"What is your condition?" he asks, and it's a public message that everyone can hear in the stadium.

But it's also a respite, and the seconds I'll gain are critical. I have to talk to buy myself some time before the battle continues. "I think I'm good. Checking the generator to make sure I can still go." A few seconds to pretend like I'm looking over power levels.

How do I deflect the rush attack? If he comes at me like that again, it's game over. I have to get to him before he gets to me. Should I attack? But I don't have my sword. I carefully think about his fighting style.

"Your generator power level is normal," the ref says. "Are you able to fight?"

"I'm able."

"You should stay down," Honda advises. "Get up again, and I'll hit you so hard, I'll knock you all the way back to Tokyo."

I clamber to my feet, annoyed by his trash talk. There is smoke coming from my chest. He's so much more experienced than anyone I've fought. Even the Javelins and NARA chimeras are no match.

Is this where the disparity in our backgrounds comes into play? He's probably received support and training his whole life. There's

no way my skill level would come close to his. But I promised Nori
a good fight. I've struggled too hard to come here and fail like this.

"Fight!" the ref yells.

The only chance I have is to make an attack of desperation. I
sprint toward him, fully expecting him to dodge. But he stands his
ground. I have to take the risk. He'll assume I'm going to come at
him and strike, so he'll prepare a counterattack. My hope is to ram
straight into him, get close, so his speed is nullified, and fight in
close proximity. It's not much of a defense, but it's an offensive
move that'll take us both down. My stampede is such a foolhardy
move, he only realizes too late what I plan to do. When he tries to
evade, it only worsens the situation for him. I crash into his body,
bringing both of us to the ground. I start smashing into his chest
armor, pounding it with my fists. Anytime he tries to get away, I
pull him back and attack more. He gets two blows into my back, so
I pin down his arms, making him unable to strike. I focus my attacks on the pivot joints, trying to damage them so his limbs can't
move. Sparks are flying everywhere, and I believe victory is mine.

That's when my mecha becomes powerless, and I'm no longer
in control, my vehicle moving away from Honda's. I don't know
what's happened until I hear the ref ask Honda, "What is your condition?"

The referee saved Honda's neck.

The crowd jeers. I'm flustered by the separation as well, but
then remember how he saved me back when I was first knocked
down. We both got one save.

"I'm ready to win," is Honda's reply.

We're both badly damaged, barely standing. I grab my sword
and check the gauges again. My mecha won't be able to survive
another rush attack. And I doubt he'd let me repeat my previous
move. That's also when I notice the right elbow on my mecha is
broken, or at least the signal isn't working because no matter how

much I move it, it doesn't work. On top of that, another red alert goes off, indicating a problem in the spinal pistons. I check what's wrong.

His earlier attack was more lethal than I'd thought. My stabilizers will soon stop functioning, and I won't be able to stand up straight. If Honda just stays away for two minutes, my mecha will collapse of its own accord. I need to find a way to balance myself, and there's only one way I can think. I move toward the stadium walls, my back toward it, and sheathe my sword. Honda must be damaged too as he doesn't strike right away. I circumspectly watch him, readying for another attack. When I'm close enough to the stadium wall, I fire two of my hooks into it. I'm hoping they can act as a sort of tension wire to help keep me upright after the pistons fail.

Honda is baffled, and asks, "What are you doing?" But as soon as he questions me, I think the answer dawns upon him. He also realizes I've found a way to keep myself upright, but he knows I'm vulnerable.

He prepares to do his rush attack.

I remember what Chieko pointed out the night before. He'll take four rapid steps before his dagger hurricane starts. Can I counterattack him right after his fourth step? Where should I attack? I might have one chance at stopping him. If I can execute the *iaijutsu* right after his fourth step, the momentum from his speed will cause him to be impaled on my sword. But the timing has to be right. Too soon, and he'll stop. Too late, and I won't be able to get my sword out in time.

Good thing it's my left arm that's still functioning.

I take a deep breath, disable the warning alarms on the console just as the stabilizers fail. Fortunately, I'm able to lean against the wall, and the wires help. But if this fails, and Honda can get me off my feet, I won't be able to recover. At the same time, he can't merely stand back and wait for me to fall on my own.

Honda skips about, preparing himself for the attack. It comes suddenly. I count the steps. They're four rapid beats, and as soon as I see the final step, I pull out my sword as quickly as I can. The sound of his mecha being pierced by my blade is shrill and painful. The impact causes the cockpit to shake. Honda's mecha powers down. There is stunned silence in the crowd. I understand them as I can't believe it worked either. I want to push Honda away, but I can't move without losing balance.

"What is your condition?" the ref asks Honda.

Honda glowers, pressing buttons on his console. It takes him a minute to acknowledge, "My mecha is down."

The bell rings. There are actually fireworks. There is a frenzied applause. I lift up my left fist and shake it exultantly at the crowd.

I've won.

A crew rushes out with the appropriate vehicles to separate us. Cheerleaders spell out my name, using their rocket packs. I climb down the cockpit ladder and wave at the crowd. It's hard for me to believe that they're actually excited for *me* this time. I don't know how to describe the emotion that surges through me. It's almost like bliss, pride, and ecstasy combined. But even the words pale in comparison to how euphoric I feel. I search my memories to recall a similar emotion. There's nothing like this. Above on the display screen, they are doing replays of the fight, and I see commentators analyzing my moves. I wave again and bow to the audience. That makes them scream even louder. I don't want to go back down into the lockers, and I stay until the officials request for the eighth time that I descend.

MEDICAL OFFICIALS DO AN X-RAY, MAKING SURE I HAVE NO BROKEN bones. "Let's check that bruise," the doctor tells me.

I look down and see the skin below my chest is purplish black. I must have gotten the bruise during the initial stages of the fight.

He checks my body for internal bleeding, presses against my stomach. It hurts like hell, but after he does a scan with his portical, he informs me, "I'll prescribe you some gels. Leave them on overnight, and you'll be healed up by the morning."

In the shower, I feel the pain on my stomach as the hot water makes the affected area sting. I decrease the heat, then think back to the crowd's reaction. I make swinging motions in the shower, recall that final sword draw that got Honda.

After I clean up, I get dressed and enter the hallway. There's a wall with some of the most famous fighters in USJ history, champions in their respective years. Legendary pilots like Makunouchi, Ayanami, Tomokazu, Torrubia, Miyada, Gensuke Okamoto, and, of course, the first Kujira.

I have to fight her son tomorrow.

I peek at last year's placard, which commemorates Noriko, and the year before that, Kazuhiro, who Ella mentioned. While there is small text indicating the runner-up and third place, I don't recognize any of their names.

I will win tomorrow, I tell myself, even though a part of me feels preposterous about the statement. I barely won today. Honda is an amazing pilot.

Down the hall, I see a group of people emerging from the other locker room. It's Honda with his family and friends. I run up to them, bow to Honda with genuine respect, knowing the fight easily could have gone the other way.

"That was a great fight. Thank you very much," I tell him.

He stares coldly at me and leaves. None of his group gives me any reaction. It is a slight, though an understandable one.

"Don't take it personally," a stranger says, exiting the locker room. "He's never fought such a good pilot before. Nicely done. I'm Kazu."

"Kazu, as in Kazuhiro, captain of the Five Tigers?"

"You've heard of me?"

"Yes."

"Nothing too bad, I hope?"

"No, of course not. But I did hear you served together with Honda."

"And he hasn't changed. He still relies too much on speed and leaves himself vulnerable to attack. Which you exploited very nicely."

"Thank you," I say, with a slight bow.

He shakes his head. "Forget the formalities," he says. "Whether you win or not, you and Kujira will get invitations to the Five Tigers." Kazu is of Spanish heritage, has purple hair elaborately crafted like a bird's crest. He walks with poise and confidence, at ease not just with himself but the world around him. He wears a necklace of bullets on top of his uniform and a red sash that brilliantly clashes with his uniform.

"Will Honda be the fifth?"

Kazu shakes his head. "There was a cadet named Chieko who technically didn't lose, so she'll get the final invitation. Speaking of which." And he gestures behind me.

It's Chieko, who gives me a fist bump. "Congratulations!"

"You too!"

Chieko bows to Kazu, and says, "Hello, Kazu-san."

"You're making me feel old," he says, "Drop the san and let me treat you two to ramen. What flavor you feel like? *Assari*, *kotteri*, *tsukumen*, or USJ-style?"

"I've always wanted to try Aiyas," Chieko suggests excitedly, "but there was a three-hour wait last time I went."

Kazu grins. "Let me deal with that."

IT'S SPRINKLING OUTSIDE, AND FOG HAS ALREADY SWARMED IN, MAKING it the perfect atmosphere for hot ramen. When we arrive, the res-

PETER TIERYAS

taurant is packed with people, and I overhear someone who tries to sign up being told the wait is at least three hours. I'm too hungry to wait that long. But as soon as the hostess sees Kazuhiro, she invites us in. Patrons are jammed together, so it takes us a while to navigate to our seats at the bar. The smell inside is making me hungry. Kazu thanks her in Japanese, and she replies, "You know you don't have to thank me."

Chieko is impressed. "How did you do that?"

"Perks of being a mecha cadet," Kazu says. "I highly recommend their spicy miso with an extra pork chashu, and if you're extra brave, you can try their mega beef ramen challenge. You drinking?"

"*Hai!*" Chieko replies.

"I'll have a drink too," I chime in.

Kazu shakes his head. "No drinking before piloting. You need to be sharp tomorrow."

He's right, of course, and I nod in confirmation.

"If you had picked a weapon other than a sword, what would you have done for Honda's last attack?" Kazu suddenly asks.

"I don't know," I admit. "I'd have to be in the situation to know."

"You should know. You should know how you'll face every opponent with whatever weapon you have. What would you have done?" he asks Chieko.

"It would depend on the weapon, but I'd do close-quarter combat where his speed is nullified, just like you did after your first fall," Chieko says.

"Honda loves close-quarter combat, and there wouldn't be any guarantee of victory."

"What would you have done?" she asks Kazu.

"I'm faster than he is, so I would destroy him before he even knew what hit him," he replies confidently, not boastfully, as though it were a foregone conclusion. "You both need to optimize your posture. You can't think like a human. You have to study weight distribution on your mecha to understand how to move quicker and make adjustments on the knee and elbow joint positions to match your fighting style. The adjustable kinematics also play a key role, depending on the terrain and the weapon you're using. That millisecond difference can change the flow of battle completely."

I hadn't thought about weight and posture specific to a mecha, though it makes sense since I do it subconsciously. I move differently to compensate for lag, gravity, and motion when I'm piloting. Practice makes it come intuitively, but hearing Kazu spell it out is interesting. A waiter brings out beer, and we make a toast to "Victory." I lift up my teacup and cheer.

The ramen arrives a minute later, and we slurp up the noodles. The broth is rich, with just the right amount of spiciness. The pork chashu is so tender, it practically melts in my mouth. They must have seasoned it well because there's a lot of flavor in every bite. The egg yolk is just wet enough to evoke a strong taste. I believe this is the best ramen I've ever had and let them know as much.

Chieko laughs. "Maybe the best ramen in Berkeley, but there's much better ramen in Los Angeles, and I won't even get into the main island."

Kazu eats only a third of his ramen and puts it aside. I've devoured most of the ramen in my bowl and stare curiously at his food.

"I have to watch my diet," Kazu explains. "Both of you have to be strictly disciplined with what you eat."

"Why?" Chieko asks.

"Diet plays a big part of being a pilot. You need a nutritious, balanced meal to optimize energy. Strict limits on carbohydrates and sugar intake. I let myself indulge on special occasions, but I strictly watch the balance through my portical."

"So you're not finishing the rest of your beer?" Chieko asks.

Kazu drinks it down.

"If you decide to join the Five Tigers, I expect both of you to follow the same strict regimen we do to keep in peak shape," Kazu says.

I think about Kujira being forced to follow a regimen and laugh.

"You find this amusing?"

"No, I am actually excited about this," I say, and I mean it. I love how seriously he is taking every aspect of piloting.

"What do you think it is we do?" Kazu asks us. "This is serious business we're involved in. Talent only takes you so far. Instincts can betray you. Cold, hard discipline is the closest you can get to something reliable. And even that can fail you if you don't have the nerves. We can't afford to fail if we're to be the bastion of the United States of Japan."

"Good point," Chieko says. "But can I gorge until I actually join the Five Tigers?"

Kazu grins. "I would be disappointed if you didn't."

CHIEKO AND I HEAD BACK TO OUR DORM TO WATCH KUJIRA'S FIGHTS. WE look for patterns, but his style is different in every match. It's almost like he's liquid adapting to anyone's attack stance. We try to find vulnerabilities and weaknesses but don't see anything.

"I don't know how I'm going to beat him," I confess.

She nods. "He's fast and good, which makes sense since he's been doing this his whole life. But his one weakness is his arrogance. If you can catch him off guard, the way I did for a minute, you might have a chance."

It's not much to go on, but it's better than nothing.

I pass Kujira's dorm on the way back to my room. I hear the

sounds of the coloring game he's been playing, *Rokkakkei*, those addictive "hexagons." I've just spent the past two hours trying to study his fighting style, and he doesn't even care. Then I wonder if there's something in that game that appeals to him and can give me a clue as to the way he fights. I'm tired when I enter my room, but I access *Rokkakkei* on my portical and play it.

What I thought was a pointless exercise is actually all about malleability, adjusting shapes and colors to match the environment. No single strategy works. You have to counter whatever the randomized AI hurls in your direction. Every round, the rules change, and what worked in the previous level can actually be a disadvantage in the next. I don't play long as I'm too tired and my arms are stiff from the match earlier, but it gives me a clue to his fighting philosophy. Then again, it's just a game. He could just be killing time.

WHEN I WAKE IN THE MORNING AND TRY TO STAND, MY STOMACH HURTS like hell. I lift up my shirt and realize I'm still heavily bruised. The gel didn't work. I have a hard time walking. I ring Chieko and tell her my condition. She comes by and brings me pills.

"What's that?"

"Painkillers. They'll get you through the day."

I thank her. We take the subway to Emeryville. I notice it's overcast and hope it'll clear up by the time our match begins. Chieko mentions Nori's back in town. "Whoever wins your fight will take her on," she tells me.

"I haven't even seen her fight yet."

"Nori is good, but you can worry about her after Kujira."

"I almost wouldn't mind losing just to see Kujira fight Nori," I reply.

"You can't start making excuses for yourself before the fight."

I separate with her at the stadium and go to my locker. I change clothes and head for my mecha when I spot Kujira. He's by the trash can, clipping his nails.

Should I say something?

He notices me and looks up. "Can you believe they've officially forbidden me from eating sausages while I'm piloting?" he asks me, eyes widening in mockery. "I told them I'd lay off if any of them could beat me in the ring. Course, none of them accepted. Put your money where your mouth is. Bastards. 'You disrespect the sanctity of the mecha.' Sanctity can wipe my ass. I don't respect people cause they went to a war zone running around like mad chickens with a gun. I've seen too many gun battles not to be able to tell the difference between real warriors and showboats desperate to show off their 'experiences' like it's some goddamn badge."

He takes out a bag full of sausages and chews on one.

"Let's get the circus over with," he says in resignation.

"What do you mean, 'circus'?"

He ignores my question and stomps toward his mecha. I don't know if he takes any of this seriously, but I can't allow his attitude to affect me.

IT'S SPRINKLING OUTSIDE, THOUGH THERE WAS HEAVY RAIN EARLIER. They could cover the dome, but they don't. The fighting grounds are muddy, making it hard to traverse. From the moment I get into my mecha, I feel the difference. The steps are cumbersome, and there's more drag. Even when I move the throttles for the manual arm control, it is less responsive. I rely on the gloves and the UI to match the proper motion. With the ground being so soft, it's hard to find balance, and I'm never quite sure how much my step will plunge into the mud. It's a less-than-ideal climate for a fight. Most of the audience members are wearing rain ponchos. The retractable ceiling has come in partway to shield them from showers. It's gloomily dark above.

I'm not sure what the fight will be like under these conditions. I wish they'd get the ceremony out of the way. The band is under a canvas, and their performance is much more subdued with the rain. Chieko's medicine is doing a good job muting the pain so the only thing hurting my stomach right now is the anxious knot that gets tighter with each passing minute.

Kujira. I've been hearing that name since I was born. My mom used to tell me stories about how great a pilot the original was. Now I'm fighting her son. It wouldn't be a disgrace to lose. As usual, all the odds are against me.

"You ready for your next challenge?" the ref confirms with me.

"I am."

"Anything I should be aware of before the fight?"

I'm about to tell him there isn't, but then I wonder if I should mention that I'm under medication. Better to be transparent and let them know my situation clearly. "My injury from yesterday hasn't fully healed so I'm taking painkillers."

"Do you want to forfeit the match?" he asks.

I shake my head. "Absolutely not."

"Good. We'll begin in eight minutes. Prepare yourself."

There's a sudden itch on my lower back I can't scratch without unbuckling everything. It's very annoying, and I do my best to ignore it, but that only amplifies the sensation. From Kujira's side, I hear an obnoxious eating sound. "Mmm, these sausages taste really good," he says over the public speakers so that everyone present can hear. "I should have brought some ketchup and relish, but too much makes me fart."

He is mocking the officials who forbade him to eat.

For some reason, I'm reminded of Griselda's quote, the "great despisers are the great reverers."

Kujira's mecha plops forward.

"Fight!" I hear.

I usually play it conservative, take things slowly and figure out what to do. While just a minute ago, Kujira was acting silly, the switch has flipped, and he doesn't give me a chance to catch my breath. He launches at me in full attack mode, using two whips to strike me from both sides. Anytime I try to attack him, he lashes at me. His assault makes the crowd go wild as he slashes my arms multiple times. Is there any weapon he doesn't know how to use? I think of Kazu's advice the night before that I should be prepared to face any weapon. My sword feels like a deadweight as I try to swing to match his whip speed. The rain is coming down heavily, damp-ening visibility. I've got to assume he's similarly impaired. I toggle between the forward-looking infrared camera (FLIR) and normal mode. Both have their disadvantages, and while the heated view does away with the rain, I'm not used to fighting in total red, so it takes me time to compensate.

I try to calculate whip speed and length. It's hard to evade when all my steps are slower than usual. How is he maintaining his at-tack velocity? I realize every time he moves, he fires his boosters. Step left, boost. Attack with whip, boost. I try it while moving for-ward and push the booster a half second too long. I am suddenly in a position where I'm close and vulnerable to Kujira. I don't think he was expecting the charge, and he hesitates. I boost backward to quickly get out of his way. The timing of these moves takes prac-tice. I try to get the hang of it, but I either boost too long or too short. This isn't working.

I ask the portical's AI to gauge the trajectory of the whip. But its calculations are too imprecise, and Kujira's attack defies mea-surement. He doesn't have a preferred hand, does short lunges and long lashes with equal acumen. I think the only thing that has helped me is the rain, which prevents either of us from moving at max speed. 'Course, it could be the whole situation with the sausages has made him grumpy and mad, driving him to vent his anger on me. There's a chance that could make him reckless and sloppy. I ponder to myself if egging him on will only rile him up or actually make him error-prone. As Chieko pointed out, the one weakness that we're aware of is his arrogance.

The rain is pounding down. I move away from him and raise my sword in a defensive stance. Does he even care if he wins or loses? Why do I care? He is right, this is a circus, and we're putting on a show. "They should add microwaves in these trainers so I can heat up my food," Kujira says.

I know this is probably a mistake, but I hope it'll give me a chance. "Shut up about your sausages and fight," I tell him.

"Wasn't talking to you, sausage grump," Kujira replies. "You got a problem, shut off your portical."

He doesn't rise to the bait. At least that's what I presume from his tone. But he uses his boosters to begin a quick series of attacks, exactly what I was hoping for. I block the first series, so he steps to the side, probing, trying to find a break in my defenses. I'm watching his timing too. I know he boosts with each attack. While it increases the strength of the whip, it'll also leave him temporarily out of control. I wait for the right opportunity, when he might be slightly vulnerable, and it looks like there's a second before his whip attack that I can get him. They're so rapid and furious, I have to get the timing just right. More slashes, more hurls. There, he's going to do a side cut. I slice at his right whip. Normally, the chain whip would bounce off. But with the power of his boost giving additional momentum, my blade slices through the whip as if it were a rope. His right side is open to attack, so I swing at him, lunging toward his arm with the blade. He still has his one whip, which he uses as a shield to block my attack. The chain holds, but this is my time to boost, which I do. My force pushes him back and breaks his left chain, leaving him weaponless. I thrust the blade at his chest. He blocks with his left hand, my sword penetrating straight through his palm.

Kujira asks, "So you really want to do this dance?"

"That's why I'm here."

He lowers his left hand, sword still lodged in. He uses his right leg to smash my sword in half. All I have is a hilt with a broken blade. Kujira pounds the upper half of the blade out of his left hand, then raises his fists. It's a pugilist's match now. Boxing has never been a strength, but with a mecha to fight in, everything changes.

He makes a few exploratory jabs. I instinctively raise my fists in front of me. I've never fought fist to fist on a mecha so I know very little about its limits, what it can take, and how best to defeat an opponent in this manner. If he attacks, I'd be easily outmatched, and I'm surprised he's not coming straight at me. Then I wonder if he's being extra cautious, trying to gauge my ability as he does not want to underestimate me again. If that's the case, I can't let him know I have very little experience and a whole lot of questions.

What are the spots most vulnerable to melee attacks? Do I go for the chest or the head? Do I try to disable his arms, legs? If I get in close, is he aware of pressure points that will disable my mecha? Can he disrupt my generators at close proximity and prevent me from even fighting? These are things I should be aware of but only have a general idea about from memorizing the schematics.

It's unacceptable, and my limitations piss me off. How can I aspire to be one of the greatest mecha pilots and not even know the basics of hand combat?

He pulls a knob from the side of his mecha. I'm not sure what it does, but once it's free of its position on his shoulder, he throws it away. The ref flags him, and asks, "Why did you remove your—"

Before he can finish, Kujira cuts in, "I don't need training wheels."

I do a diagnostic but can't determine what it is that he removed.

I do notice he no longer uses the booster when attacking. His punches are methodical, aiming for my upper body. I'm able to block, but that's when he increases the rate of his jabs. Suddenly, a left-right combo becomes a flurry of fists. Before I know it, my mecha is pounded by shotgun punches. It's an unceasingly fast attack, so much so that I can't even see it. I have my arms up, but I'm being pushed back through the mud. My alarms are going off, indicating serious damage to both my hands. I attempt to counterpunch him and lunge forward, but that ends with an uppercut to my face that causes a part of the head to cave in. The console pushes against my belly, causing pain that makes me gasp. He doesn't let up and continues his relentless barrage. I've heard of this before, a tactic used by the elder Kujira called the shotgun fists. It's one thing to listen to tales about its prowess but another to experience it directly as I've become a punching bag. His speedy attacks disable the rest of my mecha, and the scariest part is, I can't even see his fists. Did that knob somehow let him punch even faster? My feeble attempts at blocking fail miserably.

Suddenly, he kicks me. I'm unable to deflect anything, and he's on me, pounding my head. My arms have stopped functioning, and when I try to move away, I find my legs are entrenched in the mud. Next thing I know, I'm upside down, rotating in the air. I think he actually knocked the head off my mecha. I don't have long to ponder as I crash into the ground and safety balloons cushion the blow. I check the diagnostics to see what exactly happened. I hear cheering outside, so I know the match is over. That final strike was blindingly fast, and I didn't see it coming at all.

I've lost.

I feel so disappointed with myself. I thought I had a chance, but the last half of the fight wasn't even a competition. I want to make excuses, attribute it to Kujira's training from his mother. But this has as much to do with my lack of knowledge as it does with his ability. I have a long way to go, especially in hand-to-hand combat. I'm grateful to Kujira for helping me realize this so convincingly.

It's fifteen minutes before the crew comes to extract me. Just as I'd thought, my mecha's head has come clean off. Will I ever be able to live down the shame?

The rain has cleared, and Kujira is nowhere in sight. I expect jeers and scorn from the crowd, but when the medics pull me out of the mecha and onto a stretcher, I see the audience cheering for me. Their response is completely unexpected, and I try to wave gratefully to them. Only problem is my arms feel ten times heavier, and a cramp starts in my forearm. I manage to wave, but can't hold it long. On top of that, my calves are stiff and my neck feels like someone lodged an iceberg inside it. I need to rest.

IN THE LOCKER ROOM, THE MEDIC LOOKS ME OVER. "YOU SPRAINED YOUR right arm and have contusions over your body. You told the ref the gel didn't work last night?"

"It didn't."

"I'm going to send you to the vat for the next three hours. If that doesn't work, we may have to do a closer examination. I'm not detecting any internal bleeding or broken bones, but it's possible the scans might have missed something."

The vat is similar to the one I was in after my fight with the NARA and works its magic to heal my wounds. All my limbs felt like they were detached pieces of my body, and now they're slowly getting herded back into the fold.

I have flashbacks to the fight, try to determine if there was any other way I could have won. Maybe if I'd picked a different weapon from the beginning, or if the weather hadn't been so hideous, the match wouldn't have been so lopsided. I have so much to learn.

There's a knock on my door.

"Come in."

Kazu enters.

"That was a good fight," Kazu says to me.

"I lost badly."

"It was an epic beatdown," he replies, not sugarcoating it for me. "But you did the best with what you knew." His grin alleviates the sting of his words.

"I have to train to fight without weapons."

"You'll get all that training soon."

"When is Kujira fighting Nori?" I ask.

"The fight's over," Kazu replies.

"What? When?"

"It happened right after your fight."

I check the time, and it's been over an hour since the match.

"Who won?"

"It was a draw," Kazu answers.

"Draw?"

"Nori and Kujira got into another fistfight. They pummeled each other until both their mechas shut down."

"Are you serious?"

"I've never seen anything like it," he says.

"Is there footage? I have to see this."

"I'll get it for you. But for now you need to come out."

"For what?" I ask.

"The award ceremony," Kazu replies.

THE WEATHER HAS CLEARED UP, AND THE SUN IS SHINING THROUGH THE clouds. Several high-ranking officers are preparing for the ceremony, including Mayor Wakatsuki of Berkeley, Superintendent Tobo, and directing officers, Suzuki-san and Ishikawa-san. Eight of the training mechas are arrayed around us. The band is playing a festive tune, and highlights of the tournament play on the main portical screen.

Chieko and I take our respective spots on the three-level podium at numbers two and three. But the number-one spot is empty.

Imperial Guard Misato Hirono, who is presenting the medals, is visibly annoyed by Kujira's absence. While speaking to the crowd, she makes an excuse for him, indicating he is being treated for injuries and will be awarded *in absentia*. I am irritated by his disregard for the ceremony and his disrespectful attitude to the tournament. He defeated me and didn't even care. It nearly ruins the mood for me. But then the judge puts the medal around my neck and the crowd applauds, washing away any discontent. Even though I didn't win the championship, I feel very proud.

I wish my parents could have seen this.

Fireworks go off above, and it's amazing seeing our names in the lights above. Both Chieko and I wave at the crowd—my arms feel much better after that hour spent in the vat.

"That was one helluva fight," she tells me.

"I lost."

"Kujira's been piloting his whole life. We're neophytes compared to him. We did good under the circumstances," she says. "And we kind of kept our word to Nori."

"You see her?"

"Only during the fight. We'll catch her later." She lifts up her medal to me. "This is for all the RAMs."

"Do you think their spirits are looking down on us?"

Chieko shakes her head. "I don't believe in spirits anymore. There's only now. Relish it. It'll be over before you know it."

I take her advice and absorb my surroundings. A few meters from us is an assemblage of Shinto priests. The lower part of their robes are muddy, and a few of the conscientious are trying to lift them while appearing indifferent to how dirty the earthy influence has made them. In the front row, a group of students are taking our pictures on their porticals, and three of them are angling for a closer view. A murder of crows scouts the stadium for leftover scraps, relieved that the rain is over and hoping the celebratory mood will make the strange human beasts cooperative. There are so many faces staring at me, the thousands of eyes, mouths, and noses becoming a centipede of sensory motion. Academy reporters are recording our footage, talking with officials, congratulating Chieko and me. Seven of the cheerleaders check their rocket packs and confirm the weather hasn't damaged the boosters. I gaze up at the training mechas. They look less like samurai and more like robot soldiers, dented, wounded, but stiffly standing at attention for their automated duty. The headless mecha that was mine is nowhere to be seen. Will they retire it or fix it up?

I finally spot Nori. She's in uniform, unfazed by the bad weather. She's talking with Professor Gensuke Okamoto, hero of the Marjah Encounter, where he single-handedly defeated Nazi shock troops supported by the local army. He's one of BEMA's most famous graduates and lethal with the magnetic yo-yo, a surprising choice for weapon. He's wearing dozens of medals, and I marvel that each of them represents a different battle he was involved in. The professor teaches Beginning Mecha Training, which freshmen take starting their second semester.

Nori brings him over. We shake his hand, and he says to me, "I like your spirit, kid. Feel free to stop by my class anytime."

I bow and thank him. He speaks with Chieko.

"You let him kick your ass!" is the first thing Nori says to me.

Considering this is the third rebuke I've gotten, I feel bad. "I'm sorry."

She laughs. "Nah. Don't feel bad. He's excellent. I took my

match with him too lightly. I'll get him next time." She raises her brows. "How are you feeling?"

"Healing up from the fight," I answer. "How are you?"

She tries to find the right words. "Enduring," she finally states. "It's good to be back in Berkeley and in a mecha. You all have a big day tomorrow."

"What's tomorrow?"

"Initiation for the freshman class into the Tadakatsu Circle. I heard you both accepted?"

We both nod. The invitation was a bare-bones text message on my portical asking us to join them.

"It's a special experience," Nori states, and gives both Chieko and me a fist bump.

"We're going to kick some Nazi ass," Chieko says.

"Hell yes, we are."

As Nori walks back with Gensuke to speak with the other officials, I hope I can live up to all their expectations.

11

★ ★ ★

AFTER SPENDING A FEW HOURS BACK IN THE VAT, EVERY PART OF MY body feels refreshed. I wish I could stay another day. I'm about to head home, but I get a portical call. I'm surprised it's an adjutant for the Imperial Guard, Judge Hirono. "Your presence is requested."

"Yes, ma'am. I'm just about to get on the train. Can I get directions?"

The adjutant sends me a North Berkeley address.

On the subway, I'm surprised to see the highlights of our match on the *California Nippon News*. It's not fun watching my mecha's head get dismantled. But I'm still amazed to see myself on the display as the runner-up in the matches. The channel's focus turns back to the situation on the Quiet Border. They've invited two journalists to opine on the situation, and the elderly male who represents the war hawks asks, "Why haven't we obliterated the Nazis yet? They're just asking for a beating. The Fuehrer mocked the Empire during his life, and we shouldn't expect anything different from his successors. Send a dozen battalions of our mecha corps in, and they'll take Manhattan by the end of the year."

The lower part of the screen has scrolling quotes of the negative things Hitler said and wrote about the Empire, considering us the "yellow peril" and ridiculing "Oriental power" as an oxymoron. "The Aryan people have more power in the tip of their pinky than the entirety of the Orient!" he'd infamously declared.

That's followed by a roundup of German media depictions of our citizens. They usually portray weak Asians with terrible accents who are unable to save themselves and rely on "Aryans" for salvation. The Asians are usually polite buffoons too weak to do anything of merit, or "exotic Orientals" who have a "fascinatingly strange culture" and convey us in the worst light.

It'd be funny if so many Nazis didn't see it as truth.

The news cuts back to the debaters. The younger man advocating peace gets to the crux of why conflict hasn't broken out yet. "The threat of an all-out nuclear war precludes any real conflict unless we're willing to risk the end of the world."

I arrive at my subway stop and get off. There are rotating advertisements on the walls for the kite battles in Hamamatsu, bargain resort vacations in Cancún, and an underwater shopping mall they're building off the coast of Cartagena.

The Imperial Guard's mansion is four blocks away from the exit. I knock at the door, and one of the servants lets me in. He bows, asks in a formal tone if I'd like anything to eat. I decline, and he asks me to wait in the lobby. Encased in glass are four special uniforms awarded by the Emperor to the Imperial Guard for her service as part of the elite mecha corps that watches over the palace in Tokyo. There are numerous medals on each jacket. I'm marveling at them when there's another knock. The servant answers and lets Kujira in.

"Would you like something to eat?"

"Sure," Kujira replies. "What's on the menu?"

"What would you like?"

"Whatever you're serving, man. I could eat a horse right now."

The servant nods and leaves.

"They were looking for you earlier," I tell Kujira.

"I'm not into pomp and circumstance. Waste of time."

"Why'd you even bother to participate in the tournament?"

"Wanted to see how good y'all were. Y'all have a long way to go if you want to compete with me," he states.

"Sorry I didn't have the best mecha pilot in the world as my mother to teach me how to fight. Besides, I heard Nori fought you to a draw."

"Damn trainer mechas stink. How you supposed to fight in them? It's like putting you in casts and telling you to do your best in a marathon. If this were real combat, I would have easily won."

It's one thing to put me down. But Nori. No way will I accept that. "We all fought under the same conditions, so don't make excuses. She is ten times the pilot you will ever be."

"Hardly."

"We've been in actual combat. I saw her beat real-life enemies in a mecha."

"You think I haven't?"

"No, I don't."

Kujira shakes his head. "What's your problem, man?"

"Everyone who's here struggled hard to get in. I don't like the way you're so flippant about being here, like you're doing all of us a favor."

"Whatever." He raises his index finger. "You're still sore about earlier, ain't ya? You weren't bad, but you got to work on your weaponless combat. You stink without a sword," he says with a snide smirk that seems to be begging for a fight.

I'm tempted to, upset by his arrogance. Why were we invited here together? I want to leave right away. That's when the servant reenters with a tray of food that smells delicious.

"What is that?" Kujira asks.

"Horse filet mignon," the servant replies. "I took the liberty of asking for it well done."

Just as Kujira is about to eat, the servant receives a call. "Yes, ma'am, they're ready." He hangs up his portical, and says, "She is ready to receive you."

"What about the food?"

"You can eat in her presence."

The servant guides us through the mansion. Every room has a different theme, with unique art from around the world. I like the collection of woodblock prints of recent mechas and their pilots done as wondrous *ukiyo-e* as well as traditional paintings by the maestro of all things mechanical, Shinkawa. The next hall catches my attention with its uniforms and memorabilia from many of the nations we've defeated. I recognize the American ones and wonder what it was like living under their rule.

Judge Hirono is in her study, a two-story library, where all the shelves are filled with physical books. There is a holographic globe in the center, with news updates flashing continuously. She is seated in front of the globe, reading Japanese poetry, eating salted pistachios, and discarding the shells into a small bin. She signals us to sit across from her. The servant gives Kujira his food.

Kujira tries to pick up the horse meat with his hands, but it's too hot, so he uses the fork to take a bite. "This is weird, but tasty," he says. "What ya' want?" Kujira asks straightaway.

Judge Misato Hirono smiles. "It's uncanny how much you remind me of your mother."

Kujira's eyes widen, and he stops chewing. "You knew Ma?"

"Of course."

"But you were stationed in Tokyo with the Emperor, weren't you?"

"I was in the Imperial Guard for seven years. They cycle us out after seven years, so my duty ended then. They gave me the chance to go anywhere in the Empire. I chose the United States of Japan because I loved San Diego. It used to be one of the most beautiful places in the world until the George Washingtons destroyed it. I served with your mother," she says to Kujira. Turning to me. "I knew your mother as well. She served with my nephew aboard the *Kamoshika*."

I'm so surprised that she knew my mother, I blink rapidly and repeat Kujira's question, "You knew my mother?"

"She had very sharp eyes and could adapt to any situation on the spot," the judge says. "Easily one of the best navigators in the corps. But the part all of us loved was that she used to write very long reports after her missions and recount her thoughts, her dreams, even philosophical expositions on war in general. Most official reports are a page or two. Hers were thirty to forty pages. Her superiors complained about her 'purple prose,' and there were many word snobs who picked on her phrasing, insisting she stick to the basics. But her reports became the thing of legend among the ranks." I imagine it to myself and smile, wondering if there's any way I can get hold of those old documents. "She would have been proud that you're on your way to becoming a full-fledged pilot."

"Thank you, ma'am."

"Thank yourself." The judge looks to Kujira. "Your mothers were close friends."

I'm doubly stunned, but this is the first time I see Kujira taken aback. "What are you talking about?" he snaps.

Judge Hirono replies, "We all served together in San Diego. Your mom"—to me—"was Kujira-san's navigator."

"My mom never had a navigator."

"Later, when she insisted on doing everything herself, that was true. But in the early days of the conflict with the George Washingtons, she needed someone to help her navigate San Diego. It was a short tour, but I know that both of them would be proud if they knew you had taken the number-one and number-two spots in the championship." She looks at us with a nostalgia that is both comforting and alien. I never would have suspected Kujira and my mother knew each other, much less this judge. "But I didn't call you two here to wax about the past. There's something I think is important for you two to know about each other."

Kujira stares quietly, as do I, not sure what she's talking about.

"Did you know they had pistachio trees in the Hanging Gardens of Babylon?" she asks. I shake my head, and though I don't actually know what the Hanging Gardens are, don't want to confess as much.

"Never heard of 'em," Kujira sputters.

"The Gardens were an ancient architectural and engineering marvel, a complex structure with lush foliage that lasted throughout the year. It was one of the Seven Wonders of the Ancient World, but it's also the only one whose location contemporary archaeologists haven't been able to determine. Many German historians believe it's a myth. Now it could be they actually found the site and discovered something out of line with their Nazi creeds, meaning they erased its existence from the history books."

"That's what you want us to know about each other?" Kujira asks.

"The Gardens could have been the greatest structure of that time. But now people debate its authenticity. That's the way history works. People forget so easily. You start telling yourself a new version of the past, and after a while, it becomes reality. Even now, our role in San Diego is being rewritten by the scholars and politicians to be more hospitable and friendly. But I want you to know something about a certain day in 1984," she says. "The GWs were getting more brazen in their attacks. Some of us were looking for compromise. But it didn't seem possible, and I received orders to execute one of their leaders, Abigail Adams." I know the scenario all too well. Mom's mecha got sent in to destroy Adams, but she was ambushed in the process. "I ordered your mother's mecha, *Harinezumi*, to deal with the GWs," she says to Kujira, which is news to me. "But your mother was as stubborn as you and refused to follow orders. I had no choice but to send the *Kamoshika*, where your mother was navigator," she explains to me. "It was a trap. We all understood that, and that's why Kujira refused. But my superiors insisted that it didn't matter since a mecha could deal with any threat. There also was a remote possibility that the source wasn't just setting us up, and we couldn't risk giving up a chance to capture, or terminate, Abigail Adams. I understood the orders, and I also believed the *Kamoshika* could deal with any trap, so I sent it in."

"How did it end?" Kujira demands.

"The *Kamoshika* was destroyed by bombardment. They had the chance to deflect but chose to absorb the brunt of the attack so that their compatriots could survive and the civilian death toll would be minimized. The *Kamoshika* destroyed much of the opposition, but the GWs put everything into taking it down. They believed the symbolic value of destroying one mecha justified whatever the cost."

"What happened to your mom?" Kujira asks me.

"She was killed," I reply.

"When your father found—" the judge continues.

"You knew my dad too?" I jump in.

"He was a very good mechanic," she explains. "But he couldn't bear her loss. He asked to be transferred to a combat unit. He was much better at fixing mechas than he was at soldiering, so he was denied. But he went out anyway and was killed in a furious charge."

I try to imagine my bereaved father, devastated by the loss, blinded by rage. I've felt that sort of anger before, but for it to be for his wife, my mom . . .

"Kujira was furious as well," the judge continues, "but she was also filled with guilt. She was convinced that if she'd gone instead, she would have found a way to overcome the trap. I assured her that her fate would have been the same. But she couldn't accept it. Things had already been tense between her and command. But it only got worse from there, and she was eventually removed from her position at the front. To this day, I regret my decision to dispatch the *Kamoshika* instead of opposing my superior's poor strategic decision." She bows to me, and says, "Forgive me."

I don't know how to handle this sudden apology or the fact that there are tears forming in her eyes. A part of me is furious with the judge for her part in this. Another is equally angry with Kujira and his mom for not having followed orders. In the corner of my brain, the logical side of me tells me it's the GWs at fault here.

"It's not my place to forgive," I reply, feeling too conflicted to give her an answer with conviction.

"I understand," she says, and her gesture hardens. "I apologize for putting you in an awkward position." To Kujira, she says, "Your mom probably told you about many of the terrible things her commanding officers did in San Diego to both the civilians and the soldiers under their authority. They're all true. There were many who were dishonorable. I've made it my life's duty to make sure all of those officers were removed, and I've worked actively at BEMA to make sure we don't have officers like that ever again. It is imperative that the corps take care of their own."

"Too little, too late. My mom's dead," Kujira states.

"I understand."

"I'm out of here," he says, is about to leave but grabs the horse meat and exits.

I turn to the judge. I appreciate her telling us the truth and feel the enormity of her guilt. But I had to grow up without my parents because of her orders. "Good night," I tell her.

I don't wait to see her reaction. I leave quickly, hoping she doesn't call me back.

She doesn't.

Outside the mansion, I'm surprised to see Kujira waiting for me.

"We should, uh, talk sometime," he says. His hands are covered with sauce and meat.

"Yeah."

Kujira shifts uncomfortably. "I need mango juice." He skips away.

I walk through campus. My mom was just like I was to the RAMs, bait so they could attain an objective they felt more important than our lives. Would she really be proud of my being here, or would she think I was a fool?

I spot several couples on a stroll, holding hands and enjoying the evening. I hear singing and see eighteen freshmen in their underwear, running drills set by their Army Circle sempai as part of their hazing. Some restless cadets are banging on outdoor drums, purging themselves of their daily frustrations, bludgeoning insecurities with auditory clubs. BEMA is a beautiful campus, even more so lit up at night. There's a memorial with a group of hands sticking out from the ground, commemorating those who were lost and never identified in war. Each of the hand statues is of varying scale, from life-sized ones to those that are five times bigger than me.

Adjacent to it is a reflecting pool, and the lights at the bottom continually change hues from a vivid blue to a foreboding vermilion. I take a seat on one of the benches and spend the rest of the evening gazing at this tribute to the dead.

AT MY DORM, I CHECK MY PORTICAL FOR MESSAGES. KAZU HAS SENT ME a link to the video footage of the fight between Nori and Kujira.

Kujira usually fights loosely, an unorthodox style that is hard to

decipher. Noriko is the exact opposite, a rigid, almost perfect samurai pose. There's an eloquent lethality in her confidence that
brims from her guarded preparedness. The fight ensues, and it's
unlike any other battle I've seen. From the opening, they go at
each other. Noriko has opted for an electric sword in conjunction
with her *gunsen*. I've seen how deadly she can be with the war fan.
Kujira does a quick strike, but she blocks it. They exchange blows,
and the attacks become more furious. It's almost like a storm of
attacks, accelerating by the second. The sound of weapons collid-
ing and sparks flying mesmerizes the crowd. It's a ping-pong
match of blades. It goes on for three minutes. My arms get tired
just watching them. It ends when both of their limbs get destroyed.
Both of them are awesome.

I should be analyzing what I can learn from them. But I just
keep on thinking about my mom being sent to follow stupid orders. Then my dad, unable to bear his grief, getting killed as a result. It's not just the judge's bad commands, though, that bother
me. Kujira's mom refused. The *Kamoshika* should have too. But
then would someone else's kids be orphans instead? Thinking
about it gives me a headache.

There's a knock on my door. I answer, and it's Tabitha Uoya, my
floor leader.

"There's a situation, and some of your other dorm members
want to talk with you," she says in a grim tone.

"What happened?"

"You'll see when we get there."

I don't want to deal with this right now, but at the same time,
maybe a distraction would be good. We go upstairs to a study hall.
I wonder what it's about as we enter the door. I'm surprised when I
see fifty fellow cadets who pop confetti my way, and shout, "Congratulations!" the same message printed on the banner above,
though it has a spelling error and is missing the "g."

I don't know what to say.

Chieko is already there, and she winks at me. "They got me earlier."

"We tried waiting for you, but we weren't sure when you were going to be back!" Tabitha informs me. "But Kazu-sempai insisted we wait."

Kazu asks me, "You see the Kujira-Noriko fight?"

"I did."

"Both of them got machine-gun arms. I've watched each of Kujira's fights, and he has a different style to match whoever he's fighting. Boy got skills. It could have gone either way. My money was on Nori. I still think she has the edge on him. But every fight is different. He coming to this?"

"I have no idea."

He eyes me. "You look like you're still upside down in your mecha head."

"I'm—I'm sorry. I just wasn't expecting this."

Tabitha says, "Oh no! That's my fault. I didn't want to give away what we were planning 'cuz Chieko figured it out, and I didn't want to spoil it for you!"

"Thank you," I tell her. "I'm very honored by this."

Someone brings me a shot of vodka, and everyone raises their drink. *"Kanpai!"* they shout.

I take a sip and nearly spit it out because the alcohol is so strong.

"We start our training next week," Kazu says. "Lots you need to work on." He bends down and grabs my calves. "Weak sauce, man. Need to firm those up. Start walking on your toes at home."

"On my toes?"

"Strengthen your calves. Becomes huge for mecha speed. You have perfect eye vision?"

"I think so," I answer, not remembering my numbers from my last exam.

"If not, get your eyes lasered. Never know when the exterior sensors might get damaged and you need to rely on your own vision."

"Kazu-sempai, no more mecha talk for the night, *please*," Chieko pleads lightheartedly as she approaches us. "Go home to your daughters."

"You have daughters?" I ask.

"I got married seven years ago, right before I enlisted," Kazu says, and takes out his portical to show us a picture. "These are my twins. Mayu and Mio," he says, beaming. "They're brilliant. I show them all the mecha fights to get their insight. I've already sent them both matches from today and asked them for a report tomorrow morning."

"He's training them," Chieko tells me. "They know more about mecha combat than most of the cadets here."

"Can never be too prepared."

Chieko shakes her head. "And I thought my parents were bad."

Kazu puts up his fists in a defensive boxing pose, and says, "You're at Berkeley now, aren't you? You should be thanking your parents."

She snickers.

After some more mecha tips, he calls it a night.

"Finally," Chieko groans when he departs. "He's been giving me training advice the whole night. Our new sempai is dedicated to an annoying degree."

I laugh.

Chieko places her drink on the table and shakes my hand. "Congrats again on making the Tigers."

"You too," I reply to her.

She picks up her drink and downs half of it. "He was actually saying we'll all get our own training mechas in the new semester, and we can customize them. They'll be better than the older models we used for the tournament."

"Can't wait."

She grabs pretzels from a bowl. "My parents are flying in next week."

"They're from Taiko City?" I ask, trying to recollect what she'd told me before.

She nods. "They wanted to fly down for the tournament, but I couldn't deal with them and the tournament at the same time. My dad gives me an earful of unwanted advice every night on how to do better."

"He was a mecha pilot?"

"Barber. Both of them are hairstylists. But they're avowed aficionados of mecha movies. They watch them all the time and think the films are like real life. My dad actually referenced one of those animated movies to tell me how to fight, and I had to remind him they're not real." She places her hand on the side of her neck. "But they're trying. I can tell they're worried."

"Worried about what?"

"We are training for war."

"Oh, that."

She finishes her drink. "My dad is a geek. He cries over everything. A portical game is sad, he bawls. But my mom never cries. I don't think I ever saw her sad. Until after the stuff with the RAMs. There was one night I was still recovering at the hospital, and I heard crying. I woke up, and there was my mom next to the bed in tears. I didn't let her know I was awake. But it broke my heart." She takes a deep breath. Her eyelids are getting droopy, and she says, "I need twelve hours of Z time."

"I'll see you tomorrow."

"Big day, right?"

Even though she's drunk, her gait is straight and steady as she leaves.

I don't know the other cadets, and they're too busy getting drunk to pay me much heed. I have two more drinks, then head back to my room and fumble with the key.

"Hey, man," Kujira says, opening up his door.

"Hey," I answer. "Some of the cadets were looking for you."

"That's why they were knocking on my door?"

"They wanted to congratulate you for winning."

"Why?"

I'm about to explain but figure there's no point.

"That crap the judge said," Kujira throws out there.

"Crap I want to forget."

"I can't apologize for my mom. But the whole situation is screwy. I don't trust any officers. Even if the judge is begging for forgiveness, stuff is always more complicated than they put it, usually in their favor."

"Why are you so antiauthority?" I ask Kujira.

Kujira replies, "I'm realistic. No one gives a damn about anyone. If you're useful, they'll chew on you until you're not. I don't buy into their talk about family, honor, and loyalty. They'll say whatever it takes to make you do what they want. Their whole purpose is to exploit you. You're stupid if you think otherwise."

I'm all too aware of how easily the people in charge would discard me but don't want to get into all that happened at school and RAMDET. So I say, "I've experienced how little they care. But you can afford to be bitter. You're the son of a legend. I can't."

"They didn't take care of you?" he asks.

"The bare minimum."

"Sounds like them. My mom was the second-best pilot the USJ had, but when she got sick from the radiation in the old mecha engines, her superiors denied responsibility. They tried to shift the blame, said it was unrelated until all the medical proof came back conclusively that it was the BPG that caused her illness."

"The BPG? Aren't they heavily plated to block radiation?" I ask.

"Because of what happened to her, they strengthened the plating. She wasn't happy about their denials and let everyone know. Her superiors were more furious about losing face than they were that they'd denied her treatment." The whole time I've known Kujira, all I've seen is indifference and smugness. This is the first time I see something akin to sorrow on his face. "She was devastated. She believed the crap her superiors told her, thought they meant it when they said they would always take care of her. It was only on their terms. Once she stood up for herself, and they realized she wasn't useful to them like she'd been in the past, they got upset. They gave her an ultimatum to take back everything she said, accept their conditions, and die quietly. It was an insult. She'd sacrificed so much for them, put in all those years to becoming the best pilot. I know. I saw. She had so many sleepless nights because her body was in pain from her illness. At first, she tried to be a dutiful soldier, bear it stoically. Do you think they appreciated it? They didn't care. They only thought that since they'd given her the 'privilege' of being a pilot, she should be grateful to them. Despicable. None of her 'fellow' soldiers came to see her on her deathbed. I was the only one there. You know the last thing she told me?"

"What?"

"'Kick ass 'cause you want to, not because someone orders you to.' I live by those words."

"They're words to live and die by." I look up at him. "Why are you staying at Berkeley then?"

Kujira shrugs. "Right now, 'cause I dig fighting y'all. If things get boring, I'm out. Anyway, I don't want this to get cheesy and all, so I guess I'll see you tomorrow at that circle thingy."

"You'll be there?"

"They promised good food. I never pass up good food."

He shuffles back into his room.

I return to mine.

I think about the older Kujira. To find out this legendary figure had been treated like that is both shocking and disappointing. I had always believed veterans were taken care of for life. At the same time, I've become all too aware of how we are just numbers to those in charge, *go* pieces on the field that help them in their march to glory. We're young and disposable. Because of our training, I'd like to cling to the illusion we're more valuable. But ultimately, I know we're all in the same mecha.

12

★ ★ ★

THERE'S NO ALARM IN THE MORNING, AND WHEN I OPEN MY EYES, IT'S
noon. I'm not as sore as I was yesterday, but I have a hangover that
makes it feel like someone is squeezing my eyes. I recall the fight,
feel the pang of a million regrets.

Damn, I wish I could have found a way to win.

The memory of my decapitation stings worse now even though
I thought I'd come to terms with it last night when my head was
murkily dazed. Then I think about what the judge told me about
Mom and Dad, and I wish I could shoot laser beams from my fingers and burn down her big mansion. It's because of her orders
that I had to live with an adoptive father who'd beat me if I wasted
a single yen or left even one spoon of rice in my plate. My legal
mother always looked pissed off, and whenever I'd approach her to
ask for something, she'd snarl, "What do you want this time, you
little roach?"

My two adoptive brothers complained about my being in their
room, so they set up a mat in the garage with a sleeping bag. I slept
out there even though it was cold and full of roaches. After I com-

plained about the pests, my adoptive mother dubbed me Little Roach. They always fed me leftovers. Sometimes, the food had gone bad. But if I left it uneaten, they'd reproach me with, "At least the roaches don't complain about free food!"

It's weird how the bitterness of all those years comes back to me now. I haven't spoken to them in almost a decade, don't care if they're living or dead, and have no desire to ever hear from them again.

I pour filtered water into a cup, drink it. I take a shower to warm myself. There's a message from "Mecha Circle," the Tadakatsu, asking all prospective members to come to Kuribayashi Plaza at seven thirty p.m. sharp. We're to eat only snacks until then since a late dinner will be provided.

I don't feel like doing anything the rest of the afternoon, so I burn the hours playing *Cat Odyssey*. The nostalgic familiarity of the game eases all stress.

I HEAD TO KURIBAYASHI PLAZA WITH CHIEKO. NONE OF US WEARS A UNIform, as we were specifically requested to wear civilian clothing.

On the way there, we notice two students have been manacled, bags over their heads. The police are leading them away, and a group of cadets are jeering them, some even throwing food.

"What's that about?" Chieko asks a student who's watching the scene.

"They've been arrested on treason charges," he replies.

"Treason?" Chieko startles. "What'd they do?"

"Two of the professors were charged with espionage and are under house arrest until the Tokko can carry out their investigation. Many of their students are being arrested."

"I can't believe it," Chieko states.

"Neither can we."

We arrive at the plaza and are greeted by some of the sophomores and juniors.

I'm frazzled by the idea that there could be spies on campus. Chieko is also disturbed by the arrests and speculates on what they might be about. I'm too shocked to come up with an explanation. I reassure myself with the fact that if there are traitors, the Tokko will find them.

AT SEVEN THIRTY, THE UPPER-CLASS STUDENTS BLINDFOLD US AND lead us somewhere. I have no idea where they're taking us, but it's a long walk. I ask questions of my guide, but no answers are forthcoming. We eventually travel down a series of steps that seem to go on forever.

When they remove the blindfold, we're in a massive chamber lit by torche that resembles a chapel. Between the columns that run beside the walls are statues of mechas that are ten meters tall. I spot the enormous head of a first-generation Fox-class mecha behind the raised altar. The older machines were bigger because they had a hard time storing the energy required in a smaller frame. All the new cadets entering the Tadakatsu are gathered in the center. Circle members dressed in full battle suits surround us, and there are twelve attired in what looks like actual samurai armor. Closer inspection reveals that they're clad in suits meant to mimic the appearance of the first twelve mechas.

"You must swear to keep private anything we speak of and everything you see tonight, on penalty of death," a woman's voice calls out to us, the biggest of the twelve, wearing the costume of their leader, who had the code designation Narelle Z.

I don't know how serious they are about the death part, but everyone agrees.

"Welcome to the Shrine of the Twelve Disciples," she continues.

"We are deep underneath BEMA in this sacred shrine where only members of the mecha corps and the priests have access. The first twelve mechas and their pilots were called the Twelve Disciples for their devotion to the ideals and principles of the Emperor. They risked everything for the preservation of the United States of Japan. The Disciples were six women and six men, representing multiple ethnicities, united under the banner of the rising sun. They were given their power by the gods, who gave technology to the Emperor. He in turn bestowed it to the rest of humanity, so we could wield our own destiny. Many questioned the Disciples, particularly the other branches, who were jealous. But after the Twelve Disciples fought back the horde of Nazis who wanted America for themselves and died in those battles to save the USJ, all opposition faded. Posthumously, the Emperor granted each of the Disciples a position in the great Shinto pantheon."

Carved into the walls are Japanese letters describing the exploits of the Disciples, their backgrounds, what they achieved in battle. Each of their pilot suits is in an airtight glass display case. Painted on the ground is the emblem of an armored fox, snarling defiantly, ready to pounce on its prey. There is also a whole gallery devoted to their feats, painted by the famous Hokkaido artist Igarashi from his G-Sol Studios. His artistry is phenomenal, and I gawk at the treasure trove of our legacy.

"We are all part of the Empire," Narelle Z states. "But we are also the true inheritors of the American legacy, blessed by our Emperor whose vision of a unified world is prevented by the evil Third Reich. Tonight, we honor the memories of the Twelve and swear by our blood to do everything we can to protect the United States of Japan the way they did."

We're asked to cut our fingers with a ceremonial dagger and let our blood drip into the holy cup. That's mixed with a special *sake*, then redistributed into *sake* cups. We lift them up with both hands.

The priestess speaks in a dialect I've never heard though I recognize some of the words as having Japanese roots. Finally, she signals us to drink.

The *sake* is strong enough that it dominates the taste and burns all the way down my throat to my stomach. We turn the cups upside down, showing we've finished the drink. It's a symbolic move that gets approving grunts from the Circle members.

"The Navy wanted to control us," Narelle Z continues. "The Army believed they should be in charge. It was only thanks to the vision and struggle of the Twelve Disciples that we were given our own branch in the armed forces. You have all taken a blood oath to do everything you can to protect the USJ.

"But with the power bestowed on us, we must always keep vigilant as we stand watch over the corps. In our history, there are seventeen battles we never speak of, nine Excoriated that will not just be erased from the annals, but forever vilified for their treachery. Your best is not good enough. You will go above and beyond what you believe are your capacities. Empowered by the Emperor, we are eternally grateful to him for the opportunity to serve the citizens of the Empire." She points to the flag of the rising sun above and bows. We all do the same. *"Tenno Heika Banzai!"*

We shout back, *"Tenno Heika Banzai!"* as loud as we can.

"We don't haze or do pointless rushing," she tells us. "That you're here means you've shown the discipline and sacrifice necessary to get here. But there has to be trust. For the next part of the initiation, we will blindfold you, and you will feel excruciating pain for a given time. At any point, you can ask us to stop, and we will. But you will forfeit your membership in this Circle, and you will not be a pilot. There is no shame in that choice. We will respect whatever decision you make."

We are blindfolded again, escorted to another location. I wonder what will happen. It's the not being able to see that makes it worse as the sense of fear amplifies my imagination. Will they beat us? Will they drown us underwater? I've heard the Navy Circle does that. That's when we hear one of the cadets screaming. His pain sounds "excruciating." What are they doing to him?

It takes forever for it to be my turn. They take off my shirt and sit me down. Someone grabs me from behind so I'm relatively immobile. I feel something like an electrically charged knife pierce my arm. It digs deep, and I swear it's scraping against the bones under my skin. I clench my teeth and try to suppress the pain. But it's overwhelming, and my entire body shakes. I try to calm myself with long respirations. They're of little help as the muscles in my arm are being torn apart. I want it to stop, breathe in through my nose, shaking uncontrollably.

"It's okay to shout," someone assures me.

I do my best not to. But at some point, it becomes too much, and I let out a roar, cursing whoever it is that's inflicting the pain. I try to think about something else, but it hurts too much. It's become the vortex of my thoughts, and every attempted distraction gets sucked in. Just when I think I'm about to faint, it ceases.

They stand me back up, walk me to the shrine again. Everyone gets the treatment, and when they're finished, we're asked to take off our blindfolds again. I see they've all received tattoos of a hawk. But Chieko and Kujira have a tiger. I look at my own arm. It's a tiger too. I'm surprised when the Circle members begin to disrobe. They all have tattoos, even more elaborate than the ones we got. Narelle Z's entire body is covered by tattoos of different animals and weapons.

With the armor removed, all of us clasp arms in a huge circle.

Narelle Z says to us, "That is your lifelong reminder of your membership and your oath to the Tadakatsu Circle. Welcome, sisters and brothers."

We all applaud, hugs everywhere, and lots of welcoming exclamations.

"Are we allowed to look around the Shrine?" I ask.

"Only after the festivities tonight!"

"Festivities?"

"That part about there being no hazing. Doesn't apply to beer. We'll see who can drink the most tonight!"

"You better represent, brother!" Kazu yells, slapping my back hard.

"But I just drank last night!"

CHIEKO SEEMINGLY HAS A LIMITLESS TOLERANCE FOR BEER AS SHE drinks glass after glass with almost no discernible effect. Only other person I've seen drink this much without getting intoxicated is Griselda. "How do you drink so much?" I ask Chieko.

"Eat a lot," she replies as she devours a piece of toast with smoked trout and garlic cream on top.

There's a feast on the table, delicacies from all over the world. The Mecha Circle rented out space at a fancy restaurant close to campus for our celebration. Kujira is carrying around two plates of food, and the mountain of treats never seems to dwindle. I've noticed he almost always eats with his hands, even the *zhajiangmian* noodles, which are making his fingers black from the soybean paste. "Bacon-wrapped potatoes are good," he points out to me. "So are these mini–tempura burgers from S-Truths. They're my fave."

Both Chieko and Kujira fight over the sausage cheddar balls, which are vanishing before my very eyes. "I can eat ten times what you can," Chieko says.

"No way." Kujira steps up to her challenge.

"You wanna match?"

"This won't even be a competition."

Chieko and Kujira start to chug down ungodly amounts of food.

"That would be funny if it weren't scary," Nori comments, as Chieko wolfs down handfuls of cheddar balls and beef negimakis. "I've read that when sperm whales die and their carcasses drop to the bottom of the ocean, thousands of scavenging animals show up and eat from its body like a buffet."

"This reminds you of that?"

"Worse," she says, causing me to laugh.

Kujira tries to stuff three more cheddar balls inside his mouth.

"Did you hear about those two professors who were arrested on treason charges?" I ask Nori. She nods. "What could the Nazis have offered them?"

"I don't even care about the professors. It's the students who were misled that have it worse," Nori states. "They'll undergo standard punishment and be executed, all because they had the wrong teacher."

"Executed?"

"Or imprisoned for life. I don't know how professors like that could even be appointed. There have been calls for a change in the leadership and more oversight on how appointments are made."

Someone puts his arms around both of us, and says, "Politics! I love it."

"Kazu-sempai," we both greet him.

"There's a lot of history I need to bring you up to speed on," Kazu says. "But I have a question I want to ask you."

"What is it?"

"How do you know how sanitary a restaurant is?"

"I usually read the ratings and reviews on my portical."

Kazu shakes his head. "Always judge the health of a restaurant by the state of its bathrooms. I've been to posh restaurants that are very swanky, get rave reviews, but their bathrooms are filthy. I walk right out. I won't subject my daughters to trash."

"What's the bathroom like here?"

He smiles approvingly at my question. "Well kept."

He walks over to Chieko and Kujira, who are still stuffing themselves with food. "What are you guys, junior-high kids? Cut that out."

Both of them have to catch their breath, holding their stomachs.

"Who won?" I ask when they return.

Chieko holds her arms up. "I'm just getting started."

Kujira wraps his arm around his gut, and says, "I have to use the bathroom."

He stumbles away.

"I'll be back," Kazu says, and mingles with some of the juniors, including the one who dressed up as Narelle Z. She's dyed her hair white, has tattoos all the way up to her neck, and looks tough enough to be able to eat mechas for breakfast.

"How'd you eat all that?" Nori asks Chieko.

"Chew very carefully, mash it up into small pieces, then swallow. Kujira there just eats things whole, which'll make your stomach full really quick."

"It didn't look like you were chewing," I note.

"Part of it is genetics too. My mom can eat everything in the ocean, and she's still the skinniest lady I know."

"You have to name your mecha Ocean Devourer," Nori jokes, causing both of us to laugh. "Kazu's going to woo us tonight."

"Woo us?"

"He did this last year too. It's a preemptive apology for the hell he's going to put you through."

"What do you mean, hell?"

"You're a Tiger now. You have to be the best of the mecha pilots."

Kujira returns and looks like he's decreased his personal load by several pounds. He's already picked up a new tray of food.

Kazu comes back at the same time, and says, "You all need to fix your eating habits."

"I'm good," Kujira says.

"You body mass index is unacceptable."

"I don't care about that stuff, man."

"Don't force me to put you on rations."

"You can't put us on rations," Chieko says.

"Actually, I can. Your alternative is vegetables and fish, five days a week. The other two days, you do whatever you want. Try it for a month and tell me if you notice a difference."

"What about dessert?" Kujira asks.

"Fruits. I've already had your meals programmed at the mess hall, so you don't have to worry about what you're ordering. Now let's get out of here."

Chieko, who looks like she's ready for seconds, is puzzled. "We're not staying for the party?"

Kazu smirks. "We're heading to Vegas."

ONE OF KAZU'S AIR-FORCE BUDDIES FLIES US OUT ON HIS PRIVATE PLANE. It's a small plane, so it's loud and bumpy. But it also gives us a spectacular view of the strip. After Tijuana was eviscerated by the George Washingtons, many of the resorts moved to Vegas. The mass spectacle on display makes it feel like they've taken the countries of the world and encapsulated them into a series of glitzy hotels, all with various themes.

There's the Ninja Garden resort, which has shurikens and shinobis everywhere—I remember watching a video of one of their shows where ninjas run on water. Gradial Legend goes off the motif of a spaceship and is shaped like a massive starfighter, with each of the floor designs based on a galactic theme by the famous artist, Naoyuki-san. Kazu takes us to a casino called the Goldfly Jupiter, famous because it's home to the top musicals in the Empire. We attend a show based on the *Heike Monogatari*, which follows the heroism of Minamoto no Yoshitsune. Kazu has gotten us box seats that we have all to our own.

"Very fancy," Nori says. "I've wanted to see this for ages. I thought tickets were sold out for the next year."

"They are," Kazu replies. "You're welcome."

"I don't like musicals, man," Kujira says. "I'll be gambling downstairs."

"Ten thousand yen says you're going to love this in the first ten minutes. If you don't, feel free to leave."

"That's a lot of confidence."

"We wouldn't be here otherwise."

Kujira takes a seat, and says, "Get my money ready."

"Honestly, if you can walk away from this, I'll gladly pay you."

The opening music is sublime. Performers come out riding on something that looks like a mix of a chicken and a horse. The main actress lugs around a sword that's twice as big as she is. But it's when she starts singing that we're all mesmerized. They synchronize the music, and the duets become even more intertwined. They sound divine, and their voices fill the entire theater with vigor, courage, and hope. It's only at intermission that I notice Kujira has stayed the entire time. He excuses himself to go use the restroom. Kazu and Nori leave to get some air, with Nori saying, "She missed some of the notes."

"Did she?"

"It's very close, but there was a slight warble on some of the peaks, barely noticeable, but enough to distract me."

"A million apologies," Kazu offers.

"No night at the Goldfly would be complete without us getting to play critic," Nori replies. "They miscued some of the smell flashes too."

"I noticed that. Like the raspberry scent when she was cutting thr—"

Chieko looks sad in her seat, so I ask her, "How you liking it?"

"I love it . . . I just wish . . . I wish Wren were here. He always wanted to see this. We actually planned to come see it after graduation."

"I'm sorry. We probably shouldn't have come."

"No no, I'm glad I came here with y'all. Otherwise, I probably never would have seen it. It's beautiful . . . Did I tell you I failed the mecha sim exam three times?"

"You did," I reply, faintly recalling it.

"I wanted to be a pilot so badly. And now I'm here, and it's all so amazing. Honestly, beyond what I was expecting. That shrine earlier was awesome."

"I didn't even know it existed, and I thought I knew a lot about the mecha corps."

"Same here. When I was looking at the altar, thinking about the fact all of the Disciples were killed in battle, I realized, there's a good chance we'll be killed too. And I wondered, why am I so happy about joining when we'll most likely die because of it? I'm like a pig getting buttered up for the slaughter and actually looking forward to it."

"This time, we'll have actual mechas to fight the biomechs."

"You saw what that Nazi monster did to our mechas."

"Those were Sentry class," I answer to try to assure her. "Older models."

"I know what they were," she snaps.

"Sorry."

She shakes her head. "I know what you meant." She looks at the empty stage. "I never dream about Wren. I dream about everyone else. But never Wren. I don't know why."

Kujira reenters and has a basket full of onion rings. "Hungry?"

Chieko stands up and excuses herself to use the restroom.

Kujira starts to eat the rings, puts his feet up on the balcony rail, and asks me, "You any good at cards?"

"Not really. You?"

"Learning," he replies. "Wanna play later?"

"Sure."

WE GO TO A SUSHI BAR AFTER THE SHOW. THERE ARE WAITRESSES WITH purple hair and huge earphones. They're riding roller blades and wearing short shorts and thin tube tops. Almost all of them have elaborate accessories on their bodies. There's extra enthusiasm from the patrons because four professional sumo wrestlers in the WSO are here, gorging on raw fish. I recognize them. Two are ethnically Mongolian, and the other two are from the main island. It takes a lot of effort not to be like everyone else in the restaurant and gawk.

"Did you like it?" Kazu asks Kujira about the musical.

Kujira reluctantly nods. "It was fine."

"Fine?"

"What's with you and the perpetual chip on your shoulder?" Nori asks Kujira.

"What chip?" Kujira asks back.

"You know what I'm talking about. Your 'too cool for school' act. I get it. But you can drop it with us."

"This isn't an act. I don't trust the military or anyone at the academy. I'm only here because I thought there'd be good food."

"Spoken like a pastiche of your mother. What about *you*?"

"What's pastiche mean?" Kujira wants to know.

"Look it up," Nori says. "I get it. Trust is earned, not deserved. But we're not here to screw you, so stop acting like it's you against the world."

Kujira appears annoyed, but Chieko laughs in a placating manner, and says, "Wow, that's a roasting. Is it my turn next?"

"You want it to be?" Nori asks.

Chieko gives Kujira a punch. "Thicker skin, man. You need look no further than Mac as a paragon of thick skin. People give him so much grief, and it all bounces off him."

"I think you mean thin skin. Everything bothers me. Plus, my nickname used to be Cream," I confess.

"What?" Kazu asks.

I tell them its origin with the RAMs.

"Do not let that out, or I'll be forced to kick you out of the Tigers," Kazu says.

"You might as well kick me out, then, 'cause at this rate, all of BEMA'll know."

Everyone laughs at my expense.

Kujira says, "I spent the first ten years of my life without people. It was just me and mom. Some of her old pilot friends would visit, and we'd mecha spar off Catalina. But aside from that, it was just us. And then it was just me for a few years."

"Isn't Catalina a prison colony?" Chieko asks.

"Long story, but there are lobotomized prisoners everywhere," Kujira answers. "I don't really count them as company. I'd talk to them, but they wouldn't say anything back. So I'm not used to being around people who can talk. My 'guardian' tells me all the time that my manner is gruff, which is saying a lot since she's worse than I am. I wouldn't know how to be cool even if I tried."

There's a momentary silence, which Chieko breaks by asking Nori, "Why you gotta go and make him sad?"

"I'm not sad," Kujira states. "It is what it is."

Nori, undeterred, says, "All I want to know is what you really think of the musical."

"It was . . . nice."

"I guess that's better than 'fine.'"

We all laugh again.

Kazu asks, "How'd you spar off Catalina without getting caught?"

"We fought on the west side and had sensor jammers so they couldn't catch us. But even if they did see us, I don't think they would have cared. Everyone hated being on Catalina."

Our waitress brings us two large plates full of sashimi.

"This is on the house from our owner," she says, pointing to a man in a kimono, who bows to us. "He wants to thank the legendary Tigers for your service to the USJ."

"Thank you," Kazu says with a bow. The owner nods gratefully.

I don't know how the others do it, but they're able to eat more. I'm still stuffed from earlier. I can't even eat a single edamame bean. Instead, I look over at the sumo wrestlers. People are respecting their privacy for the most part, but several of the adults with kids have gone over to ask for autographs.

"Cards after this?" Kujira suggests.

"Whatever you want. I got us a suite in the New Cancún, and they have a casino downstairs," Kazu explains. "They also have the biggest indoor swimming pool in the world. They used to have dolphins, but animal-rights activists protested, so the dolphins were all moved to a preserve. Before that, I brought my daughters out, and both of them got to swim with them. They wanted to be marine biologists for a whole six months."

"Until you told them about what Nazis do to marine life, right?" Nori asks.

"Just the reality," Kazu replies.

"That's cruel," Chieko says.

"World's cruel," Kazu says, eating his kanpachi. "Sooner they know that, the better prepared they'll be."

We get ready to exit, but a waitress comes over and asks us if we wouldn't mind coming over to the sumo-wrestling table. We do.

"I just saw all of you in the tournament!" the Mongolian Yokozuna exclaims. "You're BEMA's Five Tigers, right?"

I'm astonished that he knows us, but Nori and Kazu act unfazed, like they're used to the attention.

"Can I get a photo with you five?" the Yokozuna asks.

Obviously, there's a lot I need to learn.

AFTER SOME BANTERING AND AN INVITATION TO GO WATCH THEIR NEXT match (front-row seats!), we go barhopping, visit some dance clubs, and trek through a sim booth arcade. I'm still on a high that the wrestlers recognized us. Two very attractive women spot Kujira and me, then tell us, "You're both much cuter in real life," which doubles my spirits.

But Kujira, usually so boisterous, becomes uncharacteristically quiet. I tease him about it, and he whispers to me, "I think they're trying to make their boyfriends jealous."

"What boyfriends?"

On cue, both of their boyfriends show up and aren't too pleased to see their girlfriends talking with us.

Before they can make a scene, Nori comes to the rescue, buys everyone drinks, and whisks us away.

I thank her, and she urges us, "Think of yourselves as public figures now so stay out of trouble."

I ask Kujira, "How did you know?"

"I saw them when we first came in," he answers. "I usually take notes on everyone when I enter a new place."

Randomly, I pick out a male having drinks. "What's his deal?"

"He's had three beers, and he's been practicing lines to himself for the last twenty minutes and laughing about jokes that aren't funny."

"How do you know they're not funny?"

"I read his lips."

"What about that couple over there?" I ask.

He peeks at them. "They're just friends, but he's hoping for more. She only brought him so she won't be alone, but she has no interest. She's been looking over at the guy drinking with his friends at the bar. They'll probably end up together in a few minutes."

Shortly afterward, she leaves her "friend" to flirt with the other guy.

I'm amazed and wonder how much his people-reading skills will help him at gambling. When we hit the tables, Kujira takes his chances at blackjack. Nori takes a small stack to the poker table. Kazu is talking with his daughters via portical, while Chieko plays the pachinko machines.

I stand over Kujira and watch his game. First hand, his two cards are a jack and a 4. He asks for a hit, gets a queen, and busts out. The next four hands don't go any better. He loses all of his gambling money within ten minutes.

"Don't forget you owe me 10k," Kazu reminds him as he returns.

Kujira looks at me confused. "I don't get this game."

Meanwhile, Nori, whose game face is as intimidating as her piloting one, has tripled her stack. She shows no expression and doesn't say a word as she wins multiple hands. Her opponents question out loud if she's bluffing, if she really has the superior combination of cards. Her silence melts the opposition.

"Do you always play so seriously?" I ask her when she gets up to cash in her coins.

"Only when I play to win."

THERE ARE SO MANY THINGS TO DO, FROM WATCHING SAMURAIS DUKE IT out in real sword combat, to arcades with retro portical games, that I feel like I could spend a year here and not do everything. There are big portical displays showing off all the popular shows on the strip, including the bawdy comedy act with Mr. Walrus whose punch line is, "I'd buy that for a yen!"

People can gamble on anything, from sumo matches on the main island, to bondage baseball games in the underground Minci league, and even the kyotei matches of the day. At three in the morning, Kujira wants more food, so he goes to the packed twenty-four-hour buffet with Kazu, who accompanies him. Chieko, Nori, and I end up on top of the *Matsumoto's* Eiffel Tower–sized Ai doll, which overlooks the whole city. It's hot and dry outside. We can't see any stars, but I marvel at the neon sparks of the Vegas strip below.

Nori and Chieko ruminate about perception.

"Our bodies are like simulations, but our brains are the porticals, and our eyes are the display cameras," Nori suggests. "Say a hundred thousand years ago, people could choose which virtual world to live in, and this is just the one we synced our portical brains to. On other planets, their existence isn't carbon- or solid-based like us, so they have completely different social structures. With every 'life,' you experience a full cycle according to a different set of physics. You die, you reincarnate in another world where you live as a gaseous amalgam or as an organism that thrives in liquid ethane. Repeat."

"So basically, you live as a fart or piss?" Chieko asks.

"That is a crass way of putting my metaphysical speculation."

"It's all the same, right? Stardust becomes planet becomes human who creates crap and piss that spurs growth in farms and plants and eventually, becomes Chieko Two and Noriko Two, who use the bathroom three to four times a day."

"Mac, can you please explain to Chieko why life isn't just about defecation and urination?"

"I will, after I use the bathroom," I reply.

SOMEHOW, WE ALL MAKE IT BACK TO OUR SUITE. I FALL ASLEEP AND wake five hours later because Chieko snores extremely loudly. She and Wren really were the perfect match.

Kujira is sleeping with his mouth agape and his body scrunched up. Kazu has earplugs on and is resting soundly. There are cards, bottles of wine, and paint all around us. Someone painted, "I'm a whale," on Kujira's back, and I sincerely hope it wasn't me—I can't remember.

I don't see Nori until I go to the living room and see her in a quarter lotus position, meditating. I was hoping to sleep out here but don't want to disturb her. I'm about to tiptoe back in when Nori asks me, "Did you have fun tonight?"

"I did. You?"

"Vegas is always a spectacle."

I nod in agreement. "You sleeping at all tonight?"

"I've trained myself so I can get by with only four hours of sleep a night."

"Four hours?" Is she kidding?

"You'll be amazed how much you can get out of your body with the proper training and discipline."

"I like my sleep."

"A person who lives to seventy-five years spends an average of twenty-five of those years sleeping. Twenty-five. Think how much you could do with even half of that back."

When she puts it like that, it seems an awful waste. "That's a trick you need to teach me."

"It's not a trick. It's a lifestyle. And, of course, I'd be more than glad to teach you. But it'll take years to retrain your body to maximize efficiency."

She gets back to her meditation. I reenter the room and try to sleep. Four more hours of sleep before morning would be a boon, but Chieko is too loud, so I throw a pillow at her. She wakes for a second, then goes back to sleep and snores again. I take a blanket, pillow, and sleep in the bathtub, with the bathroom door shut.

WHEN WE GET BACK TO BEMA IN THE MORNING, KAZU GUIDES US TO ONE of the private conference rooms. Only Nori looks refreshed, while the four of us look like we slept in trash cans.

"I'm really honored that you're part of the Tigers," Kazu says. "One of the biggest privileges being part of this group is we get to test mecha prototypes for the R and D department. After your classes end next week, we'll be spending our evenings doing simulation tests to familiarize ourselves with the controls on some new mechas they're developing."

"What happens after we're familiar with them?" Chieko asks, unperturbed by all the alcohol inside of her even though I'm barely standing.

"Test drives."

"In San Francisco?"

Kazu shakes his head. "Underneath the bay."

"Underneath?"

Kazu looks at Nori who explains, "There's a whole underwater facility to test out top secret prototypes."

"Nazis are so proud of what they did to the Mediterranean, they have no idea we have something even better."

He puts his hand, palm down, in between us. The four of us pile our hands on top of his.

"For Berkeley!" he exclaims.

We all yell, "For Berkeley!" as we raise our arms.

He gives us all a thumbs-up and leaves. The four of us lock

arms and help one another back to our dorms. Nori makes sure we're safely in our rooms before going to her own apartment. I literally blink and am woken by the alarm. It's Monday morning, and I have class.

13

★ ★ ★

I LIKE THE BAY AREA, BUT I MISS THE HOTTER CLIMATE OF DALLAS AND
Los Angeles. Mornings are cold and foggy in Berkeley, making
early exercises a challenge. My muscles feel bloated, and my joints
feel stiffened by the cold. We have electric heaters in our rooms,
but they take a really long time to warm the room. The only way
for them to work is to leave them on all day. But the dorms are set
up with motion sensors that shut off all electricity when we're not
in the room so I'm always too cold.

Kazu's breakfast arrangements have me drinking weird con-
coctions of fruits and vegetables that taste like blended celery with
apple strips thrown in. I hate celery. No toast, or anything with
bread, is included. The focus is on proteins, with eggs and seasoned anchovies. When I ask for replacements, substitutes, or additional food, they check my records and inform me, "Your diet is
strictly limited. We're not allowed to give you anything else."

Thank you, Kazu-sempai.

I know there are ways around it if I really wanted to try. But I'll give it a shot for a week.

AFTER THE FRENZY OF THE TOURNAMENT AND THE ENTRY INTO THE CIR- cle, daily school life is a jarring reminder that the majority of cadet work is studying and practicing. I still hate homework, though I try to be more diligent about it.

Kenjutsu class with Professor Sugiyama is still my favorite as we learn new ways to wield our sword. The lessons were invaluable during the tournament. Since then, she spends much of her time teaching us defensive parries, criticizing all of us for "relying too much on offense."

Nori recommends I join a boxing club and drop in once or twice a week so I can work on nonweaponized combat. The first class I attend, I strap on my headgear and spend the whole hour getting pummeled in the face. Even with the protection on, it hurts, and when the class is over, I have to go home and close my eyes because I feel like I'm still getting pounded.

I'm completely lost in Literature and Rhetoric because I haven't read any of the assigned material. Math is an obscure language that gets more confusing with each class. My elective, calligraphy, is a real chore. Chieko's writing is excellent. Even Kujira is good with brushes. The smell of ink oddly makes me hungry, and that's about the only good thing because my calligraphy is egregious. When my professor sees my attempts, he yells, "Are you using your toes to write?"

One of my biggest (and most pleasant) surprises is that corporal punishment isn't allowed. I ask Nori about it, and she tells me, "It was banned a long time ago. The cadets here are the most dedicated in the USJ. Hitting them won't serve any purpose."

They've started giving us voluntary mecha training on the

weekends, and, of course, everyone attends. Our teacher is Professor Okamoto, and his class is on the east side of campus, surprisingly, in the art building. His room is filled with paintings, and when he begins, he reviews the two San Diego conflicts, citing specific lessons from real battles.

"Anyone know what war actually is?" he challenges the cadets.

"Fighting our enemies for justice," someone suggests.

"It's all-out combat with other nations."

Most of the answers are along that vein.

The professor doesn't refute them, but explains, "War is the most extreme form of diplomacy. That's it. Every mecha pilot is a diplomat. We just don't use words. We use our mecha fists to achieve a political objective. In that negotiation, anything can become a weapon. The George Washingtons were short on bullets, but do you think they surrendered? No. They cut up bronze curtain rods, filled them with gunpowder they got from our mines, primed them with sulfur and carbon from coconut shells, then fired them right back at us. Sometimes your weapons will not be enough to defeat the enemy. Use their tools against them. How do you that? Understand and study your enemy." He points to several paintings behind him, powerful illustrations of the Americans and mosaics of different art styles. "I learned to paint like the George Washingtons in order to understand how they approach art. Liberto is one of the greats when it comes to warfare. Study him and the artists of that generation so you'll always keep one thing in mind. In this class, I'm training you to be a diplomat, not a brute in a big robot suit."

It's an approach I've never thought about and something I ponder the whole week. It definitely makes my military history and battle-theory classes more interesting. I can't wait until we begin the prototype testing in the underwater facility.

BEFORE WE CAN DO THAT, I RECEIVE A NOTICE FROM THE TOKKO, ASKING me to send in my portical. I send it in via the academy courier service. I spot Nori on my way to class, and inquire, "Is it normal for the Tokko to ask for our porticals?"

She assures me, "This is standard for all of us to get security clearance. They'll check your portical activity, every message you've sent, and everything you've said on the kikkai."

"Everything?" I ask, thinking back on a thousand dumb things I've said, looked at, and taken part in. I'm sure for every stupid message that I remember, there are twenty more I've forgotten.

"Everything," she confirms, and a part of me sinks. "They'll also do a sweep of your room to make sure you aren't bugged and talk to your family members and friends."

"They're doing the same for you too?"

"All five of us."

"I've said some stupid things in my messages," I confess. Maybe I'm preemptively warning her in case some of the things I've said become public.

"We all have," she says. "But is there anything treasonous?"

"No, of course not." What I really mean is, not that I remember. But I can't guarantee that some comment won't be taken out of context and misinterpreted in a negative light.

"Then you don't have to worry. By the way, don't try to delete anything because that'll only raise a red flag for them."

Scratch plan b. "Thanks for the warning."

I SPEND THE WHOLE WEEK WORRYING ABOUT MY SECURITY CLEARANCE, second-guessing myself. What if my messages to Griselda are misconstrued? Will my connection to Hideki cause any issues? All it takes is one misspoken word for the Tokko to cart me away on suspicion of clinging to a subversive ideology. No one is exempt. Not even military. I remind myself that after Hideki's death, Agent Tsukino said other agents had gone through my messages and found nothing. It's probably the only reassurance I have.

At night, I knock on Kujira's room. "What's up, man?"

"How'd you meet the Tokko agent?" I ask him.

"That's one of those things I'd tell you, but I think she'd kill you if I did," he answers.

I stare at him to see if he's serious, but I can't tell. "Forget I asked."

"Why do you care?"

"I'm worried about the security clearance."

"Oh, that," he says. He brushes his hair aside, and I see his scar again.

"You're not worried?" I ask.

"You forget? I lived off the grid for the last seventeen years. Nothing for them to check even if they wanted."

"What about your portical files?"

"I use an encrypted connection to the kikkai that erases itself as soon as the session ends."

"You need to show me how to use that."

"Use that now, and it sets off alarms," he answers.

"Then how do you use them?"

"Because I have Akiko's permission, and there's no history for them to compare me against."

"What about your family history?"

"My grandparents were from Osaka, so I guess I have some relatives there. But I haven't ever met them." He snorts at me. "I wouldn't worry too much if I were you."

"Why not?"

"If there was something on you, they would have gotten you

already," Kujira replies. "I've seen her kill a person before, man. Secret police don't kid around. But it's not you they're after, so stop stressing." He looks back down at his portical. "I got some real issues to take care of. Because of that damn Kazu, I can't get a sausage anywhere."

"You don't like the new diet?"

"It's terrible, man. Everything tastes like processed vegetables. Even the fish. I can't sleep 'cause I'm starvin' at night. Don't tell me you like it?"

"I've noticed I have more energy."

"I'm not talking to you anymore," he says, and shuts the door.

AFTER CLASSES END, I FEEL GROUCHY BECAUSE THE COLD WEATHER IS freezing my ears and giving me a headache. Plus I have several hours of homework that I don't want to do.

I enter my dorm room, and it's even colder inside than it was outside. I turn on the heater, which does nothing. The knock on my door irritates me as I wonder out loud, "Who is it?"

"Open the door, Makoto Fujimoto," a strong voice asserts.

I check the peephole, and it's Agent Akiko Tsukino.

Is she here to arrest me?

I involuntarily look toward my window. There's no escape. I calm myself and open the door. She holds up my portical.

"You're clear," she says.

I feel immense relief flow through me. "Any issues?" I ask, and regret it because I'm not sure I want to know.

"Only the ones I've already pointed out to you. Why were you so worried?"

"How'd you know I was worried?"

"Kujira asked me to look into the situation. He said you were losing your mind over it."

"Really?" I ask, surprised he would actually do something for me and that the Tokko agent would listen.

"Yes. Kujira tells me your parents were acquaintances," she states.

"It's true," I reply. She doesn't look at all surprised. "Did you know that already?" I ask.

She doesn't answer my question. Instead, she says, "You and Kujira will be taking on an important assignment."

"I don't know the specifics."

"You will learn them."

"Did you—did you know my mother?" I want to know.

"No. But the situation troubles you," she states with a certainty that makes me believe she already knows what I think.

"It bothers me a lot. My mom was sent to her death even though they knew it was a trap."

"In any profession, you will have superiors making bad decisions," Agent Tsukino says without emotion. "Even the best generals make mistakes. The reason we're officers is to learn, improve, and make a difference for those who rely on us. You can quit if it bothers you too much. But that means someone less competent will take your place."

"You've received bad orders before?"

She ponders her answer, and I'm surprised to see conflicted pain in her squint. "In any profession, you will have superiors making bad decisions," she repeats. "If you're going to quit, do so immediately as this task is too vital to be hindered by your ambivalence."

"Do you just ignore the problems?" I ask her.

"I continue my mission because bad orders don't cloud that I'm fighting to protect the United States of Japan from everyone who wants us to be as miserable and deplorable as they are."

As she's about to leave, I tell her, "Thank you."

She doesn't acknowledge my gratitude, but it's okay. I feel like the foot has been removed from my chest.

SUNDAY MORNING SLIPS IN. I EAT EGGS AND MISO SOUP ALONG WITH A protein bar. My ankles and wrists feel constricted from all our sword practice, so I stretch them out. My favorite ankle stretch is to stand on one leg, close my eyes, raise my arms out to the side, and hold the pose for thirty seconds, repeating that five times on alternate feet. It's harder than it sounds as my body has a hard time keeping balance without visual reassurance. The stress of standing stretches the ankle muscles.

After receiving orders to report for our new duties, the "Five Tigers" take the subway to San Francisco.

Nori and Chieko are talking about a new type of defensive sword style they've discovered. Kazu sees some officers he recognizes and greets them. Kujira is sitting with his arms crossed, and mutters, "How is a person supposed to live without sausages and orange juice in the morning?"

"Orange juice has concentrated sugar, which is unhealthy for you," Kazu interjects before getting back to his conversation.

"My mom survived on orange juice and sausages for three days because she couldn't get back to base, and she still kicked GW ass."

"Don't get me started on the food," Chieko groans.

"He thinks this new menu gives him more energy," Kujira says to her about me.

Chieko looks to me for an explanation.

"I like the new diet," I say. "I feel more energized in the mornings."

Chieko shakes her head. "Food is a reward, not just an energy source."

"Take it up with sempai," I protest. "What about you?" I ask Nori.

"I've been doing the diet for the past year, and it's made me a lot healthier."

"See? It's not just me," I say.

"Sellout," Chieko mutters to me.

"I heard that!"

"I wanted you to hear it," she says.

The Market Street stop is our exit.

OUR DESTINATION IS A GROUP OF OLD WAREHOUSES NEXT TO THE PIER. A young woman is waiting for us. She's wearing a khaki coat and pants, has hair down to her shoulder, and is preoccupied with her portical.

"I'm Dr. Shimitsu's assistant. Please follow me," she says, without looking up. I'm not sure who Dr. Shimitsu is, but I assume it's the name of the person in charge.

We are led inside one of the nondescript buildings. There are several bulk shipping containers inside. The red one opens up to a secret staircase we take down two floors. There's an elevator at the bottom. The five of us get onto an elevator that's big enough to fit two cars. I can't wait to see what's down here. Dr. Shimitsu's assistant continues to read as the doors close. We begin our descent.

"How far does this go down?" I ask.

She doesn't answer.

Kazu says, "Just short of the center of the earth."

"Seriously?"

Kazu chuckles. "Close enough."

When we come out from the elevator, there are three more gates we need to go through. They check our porticals, do a finger

ID, run a retinal scan, and confirm our auditory signatures. After we're cleared, we emerge into a big hub that could pass for a train station with the high density of people present. Some are soldiers, but many more are civilians heading to their next destination. The ceiling is a massive portical display colored azure with clouds streaming by. The floors are all wooden, and there's a brick fireplace where people are conversing and drinking tea. There are a variety of stores, restaurants, and kiosks that make the area resemble a shopping center more than a top secret underground base. There's even a gym, and I see a gigantic swimming pool and indoor tennis court through the glass walls. Trees are everywhere, genetically modified to be able to subsist without the sun.

We traverse into the next area, take an escalator down multiple floors. I notice that many of the people are pale and wonder how long it's been since they've been outside. I appreciate that there's a fully functional climate control, so it's very toasty.

"Welcome to Mechtown," Kazu says. "A fitting name considering the primary focus down here."

"What's that?" I ask.

"What do you think?" Kazu asks back as he points at the towering mechas in the distance.

"I can't believe this is all underneath the bay," Chieko states.

"This is a subterranean reflection of the city," Nori replies. "I've visited here every week for the past year, and I think I've seen only a small percent of the total space."

"We don't have clearance for most of the areas either," Kazu says. "There's some amazing stuff going on down here. Don't gape too much."

There are eighteen gates in the northern hall, and we have to use our portical clearance to get through 013.

"Why isn't mecha spelled with a k?" Kujira asks.

"Why would it be?" Chieko asks.

"With the 'c-h' spelling, it should be pronounced 'metcha', not 'mekka' like we do."

"That's stupid. The 'h' goes silent. You don't pronounce mechanical met-cha-nical. You pronounce it me-kan-ical."

"The spelling and pronunciation are weird," Kujira says.

"Be prepared for weird overdose," Kazu tells us.

We enter a hangar-bay area filled with mecha types I've never seen before. The first set looks like a cross of an animal and mecha, reminding me of the chimeras from the NARA, only more sophisticated. I look at the portical displays on the walls and am surprised to see human pilots on one side, animals on the other. Neural interfaces are hooked to dogs, monkeys, ostriches, and cats.

"These are the animal hybrids," Nori explains. "They've been testing to see how a human brain synced with an animal one drives our new mechas as part of Project Lightpin."

"Does it work?"

"It's in progress. Turns out animals are way more complex than we'd thought, but they're also simpler in other ways, so fine-tuning the neural link is taking longer than they'd anticipated," Nori says. She looks at Kazu, and they both look like they're going to laugh about an inside joke they don't bother to share with us.

As we take a multipassenger cart through the bay, Nori points out a mecha shaped like a hefty sumo wrestler and explains, "That's the prototype for the Sumo class. But the physical rigors of creating a mecha that could continuously fight like that was less optimal than someone who used a gun and melee weapon, so they scrapped it."

"This is an experimental playground for mechas?" Kujira asks.

Nori nods. "Pretty much if you can imagine it, they try it out here."

Past the beasts, there are mechas classified according to their specialties.

"Those eight areas represent different divisions and areas of development," Kazu says. "That's Heat, Flash, Metal, Bubble, Quick, Crash, and I forget the last two."

"Wood and Air," Nori says. "Air Division is developing a tornado cannon that ended up destroying the facility they were housed in, so they moved here three months ago."

Kazu grins. "The Flash Division is trying to find ways to adjust time perception through steroidal enhancers that make pilots respond faster."

"Does it work?" Chieko asks.

"It makes the pilots soil their suits as soon as they take the pills because they can't control their bowel movements anymore."

Each section has several dozen researchers experimenting with prototype weapons.

The mechas come in vastly different body types than the ones I'm used to seeing. Many are much smaller than the looming giants that are the norm. Chieko asks about their size, and Nori explains, "In the early phase, they'll build at a quarter scale to try to test it and pitch it to the brass. If they get approval, they move into the actual development phase. That's housed in a different section."

"We're not allowed there," Kazu adds.

"Yet," Nori says.

Kazu laughs. "You'll be running this place in a decade."

We pass through the first area and have to go through another security gate. The second area is similar except that there are just five enormous mechas. They remind me of the lethal *Korosu*-class mechas, which are usually at our front lines as the most advanced type in the corps. If you crossed a samurai with a stealth jet and gave it curves like a racing car, you'd get this new mecha. Their surfaces are much smoother than the *Korosu* class, almost no division or separating sheets. The sleeker shoulder fins probably house the antenna and a jamming system, while I'd assume the helmet crest contains the primary sensors. The BPG is contained in the gut, which looks reinforced by titanium. Unlike a completed mecha, there's no paint applied, so they're a silvery white. On each of the five mechas, parts are missing and the innards are exposed. A crew is attaching a separated arm piece. There's a new type of joint-hinge mechanism in the elbow and upper arm that makes me wonder if they've been working on speeding up motion.

Dr. Shimitsu's assistant, who hasn't said a word the whole time, looks to the woman walking our way, and says, "This is Dr. Shimitsu," before scurrying away.

Dr. Shimitsu is a short Asian female with a bowl cut, wide brown eyes that seem to absorb everything, and a mischievous grin.

"You're my testers?" she asks us.

"We are," Kazu replies.

"You all have limited mecha experience?"

"Very limited."

"Good. I want raw feedback from a fresh perspective. The experienced mecha pilots want to keep everything status quo. We have to shake it up with Dr. Günter's new program. Which of you two are Makoto and Chieko?"

"That's us," Chieko replies.

"We especially want your feedback because you've fought a bio-mech before."

"What kind of feedback?"

Shimitsu claps her hands. "What else? This is the new Leviathan-class mecha. The first five prototypes are named *Ari-kuni*, *Yoshimitsu*, *Sukehira*, *Kanenaga*, and the *Muramasa*."

"What's the Leviathan class do?"

"They're designed for one purpose. Destroy the Nazi bio-mechs," Shimitsu answers. That's exactly what I want to hear. "Don't talk about anything that you see here outside of these walls," Shimitsu warns us. "You'll be shot if you do. Tokko installed audio recognition on your porticals that'll alert them if you say a word related to the research going on down here. It happened to my last assistant because she mentioned it to one of the researchers while they were eating outside Mechtown and several civilians overheard, which is why my new one never talks."

She says it so quickly, I can't tell if she just has a dark sense of humor or if her assistant really was executed for talking about the project. Her assistant's reticence seems to indicate the latter.

"What do you want us to do?" Kazu asks.

"First thing I need you to do is run the simulations. We need as much test data as we can get. Try everything. We'll attempt to mimic simulation information on the Leviathans. We will perform stress testing, unorthodox motion, and combat beyond what my group has been doing. I've already requested temporary habitats for all five of you here."

"What about our classes?" Nori asks.

"You've been excused from your classes for the next four weeks," Shimitsu replies. "This testing is of vital interest to the Empire." She leads us to a circular room with ten simulation booths that are facing one another. "This is the test pit," she tells us. "Everything's been reprogrammed to match the Leviathan's protocols. Strap yourselves in."

Before we do, Nori reminds us, "Clean your gear thoroughly with alcohol and disinfectant before you put it on. I got pinkeye last year during the tournaments, and it wasn't fun."

We wash our equipment and put on the basic gear. Plugging in, I'm surprised that the interface and its functionality are similar to the ones we used for the tournament. But there are improvements. In the past, if I wanted to check something on the sensors, I'd have to mark it and query. Now, wherever I look, the system will automatically track my eye movement and show the relevant data, erasing anything that's fallen out of focus.

Shimitsu tells us, "When we extend past the initial testing phase, we'll get you a crew to help you aboard the Leviathans. For the purposes of this initial test, we've simplified the interface so you can get by without a navigator, munitions officer, and engineer. We want to see how you fare against a biomech in a standard mecha versus the Leviathan. We've been modifying the behavior of the biomech so that it's as accurate as we can get it. So far, none of our researchers has been able to defeat the biomech without the Leviathan, so we'd like to do a test comparison of how you fare with and without the new mechas."

We talk to one another through communicators installed in the sim. Shimitsu asks us to customize proportions according to our needs.

"Why does it matter?" I ask.

"Adjusting things like arm length is critical," Nori replies. "Arm length affects your speed with weapons as well as your mobility and defenses. You can give it a general range that can be adjusted."

"A factor you young'uns have to consider for longevity is repetitive stress injuries," Kazu says. "You keep on doing the same motion over and over again, and you get hurt." It reminds me of Spider's pain. "You have to work with the architect program to get the right seating configuration and make sure your posture remains upright. Last thing you want is to get a pinched nerve that puts you out of operation."

We end up spending the first four hours customizing all the parts and scaling them appropriately. Every time I make a change, I take my Leviathan for a spin, running around the simulation course. There are dummy targets I destroy with my sword. Shortening arm length means I get a quicker attack but lose length and reach. Longer arms translate into greater reach but a slightly slower swipe. I make the arms a little shorter than the default, which seems to strike the right balance. Knee positioning is critical for mobility, and I adjust that about eighteen times. Same for hand scale, finger length, and overall height in proportion to the others. When I actually compare my updates to the default, they're not far off. Kazu and Nori bulk up, increasing limb lengths by about twenty percent. Chieko keeps the defaults but asks for bigger hands and fingers.

"This thing doesn't feel right," Kujira says.

"What doesn't feel right?" Shimitsu asks.

"Everything feels too light."

"Response times should be more reactive than any training mechas you may have used."

"I mean compared to the *Korosu* class," Kujira replies. The *Korosu* class is what his mom used.

"Those old things are junk compared to the Leviathan. Their reaction time is a tenth of the Leviathans."

"That 'junk' would handily destroy any of your Leviathans."

"Kujira, let's save this debate for later," Kazu jumps in.

"There's no debate to be had," Dr. Shimitsu says. "The Leviathan is far superior. There will be another day to lock down proportions in case you want to adjust it after starting the simulations. I've uploaded the 'Lygar' program, which will pit you against a biomech using pre-Leviathan mechas. Please do your best to defeat it even if you feel it is impossible. It's important for us to assess your fighting methods. You can also start testing out direct voice input."

For some reason, I've screwed up the interface so that changes on the left side don't mirror properly to the right. I toggle the symmetry controls, but everything is out of sync. I have to ask Dr. Shimitsu, who says she will take a look.

"Done!" Nori shouts.

"What's done?" Dr. Shimitsu asks.

"Biomech is defeated," Nori replies.

"That's impossible. You're still playing in pre-Leviathan mode." But when Kazu, Chieko, and Kujira also defeat the biomech, Shimitsu is surprised. "None of our testers have been able to defeat the biomech in this mode."

"This biomech needs to get a lot tougher," Chieko chimes in. "The thing we fought dismantled the Sentries like they were scarecrows."

Shimitsu resets my finger positions, and I have to readjust them with the symmetry reactivated. This time, the coordinates are appropriately mirrored, and I plunge into the biomech fight via simulation.

I'm in San Francisco. Skyscrapers are all around me. There are people inside the windows and cars are driving down the street. The biomech is in front of me. It's not as intimidating as my confrontation, both because I know it's not real and I'm at the same level as it is. Its movement is all wrong and looks more like a mecha with a black texture applied to it, not like the biomech with living skin as its armor.

I expect it to be an easy fight and charge headfirst. But before I can strike, it punches me hard. Its length is longer than mine. I raise my defenses, but it charges into me and starts cutting me up. Before I know it, my mecha is destroyed.

I try again, and the result is the same.

"Something wrong, Mac?" Kazu asks.

"Just warming up," I reply.

In the next simulation, I don't charge it. I try to draw it close to me. I have my sword up, hide between the buildings. The biomech destroys everything in its wake and jumps on top of me, destroying my mecha.

I'm boggled.

"What's going on?" I ask.

"I've increased the difficulty level," Shimitsu says. "You all can try again."

Even with the higher difficulty, the other four breeze through it. It's a struggle for me to keep up, and eventually, Kazu suggests I watch the others fight. Nori is excellent with her spear and uses her length to pierce the biomech to death. Kujira uses his sword arts to slice the biomech to pieces. Kazu swings his magnetic yo-yo, which has deadly blades that are also charged and melt the biomech's skin. Chieko actually gets up close and personal, using daggers and her combat skills to choke the biomech to death. I realize its neck is its weak point and am able to take it down on my eleventh try. I feel embarrassed, but I'm also getting used to the controls.

The day passes quickly, and by the evening, we're sent to our temporary housing in the residential quarter, apartments inhabited by workers and their families. There's a school down here, mess hall, clubhouse for people to congregate and watch portical shows together, as well as a twenty-four-hour market.

My eyes are strained from the simulation and I grab my dinner to go so I can eat in my room. It's a studio with a bed, a kitchen, and private toilet. I eat dinner, drink two glasses of water, and take a hot shower. I shave the stubble on my chin, tell myself I'll do better tomorrow, then lie down in bed for sleep.

UNFORTUNATELY, DAY TWO DOESN'T GO ANY BETTER.

"Based on the exercises yesterday, we've revamped the biomech intelligence and made updates to the mecha controls," Dr. Shimitsu tells us as we arrive. "We'd like you to switch to the Leviathan today and document any bugs, issues, and suggestions through our database."

The menu for filing bugs has multiple categories including priority, type, importance, affected section of the mecha, and other information for the engineers. Once the simulation commences, we find that the biomech is a much more competent opponent. But the upgraded armor in the Leviathans proves too much for the biomechs. Chieko has plenty of suggestions for ways to improve. Nori finds major kinks in the way the limbs respond to our controls. Kazu has more philosophical ideas about the broader scope of the project. Kujira complains about everything. I'm struggling just to survive against the updated biomech. Even in the Leviathan class, my mecha is defeated by the biomech. I launch, reset, launch, reset. The final result is always my destruction. I think I'm prepared for the assault and try to defend myself. The monster always gets me before I can get it. There's no way for them to revert the difficulty level of the biomechs either so that I can practice.

At lunch, everyone gathers to throw around ideas about how to improve the Leviathan. Dr. Shimitsu and her team of engineers are excited to hear our input. Everyone has suggestions except for me. Dr. Shimitsu actually asks me, "Do you have anything you'd like to add?"

I shake my head. "Not at the moment."

I feel comfortable with the controls. When I practice by myself, the sword reacts the way I expect it to. But whenever I go up against the biomech, my response time isn't fast enough to react to its vicious attack. Are the others just that much better than me? I don't know why I'm struggling so much.

The four times I do find a minor problem in the mecha, I do a search in the database and see someone has already logged the issue.

I feel useless here, like I don't really belong. By the end of the second day, I've nearly defeated the biomech but still haven't done anything to contribute. The others have reported a combined 217 bugs. I have three, and they're suggestions about how to improve the biomech's appearance.

Maybe it's being underground or maybe it's just not having seen the sun for three days, but my dreams are vivid that night, and I have a hard time breathing. All my old RAMs pile up on top of me. I try to push them off, tell them they're suppressing me, but they won't budge. Spider, Botan, Wren, Sensei, Olympia, and all the others have blank faces though they're staring in my direction. Their eyes get wider and bloodshot. I struggle with their weight, try repeatedly to extricate myself. My alarm wakes me, and I realize I've been wrestling with my blanket.

I'm extremely frustrated on the third day, and by the fourth day, I want to destroy my console. I try to fight, attempt to master the use of the Leviathan. But after getting beaten eight times, I unstrap my gear and pop out of the booth. I need to get out, need someplace I can breathe. Dr. Shimitsu meets me, and asks, "What are you doing?"

"I need fresh air. I need to go up to the surface."

"You can't leave right now."

"I'm not staying here!" I shout, and rapidly march out.

It's a long trek back up, but I don't care. I go through all the security gates, past everything we saw on the way in. When I reach the surface, I welcome the cold breeze of the bay. I breathe in deeply. I feel embarrassed that I broke down and left the way I did. Will they kick me out of the Tigers now? Will they say I wasn't mentally tough enough? I suck in the bay air, let it refresh my lungs. Why am I having such a hard time with the program? Am I more disturbed by the presence of the biomech than I'm admitting to myself? I give myself half an hour to cool down. I feel a hundred times better. But I don't know what to do now. Go back to my dormitory? That seems silly. But I don't want to go back down and try to explain myself to them when even I don't know why I'm doing so badly.

I think it's the sense of helplessness that's getting to me. I hate feeling like there's nothing I can do to stop that biomech again. Is it my fear that's locking up my movement?

I'm fuming to myself when Nori arrives. I expect her to say something to me, either a reprimand at my childish departure or some type of cheesy encouragement. But she doesn't do either. She's holding a *nashi*, which she starts to peel with her dagger. The yellow skin slides off, hanging from the side. She makes her way around the pear until it's bare. She cuts off two half-circle slices and hands them to me. I take them, and she starts eating her pieces. I take a bite out of mine. It's very sweet and tasty, and I'm grateful she peeled it for me as I've never been able to do it without cutting my fingers. We spend the next two minutes chewing on our pears. I appreciate that she doesn't lecture me or tell me what she thinks I should do. By the time we're done, she heads back. I follow her. No one mentions anything. I jump into the sim booth.

"Let's calibrate your mecha," Nori suggests to me.

"What'd you have in mind?"

IN THE BIG SCHEME OF THINGS, THE CHANGES SHE SUGGESTS TO ME ARE minuscule. Shorten the arm length by 3 percent. Adjust the elbow location so that it's slightly more equidistant between the shoulder and wrist (1.8 grid units in X). Scale out the shoulder spans by 2.4 percent. And bulk up the chest by 1.7 percent. But it makes a huge difference when it comes time to fight the biomech. My swings are faster, as are my defensive parries, because my reaction time has been optimized. When I confront the biomech again, I'm able to deflect its first set of lunges. I see an opening and plunge my blade into its left armpit, slicing the arm away from its shoulder socket. It swings at me with its right arm, but I'm able to block it and pierce it with my sword. It gets a few more attacks in that damage my hull. But I lop off its head and score the victory. I hear cheers from the other Tigers that make me realize they were closely watching my fight.

I input a few suggestions related to the proportions, recommending they find a way to compare the different ranges for scale and provide alternatives that'll give pilots a clearer idea of what might work better for their skill set. It's not much, but I feel like I can breathe in peace.

"I didn't know those changes could make such a difference," I tell Nori later.

"It's a matter of life and death," she replies.

"Your ass just needs to get faster!" Kujira snaps at me.

THURSDAY NIGHT, KAZU SUGGESTS WE GRAB DINNER TOGETHER AND EAT in a private lounge. I'm not a big fan of the salad and dried fish, but at least there are pineapple slices.

"What do you all think of this place?" he starts.

"I knew lots of research took place into mecha development, but I never knew it was this much," Chieko replies. "One of the scientists was saying she's being transferred to the space division, onto a project called Cybernater."

"That's 'cause the Nazis are focusing so much on space development and building those huge satellites," Nori replies. "If they want a war in the stars, we've got to be ready for them."

"How big is Mechtown?"

"Big," Kazu answers. "Berkeley has the largest mecha research facility in the USJ."

"There are two bigger ones in Asia. But none are as advanced as here," Nori adds with pride.

"How you liking the place?" Kazu asks me.

"It's been a steep learning curve," I reply. "I'm trying to absorb everything. But it's awe-inspiring. And they have very nice bathrooms."

Kazu laughs, acknowledging my reference. Then to Kujira, "Let me guess. You're not impressed."

Kujira shrugs. "Lot of money being wasted here on pet projects and mad-scientist chicanery."

"That's what they said about the very first mechas."

Kujira can't deny that, so he says, "I don't care where the powers that be waste their money."

"What do you think about Mechtown?" Chieko asks Kazu.

"This is high-tech royalty," Kazu replies. "I started off as an enlisted soldier, so everything here is posh compared to what I'm used to."

"How'd you go from enlisted to BEMA?" Chieko asks.

"Same way you jumped from the RAMs to BEMA. Fought my way in."

"What was it like driving tanks?" I ask him.

"Wild," Kazu replies. "I was stationed together with Honda in the Singapore Province. Local dissidents were stirring up trouble, so we were sent in to pacify. It's weird—the things I remember most are the heat and the ants. If you left any food around, it'd be swarmed by ants."

"Killer ants?" Kujira asks.

"Fortunately, nonmutated and not lethal to people. But they were everywhere, just like the rebels. They'd blow up everything they could. We'd try to track them down, but they'd blend in with the civilians. One time, we think we've found a shipment of arms, so eight of us chase them down. It's a trap, and about a hundred guerilla troops surround us. They got antitank personnel in place too, and I swear it's over for us. I make peace with the Emperor.

That's when a mecha came to our rescue. Just when one of the guerillas is about to shoot me, the mecha swoops down and crushes him with his hands. It killed the rest, took out their vehicles, and even destroyed three of their helicopters. I got to thinking, what am I doing in this tank? I should be up there in that mecha. It's tough for enlisted to transfer. Outwardly, there are opportunities for everyone. But it's about connections and what your superior officers are willing to do for you. I wrangled some heads, got a transfer to work as a service technician aboard the *Morikawa*. It was an auxiliary mecha that got sent all over. But those two years traveling through Asia on the *Morikawa* will always stay with me. You all ever been to the Khyber Pass?"

None of us have.

"It's a bleak, mountainous road where old military leaders like Alexander the Great and Darius passed through," he informs us.

"Who are they?" Kujira asks.

"Warlords of the past. You know Genghis Khan, don't you?"

Kujira shrugs. "I got too many problems of my own to be interested in ancient history or dead people."

Kazu laughs. "It's a special experience visiting some of the most important sites in Asia on a mecha, even if they're only about dead people and ancient history."

We swap stories before breaking for dinner. I catch up with Kujira in front of his room as there's something I've wanted to tell him.

"Thank you for talking to Agent Tsukino."

"Why?" he asks me.

"Why what?"

"Why thank me?"

"I—I wanted to express my appreciation," I say.

"Why?"

"It's—I guess it's the polite thing to do. You don't want me to thank you?"

"It's quaint, man."

"Quaint?"

"If you're really grateful, get me some junk food. Otherwise, no thanks."

He enters his room and shuts the door. I laugh to myself, wondering what response I was expecting.

SIXTH DAY IN, THE SOUND OF DRILLS WAKES ME. I GET UP AND FIND MY-self inside a hangar bay with unfamiliar test mechas. I have no idea how I, or my bed, got here. An officer I don't know asks, "What are you doing here?"

"I actually have no idea," I answer truthfully. "Where am I exactly?"

It takes an hour and the help of one of the assistants to get me (along with my bed) back to my dorm. I'm late for the training session, but I wonder if I sleepwalked out to the hangar. When I arrive for the testing, I see my fellow Tigers eyeing me.

"Have a good night's sleep?" Kazu asks.

"Wonderful," I reply.

They all burst out laughing.

"How did you get me out there without waking me up?" I demand.

"That's something you should ask yourself," Kazu says.

"You slept like a mummy," Chieko says. "Nothing woke you."

WHEN WE REACH THE ONE-WEEK MARK, THEY GET US INTO THE PHYSICAL Leviathans. I get the mecha designated as the *Arikuni*, and the engineers have matched the parameters we set up in our simulations to a centimeter. The bridge is similar in size to the quad mecha and is placed inside the stomach, where it gets maximum protection. It can fit seven crew members and has ladders extending up and down through the mecha for maintenance. I take the pilot's seat, which can be pushed into the ground if I want to control the mecha from a standing position. Next to me is a console with maps, sensor schematics, and communication relays that are traditionally used by the navigator. On both sides of the bridge, they have a spot for the two munitions officers who control the left and right side respectively. Toward the back is the seat for engineering, which directly connects with another engineer near the BPG. They've simplified functionality for these tests so we don't require a full crew. They also have global optics on the goggles, which can make the bridge turn invisible. I feel like I'm floating midair with the arms and legs visible for combat, similar to many of the first-person portical games I play.

We're testing our mechas in an underground version of the Coliseum where we had our tournament, but it's double the size, and there isn't any stadium seating. We're able to move our Leviathans freely around, and I'm amazed at how well they respond to our commands. I swing my arm with the controls, and the mecha corresponds to my motion. The harder I swing, the harder my mecha punches.

They've built a life-sized version of the biomech. Unlike the simulation, this one has the regenerative skin that oozes around it. The biomech doesn't move, but if it did, it'd be indistinguishable from the Nazi version. Did they capture an actual biomech? How were they able to re-create it so perfectly?

"Attack it with your weapons, please," a new voice asks us over our communicators. I notice his *w* sounds like a *v*. *Attack it vith your veapons, please.* Is he German?

"Who is this?" Kazu asks.

"I am Dr. Günter, and I am assisting you in this operation."

"Who would like to go first?" Dr. Shimitsu asks, without introducing the previous speaker further.

"I'll take care of the vomit monster," Chieko volunteers.

She doesn't wait for confirmation and plunges her daggers into its belly. But the regenerative skin swallows the blades. Chieko tries to punch it, but the black ooze blocks her fist. She attacks it several times but only ends up denting her fingers. She pulls back, strategizing what to do next.

"Thank you," Dr. Shimitsu says.

"What do you mean 'thank you?' I can take this thing down."

"Any further attacks will only result in more damage. We'll try someone else now."

Kazu is very fast with his yo-yo, able to swing it and lacerate anything in his way. But when he attacks the biomech, the ebony skin actually latches onto his weapon and sucks it in. "What the hell's going on?" he demands.

The results are the same with Noriko's spear, Kujira's sword, and my own blade. Nothing we have pierces its skin. The harder I thrust, the stronger the resistance. They have to turn off the biomech so we can extract our weapons. But even then, they're damaged and will need replacement. My own blade is skewed, the sharp end blunted.

"Is this the Nazi superweapon?" Kujira asks.

"We call it a biomech because it fuses biological components on top of a mechanical skeletal structure," Dr. Günter explains.

"You pronounced 'mechanical' wrong," Kujira notes even though Dr. Günter pronounced it correctly.

"Did I?"

"Please try guns next," Dr. Shimitsu asks us.

We're each given machine guns with grenade launchers. We take turns unloading our bullets into the biomech, but it doesn't affect it at all. That's not a huge surprise since our melee weapons were ineffective as well. The gun has an alternate launcher built in so we switch to it. The grenade launchers make huge explosions, but even with acid shells, not much damage is inflicted on the biomech. It's no wonder our Sentries were so easily destroyed.

Noriko tries out her sniper rifle, and even though the distance isn't great, she aims at its head and fires. The biomech doesn't even flinch as the black ooze absorbs the bullets.

It's an afternoon of futility.

Kazu suggests to Dr. Shimitsu, "Can we give this one more go?"

"What would you like to try?"

"A simultaneous attack by all five of us."

There is no response for a minute. They must be talking about it.

"Go ahead," Dr. Shimitsu gives her approval.

Kazu says, "I'm sending each of you a vector of attack. If we strike the biomech simultaneously, we should be able to destroy it. But the timing has to be precise, so make sure you stay in sync."

He sends us over the thirty-six-degree spread we're covering. I have the back left. I grab a new sword and prepare myself.

"Timer ready," Nori says. "I've done an analysis on the points which should cause maximum damage."

The vulnerability I'm shown is in the shoulder. I overlay her graphic representation on the actual biomech and lock onto it as a target.

"Let's do it!" Kazu yells.

The countdown begins. Fifteen seconds. I rush toward the biomech. Ten. Sword is in the air. *Don't screw this up, Mac!* Syncing with the others. Five, four, three, two, *wham*! The Five Tigers strike the biomech at the same time. The impact from all directions shakes the biomech. My blade feels like it's going deeper than it did before. The surface is being stretched to compensate for the multidirectional blow. For a second, I see through the black ooze to a metallic shoulder plate underneath. I push harder, hoping to penetrate. But I see a surge in the armor, and the biomech's armor surrounds my sword. I try to withdraw, but only a third of my blade remains—the other two-thirds have dissolved inside its armor. Nori is the only one who cuts through the ooze and pierces into its armor, causing it to suffer an overload in its circuitry. Its right arm goes limp. But Nori can't pull her spear out, and the ooze overtakes it. If this were a real-life fight, we'd all be dead now.

"Good effort," Dr. Günter says. "But no regular attack will work against the Nazi biomech because it'll absorb it, dissolve it, and redistribute it as part of its armor."

"How do you know so much about them?" Nori asks.

"Because I helped design them," he replies, which surprises the hell out of me.

If one of the principal designers of the biomech has defected to our side, it would be a huge blow to the Nazis. I'm certain they'd be doing whatever they could to get information about him and am reminded of the professors who were arrested earlier. Is there a connection? "Now let me show you an alternate method."

The crew rolls out a crate full of new shells and a massive bazooka.

"Please equip the M87 sonic antimecha rocket launcher and load up the ablative shells," Günter tells us. "You'll need to feed it energy from your BPG. I'm sending over the necessary schematics so you can see where to connect to it."

There are wires in our arms that connect with the M87, and I see the gauges activating, showing me how much power is being channeled into the weapon. I've never seen a bazooka require this much juice.

"Who'd like to go first?"

"Me," Chieko volunteers again.

She places the M87 on her shoulder, where the pad actually has a spot for it to lock onto.

"For the purposes of this test launch, I've disabled the automatic aiming syste—"

There's a deafening burst, a sonic boom rocking the coliseum. The ablative shell launches at the speed of sound into the biomech, shattering the black components. The whole front is exposed and vulnerable to attack.

"Whoa," Chieko says. "That's sweet. Barely any recoil too."

"I'd like for each of you to try using this. But please wait for my signal before firing so we can take the appropriate measurements."

"Sorry!" Chieko chimes in, though from the glee in her voice, I can tell she's not at all sorry.

We each get a turn as they roll out a new biomech. I'm last, and after I position the antimecha launcher, I use my visual display to aim. As the red target lights up the biomech, I fire. Just as Chieko said, minimal recoil. I've dampened the audio from the blast, which is good, as my ears are still ringing from the first shot. The ablative shell hits and dissolves the biomech's armor. All that's standing is a metallic skeleton, vulnerable to our attack.

We do a few more drills and run some tests for Dr. Günter. But I have a solemn feeling like I'm witnessing history. If this works in combat, it means the balance of our two empires is going to change. What that portends, I have no idea. But it's exciting and intimidating to be part of.

AFTER OUR PRACTICE, WE'RE HEADING BACK TO OUR DORMS WHEN A message arrives for Kazu. He takes it, talks for a minute, then leads us to a private conference room.

"You might have noticed our police have been arresting a lot of spies on campus recently," he says. "The Nazis have been activating their sleeper agents in an almost reckless way. But I don't think they care right now because they'll sacrifice anyone in their attempt to find Dr. Günter."

I'm disconcerted to hear that the Nazis have many sleeper agents in Berkeley. "Who exactly is he?" I ask.

"The foremost specialist in the Nazi's biomech program."

"Why did he defect?"

"I don't know. I actually asked, but they didn't tell me."

"When'd this happen?"

"In the past year," Kazu answers. "The Nazis are afraid we'll find a way to undermine their entire biomech program, which, from the looks of it, we have. That's why they're doing everything they can to find Dr. Günter and neutralize him."

"Did his family defect with him?" Chieko asks.

Kazu shakes his head. "His father is an important officer in the Reich. I don't know about the rest of his family or what the fallout will be."

"If this is so important, why are they using cadets to test his weapons?" Nori inquires.

"I want to be real with y'all. I think it's because they still don't trust Günter, and we're more expendable than the other pilots."

In my head, I was envisioning something like *Only cadets with their unbiased perspective could be entrusted with this matter.* Reality is always more sobering.

"I want to emphasize how crucial it is that you mention nothing about what we're doing to anyone. Nazi spies are everywhere, so we have to be extra vigilant. If anyone asks what you've been up to, tell them a special assignment testing out training mechas. Even after the testing ends, and we break for the national holidays, be mindful."

All of us agree.

"Tonight, we've been summoned for a dinner at the Gestahl Ball-room," he continues. "They want us to come in full dress uniform."

"We don't have our full dress uniforms with us," Nori replies.

"They've been sent to your rooms. Wash up and meet in the hall at eighteen thirty."

"Do you know what it's for?"

Kazu shrugs. "Maybe they want to celebrate our new weapon. You all can bring guests if you'd like. I'm sending you contact information to get clearance. We don't have to report for testing to-morrow either, so you have the day off."

"Will there be real food?" Kujira inquires.

"I don't know the dining menu, but I assume there will be," Kazu answers.

"You're not policing us tonight, right?"

"You have free rein to ruin your gut tonight."

"My gut thanks you."

We split off except for Chieko, who asks if she can speak with me in my room.

"Are you excited?" she asks me.

"It'll be great to eat something new," I reply.

"I mean this is our chance to finally avenge everyone," she states emphatically. "We don't have to be afraid of their biomechs anymore."

"We're going to blow them to high hell," I reply, but as I do, her enthusiasm reminds me of all the bad decisions I made the day of the biomech attack. I know it was our superiors who put us in that impossible situation. But then I think, wasn't the biomech pilot doing the same thing as us, following his orders?

"I'm worried that it works fine while we're testing it but using it on the field will be different," I reply.

"It's always different on the field," she says. "And Command is smart to be cautious with Dr. Günter. Nazis have sent fake defectors before. But if he's the real deal, they'll keep on improving our antibiomech weapons, and we'll make sure it works out there." She looks plaintively at me. "I hope this means we're going to see some real action soon."

Real action? Fight a real biomech? I should be thrilled, but dread fills me instead. It's an involuntary reaction that makes me slow to respond.

"You look shell-shocked," she says.

"Last time we fought the biomech, the results weren't so great."

"This time'll be different." She gives me a wake-up sock. "I'll see you at the party."

She exits. I check our dress garments in the closet. I take a long shower. Even with weight training, controlling the mecha all day takes a toll on my muscles. Fortunately, the hot water works its magic. I look forward to relaxing for the night and eating tasty food again.

I THOUGHT THE GESTAHL BALLROOM WAS PART OF MECHTOWN, BUT IT'S actually aboveground at the Berkeley Marina, overlooking the bay. It feels nice to come up for the night breeze. I think we'd all been under the impression that we were celebrating our test today, but it's a party commemorating Tagomi Metal Works' thirty-fourth anniversary.

"Once the national holidays start, Berkeley will become a ghost town," Nori says. "Which makes it perfect to visit all the touristy places in the bay."

"You sticking around?"

"Of course. I get extra training in and catch up on all my schoolwork. You?"

"I think I need more than a week to catch up on all my schoolwork," I confess.

The security is tight, and we walk past a thermal wall that scans our bodies for weapons. There are several hundred officers present on top of the plethora of civilian researchers and scientists. There's a chandelier with more than thirty-three thousand crystals shaped like a mecha. Trees made of colored glass intertwine with plants that are shaded violet and fuchsia. A live band is playing popular songs from the USJ, and the glass dance floor extends all the way out over the water. There are several open bars and tables full of food. Kujira is piling up.

"You know what everyone in the room is doing?" I ask, wanting to test his social skills again.

"No time for that nonsense," he replies as he ignores the chopsticks and uses his hands to pick up the sushi rolls.

"I just want to know who you think the most important person in the room is."

"Me," he quickly responds.

He loads up on fried cod and snatches several garlic beans, munching on them before some female cadets whisk him away to ask him about his victory at the tournament.

I'm by myself, and I actually don't know who to talk to. I fidget nervously, look for food, and grab a plate of zucchini fries just to keep busy. Near the main podium, I spot Dr. Shimitsu speaking with Colonel Yamaoka and a few other officers whose insignia designate them as generals. I didn't know that the colonel was here, but it makes sense he'd attend the event. I should try to thank him sometime tonight.

"Mac!"

I turn around. Kazu is with two young girls, who I assume are his daughters.

"Say hi to Makoto-san," Kazu orders them.

They both bow to me.

"I'm Mayu."

"I'm Mio."

They're both clad in black dresses and red sashes.

Kazu grabs onion rings from a waiter passing by with a tray full of them.

"Dad, you're over your calorie limit!" Mayu yells.

"And your drink limit!" Mio states firmly.

"Just one more snack for Dad," Kazu pleads.

But his daughters grab his rings and take them away.

"It's curfew time in twenty minutes," Mayu says.

"Girls, party night today. Exceptions allowed."

"No exceptions!" Mio shouts. "You promised to go over the Komatsu Type 932A tomorrow morning."

"Four RCL 106mm recoilless rifles and 12mm armor with dual GX Missile Launchers and—" Maya starts, and spouts off a series of statistics.

"You interested in an antimecha-vehicle tour tomorrow morning?" Kazu asks me.

"I think I'm sleeping in."

Behind me, a woman says, "I don't know who's the boss in our family."

"It's them," Kazu says about his twins. "This is my wife, Eileen."

We bow to each other. The twins give Kazu more orders.

"Now now, girls. Take it easy on Daddy," Eileen tells them.

"I think my girls want me to leave," Kazu says. "Gotta listen to the little tyrants."

"Your usage of the word *tyrant* is inaccurate," Mio says.

"Tyrant means an absolute ruler who is oppressive and cruel."

"Only a cruel ruler would prevent their dad from indulging in a few cocktails," Kazu whines.

"No exceptions!"

I can't help but laugh.

"One day, brother, you'll have your own kids, and you'll get what all of this is about," he says to me. "We don't just fight for the Empire. We fight for family."

I admire him and his entire family. I haven't even thought about what having a family of my own would be like as the only thing I've aspired to was to become a mecha pilot.

The twins lead their parents out. I wander the ballroom and see Colonel Yamaoka by himself. I approach him, bow, and state, "Colonel, I wanted to thank you for all you've done for me."

He looks at me and appears confused. "You are?"

Not the response I was expecting, which causes me to stammer, "It's—it's me. Makoto Fujimoto? You—you recommended me to BEMA last year?"

He stares at me for a few seconds, checking his memory banks for a match. "Ah, that's right," he says in an unconvincing voice that makes it obvious he has no idea who I am. He puts his hand on my shoulder. "How are you doing?"

"I'm good, sir."

He checks my rank. "You're in your first year?"

"Yes, sir."

"Excellent. Make sure you study hard. The fate of the Empire depends on cadets like you."

His aide returns and takes him away to his next appointment.

"Smooth of you to mingle with the brass," Chieko says to me.

"He's the one who got us in," I say to Chieko. "But he had no idea who I was."

She laughs. "Officers like him meet thousands of people in a year. Don't take it personally."

"I know," I say, but I still feel disappointed.

"You think galaxies have gender?" Chieko asks, maybe trying to divert my mind.

"That's assuming galaxies are alive."

"Aren't they? Everything in the universe has the same courting rituals, inevitable breakup, or eventual destruction."

We talk for a bit about singularities and galactic dynamics. Chieko sees a friend and goes to greet her. I'm about to grab a drink when a waiter crashes into me, spilling ceviche all over my uniform. It causes a huge clatter. Everyone in my vicinity turns to stare. The waiter appears annoyed. I rush to the bathroom and try to wipe away the stains. But it's all over my uniform. First time wearing formal wear, and it's ruined. Probably a sign it's time to call it a night. I wipe where I can, grab a bottle of *sake*, and head back to Mechtown.

14

★ ★ ★

IT'S A LONG TREK, BUT I LIKE THE TIME ALONE TO REFLECT ON THE LAST couple of weeks. Rather than go back to my dorm, I take a detour and walk to where the Leviathans are secured. I'm tipsy, but I can still manage the cart to the hangar.

I stand at the feet of the *Arikuni*, in awe at its size. The toes alone are twice as tall as I am. I suddenly recall my earliest childhood memory, staring at the massive mecha parts in a Long Beach factory. My parents were pointing out each of the pieces, excitedly describing them to me in detail even though I didn't understand most of the technical jargon.

I feel joy now that I'm finally getting to drive mechas at BEMA. But as my eyes follow the mecha up to its beltline, I see the holster and scabbard. A mecha's primary objective is to destroy its enemies, which, technically speaking, makes me an executioner.

"Hello, stranger," a familiar voice says to me.

I can't believe my eyes.

"What are you doing here?" is my response.

It's Griselda. She looks thinner than when I last saw her, stress carving wrinkles of woe into her face.

"Miss me?" she asks.

"How are you here? Don't tell me you're an exchange student to BEMA."

"I wish it were that simple," she says wistfully. "I've defected."

"What?" I say, incredulous. But then I remember the biomech technology that we have. "You came with Dr. Günter?"

She nods. "He was a friend of my family. He asked for my help since I'd spent time here."

"How'd you get here?"

"A group of Spanish mecha pilots smuggled us out. It's—" she's about to say, then smiles. "It's a complicated situation."

"I bet," I say, and hug her, feeling ecstatic. Her arms are sturdier than they were the last time I saw her. "I don't care what the situation is. I'm thrilled you're here."

"I saw you earlier in the week and wanted to say hi, but I wasn't sure what your friends would think if they knew you were friends with me," Griselda says.

"They wouldn't care," I reply.

"You speak with a lot of confidence about that."

"They're my friends." She puts her hand on my stomach, where Orwell and company branded me with the swastika symbol, reminding me she hasn't forgotten what happened. "It's been removed," I tell her.

"Scars like that can never be fully removed."

I'm about to ask her something, but then a thought hits me. "What about your parents? Won't they be in danger?"

"They were killed a few months ago."

"Why?"

"I don't know. There was no official explanation. They called me one day and told me my parents had been cleansed, and I didn't need to worry about them anymore."

"I'm sorry. I remember what you told me about your mother," I say, recalling Fargo Station, her refusing to fire on civilians, then being required to report for reeducation.

"I wasn't allowed to mourn them," she says in an emotionless voice. "I wasn't allowed to even mention their names. I was ordered to act like they were still alive."

"I'm so sorry."

"We're both orphans," she says.

I lift up my bottle of sake, and ask, "Drink?"

"*Sake* never gets me drunk."

"I'm not trying to get you drunk."

She laughs. "Do you have a cup?"

"Drink straight from the bottle."

I take a small sip and hand it to her. She does the same.

"That's strong *sake*," she says.

I take the bottle back from her.

"I always wondered why so many of the heroes in legends are orphans," Griselda says.

"What was your conclusion?"

"They have nothing to lose, so they're willing to put everything on the line."

"That's the way you are?"

"It is," she replies.

"I didn't know it was legendary status you were after," I tell her.

She smiles. "I want peace in the world."

"Peace between the Empire and Reich is never happening."

"Your Colonel Yamaoka has a very unique vision for the future of the United States of Japan."

I bristle at his mention and the reverence with which she speaks his name. "He gave you his spiel too?"

"What do you mean, 'spiel'?"

"He's a big charmer, but all he cares about is his own glory," I say, and feel petty afterward.

She looks disappointed. "That's unfortunate to hear." She takes another swig of *sake*.

"Ignore me," I say, wanting to cover up. "I'm a little drunk."

"This is good stuff." She grins at me. "You handle your drinks better."

"Learning. You've been given the tour around the campus?"

"You offering?" she asks.

"I am."

She shakes her head. "We had to be careful not to be seen, so we haven't left the premises. Maybe in a year or two, if things cool down, I can sneak out and get an actual tour."

"That'd be great. There's so much I can show you. I recently found out there's a whole shrine to the Twelve Disciples—our first mecha pilots—underneath the academy, which is amazing. I'm not sure if I can take you in, but I'm sure we can get special permission." My mention of the Twelve Disciples causes her to wince. "Did I say something I shouldn't?"

"I might be mistaken, but the people you call the Twelve Disciples—I think they're the ones we know as the Twelve Executioners."

"Executioners? But they're heroes."

"They killed thousands of Germans," Griselda says, "including civilians during their attacks. There's a collective fear in the German Americas about all the destruction your mechas have caused."

"I . . . I've never thought about it from the other side. I guess when I show you around Berkeley, we'll skip the shrine."

She shakes her head. "I want to see everything." She gazes up at the *Arikuni*. "We grew up our entire lives learning to hate the Empire. But there are many of us who hate what the Nazis do more. The Nazi ideology doesn't represent us. We're under its yoke, but we want the tyranny to end."

I remember her mentioning this last year. "Do you remember that fight at the bar, when those soldiers insulted Germany—"

"It was a charade. If we allow anyone to publicly malign the Reich and don't stand up to it, we'll either be tortured or executed."

"Are you serious?"

"Everything is regulated. The only reason the Nazis don't kill everyone who isn't Aryan is because they need a steady pool of slave labor. They persecute those of Asian descent but don't outright murder them in fear that it will provoke the Empire into an all-out war. But there's a huge sect of hawks who want a fight with the USJ. With the recent developments on the biomechs, they thought they'd have something your mechas can't handle. That's the main reason we're here."

"You said 'your,'" I point out. "It's 'our' now."

She stares glumly at me before forcing a smile. "I hope so."

WE SPEND THE REST OF THE EVENING CATCHING UP. ACTUALLY, IT'S MORE her asking questions about me. I can feel her not wanting to talk about what she's been through. I respect that and tell her about BEMA, the tournament, traveling the Empire. She deflects any probing questions about her journey to the USJ and turns it around on me. I don't press her too much and get into my BEMA life, the rigors and joys of pilot training.

"Never seen you so happy," she notes.

"It's the first time I feel like I belong."

"I sometimes wonder where I belong," she says.

"You belong here now."

She smiles at me, and says, "If only it were that easy."

Before I know it, it's morning. It's a good thing we have the day off.

"You should get some sleep," she says.

"You too. What's your portical number?"

"We don't have porticals. But I'm always here."

I don't want to part from her, so I say, "Actually, I'm not that tired. A little tea should wake me up. Want to grab some breakfast?"

She laughs. "I need some sleep. There's a bunch of work I need to help Dr. Günter with in the afternoon." But just as she's about to leave, she suggests, "Want to do a late dinner?"

"Sure," I reply, elated. "Anything you feel like from the outside world?"

"Can you bring squid casserole?"

I try to think where they have good squid casserole. "Done."

She tells me her dorm number, and says, "I should be done by eight."

"Every day, you pick a food, and I'll bring it to you."

"Don't you have to study?" she asks.

"I can study while I eat," I reply.

"What if you get in trouble?"

"How can I get in trouble for having dinner with a friend?" I ask, even as I recall the Tokko agent's warning. Still, seeing her is worth the risk of whatever may come.

She holds my hand. "I'm so happy you're here."

"I'm so happy *you're* here."

"See you tonight."

IT FEELS GOOD IN THE LEVIATHAN. I'M GETTING A COMFORTABLE GRASP of the controls, and we practice combo attacks to coordinate defeating the test biomechs they've constructed. Since Kujira and I both use swords, we deploy an "X-Attack," simultaneously attacking our opponent in an x pattern with me starting on the left and ending on the right flank of the biomech. This incapacitates the enemy, allowing Nori to close in with her spear and pierce it in the forehead for the finishing blow.

Kazu is so fast with his yo-yo, none of us can get within two arm-lengths of his mecha. Anytime we even try to step in for our "friendly" competition, the yo-yo hurtles our way. Chieko prefers close-quarters combat but for the testing begins using the proto-type laser rifle to shoot from afar. It fires bursts of laser bullets rather than a continual stream and can disintegrate most armor. The two of them work on a combination, which they coin the "Omega Flare," to use against enemy parties. Their first attempt is against seven homunculi, which are smaller, portical-AI-driven mechas. Since they're older models and pretty much worthless in combat, they've become cannon fodder for mecha pilots to train on. Chieko opens with a string of laser fire that immobilizes half of them, the others shielding themselves as best as they can manage. Kazu sweeps in and knocks out any survivors with his yo-yo storm. The two of them mop up the homunculi who survive.

We try to marry the two combinations together, but we can never get the timing quite right.

We destroy over fifteen of the biomechs. I tweak the calibration settings on the arms and legs to get optimal motion. The traits I'd seen in each of the fighters comes out even more in the test battles. The Leviathans are easier to drive than the test mechas or the quads. The portical AI learns from our tests and adapts to respond even faster to our preferences. Nori leads the charge in that aspect, pointing out minutiae like if a forearm feels as though it has too much weight or the head isn't turning fast enough. On the oppo-site end of the spectrum, Kujira somehow is always eating food even though food isn't allowed aboard the Leviathans.

In terms of combat talk, Kazu almost never speaks. Nori usually gives the instructions. Kujira talks trash to everyone. Chieko is generally reserved but will berate anyone for messing up.

"Mac! What are you doing?" Chieko yells at me. "You were off by a full second."

"My bad," I reply.

"Yeah, it's your bad. Keep up!"

I'm the one who's continually apologizing for screwing up.

DURING ONE SPARRING SESSION, KAZU KNOCKS THE SWORD OUT OF MY hand. Nori and Chieko have given me boxing lessons, but I feel defenseless as he swings his yo-yo blade at me. I withdraw every time he tries to attack. He puts his weapon away and challenges me to a fistfight. A few punches in, and he clearly has me at a disadvantage. He's much faster, and my defense stinks without a weapon. My mecha gets a severe beating.

"Every part of you is a weapon," Kazu sternly tells me. "*Every* part. Your brain, your eyes, and your fists. On board your mecha, your fists are more powerful than regular artillery shells. If you can't fight with them, you'll be pulverized!"

"I'm sorry," I reply.

"Don't be sorry! Get better. How long has it been since you lost to Kujira for this very reason?"

From then on, I have to spend a few hours every day practicing without weapons.

"Use your momentum," Chieko chides me. "Don't just punch from a static position. Step in."

I do my best.

THAT WEEK, I BRING GRISELDA DIFFERENT MEALS, STARTING WITH SQUID casserole and a full slab of pork BBQ ribs with potato salad and dirty rice. On the following days, I bring smoked shrimp gumbo, beef brisket, codfish stew with oysters and tofu, smoked furikake and shishito peppers, pollack spawn *jjige* in kimchee sauce, and grilled duck heart. In the past, right before eating, she'd always exclaim, *"Itadakimasu!"* But I notice she doesn't say it anymore. Her room is similar to the apartment in Dallas in being bare. But she does have some baseball equipment, including a bat and a mitt.

"Do you play baseball?" she asks me.

"No. You?"

"Trying to learn so I can keep myself busy. I bought you a gift," she says, handing me a utensil I don't recognize.

"What is it?" I ask her.

"A fruit peeler. Now you can cut your own pears without hurting yourself." She actually has a pear and uses the peeler on the skin, which causes it to slice right off. "Try it," she tells me.

I do, and it's very easy to use. "This is what I've needed my whole life." I cut up some pears, which we have as dessert to cool our tongues after our spicy mentaiko.

"You have any pets growing up?"

I shake my head. "What about you?"

"I had a tarantula."

Thinking about it gives me shivers. I'm not a fan of big hairy spiders. "What was that like?"

"They're very low maintenance. Did you know female tarantulas live longer than the male ones?"

"I didn't."

"Female tarantulas are more valuable than male ones because of their longevity. I fed her once a week. Right before they molt, they stop eating so they can shed their old skin, and they're very vulnerable when they're undergoing the metamorphosis. But it's the only way for them to grow up."

"Wonder what it'd be like if humans had to molt their own skin," I wonder.

"Someone would probably find a way to commoditize the skin of famous people," she suggests. "They'd dig up the molted skin of historic figures and put them up in museums. They'd even have one dedicated to the old Americans."

"I faced some of the new Americans in the Quiet Border," I say.

"These new ones are nothing like the real Americans."

"They're not?"

"The old Americans had an uncanny strength about them. They believed in freedom, and the people chose their own leaders," she says.

"What if they picked the wrong leaders?"

"That's why they had a system of checks and balances to temper any one side from becoming too powerful. But there was also a fundamental faith that whoever was elected would respect that system. If someone came along and threw it all aside, the whole thing would crumble."

"It's a good thing our leaders are chosen by the Emperor," I say.

"The Emperor has never made a bad choice?"

"I wouldn't know," I reply. "But he is all-knowing, and I doubt he'd appoint someone who wasn't right for the position."

She smiles. "You can be so naive."

"If I weren't naive about life, I'd have given up trying to be a mecha pilot a long time ago."

"It's true, naive people tend to be persistent."

"You mean they never give up even though it makes sense they should."

"Is that why you've come this whole week?" she asks.

"I just wanted to make sure you get good food," I reply.

She comes close to me and kisses me on the lips.

I'm startled.

"What's wrong?" she asks.

"I haven't done this before," I admit.

She kisses me again.

Our lips caress for a few seconds. I wish it could last longer. She puts her hand on my cheek, and says, "Pick some German food for tomorrow. Doesn't matter what. I just miss home cooking."

I skip back to my dorm, jubilant.

IN A MOCK BATTLE, KUJIRA HITS ME WITH THE SWORD TOO QUICKLY. I block the blow, but the force causes me to fall to my mecha's knees. When I try to get back up, the knee buckles, and I drop back to the ground. Something's wrong with the piston. Normally, this is where my engineer would run a diagnostic and try to figure out what's faulty. But since I don't have one on board, I have to wait for someone from Dr. Shimitsu's crew to evaluate the problem.

As I'm down for the count, Kazu is pitted against Kujira. It's a fight I've long wanted to see. Even though they're not fighting "for real," the battle gets heated. Kazu's yo-yos move so fast, I almost can't see them. Kujira uses his sword to parry and defend himself. But Kazu's attacks remind me of Honda's rush attack, only much faster, with that deadly yo-yo. He swings that weapon around as if it were weightless, whipping Kujira as soon as he's within range. Kujira has to assess his situation. They hold their distance for over a minute. Kazu takes a tentative step forward, causing Kujira to step back.

"Whoa. Is this what I think it is?" Chieko private messages me.

"I think so."

"I'd actually pay money to see this."

"Me too."

"Who do you think's gonna win?"

"I have no idea," I reply.

Kazu puts Kujira in a corner and begins a flurry of yo-yo attacks. Kujira somehow deflects all of them, but when he tries to strike, gets hit in the hand, slicing off two of his fingers. The sword drops, leaving him vulnerable. Just as Kazu is about to come in for the kill, Kujira times a perfect kick to knock Kazu back. Kujira uses the opportunity to pick up the sword, and they're about to continue the fight when Dr. Shimitsu stops them to do a maintenance check "on your hands."

A crew goes to inspect Kujira's sundered fingers. Chief Engineer Nobusue checks my knees and determines that several parts that have short-circuited need to be replaced.

I'm done for the day.

"You're lucky the fight got stopped," Kujira says to Kazu.

"Don't chirp to me, brother. I will annihilate you."

"Let's do it tomorrow. No stopping until one of our mechas is down for the count."

"Be glad to."

"Now, boys," Nori jumps in. "We're not here to prove who's a better pilot. We're here to test out the mechas."

"The best way to test it is with a fight," Kujira states.

"Agreed."

"We'll leave it to Dr. Shimitsu."

Dr. Shimitsu says, "Absolutely not."

But that only ignites the sense of competition between the two.

EVERY NIGHT, NORI SENDS US A PORTICAL REPORT ON HOW WE DID. I don't know how she finds time to make the detailed analysis using film footage from our fights. For example, if a practice swing is off, she'll actually paste in the recording, draw out the arc she'd expect, point out where the pose is off, and offer suggestions on improvement. (Ninety-five percent of mine involve suggestions to improve weaponless combat.) She also measures energy expenditure and points out inefficiencies that may be overutilizing power where less could get us further. The concrete feedback is very helpful.

THE HOLIDAYS CELEBRATING THE EMPIRE'S VICTORY OVER AMERICA starts tomorrow on July 2, which is a Tuesday. It'll go through the whole week until the seventh, though the main celebration will be on the fourth of July. Lots of military personnel and workers have traveled away to visit family. One of the unexpected absences is Dr. Shimitsu, who had told us earlier she was staying to work with us, then abruptly decided to leave. Many of our soldiers are going down to Los Angeles to take part in the annual military parade. A dozen of our newest mechas have already been transported south for the celebrations.

I ask Griselda what she's going to do.

"I've never actually celebrated it," she says. "What do you traditionally do?"

"BBQ lots of food, watch fireworks, and see kyōtei or baseball on the portical. Lots of people visit distant relatives."

"What about your family?" she asks.

I tell her what I recently learned about my mother and her death.

"That's terrible," she says. "I know it doesn't make it better, but it's the same in the Reich. We're all disposable fodder."

"Unless you're one of the chosen," I say.

"Even chosen ones can be sacrificed if someone wants to stay in power bad enough. What about your legal guardians?"

"I've told you about them."

"They've never reached out?"

I shake my head. "They better not. I never understood how they could be so cruel to me."

"What if you saw them now?"

"They better hope I don't."

She holds my hand.

"I want to show you something."

"What?"

She guides me to Mechtown's underground subway system. It looks just like the BART, except there are no advertisements. I'm curious where we're going. There aren't too many people taking the train, as it's the evening and most are away for the holidays. There are many other routes going underneath San Francisco, intertwining with the public subway system.

It's six stops to our destination. Once we get off, we take an elevator to exit. We emerge in the mountains at a Shinto shrine that overlooks the Golden Gate Bridge. There isn't actually another road up here, so I assume it's accessible for military personnel only.

"This is the Sausalito Shrine," Griselda says. "It commemorates all the Americans who were killed in the Holy War fighting against us."

"A shrine to our enemies?" I ask, surprised by its existence.

"Hard to believe, right?"

We wash our hands at the water basin before we enter. Inside, it's just us and the dozen or so priests who are dressed in white robes. Portical display screens show the names of those who were killed in the atomic blasts that destroyed Sausalito, Sacramento, and San Jose in 1948. It smells of incense, and there are candles burning everywhere.

"I've come here to pray often," she says.

I look at the names of all the dead. "No one listened to their prayers."

"That's why the shrine is here, to appease them."

"The dead don't care who listen to them now."

"How do you know?" she asks.

"I guess I don't."

We both pick up candles with the names of victims on them. We blow out the light and say a private prayer.

She leads me out to the observation deck. It's windy and cold, but the view is spectacular. They rebuilt the Golden Gate Bridge in 1950 after it was destroyed during the war. It's supposed to be an almost exact duplicate of the bridge before the Empire's victory, only twice as wide. It's majestic, the orange-vermilion gleaming in the nighttime lights. I'd always seen it from the east bay, but seeing it from up here, I'm awed by its scope and size.

"I hate war," she says. "I hate that so many people have to die for the dumbest reasons."

"Let's pray that one day—"

She puts a finger to my mouth. "You can't tell me your prayers."

"Why not?"

"If you tell anyone else, they won't come true."

"Then I won't tell a soul."

We stay out for half an hour, not talking, just watching the surroundings, seeing what it is that we're training to protect. I still can't believe she's here and hold her hand tightly, praying that she never leaves.

I GET BACK TO MY ROOM LATE AND SEE I HAVE A MESSAGE FROM KAZU ON my portical, asking me to meet them in the morning. I wonder if they have something scheduled for the holidays. I take a hot shower, think about Griselda, and go to sleep.

ALL FOUR TIGERS ARE WAITING FOR ME IN A CONFERENCE ROOM. KAZU talks as the other three are sitting down, arms crossed. "I don't care who you date, but Dr. Günter's assistant?" Kazu asks, raising his arm with his hand flat to me in a questioning gesture. "Brother, you are really pushing the boundaries. I know I mentioned you should think about family, but this isn't what I had in mind."

"Did someone say something about me and Griselda?" I ask.

"Of course," Kazu snaps. "You're bringing in food from outside every night and going to her dorm. The security cameras recorded it and flagged it. Security officials asked Nori about it the first night, and she explained you were friends from high school. But every night, man, you look like you got a hook on your nose. You got to think carefully about this. We still don't know what her real agenda is."

"You know her, Nori. It's peace she wants," I state.

"So she says," Kazu continues before Nori can reply. "And from all appearances, I'm inclined toward believing her. But we won't know until some time passes. She could be carted out of here any minute. Just 'cause she defected doesn't make her a free citizen in the USJ. You've put the Tigers in an awkward position. More specifically related to you, if you choose to pursue a relationship with her, the security concerns make it hard to trust you with a mecha since it puts us in a compromising position."

"What's that mean?" I ask.

"Don't play dumb. You know what I'm saying."

"There's a lot about Griselda you don't know yet," Nori says.

"I assumed as much," I reply.

Irritation flashes across her face. "A Nazi is a Nazi no matter what."

"Griselda hates the Nazis."

"That's what she says. You still don't know about her role in your friend's death?"

"Who are you talking about?"

"Hideki," Nori replies.

The name hits me like a brick. I take a second to gather my senses. "Th-there's no connection there."

"Why don't you ask her about it?"

"I—I will," I stammer.

"Like I said, who you date is normally not my business," Kazu emphasizes. "But a Nazi defector is a different ball game. If the Germans even got a hint they're here, they'd attack right away. We've been shielded off, but things are super tense above, especially because Dr. Shimitsu has gone missing."

"What?" I ask, stunned. "I thought she was on vacation?"

"No one can get hold of her or her family. Their entire apartment was ransacked, and it looked like there was a struggle. That's why word has come down, and it's simple. You need to cut off with Griselda if you want to be part of the Tigers." He puts his hand on my shoulder. "I get it man. High-school crush. She's smart, attractive, you guys have a connection. But this is the Empire's fate at stake here. It's not the time for romance. We talked to the officers, and they're willing to let it slide as long as you do the right thing."

Kazu and Nori exit.

Chieko's face is stolid, but when I try to speak to her, anger hardens her eyes, and she shakes her head. "A Nazi monster killed our friends."

"I know."

"Do you?!" she rages, and leaves.

The only one left is Kujira. "Ignore them, man, and do whatever you want," he says.

"Even if it means getting kicked out?"

"So what?" Kujira asks. "Get your priorities straight."

"They are."

"You sure about that?"

"What if things go wrong?"

"What's the worst that can happen? She breaks your heart, betrays you, causes you to be miserable, and makes you want to jump off the bridge? That's what love is, man."

"Didn't know you were an expert."

"It's not hard. Ain't nothing worth dying for more than love."

"I'm not in love."

Kujira chuckles and states, "It was fun piloting with you," as though he's read my mind and knows my decision.

But I won't make one. Not until I understand what Nori meant when she asked about Griselda's connection to Hideki. I don't want to ask, although a part of me begins to suspect. I force the doubts out of my head and wonder what in the world I'm supposed to do.

15

★ ★ ★

I GET LITTLE SLEEP. I HATE FEELING JUDGED. THEY WERE RESPECTFUL about it, but it seems no matter what I do, there's always criticism, whether it's wanting to be a mecha pilot, the actions I took on the Quiet Border, and now even the friends I make. They should trust that I know what I'm doing. But do I?

I think about my kiss with Griselda and recall the first time I met her. She was in my homeroom, though we hadn't actually talked. I saw her at the Gogo Arcade one day, playing a game called *Dual Dragoness* about two friends, Cindy and Mindy, who have to fight their way through yakuza thugs to retrieve Cindy's boyfriend, Bimmy. I joined her, and we made it all the way to the end before being pummeled to death by the rail-gun-wielding boss. No continues were allowed, even when putting in more money, a conscious choice by the designers. We were outraged.

"We almost had that!" she exclaimed.

"I don't think I've ever seen anyone get past that final boss."

"We have to do it tonight! I won't be able to do anything else if we don't beat him."

"We can try."

We tried three more times before finally beating him. But before we could save Bimmy, we were required to face off against each other for Bimmy's love.

"It's all yours," I told her.

"C'mon, you got to fight me."

"You deserve it."

I let go of the controls, but she refused to kill my character. Instead, we let the timer run out, and we both lost.

"Why did you do that?" I asked her.

"Friends come before anything," she replied, and put her hand out. "I'm Griselda."

"Makoto. Most of my friends call me Mac."

"What other games do you like, Mac?"

I smiled. "Pretty much anything except those mindless puzzle games that suck up all your time and you don't even remember what you just did."

She laughed, and said, "I'm starving. Feel like dinner?"

I RETURN FOR LEVIATHAN TESTING. DR. SHIMITSU'S ABSENCE FEELS OM-inous.

None of the Tigers mention Griselda. Even after our practice time aboard the Leviathans ends early, at three, for the holidays, they talk about dinner plans like it's business as usual. Except it's not, and I have to go see Griselda.

I pace in front of her door, unsure what to say if it turns out she knew more about Hideki than she let me know. When I do knock, there's no answer. I call her name a few times, but I don't think she's in. I feel relieved that I don't have to confront her yet and am about to leave when I see her come around the corner with a gloomy disposition.

She brightens when she sees me. We hug tightly, and she says, "You have no idea how happy I am to see you. It's been a looong day."

"Same for me."

"Where do you want to grab food tonight?"

"Something I need to talk with you about first."

"Sure, sure."

We go inside. She takes off her jacket and asks, "Do you want some tea?"

"Thanks."

She turns on a tea burner, which slowly fills the room with the aroma of green tea. "What'd you want to talk about?" she asks as she takes a seat.

"I wa—"

There's a knock at the door, which catches both of us off guard.

"Housekeeping," a voice calls.

"Housekeeping?" she says, puzzled.

"Your dorm is scheduled for a cleanup."

Griselda looks at me and shrugs. As soon as she opens the door, a man rushes in with a broom. From the broom's edge, a blade pops out. He's about to stab Griselda, but I pick up her teacup and throw it at him. He blocks it. I grab the lamp and attack. But the lamp breaks like brittle glass when it collides with his arm. He punches me, and I swear it's like he's hitting me with a metal cane. I get thrown to the floor. I look around and see Griselda's baseball bat. Just as he's about to hit me again, I grab the bat and block. The bat gets dented badly. Is he superhuman? Or are his arms robotic? He hurls the bat away and is about to smash my head in when Griselda grabs his arm from behind. She has as much strength as he does, which makes no sense. Unless her arms are artificial as well. She starts pounding his face until he falls to the ground.

"Who sent you?" she demands.

He refuses to speak.

I'm surprised by the turn of events, but more by the sight of his metallic arm with loose wires, which looks identical to Hideki's arm. She punches the assailant in the face, rendering him unconscious.

"We're in danger," she says.

"Are they German spies?"

She looks at the artificial arm. "Very possibly."

"I've heard that Dr. Shimitsu and her family are missing."

Griselda's eyes widen. "We have to get to Dr. Günter. *Now.*" She sprints out of the apartment, and I chase after her.

"What's happening?" I yell as I catch up with her.

"If German intelligence got to Dr. Shimitsu, then they know about us, and we're in danger," she replies.

"But we're in BEMA. There's no way for them to even get here."

"They could launch a Longinus Strike," she says.

"What's that?" I ask, as we run up the stairs and down the hallway.

"The *Luftwaffe* developed freighter jets that go high up in the atmosphere, travel at supersonic speeds, descend, and drop off their cargo. They could deploy multiple biomechs in a quick and dirty attack on any given target before you could retaliate with atomics."

"They could use atomics too."

"They could. But chances are, if they launch a Longinus Strike, it's to deliver a biomech so they can retrieve something they want."

"What's that?"

"I have to ask Dr. Günter."

"If they attacked, isn't that a declaration of war?" I ask.

"If they resort to that, it means they don't care."

"Dr. Günter is that valuable to them?"

"Yes. Or, not so much the doctor, as any countermeasures the

USJ has developed against the biomech. My people would do anything to destroy it."

"They're not your people anymore," I remind her.

As we arrive at the doctor's dorm, we knock on his door. There's no answer. Griselda gets her portical and overrides the lock. Inside, we find a dead soldier with his neck snapped.

"That's Dr. Günter's personal guard," she says. She examines his skin. "He hasn't been dead long. But chances are they have the doctor."

"Security cameras would catch them, right?"

"Not if they have inside help."

"What was the deal with the fake arm that guy back there had?"

"It's Nazi technology."

"I thought it was something the NARA uses," I say.

"Nazis gave it to the NARA."

"Do you have them too?" I ask.

She glances at her arms, then back at me. "Both my legs and arms are artificial," she says.

"Why?"

"Because"—and she takes a deep breath—"I was a biomech pilot, working with Dr. Günter after he devised his plan to defect."

"A biomech pilot?"

She removes her jacket, presses her skin. A small panel comes loose. She takes it off and exposes her artificial arm.

"For us to reach synchronicity with the biomech, we have to physically join with it," Griselda says. "That means removing all our limbs and connecting directly to achieve a perfect biological and mechanical fusion."

"Were you always like this?"

"Not until after the last time you saw me," she says. "That's when I had the surgery. When Dr. Günter told me about his plan to defect, I agreed to aid him. But there was no way he could escape with a biomech unless I agreed to help. So I volunteered for the program."

"But you had to sacrifice your body parts?"

"It was the only way they would trust me. It was three months of hell until I could even get the biomech to move." She shuddered, remembering. "It's a total mental and physical invasion. They put needles in your brain, and the sync requires them to calibrate with your nerves so that you can even feel the biomech in your dreams. And the shell . . . The whole shell is made up of organic tissue from the dead."

"The dead?"

"All victims whose cells are genetically manipulated."

"You mean a biomech is a corpse reanimated?"

"A hundred, maybe a thousand corpses for each giant."

"That's scary," I mutter.

"Try driving one," she answers. "I can almost feel the cells of the dead revolting against me. But I have to channel my hate and anger to subjugate them to my will. Every time I pilot the biomech, just thinking about all those who died to bring it to life brings out the most base, feral instincts." She shudders. "It took a lot of discipline and meditation to stay in control. Dr. Günter came with me when we went to rendezvous with the Spanish pilots who brought us here."

"You mean you brought your biomech here?"

"You didn't know?"

Now it makes sense how they were able to re-create the biomech armor. "I suspected. What happened to the Spanish pilots?"

"They're independent, so they travel all over. My aunt is first officer on one of their mechas."

I need to ask her about Hideki. I muster my courage. "Were you—were you involved with what happened to Hideki?"

She blanches, a gesture that blares volumes. "He insisted on it," she finally offers, clearly not having expected the question.

"Insisted on what?"

"One of the exchange students with us was connected with NARA. We were all hanging out one night when Hideki talked about how desperate he was to pass the test. That's how it started. I told him to let it go, but he wouldn't."

I had no idea how he got in touch with the terrorists, and now that I know, I wish I didn't.

"He knew the risks," Griselda says quickly. "I told him to drop it. But he went around my back and asked my friends. I tried to stop them, but it was too late. The NARA wanted to use him for their plans."

"Why didn't you tell me?"

"I wanted to. But would you have believed me?"

"He was our friend!"

"It's your soldiers who executed him," Griselda says. "He wasn't supposed to die!"

"What'd you think they would do?"

"Not execute him. When I found out—" She doesn't finish the sentence.

"Why are you really here?" I ask, furious.

She sees the rage in my eyes and averts her own. "I told you, I want peace," she says. "But I know it'll never happen. Not without war."

"War?"

"You think my people will ever surrender? It's true, they're focused on building space colonies on the Moon. But the idea of surrendering even a centimeter to the Empire offends their belief in their racial superiority. The only way there will be peace on this continent is if the United States of Japan takes over."

"What?"

"Colonel Yamaoka plans on taking over the continent. He promised Dr. Günter peace after that happens."

"That's why you're here?"

"Why else? Dr. Günter and I sacrificed everything because of that. There are many in the German Americas who hate Nazi rule."

"But they're Nazis too."

"Only in name," she replies. "What they care about is having a place to sleep and getting enough so they can provide for their families. Ideology means nothing to them compared to earning bread."

"Your so-called German Americans who hate Nazi rule killed all my friends in the Quiet Border."

"I know," she states. "That was my cousin, Dietrich, who attacked your convoy in the Quiet Border . . . He told me he spared you for my sake."

I remember the biomech that day not attacking, letting me go.

Her cousin killed the RAMs. She helped Hideki make the connection that led to his demise. I'm shaking. I try to speak, but I can't enunciate because I'm so angry.

Suddenly, an alarm starts ringing throughout the entirety of Mechtown.

"Attention military personnel. The base is under attack. This is not a drill. All available—"

We hear a loud explosion.

"I have to go," Griselda says. "I don't expect you to forgive me."

"Forgive you? How can you—"

More blasts shake the whole base. "We'll deal with this later," she says.

I grab her arm. I'm so angry I can barely think. "You don't belong in the USJ. I thought you were different from the Nazis! But you're worse than they are. At least they're not hypocrites."

Her eyes widen in pain, and she looks like I've stabbed her.

She's about to say something but restrains herself. "I'm sorry you feel that way." She takes a deep breath, hesitates for a second, then leaves.

There is a vibration in my pocket, which I thought was coming from the base, but it's actually my portical. I check the screen and see it's Nori.

"Get here right away," she states.

"What's going on?" I ask.

"I'll tell you when you get here. How far are you?"

My portical indicates she's with the Leviathans. "Not far."

I enter the hangar bay that houses Project Lightpin. All the years developing machinery and weapons have been destroyed in minutes—a part of me realizes it's the same as my friendship with Griselda. I wish none of what she told me was true. I'm upset, not just at her, but with myself for not having realized things sooner.

The supporting platforms have collapsed, and much of the portical circuitry is ablaze. As I'm about to rush back to where the Leviathans are, I hear a loud stepping noise, then another. I hide behind one of the burning consoles.

There's a mecha type I've never seen before with multiple turrets. It looks like eight tanks stacked on top of one another with guns that can rotate 360 degrees. It is passing through on its four legs rather than searching for targets, which is lucky for me. I wait until it moves to another area before sprinting to my destination.

The pulsating heat from the fiery remains of the Sumo-class mecha scorches a part of me. I occasionally look behind to make sure the enemy mecha doesn't spot me. But it's gone. I'm relieved not to see any corpses as most of the scientists are away for the holidays.

Then it hits me, did they time this attack for the break?

When I finally get to our station, three of the Leviathans have already left. It's just Nori waiting for me. I strap into my suit, take the elevation platform up to the stomach cockpit of the *Arikuni*, and start it up. The visual display on my goggle lights up, and I see Nori's face in a faded circle in the upper-right corner. I move her image to the upper left by swiping with my finger.

"What have I missed?" I ask.

"Several mechas have gone rogue and are destroying everything inside Mechtown. We need to stop them."

"Where's security?"

"I don't know, but I'm assuming they were caught off guard. They couldn't have picked a worse time to attack. No one is around, and those who are have already been destroyed."

"I saw one coming in here," I state, and try to describe it to her.

"I have to see it to confirm, but that sounds like the Yamarashi prototype," Nori says. "Eight 30mm cannons and the main 105mm cannon with sonic boosters, which is the primary one we need to worry about."

"That sounds like the one. Do we have any idea who's driving them?" I ask.

"None. But we can assume there must be traitors on the base. I'll let Kazu know to expect a Yamarashi." She sends a message, then tells me, "Let's go."

I pick up my sword, the M87, and the pentagonal shield.

"Where are the ablative shells?" I ask.

"They should already be loaded into your arm," she informs me.

To avoid making too much noise, we switch to tread mode, which causes wheels to come out from the bottom of our soles.

"It's a good thing we have enough space to move through the base," I point out.

"Mechtown was designed so that standard-sized mechas could move through most of the main passages," Nori replies.

There's destruction everywhere along our path.

"You were right about Griselda," I tell her. "I'm sorry. I didn't know about Hideki."

"I didn't until recently, either," she replies. "I should have told you earlier, but I didn't know how to put it to you."

"How did you find out?"

"She told the Tokko during the initial inquiry when she defected. When they asked me about your relationship to her, they showed me her files."

Was it Agent Tsukino who asked her?

"I know she had her reasons, and she couldn't help what happened to Hideki," Nori continues.

"What do you mean she couldn't help it?"

"That was his decision."

"But you said she was responsible."

"I asked if you knew her role in what happened to him. From what I've gathered, he was the one who pursued that path," Nori says.

"She helped make the connection," I reply.

"I know. And that's why we don't know if we can trust her. For all we know, she could be behind these attacks."

I'm about to reply that she's not, that I was with her when it began, but then another part wonders, was all that a masquerade? She's lied to me before.

"I hope not," I answer.

"Me too."

"Did you know her back in school?"

"Not well. We had a physics class together."

"She was one of the closest friends I had in high school," I say. "I spent most of my senior year with her and Hideki . . ." I recall our nights out at the arcade, playing portical games and getting into trouble for the dumbest reasons, mostly thanks to Hideki, who could be very stubborn.

One of Mechtown's security mechas comes crashing through the wall. Beyond, pummeling another guard, is a Labor-class mecha, the muscle of the construction force. They are big and boxy, designed to carry a heavy load. They're built with thick armor to protect against possible accidents. Though they have no armaments, the one we come across has switched out its right hand for a power drill. It's using that drill on the opposing security mecha, piercing right through it. The security mechas are more like scouts and are relatively smaller and weaker. This Labor class has little difficulty puncturing its power source and hammering it into the ground.

"There you are," we hear Kazu say, as his face flashes up on my display, followed by Chieko and Kujira.

As soon as I see Chieko's face, I'm reminded of how angry she was with me for the death of the RAMs. She took out all her anger at me. Did I do the same to Griselda? I feel a momentary remorse.

"Sorry we're late," I say, as Nori and I retract our wheels and take defensive stances.

"I figured you two were taking the scenic route," Kazu states. "Come on, let's take care of Mr. Labor."

Chieko charges at the Labor mecha though it's a quarter bigger, and crashes into its torso. The Labor is knocked back, but not far, and holds its ground. Chieko is trying to grapple it, but it has its arm around her mecha as well. It's about to use its drill, but Kazu uses his yo-yo to slice it off. Chieko and the Labor get into a scuffle, swinging each other around and destroying everything that gets in their way. It's a titanic wrestling match as the two try to gain an advantage. The Labor pounds Chieko with its fist. But just as it seems like Chieko is about to be overwhelmed, she spins around it, grabs it from behind, then tackles the Labor to the ground, using her feet and gravity to assist their fall. Once they're down, she goes to work, breaking its limbs and disconnecting its power generator. Anytime the Labor tries to resist, it only aggravates its own situation.

Chieko rips off the cover to the bridge. There's a male inside. Chieko's fist hovers above him. His face shows up on our display on a communication channel.

"How many of you are there?" Nori demands of him.

The man yells, "For the Reich!"

"Chieko!" Nori yells. "Draw back!"

Chieko realizes what's about to happen and raises her arms. The Labor's bridge self-destructs, and the blast forces Chieko's mecha to fall on its back.

"Chieko!" we all yell, as her display temporarily cuts out.

But it's only a second before Chieko is back. "I'm fine."

"How bad is the damage?" Nori asks.

Chieko checks her sensor reports. "Could be worse. This armor is tough." She gets her mecha to its feet. "I'm using the self-repair module to do automatic diagnostics and fix any issues it detects."

"Good," Kazu says. "I looped into the security cameras, and it looks like there's a Scorpion-class mecha in the hangar next to us. This should be our priority as it can cause the most damage."

Nori chimes in, "The Scorpion class has scale armor and a tail with a prototype laser blade. We need to dismantle that tail first."

"How do we do that?" Chieko asks.

"Chop it off," Kujira says.

"Oh, very clever," Chieko mutters.

We enter the adjacent hangar. I've never been to this area, but it's as large as the previous one. The Scorpion is actually bipedal, though it has a massive tail behind it. It's bulkier than a standard mecha and slightly hunched. It wields two scimitars, and there are cannons in its shoulder plates. The face mask has sharp, fanglike protrusions covering it. The defunct bodies of four security mechas are on the ground, sliced up. Multiple human corpses lie next to them, having died doing their best to protect the base. I feel sickened by the idea that someone betrayed us. I stare at the Scorpion, furious with the pilot. What the hell are they thinking, supporting the Nazis against the Empire? Even death wouldn't be a sufficient punishment.

"The tail has ninety-six jointed segments with a stinger at the end that has the laser blade," Nori informs us. "It's fast. I don't know maximum speed, but it's designed as an antimecha machine."

"Fire the M87s," Kazu orders.

We're about to take out our guns when the Scorpion sprints at us. The tail punctures Chieko's gun, leaving it dysfunctional. Kujira tries to swing his sword, but the tail evades. I can't get a clear shot without hitting one of the others because it's moving so fast. Nori gets a few shots in, but the shells bounce off the thick armor.

Kujira tries to chop off the tail, but it hits him in the flank, causing his mecha to crash into the wall. Kujira does get a swipe in, but the sword isn't able to penetrate. Chieko and I strike, but the tail whips at my sword, knocking it out of my hand. Chieko clutches the tail, but it releases an electrical volt that causes her to momentarily lose control of her mecha. She capsizes. The tail goes up and is about to strike her. But Kazu flings out his yo-yo, causing a big spark. Nori thrusts her spear into the tail, forcing it back. The Scorpion tries to attack again, but Kazu deflects it. A series of rapid attacks are countered between the two as the lasers seem like light trails against the magnetic blades of Kazu's yo-yo. I can't figure out how the yo-yo isn't getting sliced up, until I realize Kazu is timing it so that his blade actually hits the stinger before the laser blade can connect. I pick up my sword again and scan for any possible weaknesses. Nothing is exposed, and the only thing holding it at bay is Kazu. Nori and Chieko try to attack, but the Scorpion's scimitars act as claws to block them.

I see Kujira getting back to his feet, dislodging himself from the wall.

"What's your status?" Nori asks him.

"Annoyed," Kujira replies.

"I have a plan. Chieko, when you have an opening, I want you to grab its tail again."

"It'll just shock me again," Chieko points out.

"Yes, but it requires a power surge at its stinger to do it. Use the grappler on your arm and hold on."

"Why?"

"If we can drain it of enough power, it might be vulnerable to an attack," Nori explains. "Kujira, Mac. You ready for an X-attack?"

"Sure," I answer.

"When I give the signal, X-attack its tail."

"Will that work?" I ask.

"I believe so."

"You kids have the plan down?" Kazu asks.

"We do."

"Good."

Kazu launches a quick flurry of yo-yo attacks that the Scorpion blocks. As it does, Chieko vaults at its tail, grabbing it with both arms. She fires the grapplers onto one of the segments, latching herself on. As predicted, the volts begin. Normally, this would cause her mecha to automatically retract. But with the grapplers tying them together, the volts continue.

"What is your condition, Chieko?" Nori asks.

"I'm insulated, but I don't have control over my arms."

"Can you release the grappler?"

"I can. Do you want me to?"

"Not yet." The electrical charge begins to weaken until the scorpion's tail goes limp. That's when Nori orders, "Now."

Chieko detaches, and her mecha, which she no longer has control over, drops straight into the ground.

"Mac, Kujira!" Nori yells.

We plan our trajectories and run in a cross pattern, striking simultaneously and slashing it diagonally. The timing is perfect, and the tail is cut in half.

Nori uses a spear straight to the Scorpion's neck, while Kazu's yo-yo knocks the scimitars out of its hands. The Scorpion loses all power and comes to a standstill.

"Nicely done!" Kazu exclaims.

"How'd you know that'd work?" I ask Nori.

"There were power-generation issues with the tail, which is why it's still in the prototype phase," Nori replies. "Chieko, what is your condition?"

"I still don't have any control."

"I'm going to try to track down the chief engineer and see if he can get you up and running," Nori says.

"Now let's see who's driving this thing," Kazu says, and motions Kujira to do the honors of ripping off the bridge panel.

"Watch out in case it self-destructs," Chieko reminds him.

"Got a fist ready in case they try any funny business," Kujira answers.

But when Kujira tears it off, there's no one inside.

"What the hell?" Kujira asks. "There's a ghost in the machine?"

"It must be remotely controlled," Nori says. "Which might be a good thing."

"Why?"

"If we can track down the source, we could take out a whole lot of rogue mechas without having to fight all of them."

"Can you find the source?" Kazu asks.

"I'm trying right now," Nori replies, anticipating his question.

Kujira gets up and lifts the sundered tail. "Can I ask for a tail upgrade? I want that laser tail," he says, chewing on food.

"Are you eating something?" Chieko asks, as we watch him bite a piece of something.

"Turkey dogs," he says, holding one up.

"How did you get turkey dogs?"

"I installed a minifridge in back," he says, scrumptiously biting his meat.

"You what?"

"Mute your communicator," Kazu orders. "You're making my ears hurt."

"Yes, sir!" Kujira shouts, taking a few more loud chomps before muting.

We stand there, waiting for Nori's search.

"If someone could take over any of the mechas, why didn't they take over the Leviathans?" I ask.

"Remote control hasn't been established on them yet," Kazu replies. "Most of the prototypes on the base don't get far enough to have those controls installed, but since Scorpions are antimecha units, remote controls are essential to their functionality. Normally, even when they have remote leashes, it's hard to break in because each one has a pair of distinct codes and an override."

"That means whoever did this has to be high enough up the food chain to know the codes," Chieko assumes.

"And be a decent pilot. Not just anyone can drive a mecha remotely."

Kujira unmutes, and asks, "Do any of you know why they call them hot dogs when there's no dog meat in them?"

I have no idea. Chieko shrugs. Kazu looks baffled not just by the answer to the question, but by the fact that Kujira asked it at this moment in time. Nori says, "According to this signal trace I put out, the source of the control is very close by."

"Kujira. You stay and guard Chieko. Nori, Mac, let's hunt this traitor down."

Nori tells Chieko she got hold of Chief Engineer Nobusue, and he'll arrive soon. We switch to tread mode again and accelerate to a nearby corridor.

When we get closer to the source of the remote controls, there are two stalwart Hornet-class mechas in our path. They're similar to the *Korosus* though not as powerful. They're primarily designed for urban warfare by local police for pacification purposes, designed to intimidate and disarm foes. When the Hornets spot us, they raise their batons.

"Let me handle this," Kazu says.

He runs at them, swinging a yo-yo in both hands. One tries to hit him with the baton, but Kazu wraps his yo-yo around its arm, then tugs, ripping its hand off. He ducks under the attack of the other, then gives him a backward kick. The momentum of the motion plus the kick causes the Hornet to stumble forward. Before it can turn around, Kazu lashes his yo-yo out so that it wraps around its neck. He tugs hard, causing the head to come straight off.

The handless Hornet gets up and tries to run.

"Nori?" Kazu calls for aid.

Nori prepares her spear and launches it. It impales the Hornet in the back, causing it to fall to the ground.

"Let's find out who the queen bee is," Kazu says.

The corridor branches off into several hallways that have research labs in them. The one we're going to is 239T. The doors are only big enough for humans. Sensors indicate there are two people inside the lab. One's identification comes up as Dr. Shimitsu, which explains why she'd gone missing. The other is unknown.

"Dr. Shimitsu?" Nori contacts her. But there's no reply. "Switching to thermal view."

"It looks like she's being held hostage," I note, as the person behind her is carrying a gun.

"I think you're right," Nori confirms.

"You got this?" Kazu asks her.

"I got it."

"Got what?" I ask.

"Watch," Kazu says.

Nori lowers her mecha, balances one arm against the wall, then uses the other to punch straight through. The wall shatters like glass. I check my thermal view. The fist goes straight through and smashes the unidentified person while leaving Dr. Shimitsu intact. I'm amazed she could make so precise an attack.

"Dr. Shimitsu. Are you there?" Nori calls again. "Dr. Shimitsu?"

In the thermal view, she is moving. "Is her communicator broken?" I conjecture. "Maybe one of us needs to go down there?"

"Nori," Kazu says. "What's the status of the rogue mechas?"

Nori checks, and replies, "They've all been deactivated."

Right then, Dr. Shimitsu shows up on the internal communicator. She's in tears.

"My family . . . My family is dead now," she says.

"What happened to your family?" I ask.

"They—they took my family hostage three days ago."

"That's why you were helping them?" Nori demands.

Dr. Shimitsu appears to be in a daze. "They told me the moment they lose contact with me, they'll kill my husband and my son."

"I'm very sorry to hear that," Kazu says. "Truly. Do you know where your family is?"

"I don't."

"I have friends in the police I'll ask to go investigate ASAP. Maybe it's not too late."

"Do you think so?"

"It's possible. I'll make some calls. But I need to know, what was their objective?"

"Their objective? Their objective was to . . . was to destroy all of Mechtown. But, most important, to destroy the biomech we have."

"Why the biomech?" Kazu asks.

"That's what we based all our research on," Dr. Shimitsu replies. "You—you need to get to the surface, fast."

"Why?"

"The real attack is coming soon," she informs us.

"What real attack?"

"They're sending a group of their biomechs to wreak terror on the city."

"There's no way they could get here," Kazu says.

"There is," I say, and tell them about the Longinus Strike.

"He's right," Dr. Shimitsu adds. "We've been tracking their transport planes for the past hour."

"Do you have those sensor readings?" Nori asks.

Dr. Shimitsu relays the sensor scans.

"Nori?" Kazu checks.

Nori takes a few moments to confirm. "There are four of them, and they'll be here soon. An hour, tops."

One hour? And not just one of them, but multiple biomechs. With much of Mechtown in disarray, the destruction they'd wreak on the Bay Area would be catastrophic.

"What about my family?" Dr. Shimitsu asks.

"Your family?" I shout. "What about the whole city? You've put everyone here at risk!"

"I'm trying to reach my friends right now," Kazu calmly says.

"But—"

He cuts off the communicator, and the doctor's visual disappears.

"You going to help her?" Nori asks.

"I'll do my best," Kazu says. "But even if they're alive and can be rescued, Dr. Shimitsu will be punished as a traitor. That means her family will probably face death sentences too in order to set an example."

"They would do that?" I ask, shocked by the implications.

"They might," Kazu says. "I wonder what I would have done in her shoes if my wife and daughters were threatened."

"You would have found another way," Nori says.

"Maybe," he replies. "Can you chart out what you think they're planning, so we can notify Berkeley Command?"

His communicator goes mute as he calls someone else.

I think about my last fight with the biomech, and the idea of fighting more of them scares the hell out of me. Even with the Leviathans, we don't know how we'll fare against the biomechs.

Nori calls Chieko and asks, "What's your status?"

Chieko and Kujira appear on my display. "Nobusue-san is swapping out my hands and has fixed a bunch of circuitry that was destroyed."

"How much time will you need?"

"He says one hour."

"Tell him he has fifteen minutes."

Kazu unmutes and asks Nori, "Are you able to access external communications?"

"I haven't tried."

"I can't call outside," Kazu says.

Nori tries calling a few different places. So do I. "The only places I can contact are those on Mechtown's internal system."

"Then all communications are blocked outside," Kazu states.

"That'd be a safe assumption," Nori affirms.

"That means we can't call for help," I say, confirming the obvious. "They might have no idea what's going on down here."

"Have Chieko and Kujira meet us at the Treasure Island Emergency Exit when they're ready."

"What should we do about the doctor?" Nori asks.

Kazu replies, "Leave her to me."

WE REACH THE EMERGENCY PLATFORM. CHIEKO HAS BROUGHT M87S AS well as replacement weapons for us to wield. I grab a new sword and a *wakizashi* blade. Chieko is wielding her chain whip. Kujira picks up an electric sword, while Nori sharpens her spear. Kazu has his yo-yos. We each put the shields on our backs. The platform elevator can only take one mecha up at a time. Kazu hooks his Leviathan first, locking in his spinal clamps and bootstraps.

"Where does this go?" Chieko asks.

"Underneath the Bay Bridge," Nori replies.

There's something I have to say to them. "Before you all go, I have to remind you, we're in prototype mechas. These aren't battle-tested, and there are going to be biomechs up there. I've seen one in action. It's nothing like the sims. It single-handedly destroyed three Sentry mechas. There's a high probability we'll be killed. Even if you were soldiers, a wasteful death is a stupid one. We're cadets. I know it doesn't look like there's much up there to defend against them, at least not yet. But I want you all to know what it's gonna be like."

"He's right," Chieko chimes in. "The biomech is horrifying. I don't care because I'm ready to die. But you all should be prepared."

"Thanks for the spirit lifter," Kujira says. "Are you two going to go?"

"Of course," Chieko answers.

They look to me. I take longer to reply. Am I ready to die? That's a dumb question, isn't it? Who's ever ready to die? But am I willing to risk death if I fail? "Yes."

"I think most of us know of soldiers having their lives thrown away because a stupid officer charged in without thinking or consulting those under their command," Kazu says. "I became an officer because I wanted to make sure I would never have to follow or issue terrible orders again. Let's take a vote. We're the Five Tigers. Unanimous decision to go or not. Who's in?"

"Do you even need to ask?" Kujira snaps.

"I'm ready to kick some Nazi ass," Nori answers, with a rage that goes beyond the moment.

"You know my answer," Chieko says, and I can hear the conviction of all the RAMs behind her.

"Same here," I say.

"Then it's unanimous. Let's go," Kazu states.

FROM ITS INITIAL CREATION AS AN ARTIFICIAL ISLAND IN THE MIDDLE OF the bay, the Empire has greatly expanded the size and scope of Treasure Island. There is a full naval base, which is often used in collaboration with the mecha base in San Francisco for joint exercises. Its accessibility to both San Francisco and Berkeley has made it integral to the area's defensive forces. We don't know if the biomechs will target the East Bay, the West Bay, or both. This puts us right in between. As soon as I ascend, I move away from the launchpad so that Chieko can come up next. We're on an airfield to the west side of the island, and there are jets parked below us. There are eight buildings nearby, and I'm detecting people in them. We're close to the Bay Bridge, and there's reconnaissance equipment, though none of it seems to be working. The water is choppy from all the wind, but there are still western gulls casually cruising along. There isn't a beach; instead, a small, rocky shore separates the island coast from the water.

Nori and Kazu are scoping out the area, trying to determine the current situation. I take several steps in the *Arikuni* and look out at San Francisco. I switch the camera so the whole bridge vanishes and it looks like I'm floating in the air with wireframes of my arms and legs visible. There's a special sunscreen that compensates so that the solar light won't be blinding. Audio is also in full-immersion mode, and I can hear the water in the bay. It'd be one of the best experiences of my life if I didn't know what awaited.

"There are three Guardian-class mechas and nine Labor-class mechas on sensors," Nori says. The three Guardians are standing along the piers of San Francisco. The Labors are inactive but stationed at Oakland Port alongside the gigantic container cranes that look like quad mechas themselves. "None of them are responding to our communications, but they're on a different communication network from ours for security purposes, and I think their system is down."

"Is anyone aboard?" Kazu asks.

"The Labors look empty, but there should be crews on the Guardians."

Guardian classes are offensive mechas that are midsized and older generation. No surprise they're stationed here as the Bay Area is generally considered a safe haven.

Behind us, the ground begins to shake. A Guardian mecha is approaching from the airfields, probably the one stationed in the base. I look over at the communication console. It looks similar to the setup I had on the quad mecha.

"I think I might be able to contact them on a public channel," I say. "Though that means anyone can hear us."

Kazu considers it. "Do it."

I get out of the driver's seat, walk to the communications console, turn it on. There's a general system used in case of emergency situations. The links tend to be weaker, but they're useful if you want to make free calls throughout the USJ. There's only one external signal aside from the Leviathans, which I assume to be the Guardian. I call them. The communications officers on the Guardian answers in audio only: "Who are you?"

"I'm Cadet Makoto Fujimoto," I answer. "Those two with me are fellow cadets."

"This is Captain Mizoguchi," another voice chimes in. "Your communicators are down too?"

"Yes, sir."

"What in the world is it that you're driving?"

"It's a prototype, sir," I answer.

"Prototype? You have weapon systems on board I've never seen before."

"Yes, sir," I say, wanting to get to the more pressing issue. "Captain, are you aware Mechtown was under attack?"

"Attack? By who?" he asks, stunned.

"It was an internal attack, and we have reason to believe that German biomechs will be attacking the city soon."

"Is this some kind of practice drill?" the captain asks.

"No, sir. This is real."

There is silence for a long minute. "Most of the mecha corp is away for the holidays."

"Yes, sir."

I'm about to explain more when we hear a strange sound, a dismaying rumble, like someone has taken a hammer the size of a building and is whacking the ground repeatedly. But it's coming from the sky, and the noise turns into a ghastly warble. We see what looks like an enormous horde of locusts descending. They are four long aircraft, an eerily alien black, each carrying a massive shipment.

"That's the Nazis?" Captain Mizoguchi asks.

"I believe so, sir."

"I'll send an SOS message to Berkeley Command. In the meantime, I want you three to stay out of the way while I handle this."

"Sir, you'll need our assistance. Our mechas are designed to fight the biomechs."

"You're cadets, not soldiers. Leave this to me and my crew. There isn't a Nazi alive who stands a chance against us."

"But, sir—"

"That's an order, *cadet*."

I get back to the pilot's seat and inform Kazu and Nori of what the captain said.

"For now, we let the captain take the lead. But as soon as they need assistance, we'll give it," Kazu concludes.

When the planes open up, four pods are dropped into the bay at a high velocity. They shriek as they fall, two of them landing close to our current position. Right before they hit the water, rocket boosters fire, easing their fall. It is less a cannonball dive and more a finessed descent as they open up and release a nebulous shape that has the contours of something I recognize all too well.

Nazi biomechs.

Just then, Chieko comes up, and the platform goes back down to get Kujira.

"So this is the Longinus Strike," I say.

But no one's listening as the four biomechs take shape and emerge from the water. They're even bigger than I remember. Just the part above the surface means they must be around ninety meters, putting it at equal height with the Statue of Liberation. In comparison, our Leviathans, which aren't built at the final size, are only forty meters tall. Big, but the biomechs are at least double our height. Kujira arrives just as the biomechs take on their full shape.

"What'd I miss?" he asks.

"Four biomechs just landed," I reply.

"At least the party didn't start without me."

The two biomechs close to us come our way. The other two head for Berkeley.

The Guardian steps ahead of us into the water.

"Whoever you are, you've illegally set foot on United States of Japan territory. Withdraw immediately or we will be forced to destroy you," Captain Mizoguchi commands on the mecha's speakers.

The two biomechs appear different from each other, their flesh oozing like one of those Jupiter storms. The one on the right is taller and has a familiar purple protrusion on its back that resembles a dorsal fin. I could swear it's the one from the Quiet Border. Both resemble bipedal creatures, but it's more like a dissolving combination of flesh that somehow remolds itself and is bound by an elastic sheath.

"That's the one, isn't it?" Chieko asks me.

"I think so," I reply.

The biomech doesn't give a verbal response to the captain but instead, launches hives of missiles oozing with the black chemicals. At first, I think it's the gnats, but they're much smaller and faster. All we can do is raise our shields and brace for impact. As soon as they hit our surroundings, everything metallic dissolves. That includes the jets, buildings, and the Guardian mecha. Right before their mecha is destroyed, the Guardian launches a final volley of missiles that sprays the biomechs with its fiery projectiles but does no visible damage. The captain and his crew are killed. But when the biomech's weapon hits our shields and armor, the chemicals have no effect other than to splatter against our plating.

"What is that?" Kujira asks.

"I can't determine the composition yet," Nori says. "It's some type of acidic solution that melts whatever it hits."

"Looks like Dr. Günter knew about it," Kazu states. "We're impervious to it."

I think about the Guardian's crew and wonder what was going through their minds as the biomech's weapons destroyed them.

Off in the distance, I spot the two other biomechs launching a fusillade of their chemical weapons on the buildings in Berkeley. The damage is much worse, and I see several buildings topple over.

"Get your M87s ready," Kazu orders us. "Remember the training. Dr. Günter has built our Leviathans specifically to combat the biomechs. If we follow the training, we will beat them."

The two biomechs launch more of their weapon, but this time target the columns holding up the Bay Bridge. As soon as the missiles hit, they corrode the steel. The dissolution happens quickly, and the part of the bridge connected to Treasure Island's southernmost point begins to collapse.

"Is anyone on the bridge?" Chieko asks.

"Even if there is, we'll have to deal with a rescue later," Kazu replies. A hard fact, but an all-true one. We couldn't perform rescue operations even if we wanted. "Target the biomechs."

We all do. Behind, I notice the emergency platform submerge. There's no escape now even if we wanted to leave.

"Do not fire until they reach land," Kazu orders. "All the M87s do is strip them of their armor. We still have to deliver the finishing blows. And I want to wrap this all up soon so I can get home for dinner. Eileen's cooking my favorite, *hong shao rou*."

"Can I come over too?" Kujira asks.

"You're all invited."

"Not that I doubt your wife's ability, but I'm very picky about braised pork belly," Chieko says.

"I guarantee it'll even satisfy you. Let's kick some ass first to whip up an appetite."

The biomechs don't take a long time to come. Even with two-thirds of their bodies submerged under water, they move through it quickly.

They are even bigger up close, essentially being mountains that can walk. Even residing inside the Leviathan offers little comfort when they dwarf us in size. Once they reach Treasure Island, they rush up the shore and charge toward us with a speed that catches us all off guard. I wasn't expecting them to be so fast. We begin firing, but unlike the simulations, the Biomechs deflect the ablative shells with their arms, using them like a shield to swipe them away. A few shells do hit, causing parts of their regenerative skin to dissolve. Despite the slight retraction, within seconds, other parts of the armored skin cover it. At this distance, our shells won't be anywhere near as effective. The one with the purple dorsal fin is quickly upon us and is about to seize Chieko and Kujira. They try to force it back with shots from the M87, but their weapon has little effect. The biomech punches Kujira, then grabs Chieko. It's about to throttle her neck when Kazu charges into the biomech from its flank. Using his mecha's weight, he collides into it, taking it down with him.

The biomech gets back up and starts pummeling Kazu's Leviathan, which doesn't react in any way. Has Kazu lost control? The monster grabs the mecha's arm and rips it out of its socket.

Kazu yells, "Fire on it!"

Kujira and Chieko shoot from their M87, and at this closer distance, the shells are penetrating the armor, causing much of it to rot off. But it's not enough to stop the biomech from dismantling Kazu's Leviathan.

"Kazu-sempai, eject!" Chieko yells.

"There is no eject on the prototype," Kazu answers. And for the first time, I see fear in his eyes.

The biomech wraps its arms around Kazu's neck and puts it between us as a shield, preventing us from firing anymore. Chieko and Kujira sprint forward to try to grab the biomech and pull him away by hand. That's when the biomech squeezes the Leviathan's neck hard.

"Tell Mayu and Mio—" we hear Kazu say.

But before he can finish the sentence, the head explodes, causing a reaction all the way down to the stomach, where he's positioned.

Kazu's Leviathan has no power. The biomech rips its guts out and eviscerates it. The bridge is completely destroyed. Kazu's life signs are blotted out.

Our four Leviathans come to a stop.

I don't think any of us can believe sempai is dead.

The biomech hurtles Kazu's Leviathan at Kujira, then takes rapid steps forward and knocks the M87 out of his hand. Kujira swings his sword at the biomech, but the blade gets swallowed up. Nori thrusts her spear into the biomech, while Chieko fires ablative shells. This lets Kujira withdraw his sword. When an opening appears in its head, Nori is able to pierce it. Chieko slashes it with her chain whip, slicing quickly across what could be called its head. The biomech is weakening but not fast enough for the three Leviathans to defeat it.

My attention turns to the second biomech, which has taken a slower approach but is moving toward us like a hunter stalking its prey.

Red blips are catching my attention. I scroll through the visual interface, trying to determine what they are. IDs show up indicating all of those blips are people in the remaining buildings. The scanners indicate they're military personnel, but I can't get any communications through to them when I try.

"I think there are peo—" I start to say, when the biomech uses a swirling slash attack to force us back. With the space it's been given, it fires its gnats. But they're not aimed at us. Instead, the buildings full of soldiers begin to disintegrate. Many of the red blips vanish.

"Mac," Chieko calls.

"Yes?" I ask her.

"I've been waiting a long time for revenge," she says to me. I think back on all the RAMs who were killed and that moment in the Crab mecha when we were first attacked.

"So have I," I reply.

"I've missed Wren," she says with a wistful smile. "It was an honor to be among the Five Tigers. Now I need all of you to withdraw."

"What do you mean, withdraw?" I ask, confused by her request.

Chieko turns off her communicator and charges at the biomech. She gets it in a choke hold and uses her grapplers to cling to it. Whenever the biomech tries to get her off, she deftly maintains her grip. They wrestle across the airfield and end up crashing into one of the towers. There is rage in her every motion that blazes even through the mecha armor. But it's a controlled anger that moves as fast, if not faster than the biomech.

"Chieko. Your BPG generator is overheating," Nori calls. "You need to shut it down." But even as she says it, I see the heat level rising rapidly.

"Is it damaged?" I ask.

"I don't think so. She's shut off her communicator."

"Why's her generator overheating?"

But as I ask it, the answer dawns on me.

"Chieko!" I yell. "You don't have to do this!"

Our scanners keep on alerting us to a power overload in her mecha when the biomech's fist goes straight through her Leviathan's head.

We survived that first biomech together. I can't bear to think of losing her.

"Mac, we need to retreat," Nori says.

"What about Chieko?" I demand.

"Her generator is going to explode any second now."

"But—"

"Wake up man!" Kujira yells. "She's holding on for us. We need to withdraw."

Kujira, Nori, and I have no choice but to get as far away from her as we can.

Chieko's mecha self-destructs, and the blast from the BPG incinerates the biomech in a fiery rapture. I check the sensors, hoping somehow she might have survived even though all that remains of the Leviathan is a charred husk. The explosion has caused a big hollow in the Leviathan's body, and the biomech's skin melts away, the inner skeleton, destroyed.

Both fall over.

"Chieko! Chieko!" I shout.

I scour the Leviathan in the hope that, somehow, she might have survived.

"I'm not picking up life signs," Nori says.

We don't have time to grieve because the second biomech attacks.

I lift up my M87 and take aim. I'm furious and can't think straight. I am repulsed to see that its flesh is alive, oozing all over its body. The ground is shaking with its every step. Chieko, why did you do that? We would have found another way.

I make sure to lock onto the target before firing the ablative shell. A projectile launches toward it at the speed of sound, and the burst is loud. The shell hits it hard, knocking it down. Direct hit for once instead of a deflection.

The smoke clears, the biomech's skin is scrambling all about, some of it rotting off. There are parts where I can see the metallic skeleton underneath. But it stands back up. And while it's clearly damaged, it's not enough to stop it.

Do I stand my ground and fight it, or do I run? My initial instinct is to withdraw, find a better place to fight, then engage. But then I see Kujira and Nori behind me and think about all the remaining civilians on the ground, unprepared for the attack. Do I follow Chieko's example and take both of us down?

That's when I realize I'm in the exact same position my mother was. But they had the whole crew to think of, as well as families behind them. I—I don't have anyone. If I die, it won't be as grave a loss as those people below. It's not even a choice. The only thing I have to decide is whether to run to face it, or make a quick coun-terattack as it rushes me. I get my sword ready. I'm not as good as a wrestler as Chieko, but I feel confident I can take it down. I've never set off an internal self-destruct on the Leviathan and need to figure it out quickly. I bring up the BPG controls on the display screen and get my grapplers ready. Alarms are going off on my scanners. I shut them down because I already know what's coming my way. I brace for the impact, haunted by the idea that its regen-erating skin is created from the cells of the dead. For some reason, Griselda comes to mind. I wish I could have spoken to her one last time.

Just as we're about to collide, something smashes the biomech in the side of the head. It's a spear going through its temple. From the opposite side, a sword plunges into its abdomen. Kujira's on one flank with the sword, and Nori has impaled it with her spear.

"Wake up!" Nori yells to me.

"The—the ablative shells don't work well," I tell them.

"Try again," Nori orders.

"More than once!" Kujira reminds me. "Don't blow yourself up or I'll kick your ass in Shinto hell! No more Tigers die today! We'll find a way to beat their biofreak asses!"

They're holding the biomech in place with both their blades. I fire a round from my M87, reload, and fire again. The short dis-tance causes a big part of it to dissolve, but another stretch of its skin scales to cover the rest.

If I can hit it in multiple locations, it might not have enough skin to fully regenerate over the gaps. I fire rapidly, relying on Nori and Kujira to hold it in place. The chemicals start having their ef-fect, and half of the body is exposed. Kujira and Nori don't wait. They slice it up, cut up its shoulder, its nose, and finally lop off its head. For good measure, I aim at its chest and unload a stream of bullets that finally penetrate. Just as I'm feeling that we've possibly defeated another biomech, it starts swinging its arms madly. All three of us are knocked back, crashing into the ground. Kujira's sword has been flung away, as has Nori's spear. My M87 is out of reach.

The biomech looms above me and gets ready to crush me with its foot. I don't close my eyes. I watch, wondering what death is. Right when it's about to smash my stomach, another biomech emerges from the emergency platform. It's not very big at first, but begins to scale in size. The biomech that was about to kill me turns its attention to the new presence, warily confronting it. The other biomech seizes the assailant and violently hurls it to the ground.

What in the world is going on? Who is this biomech?

I'm confused until a face shows up on our communication display. "I'll handle this," Griselda tells us from her cockpit.

I can see that she has no physical arms or legs, everything fused with the organic material inside the biomech's chambers. It's a serpentine set of sinewy, veinlike wires that connect to her entire body. Even her hair has been hidden by a crown of ebony circuits covered with a gelatinous coating.

"Griselda," I call.

Despite all my harsh words to her earlier, she still saved my life. I think again of Chieko and her willingness to forgive me even though I'd made the decision that led to Wren's death.

"Stay back," Griselda warns us.

I watch as her biomech battles the enemy. Since we've already damaged the monster, her biomech has a clear advantage. But it's unlike a mecha samurai, which even at its most ferocious has a mechanical precision to its attacks. Griselda's biomech is feral, savagely brutalizing its opponent. Every fist causes tremors along her opponent's skin. She shreds its chest armor, crushing the conglomeration of skin underneath her feet. The match is violence at its most raw, and she's even using her jaws to bite her opponent. It's not a machine getting destroyed but the cells of all those sacrificed to create the monstrosity being channeled through the pilot. The biomech tries to defend itself, lashing out and diving claws into her clavicle even without a head. To my surprise, Griselda screams in pain, and I see blood forming in her actual clavicle. Does the pilot of the biomech feel physical damage? The next attack confirms it as I see Griselda wince and grunt loudly. The impact of tissue being crunched is gruesome and visceral.

"How many ablative shells do you have left?" Kujira asks me after he picks up his gun and sword.

I retrieve my M87. "I have nine. You?"

"Three dozen," he replies. "We need to save them for the two other biomechs. Ready to kill this thing?"

I nod. We both approach the fight.

Kujira swings his sword around, waits for an opening, then lunges toward the biomech. He is able to pierce its back, cutting through its hip. I attack its other hip, causing black liquid to gush out and stain our armor. The biomech lets out a howl that sounds like a wolf's throat being torn apart and repeated as an echo. Griselda's biomech punches her opponent until there are only broken bones and mutilated flesh on the ground.

I look at her face. Her nose is flared, she's covered in sweat, and there's blood over her body.

Her biomech stands up. It has gills and webbed fingers, unlike the individual digits of the others. It's slightly smaller at about fifty meters and has more amphibious features. If it wasn't for her face showing up on my display screen, I wouldn't believe it's Griselda.

"We need to stop the other two," Nori reminds us.

But it's the last thing I want to hear. "We barely survived these two. We'll be killed if we go against the others!"

Nori remains expressionless as she says, "I'm aware of that. But if we don't stop them, they will kill tens of thousands of people. Maybe more. We have to destroy them before they do."

The conviction with which she speaks makes me both ashamed at my lapse and inspired to fight.

To Griselda, Nori says, "We'll have to count on your help again."

"Of course."

"I'll see if I can arrange transportation," Nori says, then bolts away in her mecha.

That leaves Kujira, Griselda, and me.

Kujira, who is eating a turkey dog, stops chewing and says, "Glad you're on our side."

"I thought there were five of you," she says.

I point to the remains of the other two Leviathans.

"I'm sorry," she says.

I can't think about them now.

"I rushed here as soon as I was alerted to your launch," she explains. I know she would have been justified in not having lifted a finger to help us after what I said to her earlier. "These Leviathans are still prototypes, and they don't have the full equipment you need to take on a biomech."

"Why aren't these ablative shells working?" I ask.

"The shells were optimized to work against my biomech," Griselda answers. "Each biomech is different because the cells that make them up are different. Dr. Günter was working on a modulator to work against as wide a range as possible, but we weren't able to implement it before the attack. There is a modulation code that might improve their effectiveness. I'll send it directly to your porticals, so it can implement them."

I realize that these shells worked better against the second biomech than the first. "Did you—did you know the pilot?" I ask, pointing at the fallen biomech.

"I did. He was a friend. A good pilot, like my cousin." The pain in her voice reminds me she lost two people close to her as well. She actually had to kill one of them to protect us.

"I'm sorry for your loss."

"You shouldn't be. It's the Nazis that made us fight like this. They're the ones in the wrong."

She didn't blame me for her friend's death the way I blamed her. I feel embarrassed for the second time today.

Our eyes turn to the destruction taking place in Berkeley. I can't see the biomechs, but there's lots of smoke.

"Do you feel pain when the other biomechs attack you?" I ask her.

"My nerves are fused with the biomech, so I can feel everything it does, even how windy and cold it is outside."

"Can you turn it off?" Kujira asks.

"No," she replies. "But I wouldn't want to. I fight better this way."

"What happens if the biomech gets heavily damaged?"

"Any damage to the biomech happens to me too."

"Do the biomechs have any other weaknesses than the ablative shells?" Kujira asks.

"Most of our pilots are placed in an area close to the liver." I notice her unconscious use of the word "our" even though she's no longer with them. "If you use a thermal scan, you should be able to spot an area with a lower level of heat than its surroundings. That's because of the special coating protecting it. Use the M87 on that point, and if the skin responds and retracts, use your weapon to pierce through and kill the pilot. It'll shut down the biomech."

"Cool. Any chance I could try driving your biomech afterward?" Kujira asks.

"If you're willing to cut off your arms and legs and get a direct nerve connection, yes," Griselda replies.

"There isn't like a driving wheel?"

Nori's mecha, which is being carried by four tilt-rotor aircraft in a slung load, calls to us from the air. There are eight more of the planes designed for heavy-duty loads.

"What about Griselda?" I ask.

"We don't have any way of hooking her biomech for a lift."

"Don't worry," Griselda says. "I'll meet you over there."

She begins running through the bay.

"It'll take her time to get there," Nori says.

The tilt-rotor aircraft lower their belly hooks, which automatically clamp onto our shoulders upon contact. When all four make their connections, they do a diagnostic test to ensure they can handle my weight, then lift me up. I relay the new modulator information for the shells to Nori.

"This'll be helpful. I was able to communicate with a colonel on the base. They've just started reestablishing their network. She wasn't able to call Berkeley Command directly, but she sent them a telegraph. Another two biomechs attacked Yamaguchi Airport, and since a huge part of our force is down in Los Angeles, it'll take time for them to send the necessary backup without the main airfield."

"So there are four total left?" I ask.

"At least. There may be more. It's hard to tell. When we land, our primary duty will be to defend the city against the biomechs until Griselda arrives. We can't defeat them by ourselves."

"There's one way," I say, referring to Chieko's sacrifice.

"Neither of you are as good a wrestler as she was," Nori admonishes us. "If the biomech gets hold of you, there's a higher chance of your being killed before you can do anything, which would be a waste. All three of us need to survive and let Griselda destroy them."

"Not to be the optimist here, but even Balaam's Donkey collapses under one too many straws," Kujira observes.

"What?"

"What if she fails?"

"I won't fail," Griselda, who's still linked with us, states firmly.

"I'll devise a contingency plan for that scenario," Nori replies. "For now, our plan is something right up your alley."

"What's that?" Kujira asks.

"I want you to go ahead of us and see if you can lead the biomechs away from the civilian area."

"How?"

"Annoy them and get their attention."

"I sense you're trying to tell me something."

"Sense?"

Kujira laughs. "Do these things come with speakers?"

"They do," Nori replies.

"I can also give you their direct channel," Griselda replies.

UP IN THE AIR, I TAKE A LOOK AT THE WHOLE BAY, SKYSCRAPERS AND houses on the north and east side as well as San Francisco proper. It angers me that many of the architectural marvels are being destroyed by the two biomechs in a swath of devastation. I would have presumed their destination would be BEMA, but they're heading into Oakland, which is puzzling. What would they want there?

About seven years ago, there was a massive earthquake that caused heavy damage and necessitated reconstruction of several of the major freeways. I see the areas where older buildings have been supplanted by new ones and the roads have likewise been updated. I think about Griselda, wonder what the surgical process was like as she had parts of her body excised. If the same had been required for me to become a mecha pilot, would I have done it? A year ago, the answer would have been a definite yes. Now, I'm not so sure.

I look at Griselda, Nori, and Kujira on the communicator. Nori is stoic, Griselda is suppressing pain, while Kujira actually looks eager and impatient. Even though I've achieved my dream of being a mecha pilot called on to protect the city, I don't feel any excitement. Dread has usurped all other emotions. I try not to think about Chieko and Kazu, but I can't help myself. They deserved so much better. Kazu's expression the moment he realized he was going to die is still clear in my head. Chieko's words were melancholy, but determined, and I could feel how the burden she'd been carrying this whole time broke free in her final sacrifice.

"Griselda," Nori says. "Do you know what their target is?"

"They've already achieved their main one since they've extracted Dr. Günter. When I was piloting for the Reich, we were always told our secondary goal was to cause as much destruction as possible," Griselda replies.

"Then why don't they attack BEMA?"

"Because they want to make sure the USJ can respond," Griselda explains. "Their ultimate hope is to provoke a war between the Empire and the Reich."

"Mac, Kujira. Our priority is to protect the civilians," Nori reminds us. "Since their chemical weapons are ineffective against us, we need to keep our distance and draw them back to the bay. Avoid engaging them in direct combat if possible."

On the sensors, I see Griselda racing in our direction. Her biomech is fast for its size, but it'll still be a few minutes before she reaches us. Ahead of us, the two biomechs are engaged in a fistfight with four Guardian-class mechas. I should actually call it a beatdown. Our mechas, whose guns are ineffective, are trying to fight them in close-quarter combat. But the Guardians are no match for the biomechs, which have already battered two of them to death and are crushing the remaining two with their bare hands.

Kujira lands first in a commercial area full of warehouses that's not far from where the biomechs are.

"Hey, Nazis!" Kujira yells over the Leviathan's speaker, which I presume is also connecting directly with their cockpits. "Yes, you two big tall ones with rooster heads and toxic-waste skin. You ever hear the story of Balaam's Donkey?" The biomechs, which were attacking the Guardians, turn toward Kujira. "No one listened to the dude. His owner beat him for speaking the truth. Donkey has more guts than y'all, targeting civilians. You know what the best toilet paper I ever used was? These smooth ones that had the pictures of famous Nazi leaders on them. I used to wipe my ass with Hitler's face, and it felt gooood. I hear German toilet paper is tough and coarse, so y'all prefer using old issues of the *Volkischer Beobachter*. I don't think I'd want to use old newspapers to wipe. I don't want ink on my butt."

The temporary reprieve allows the two Guardians to withdraw, but the biomechs don't seem to care. They stomp in Kujira's direction.

Nori gets dropped second, and asks Kujira, "What's with Balaam's Donkey?"

"'Cause that's one sharp donkey that doesn't get enough credit where credit is due. Want me to stop?"

"Please continue."

They both start firing their guns at the biomechs, but all along, Kujira doesn't stop vilifying the biomechs. "Cock a doodle, you f—"

Just as I land, the biomechs fire the chemical missiles. The ones that hit us are ineffective, but a few strays hit the tilt-rotor aircraft. Three of them spin out of control and crash into the ground. Two others are incinerated in the air.

How many more will have to die today?

"I heard Nazi leadership is being controlled by a race of reptilian lizard aliens who taught y'all to build spaceships in Antarctica. Is that true?" Kujira asks.

The biomechs run in our direction. The one on the left does look like it has a rooster head with a huge crest running down its spine. Its partner has a massive protrusion behind its back that resembles wings, almost like a moth.

"What do we do?" I ask.

"Retreat and rendezvous with Griselda."

Nori runs toward the bay. Kujira and I follow.

"It makes sense that y'all are controlled by reptiles," Kujira continues, as we're running. "But you realize reptiles would have a helluva bad time in space 'cause they're cold-blooded? You'd have to have heaters on all the time, and it'd be hot and humid. This girl I met from Osaka used to have a pet lizard, and she'd feed it crickets and cockroaches. Do your masters eat bugs? I personally am not a fan of eating bugs. But damn, lots of bug eaters in the world. Your reptile bosses can have all the bugs. It'd make sense, though, if it turned out all your older leaders were related to snakes. My ma used to cook up fried snake and eat it. I hated it, but she'd dip it in vinegar and soy sauce and force me to have some. It was gross."

Nori has calculated the path so we only pass through areas with minimal residential properties. Still, the footsteps of biomechs alone destroy most things in their path. They're fast, but we're even faster than they are. I'm actually amazed at how smooth the controls on the Leviathan are and how running feels so intuitive. I feel superhuman.

That's when the Moth biomech veers away. We calculate its trajectory, and it's heading for one of the condominium skyscrapers. It ignores Kujira's mockery, so Nori yells, "I'll head it off," and runs in pursuit.

Rooster continues to chase Kujira. Fortunately, Griselda arrives and charges straight into Rooster. They ram each other hard, and their fists start swinging.

"Mac! Go help Nori!" Kujira orders. "We'll join you soon."

I run in the direction of the condominium. Nori has caught up with the Moth. Moth tries to fire its missiles, but none of them work on the Leviathan. It ejects fumes and propels additional limbs from its back. Nori blocks each of the attacks, using her spear. There are multiple blows, but she anticipates each of them. It's almost like she has another set of arms, helping her to defend against the biomech's assault. Even though it's twice as big as she is, she doesn't show an ounce of trepidation. She is parrying brilliantly, refusing to budge. I scan the condominium behind her. There are 242 people inside. Nori doesn't try to take the offensive, possibly because her primary objective is to delay. I want to see if I can give her a little assistance. I take aim with the M87 and fire three rounds. They hit the Moth's wings, which causes it to flinch, then let out a gut-wrenching bellow. The Moth turns toward me. Part of its left wing has dissolved, surprising me that the M87s worked so well. Griselda's modulation update has helped.

Nori thrusts her spear into the Moth's neck. The spear goes all the way through, and her blade is covered in blood and ooze. She pulls it back out and kicks the Moth. It falls to the ground. As it does, the ground begins to shake.

"What's going on?" I ask Nori.

The Moth gets up abruptly and uses its wing to attack Nori. Nori evades it, but now the Moth runs back toward the Rooster biomech. I fire my M87, causing it to stumble. But it limps on to its companion. We follow the short distance to meet with Griselda and Kujira. Griselda's biomech has dismantled the Rooster, ripping out both its arms. The biomech lies on the ground, defeated.

A wan face appears in our visual display, a Eurasian pilot whose body is covered in a black web of the chemicals. The source is the

Moth biomech. Unlike Griselda, where we can see a clear division between her and the biomech, this new pilot appears completely fused. Even his veins are bulging with black fluids. The scariest part is that I swear he's younger than we are.

"Griselda!" the Moth biomech's pilot yells. "How could you do this to us?"

"I no longer believe in the world the Marshal promised us," she replies.

I recall Colonel Yamaoka talking about the Marshal, the new leader the Nazis were growing suspicious of.

"Many must be sacrificed so many more can live," the pilot answers. "That's what we've fought for all our lives!"

"The Marshal is a homicidal maniac. How many have we killed in his name? I won't kill anymore!"

"You want the world to be plunged into this unending cycle of Empire versus the Reich! This is the only way to end it."

"There are other ways!"

"There is no other way. You've let your personal weakness cause you to stray from the righteous path. History can only be changed by blood."

The Moth lets out a scream, and there's a blast, some type of powerful electrical wave. Before I even know what hits me, my right arm is sundered straight off. Nori's mecha loses its head. Fortunately, she's in the belly, so she is okay, just unable to control the Leviathan until she can reroute the circuits for motion. Griselda's biomech is crippled, though. She absorbed most of the attack, shielding Kujira, who appears untouched. The Moth biomech powers down, having used what remained of its energy in the ring attack. The regenerative skin drops off, and only the frame is left, which is immobile. The communicators have all shut down, and the visual display of the pilot has vanished. But I see something ahead of me.

The biomech Griselda had earlier destroyed rises up. It latches onto her back and rips her skin off. Griselda's biomech screams in pain and falls to the ground. Black ooze is spraying everywhere. It's sucking her armor off of her, absorbing it into itself as it regrows its arms. It throws her aside once it's reinvigorated with a new shell, the crest drowned in a suit of tumors.

Time slows.

Now it's just me, my sword in my sheath, my M87 in my one good arm, and the Leviathan against the biomech. I remember what Griselda told me. I flip to a thermal scan and sure enough, where its liver is, there's a drop in the heat signature. I think about Chieko and Kazu, then think about what might happen to Griselda if I don't act. I no longer feel any fear or anger. Just an awareness of how feeble life is. The biomech is one permutation of that awareness, a manifestation of someone's fear of the Empire.

I aim the M87. But I don't fire. I wait for the biomech to get close to me. I have to time this perfectly. The biomech is wary but, seeing that I'm not firing, steps closer. That's when I shoot the ablative shell at its chest, causing its skin there to break away. This infuriates it. I realize the shell is even more effective because it has absorbed Griselda's armor. I put aside the gun as I'm out of shells. The biomech charges. I hold until the last second before pulling out my sword. Unfortunately, the biomech anticipates me and raises its arms. Regenerative skin from its forearm flares out like a web, covering my blade and dissolving it. I'm weaponless. The biomech punches me in the face. I only have one arm to protect myself. The biomech is too fast and batters my head.

Kazu-sempai said every part of me should be weaponized. I try to fight back, but I'm no match.

Every part.

I sink my arm into its chest and try to grapple with any piece of it I can. My fingers latch onto something. I tug and use my knees to attack. I've always thought of combat as something more elegant. But there's no finesse here. This is a brawl for survival, and I have to think of myself for what I am. I pull my arm out, hammer at it, kick, even try to head-butt the biomech. I'd bite it if I could. The biomech is stronger than me, even in its weakened condition. I lose pieces of my armor with every jab. *What are you thinking?* I wonder about the biomech pilot. *Or is it pure impulse now?* That impulse makes it surge in rage as it swells up and hurtles itself at me.

Just as it's about to cut me up, a spear goes through its wrist. Nori has held up its right arm. Its left arm moves to attack, but Kujira cuts off its hand. I scan again for the area where the heat levels dip. It's not a sword, but I use my fists to punch it as hard as I can. I repeat the motion until my hands penetrate the spot where the pilot theoretically is. I don't even care if it'll work. I just release all my rage until the biomech crumbles in front of me. My fists are stained with the blood of the pilot.

I've killed him with my hands.

Every part of me is a weapon.

Nori, Kujira, and Griselda's visual communicators all turn back on. I'm happy to see them alive. "How are you all doing?" I ask them.

"Alive," Nori answers.

Kujira answers me with a bite from his food.

Griselda smiles weakly. "I'm alive, but I do need to get out of the suit. Are we in the clear?"

"I'm not reading any life signs from either biomech," Nori replies. "It's over."

I feel immense relief. We've won.

I recite a short prayer of thanks.

Our communicators suddenly light up. Messages are rapidly

being relayed back and forth. There are all kinds of requests for assistance coming from throughout the bay.

"External communications are back," Nori says.

Only one is directed toward us. An unfamiliar face shows up on our screen, and her identification marks her as Major Usagi Higa of the 715th Mecha Battalion.

"What is going on here?" she asks us.

The cavalry has arrived, though it's too late. The battle is over. At least I think it is. Nine *Korosu* mechas land via tilt-rotor aircraft accompanied by four Lightning-class models, which are designed as speedy killers.

"We just got through kicking some Nazi ass while y'all were asleep," Kujira replies. "You're welcome."

"Step away from the biomech," the major orders us.

"They're all dead."

"The one standing next to you is still alive."

Does she mean Griselda?

"You have her mistaken," I try to explain. "She's on our side. She helped us win."

Major Higa states, "It is a threat to our forces and will be eliminated."

"But—"

"This is not a negotiation. Move out of the way."

"Hey, Major," Kujira says. "Are you all daft? Maybe you misunderstood my friend. We beat the biomechs already. This one's on our side."

Higa raises her arm cannon. "There's no misunderstanding. That biomech must be destroyed. Step aside."

If I comply, the 715th will attack the biomech. In her debilitated state, I don't know if Griselda would even be able to defend herself.

"Forgive me, ma'am, but I can't," I reply.

I stand in front of the biomech. With my one arm, there's not much I'd be able to do in her defense, but I don't care.

"You're disobeying a direct order."

"Not just him," Nori says, as she somehow moves her headless mecha between the *Korosus* and Griselda. "This is Cadet Noriko Tachibana. I can confirm Cadet Makoto Fujimoto's statement that the biomech is our ally. She defected from the Nazis this past year and is assisting us."

"This is not the time for insubordination. If you do not move, we will be forced to attack."

"You can try," Kujira jumps in. "I promise, y'all ain't getting through. She's on our side, and we protect our own." Kujira's mecha moves to protect Griselda. "Everyone still accepts lies as truths even though the truth stinks like a smelly fart."

"Thank you all," Griselda says, and bows to us on the display. "But I can't let you do this. I'll power—"

"Griselda," Nori says.

"Yes?"

"You're a Tiger now, and I'm in charge, so shut up."

More *Korosus* arrive, as do other combat models. I can see half of them charging their weapons, the others awaiting orders. The major is glowering at us, but she's trying to assess for herself what's going on. Nori is determined, Kujira appears as though he's itching for a fight, and Griselda looks like she feels guilty about the whole situation. I don't know how the Leviathans will do against the *Korosus*, but no matter how powerful we are, there are more than twenty of them. We might be able to defeat the first wave, but they could launch a directed nuclear attack, which would spell the end for us. Even if, by some miracle, we survived, we'd get a court-martial and be executed for attacking our own mechas.

"You leave me no choice," the major begins, shutting off her communicator.

The *Korosus* prepare their weapons. We get into a defensive stance.

"It was nice fighting with all of you," I say.

"Don't talk in the past tense," Kujira replies. "Y'all injured. Leave this to me."

"Don't get cocky," Nori cautions Kujira.

"It's not cocky if it's true."

"What should I do?" Griselda asks.

"Don't give them an excuse to fire on you," Nori orders. "Let us handle it."

"Thank you everyone," she says.

"We should thank you for saving all of us," I say to her.

The *Korosus* fire on me first, destroying my other arm and the balancing system in my chest. I fall to the ground, unable to stand. I try to lift myself up, but I feel like a turtle on its back. Without arms, there's no way I can get to my feet. Nori maintains her defensive stance.

I hear Kujira gleefully remark, "Finally, it's my turn."

He actually grabs my broken sword before he leaps straight into the mecha swarm and does an arc swing with both weapons. The whirlwind attack hits three of the *Korosus* in the chest, causing them to stumble back and crash into the mechas behind them. Our electric swords are much more powerful than the older models can handle, and he's so fast, it's caught the mecha pilots off guard.

"Kujira!" Nori yells. "Try not to kill anyone if you can."

"These jerks fired first! Just defend Griselda, or this won't mean anything."

"What do you think I'm doing?"

Kujira actually seizes one of the smaller Lightning models and uses it as a shield, hurtling it at the bigger *Korosu*. Two of the *Korosus* try to pierce him with their swords from opposite directions. He ducks so fast, the two mechas impale each other. Meanwhile, some of the mechas try to attack Griselda. Smoke is everywhere. I'm terrified and look to Noriko. She doesn't looked frayed at all. She's focused, planning ahead for the next step. Her calm reassures me, and I'm glad I'm on her side. The long length of her spear keeps the opponents at bay. She also uses her war fan as a shield.

I wish there was something I could do other than helplessly lie here. But Kujira seems invincible, mowing down the mechas with ease. His mastery over the Leviathan's body is amazing as he moves like a gymnast, slashing arms, legs, chests, and helmet pieces off. One approaches with a morning star, swinging it above its head. Kujira races fearlessly toward the *Korosu*, slicing the chain with his sword and dropkicking the mecha in the belly. His spin attack makes it seem like he's on roller skates, and I realize he's using his treads to move in a smooth circle, arms straight out in a cross pose, with swords destroying everything in its wake.

Just as he's about to engage Major Higa in direct combat, several mechas fire at him with their cannons. He deflects most of them, but one of the shells pierces his leg. His knee buckles, and I realize he's about to topple over. Kujira stabilizes himself by clutching onto a nearby *Korosu*. Major Higa attacks, lunging with her *naginata*. Kujira isn't able to avoid the thrust as it impales his shoulder. He grabs onto the shaft and holds tightly, pulling it forward. The major tries to pull it out, and when she finds she can't, exerts more strength. Kujira releases, causing the major to stumble back. Kujira hops forward on one leg and swings his sword hard into the major's flank, cutting halfway through her elbow. Several *Korosus* surround Kujira.

Kujira cockily asks, "Can't handle me one-on-one? I only have one leg and the other arm is messed up." I've spent enough time with him to detect something I've never heard before. A hint of fear. How bad is his mecha damaged?

The major replies, "This is not a contest of honor. Our first duty is to defend the Empire and dispose of our enemies."

"Big talk. I only have one leg, and I'll still take you all on."

The major orders, "Fire!" A volley of shells bombards Kujira. Though they cause heavy damage, the armor holds. What causes him to fall is the lack of stability in his other leg. But even as he topples over, somehow, he balances all his control and catches himself with his arms. He gets back up, defiant as always. I hear something that sounds like chewing from his cockpit.

"I saved this turkey dog for you," Kujira says. "It tastes really good."

"Fire again!" the major orders.

Just as the *Korosus* are about to comply, a new communication comes through.

It's Judge Misato Hirono, and the former Imperial Guard is visibly irritated. "Major!" she yells. "Stand down. The biomech is under the jurisdiction of the USJ, and I'll confirm the pilot is on our side."

"But ma'am—"

"Do you have a problem taking orders? You were just about to destroy one of our own. I commend these cadets for bravely standing by their own."

"They've attacked my battali—"

"They attacked because you gave them no choice. And I must point out that these cadets have been giving you a handy beating even though they have been badly damaged."

Major Higa is not happy, but she can't ignore the judge's direct relationship with the Emperor. She tries to protest one last time, but the judge won't have any of it.

"Stand down, Major!"

Major Higa sighs. "I will take this up with USJ Command."

"Go ahead. Meanwhile, I'm sending in a rescue team to extract them."

"Judge. What about the biomechs at the airport?" Nori asks.

"The 790th, assisted by Professor Okamoto, defeated them."

Higa stands down, as do the mechas around them. The judge looks at Kujira and me over the communicator. "Well done," she says. "Both your mothers would be proud."

"Thank you, ma'am," I say, grateful for her arrival.

Kujira grunts in reluctant acknowledgment.

The judge's communication ends.

"Is it finally over?" I ask, apprehensive that it isn't.

"I think so," Kujira replies. "Told you I got it."

Nori, who this whole time has remained emotionless, takes a long breath. I see her eyes getting wet. "Good job, everyone. I am honored that we've been able to maintain the Tiger's undefeated record." She looks back toward Treasure Island and bows. "The sacrifice made by Chieko and Kazu-sempai will never be forgotten."

Griselda doesn't hold back on tears. I assure her, "We're safe now. It's all over."

She looks at me plaintively. "Don't you understand? For people like me, it's never over."

A medical quad mecha arrives with an emergency crew to extract us. I look back at the biomech I killed, then think about what Griselda said and wonder whether it's like that for all of us.

16

★ ★ ★

WE SPEND TWO DAYS RECOVERING. ON THE THIRD, WE'RE DRIVEN TO THE funeral at the Imperial San Francisco Cemetery in Golden Gate Park.

We all bow in front of the caskets of Kazu-sempai and Chieko. Both of their bodies are dressed in kimonos and given six coins for their journey across the River of Three Crossings. Their families are present, and we look at the huge portical displays of both on the wall, flipping through images every fifteen seconds. Kazu's wife puts on a brave face, but her daughters are weeping. I am reminded of myself as a child. I didn't understand back then what the death of my parents meant. I can't help but feel like I've failed. Behind us, there are several thousand cadets and soldiers, all dressed in ceremonial uniforms, standing in formation.

Three generals give speeches. But it's Colonel Yamaoka that everyone wants to hear. He gives an impassioned plea for action, desiring to honor those who've passed away. Kazu-sempai and Chieko are publicly commemorated. The other branches will have separate funerals for their fallen soldiers. The thousands of civilians that were killed in the attack will be privately buried by their families or cremated. I've heard reports that Dr. Shimitsu has disappeared, taken away by the Tokko. I don't know what happened to her family.

"All of us here are orphans. All of us have lost someone dear to us. You've seen how far our enemies will go to destroy us," Colonel Yamaoka says. "This brazen attack on USJ territory, targeting cadets and civilians, shows the Nazis have no conscience, no boundary they won't cross. How long before we take action?"

The audience is entranced. I think about all those who died, starting with my parents, Hideki, the RAMs, Kazu-sempai, Chieko, and the civilians in Berkeley. What is really on Colonel Yamaoka's mind? Conflict seems inevitable between the Reich and the Empire, but do I want to be part of it? I look back over at Kazu's daughters. They're still crying.

Once the funeral ends, all the guests stand in a line to bow to the two fallen. A few people express their condolences. Nori is with her parents, and they greet me. I respectfully bow to them. Nori sidles up next to me and says, "I found out the German embassy actually notified the USJ two weeks ago that one of their biomech corps had gone rogue and was planning on attacking Berkeley over the holidays."

"They knew?" I ask, stunned.

"Either our leaders knew and didn't believe it, or they wanted it to happen."

"Why would they want it?"

"I don't know. But I don't think it's coincidence that the most important mecha units were absent during the attack and only showed up after the biomechs had done their damage. Agent Akiko Tsukino of the Tokko is leading an investigation into it. She might be in touch with you soon."

I head back to my dorm, perturbed by what it might mean. Is it still really no different here than from RAMDET? Could Chieko's and Kazu-sempai's deaths have been avoided?

I'm surprised when I hear digitized gaming sounds from Kujira's room. I knock on his door. He opens up.

"You didn't go to the funeral?" I ask him.

"Nah. I don't do that kind of stuff."

"Why not?"

"The dead are already dead. Pack it up, move on." He looks up from his game. "I'll miss sneaking out to eat with Chieko."

"At least you won't have to sneak out anymore."

"I might give Kazu's diet a real try," he says, and his eyes drop back down to his puzzles.

"It's not bad."

"Traitor," he says again.

I laugh and say, "I'm glad we were able to fight side by side . . . The way it should have been for our moms."

He looks up at me intently, and says, "Likewise. You're not half-bad as a mecha pilot." I see his scar again and remember how little I actually know about him.

"From you, that's high praise," I say.

As I'm about to leave, he asks, "Where's your friend, Griselda?"

"Not sure."

"You really need to get your priorities straight."

"What's that mean?"

But he goes back to his game and doesn't answer when I ask him again.

I ENTER MY DORM AND SPOT A MESSAGE ON MY PORTICAL FROM GRISELDA that just came in. She'd like to see me up at Point Richmond.

I take an automated taxi there. There's been lots of discussions on how to improve defensive fortifications, and they're strengthening Mechtown to make sure nothing like this can happen again. I spot the Gestahl Ballroom, where we had that fancy celebration with Chieko and Kazu-sempai.

On my portical, I read an article describing our battle, but it's so far from reality, I don't even know where to start with corrections. It sounds more like a portical-game synopsis or glorified propaganda than an account of what actually happened to us. Griselda's aid is highlighted as the turning point of the battle, which is the most accurate part of the account. Then I wonder if all wars are like that, with writers changing the nature of the battles after the fact.

The ride feels like forever, and I'm anxious about seeing Griselda. I think about the last conversation we had before the battle and regret every word. When I do arrive, I see several big mechas working on clearing the debris. The fires have been contained, though there is still a lot of smoke and ash in the air. I spot Griselda, who's at ground level, coordinating via her portical. She's wearing a long coat, gloves, and a beanie. She waves when she sees me and walks over.

"I wanted to say this earlier, but I'm sorry about what I said about Hideki," I immediately state. "It was unfair of me to blame you. I know you were in an impossible situation."

"I can't absolve myself of all blame. But that's kind of you."

"I mean it," I state. Then I think about the pilot I killed—another one of her friends. "I was an idiot and I—I shouldn't have said it."

"Hideki died because of my connection. I didn't know better, but that's no excuse."

"That's not fair to you."

"Isn't it?" she asks.

"No, it's not," I reply.

"You, Nori, and Kujira have been so kind. Since the battle, everyone's gone out of their way to make me feel welcome."

"You saved the city."

"We all did." She looks past me toward the beach. "Colonel Yamaoka has a vision for a completely different world. Not USJ. Not Nazi Germany. Just free."

"You mean like America was?"

"Different," she says. "It'd be a new world order without boundaries of country, ethnicity, or religion, where people would never be imprisoned because of the color of their skin or their ideology."

"It sounds like the only difference is the name."

"People have killed since the beginning of time for names."

"You believe in that world?" I ask her, unable to really understand what any of these officers have planned or the complex machinations behind them.

"I believe in a world where names no longer matter. I betrayed the Marshal because I believed in it. But I realize our presence here only gave the Marshal the excuse to attack. Maybe he planned it together with the colonel. I think I've been very naive about the state of affairs."

"Our superiors will always treat us like pawns. My mom died because of it. Most of my friends died following orders." I think again about Kazu's daughters and how the cycle has been repeating with every generation. "I realize now—I guess I've known for some time—I don't want to go down that same path."

"What else can you do?" she asks.

I don't even know if it's possible, but I answer, "Try to work from within to change it. If that doesn't work, fight to make sure it does. What about you?"

She's about to answer when four mechas approach us. They're unlike any I've seen before and appear designed for water combat. They somewhat resemble the samurai template, though they have legs that resemble fins and extra limbs like an octopus. They're also much longer than our mechas, similar to a submarine, with dolphinlike features along its torso.

"These are the *Furioso*, *Alexander*, *Odo*, and *Carlex*," Griselda says. "They used to be U-boat hunters for the Spanish navy, specializing in tracking down German subs. But they're independent now and were helping with the rescue effort. They'll be leaving soon."

"Are you—are you thinking of leaving too?"

"Do you want me to leave?"

"Of course not!" I exclaim a little too emphatically. "I'm sorry," I say again. "For everything."

She shakes her head and is about to reply. But the kneepad opens up on the *Furioso*, and a staircase drops down onto the beach. Several crew members come out and greet Griselda.

She introduces me to her friends as well as to her aunt Marta.

They say hello, each giving me a warm hug. They have to leave to rendezvous with their fleet, as it passes the bay in a few hours.

"How many total on board?" I ask.

"Fifty-six on the *Furioso*," Marta tells me. "Fifty-seven with Griselda. You can still come with us," she says to Griselda.

Griselda shakes her head. "I would love to, but this is my home now."

I'm surprised by her words, as I still remember her telling me back in Dallas that she didn't feel like anyplace was her home.

She hugs each of them good-bye.

The crew members reenter their mecha. The *Furioso* and the three accompanying mechas march back into the bay. We walk past the damaged buildings. I ask, "What made you decide to stay?"

"I can't leave without driving one of your mechas," Griselda says with a grin. It's true that she's piloted only the biomech, but I know there's a deeper meaning behind her choice.

"You'll learn quickly," I reply. "It's kind of like playing a more advanced version of *Cat Odyssey*."

"You know I'm a much better *Cat Odyssey* player than you, right?" she asks.

"I've gotten better," I insist.

"We'll see about that."

We walk down to the water. She points at Berkeley and the Labor mechas that are working around the clock on reconstruction. Despite all the city has suffered, it feels reassuring to know we'll build it back up.

To my surprise, she holds my hand.

I know things will be complicated for us, that there will be many challenges, but I remember Kujira's words about priorities.

I finally know what mine are.

ACKNOWLEDGMENTS

There are so many people I want to thank for *Mecha Samurai Empire*.

First off, thank you to all the amazing readers and reviewers of *United States of Japan*. I appreciated every single review, tweet, and e-mail. I never thought *USJ* would get the reception it did, and that's a huge part of why *Mecha Samurai Empire* exists.

I want to thank my incredible Japanese publisher, Hayakawa. I'm lucky to have an incredible editor, Aya Tobo, and fantastic translator, Naoya Nakahara. They gave so much valuable advice and input into the creation of *Mecha*, and I am so grateful to call them both colleagues and friends. Also, a big thanks to Akira Yamaguchi, Marie Umeda, and *S-F Magazine*, many of the Hayakawa staff, whose names appear as cameos throughout the book, as well as Atsushi Hayakawa, Ryoko Hayakawa, and to the amazing Hiroshi Hayakawa. Meeting him was a real honor and privilege.

G_P Solo, you're an amazing artist and it always makes my jaw drop to see the unbelievable mecha models you make and the way you bring the world to life. I never know how to fully articulate my gratitude!

I almost cried when I read Ohmori-san's introduction for the Japanese version of *United States of Japan*. Thank you so much for your insightful essay, which I feel undeserving of!

To the readers in Japan, as you can see Mac always says thank you in Japanese when he's being very serious. So likewise, *Domo arigatou gozaimasu!* It was an honor to meet many of you at Donburacon for the Seiun Award as well as to interact with you online. Thank you, everyone, for your incredible support! Also, a big thanks to Haruna-san, Hirohide-san, Coco-san, Nishida-san, Onitsuka-san, and Sakai-san!

144, thank you for sending me my first ever USJ mecha. I'm so honored, and it was a thing of beauty!

Sabatruth, your Kujira art is so great, and your postcard really touched me!

Ryuji Umeno, your graphic art of USJ, and especially Akiko, was really wonderful!

The Nova and Ediciones crew were fantastic and so incredibly supportive. I was so grateful to share the world of USJ/EUJ with Spanish readers. I want to thank Alexander, Marta, Berta, Esteban, and many others who make cameos in the book.

Antonio Torrubia is one of the most thoughtful and enthusiastic people around and I love hearing about his many adventures and stories! Rock on!

I think I watched Geek Furioso's video review of EUJ about a hundred times. That guy is a genius and one of the coolest people around. We're not worthy!

Thank you Ife Olowe, one of the most brilliant engineers at LucasArts. When I was just starting in LucasArts, you were a friend, a mentor, and a role model.

Alonso Martinez, damn, man, you're such a phenomenal artist, I sometimes feel like I am in the presence of a contemporary Michelangelo. Your talent is matched by your generosity, and I learn something new from you every time we talk.

Ken Liu, your work has always inspired me, and your friendship and advice throughout the creation of *Mecha* were deeply appreciated. Thank you so much!

To Riley MacLeod, you always push me to dig deeper into my stories and see beyond the surface, then dig a little more. It's helped my fiction a bunch, and your sincerity and big-heartedness have always touched me.

Shinichiro Hara, you were an amazing boss, friend, and leader. You brought me along for the most amazing, and surreal, ride, and you always found the humor in some of the most difficult situations. There are lots of nods in the book, some of the more obvious being Mike Tyson's Punch-Out, Neon Genesis Evangelion, Fighting Spirit, Patlabor I and II, Phantasy Star IV, Yakuza Papers, Castlevania: Symphony of the Night, Herzog Zwei, Bionic Commando, Legend of Zelda: Majora's Mask, Super Mario Bros. 3, the Shin Megami Tensei and Persona games, Battle Royale, Stray Dog, High and Low, Sympathy for the Underdog, Fatal Frame II, Daredevil 181, Mega Man 2 (aka Rock Man 2), Final Fantasy VI–VII, Terranigma, Ninja Gaiden NES, Chrono Trigger, *Do Androids Dream of Electric Sheep?*, *The Man in the High Castle*, stories by Cordwainer Smith, and so many more referred to throughout the book. Thank you for inspiring my childhood as well as *Mecha Samurai Empire*.

A big thanks to John Liberto! It is such an incredible privilege to get to collaborate with you again. I have been totally in awe of your mecha art from the moment I first saw the USJ mecha to the early sketches of Mac holding his sword. I'm time and again blown away and feel so lucky to work with such an awesome generational artist! You really bring the world to life and I'm always so impressed at the way you impart authenticity and realism to every work of art!

Thank you to the amazing Misa Morikawa of Tuttle Mori Agency! I often call her my superagent, who works magic behind the scenes. She is so thoughtful, considerate, and caring! I also thank her for helping me to decide on the final title of the book as *Mecha Samurai Empire*.

I'll be honest, there were some rough times in relation to the book. My agent, Judy Hansen, steered me through all the storms, and I honestly don't know if I would be here without her. I am extremely grateful to her for being the best agent an author could hope for.

How can I even begin to express my thanks to the team at Ace, starting with my amazing editor? From my first conversation with Anne Sowards to all the amazing editorial sessions we had, she helped refine *Mecha* into what it is. I am so honored and grateful to collaborate with her as she crafted the book into the best mecha it could be. Thank you very very much! Also thanks to Miranda Hill!

There are so many people I need to thank, and many of them I do through cameos in the book. If you see a reference, you know it's a big shout-out your way. Thanks to Sajan, Domee, Rona, Dave M., Mara, Mary, Sal, Joe, Rachel, Arthur, Paul A., Ian, Aaron H., Aaron P., Narelle, Ben, Patty, Tyrone, Kiyomi, Marlina, James, Geoff, Janice, Jimin, Bridget M., Chris L., Joel C., and many others. And of course, I always thank God.

I wanted to give a big thanks to Hideo Kojima. Kojima Kantoku has been a huge inspiration in my life, one of the most brilliant and innovative writers/designers/creators of our generation. I actually got to meet him in person when I visited Tokyo. It was an amazing experience, and he imparted some incredible wisdom, including a story about *Zone of the Enders* that I've often thought about in making choices for this book. If you see nods to his work throughout my writing, it's because he's been such a huge influence.

Also, thank you to Ayako Terashima for being so thoughtful and kind!

Finally, to Angela, my wife, to whom the book is dedicated, words are insufficient to convey my gratitude and love. It's been a long journey together, but there's no one else I'd rather be together with in the bridge on the mecha of life. Thank you for your patience, your thoughtfulness, and for believing in me through the tough times, of which there were plenty.

I hope readers who enjoyed *Mecha Samurai Empire* will come back for the next book to find out more about the looming Nazi-USJ war, who the Marshal is, and what Colonel Yamaoka is really planning.

Photo by Angela Xu

PETER TIERYAS is the author of *Mecha Samurai Empire* and *United States of Japan*, which won Japan's top science fiction award, the Seiun. He's written for Kotaku, *S-F Magazine*, Tor.com, and *ZYZZYVA*. He's also been a technical writer for LucasArts and a visual effects artist at Sony, and currently works in feature animation. He can be reached on Twitter at @TieryasXu.

Ready to find
your next great read?

Let us help.

Visit prh.com/nextread

Penguin
Random
House